DAUGHTER

OF

AIR AND STORM

DAUGHTER

OF

AIR AND STORM

Book I of the Dark Moon Trilogy

Sherryl King-Wilds

Bad Girls Publishing
Nashville, North Carolina

DAUGHTER OF AIR AND STORM

All characters and events in this book are fictitious. Any resemblance of characters to persons either living or dead is purely coincidental.

With the exceptions of mental anguish and beating her head against a wall, the author was not harmed during the creation of this book.

Cover art copyright © 2006 by Bad Girls Publishing
Book design and layout by Stephanie James
Edited by Jonathan Stillwater, Angela G. Wilds, and A. Daphne Douge

ISBN-10: 0-9789514-0-9

ISBN-13: 978-0-9789514-0-5

LCCN: 2007927128

Published by
Bad Girls Publishing
P.O. Box 275
Nashville, NC 27856
www.badgirlspublishing.com

Printed in the United States of America

To Andrew, Forest, and Terri for giving me the courage and the reasons.
To Mom and Dad for giving me life and their wild imaginations.
To Melany and Ashley for their laughter.
To Frieda for being there.

ACKNOWLEDGMENTS

Words of thanks go to Angie for her patience in slogging through an early draft of this novel, offering her advice, and instilling within me the confidence to finish. Thanks to Jon and Daffs for their final tweakings on this project.

Words of thanks also go to Dad, Ashley, Melany, and Terri for cheering me on and being the best mirrors I've ever had!

Also, thanks to Mom, Elsie Singley, and E.C. Bassett for recognizing the writer within me all those years ago.

I'm ever indebted to all of you.

CONTENTS

"One must question the ambitions of the elements, for

nature is both kind and deceitful."

~Anonymous

EYE OF THE STORM

feeble torch fought for survival under the darkest of moons, its flame lilting through the ancient trees. Wind blew through the torchbearer's blue-black hair, blending long tresses into the opaque shadows behind her. The sound of gravel crunched underfoot as the torchbearer reached an area clear of trees on the river's bank.

A strong gust failed the torchlight. Breath caught in the woman's throat. She closed her eyes, wishing the umbrage away. Still, eyes opened or closed seemed to make little difference under this new moon, not even starlight to guide her. She let the torch fall from her hand to clunk on the ground. Its ember ghosted into blackness, leaving her to the echoing night.

It was to this desolation that the woman opened her eyes.

And cursed her luck that the contractions had struck her this day. Cursed the truth of the weather witch's predictions that tonight, of all nights, would be of a dark moon. Cursed that her husband had shoved her out the door the moment her water had broken. With the looming clouds, no one need have known of the sky's darkness except for what the witch's calendar foretold.

Another round of pain ensnared her uterus. She plummeted to her knees, catching herself on her hands, rocks cutting into her palms. She rose to a squat. The time had come. She pushed, teeth gritted, hands fisted. The baby slipped out and gave a hearty cry, caught as it was in the woman's skirts.

The woman thanked the deities that this birth was not her first and the child's passage through her birth opening had been uncomplicated.

She filched the baby out of the skirts of her dress while, around them, vegetation chuffed in a rush of air scented with oncoming rain. The woman had no sooner cut the umbilical cord than it and afterbirth were snatched out of her hands and whisked away on a mischievous wind. She reflected on the swirling wind but a moment, thinking the gust perhaps aberrant, hoping it was not.

She groped beneath the cloth of her dress and pulled out the blanket she had concealed there earlier. The woman hastily wrapped the baby in that thin material, tactile senses telling her the babe's face poked out of the blanket.

A bolt of lightning slashed through the air and zapped over the woman's head; thunder snarled in response. A strong gale ripped the blanket off the baby, setting it a-sail. The storm stomped this way.

The woman shuddered, gaping at the sky. The lightning had been too close.

The woman retrieved the blanket, not recognizing her source of illumination, then gasped before she could wrap the cloth around the tiny girl. Sparks of smoky-blue light coursed around the infant's form.

The woman stared a long time, even after the dancing light had faded. Perhaps it would be best to fulfill her husband's wishes; the deities knew the villagers would if she did not. She placed her hand over the babe's mouth, yet she could not press down; her hand shook as if in spasm. A jolt of lightning struck near her feet, rendering a deafening clap, and the smoky-blue glow reappeared around the newborn.

The woman removed her hand from the babe's mouth then cast her vision into the galvanized sky.

"I can't do it. I can't," she murmured and embraced her child, kissing the small head and swathing the quiet babe in cloth anew. She contemplated keeping the infant, not going home, but they would surely hunt her down if she did not return, and her other children would be without her protection. She, however, would die before she killed this babe. Her husband and the rest of that lot be damned!

The mother tottered away from the river's edge through the shifting trees, almost grateful for the glow her newborn provided as the winds caressed the babe's skin until another light source winked its bleak eye in the distance. The mother's steps ceased. A fevered revulsion scurried down her spine. She glanced down at the trusting babe, set her jaw, then followed that winking eye.

She found the crone's cottage in a clearing. Dim light flowed between the slats of the windows' shutters. The mother sat on a fallen tree on the edge of the clearing, catty-cornered to the cottage's front, and offered the babe a breast, which the infant took with a meek hunger.

The mother gazed before herself into the darkness with the knowledge that the crone's Lavender Hills spread over the land in that direction. The smell of that wind-bruised herb carried on the air.

Gales whipped about them, tugging the blanket and once more exacerbating sparkling surges of blue-gray luminosity on the babe's skin. The mother sighed as she switched the babe to the other breast. The child fed not with the lusty hunger of her siblings but with a gentle politeness. The mother smiled, the wind still whipping about them.

A faint creak carried over the gushing air. The mother looked up to see the crone standing in the doorway of the cottage, wraithlike candlelight beckoning behind the bent form. A gnarled hand gestured the mother come near.

Fear promulgated the beating of the mother's heart. Yet, somehow, she managed to raise herself and shuffle her feet enough to stand outside the small doorway, the friction of each gale blast bouncing sparks off the baby.

Creaking words flowed to the mother on the wind. "What power hold you?" Hawk-like eyes perused the newborn.

"I hold no power." The mother grimaced, knowing the words an untruth as they slipped past her lips.

"Humph" came the crone's reply, her eyes latching on to the mother's.

"Come in." The crone turned and the cottage engulfed her, leaving the mother in the playful breeze.

The mother noted that the gale neither shook the trees about them nor touched anything else in the distance. If not for the sake of her sanity, she would have sworn it followed the newborn.

The baby cooed. The mother's lips trembled as she tried to smile down at her daughter. The mother swallowed then peered into the shadowy cottage and knew by the heat of the tears scalding her cheeks what she had to do.

CHAPTER 1

THE WHIPPING GIRL

*L*arka bent slightly and cut a spike of tubular, purplish flowers from its stalk, forever severing it from the life-sustaining juices the rest of the plant offered. She tucked the spike into the basin of an elongate, open basket. She snipped and tucked until, inhaling deeply the sweet yet pungent smell of lavender, she put the scissors and the last bunch on the burgeoning pile and turned back toward home.

She loved lavender, its scent, its color, the wild freedom of it. She smiled. She had been told that many thousands of years ago this mint had traveled over the seas and been planted in the gardens of her homeland. The lavender had escaped cultivation and now grew wild in patches in most areas but in profuse sprawl around her home. How she wished to be like that—wild and free with the laughing wind in her blue-black hair.

Old Gilly had plenty of lavender planted around the cottage too, but it was not enough to supply the crone with the abundance of flowers necessary to make the essential oil the people of Jaunty Village prized for its antiseptic qualities. The Lavender Hills did that.

Here, atop this gentle slope and as far as Larka's eyes could see, waist-high lavender's nearly linear leaves undulated over the hills in silvery-green abundance, the full sun setting that color ashimmer.

Larka tied the strings of her straw hat beneath her chin. Gilly would be angry if Larka lost another hat to the wind, though she had lost

15

only one in her fourteen years. Larka ran as fast as she could without spilling the lavender, the parting air flapping her loose britches and shirt. She had so many chores to complete this day, yet she slowed as she saw the fieldstone cottage rolling into view.

She topped the adjacent hill—Last Hill she had dubbed it—and stood for a moment, examining the cottage. The structure looked like a fairytale creation with a window box spilling green herbs, blooming flowers wafting their scents along the stone walkway leading to the front door, and the sun dazzling over the swaying forest behind it.

Not so long ago the forest had grown on the north and south side of the cottage, but Gilly had insisted on having those portions cleared to make more room for her gardens.

Larka stretched her legs in a run to the cottage, her left hand holding her pickings in place within the basket. At the cottage's fore, a vat of hazelnut oil rested on one of the benches the village carpenter had built several years ago. A bucket of water nestled beside the other end of that bench. Larka took a seat between the vat and water. She breathed in the perfumy scent of lavender as she ladled water from bucket to mouth.

"Are you addled, girl? Put the flowers in the oil and be off with you."

Larka started, nearly spitting the water from her mouth. She peered over her left shoulder around the north corner of the cottage. Gilly sat on a bench in the partial shade of a lone sugar maple, the late afternoon sun peeking beneath its leaves and spotlighting the bent, shriveled body Gilly had enshrouded within a shapeless, sleeveless dress.

"I . . ." Larka decided not to waste time explaining and plunged the flowers and their shortened stalks into the oil.

"Didn't pick the ones that were already to seed, did you?" Gilly prodded.

"No," Larka murmured. "None have yet started to seed, and I didn't pick clean any one patch. They do spread without seed." Her hands crept to her hips as she spoke, arms forming a defiant crook before she thrust them flat against her sides.

An odd rattling noise met Larka's ears—Gilly's snickering. The crone's whole body shook with the effort it took to expel such mockery.

"You're a touchy one today," Gilly remarked and stood, joints cracking and popping.

Larka cringed, and her nose crinkled at the sound of Gilly's rickety body.

"Well, get to the garden then." Gilly waved Larka off as she hobbled around the girl to enter the cottage.

Larka headed around the south side of the cottage where beans grew up vines poled to the building's very walls. Many pods hung there, cylindrically fat and ready for picking. Larka's stomach gurgled. She had been in such a hurry to escape to the lavender, she had not eaten lunch at noon.

She tarried not, gathering only the plumpest pods to set inside the cottage entryway, so Gilly could prepare the beans for dinner. Her stomach grumbled. The thought of a plate filled with tender, steaming beans flavored with garlic teased her. She dismissed the thought and tightened then released the muscles of her abdomen over her stomach several times. That trick usually quieted the hunger.

She set to work in the herb garden, pulling out stubborn weed and tender grass blade alike. Under a section of the herbs she poured a basket of drying bean hulls. That would prevent more weeds from clamoring for space beneath these valuable plants as well as feed them. Larka beamed at her work and began to weed around the amaranth plants.

So bent to her task was she that she did not hear Gilly behind her, not until the pain sliced through her back. She yelped and fell to her bottom, tucking her legs and arms against her trunk, rolling to her side as something familiar slashed toward her again and again.

The slashing relented. Larka rolled onto her back and held her hand over her face, shielding her eyes from the stabbing rays of the nigh-setting sun. Gilly stood above her, silhouetted in that light, rawhide whip in hand.

"Look at this, *girl*." Gilly threw a handful of bean pods on Larka's spare chest. "Do those look ready to you? Look! They're skinnier than you are."

Larka held a pod before her eyes. It was skinny, the seed in it unripe, yet she had been so careful to pick only the fullest pods. She squinted up at Gilly.

"Were these in the basket beside the door?"

"Yes." The word slithered out of Gilly, and Larka surveyed the glare in those hate-filled eyes before the hanging skin of the crone's upper arm flapped with the renewed lift of the whip, the rawhide slashing up and back.

With a hiss, the wind collided against the rawhide and sent it hurling through the air to rest it atop the mildly slanting roof of the cottage.

Gilly's head snapped back, a mutinous flare in her amber eyes.

Larka sat there, unable to speak, hand over her gaping mouth. A kind zephyr caressed the wounds of her back. Though she could not see it, sparks glimmered where the wind touched her, and the pain began to fade.

"Get out!" the old woman bellowed.

Larka got her wobbly legs beneath her and backed away from Gilly. She turned hastily and strode away but a rock struck her injured back. Air propelled from her lungs as she fell to her knees. Larka clambered to her feet, and this time she did not hesitate to run as the rocks from old Gilly's garden zipped by her. Air also rushed around the fleeing girl, hissing as it deflected the best-aimed rocks before they could hit their target.

Larka sat atop Last Hill, watching Gilly's cottage. She stared disbelievingly at the whip's insignia scrawled across the roof until sunset allowed darkness to fill her part of the world and, still, she stared.

The crone always came for Larka at dawn after forcing her into an unsheltered night, but never had anything like this happened. Larka could not dismiss how the rawhide whip had come to rest on the roof. The image of Gilly's enraged expression spilled over her once more.

With dawn, would Gilly come for her this time?

"Let her come," Larka breathed. She would not be there awaiting more abuse for folly not her own. "Pick your own beans," she croaked, for her voice had become hoarse with the urge to cry yet surprisingly no fear, not the fear of Gilly that had for so many years possessed her. It was as if the wind with its one act of kindness had washed away all the panic that had clenched Larka's mind in the crone's presence.

Larka rubbed her head and realized it bare. At some point during Gilly's attack, that ill-fitting straw hat had been lost. Tears pricked her eyes; she gritted her teeth. It was just a stupid hat.

She again gazed brokenly at the home that had never been hers. The light in the shuttered windows comforted her until Gilly's hand slew that spark of happiness, too.

In the darkness, Larka lay back and shut her stinging eyes. She began to dream as she always did of the black-haired woman who had brought goat milk to her, the same gentle woman who had brushed Larka's dark hair and sang to her almost daily until her fourth birthday. Then, with great tears in her eyes, the woman had told Larka she could visit no more. The woman's husband had become suspicious of her walks in the woods. The woman had caught him following her the day before, and she had acted as if she were simply gathering wild herbs before returning home.

"Mother," Larka called, nearly roused, then drifted into another dream, that of Gilly screaming while Larka lay abed in the adjacent room—the first time she had heard the crone scream. Another voice roared over Gilly's, that of a man's. Larka could not understand their words, but Gilly appeared the next morning with a thorny switch in hand and dragged Larka out of bed, screeching antipathy; about what, the dream would not recall—the first time she had beaten Larka.

Larka's eyes popped open. Dark skies had begun to lighten to gray. She jerked upright to view Gilly's abode. The door to the cottage snatched back on its hinges. Air caught in Larka's throat. She leapt to her feet, scampered down the opposite side of Last Hill, and fled to Jaunty Village.

CHAPTER 2

GOSE INN AND TAVERN

The crusty streets of Jaunty complained each time Larka a took a step, making her feel even more conspicuous than she already did. She had received enough furtive glances over the last two days to make the boldest person jittery.

She had visited every business in the village, and no one thus far would give her a job—no matter how she begged. One man had even gone so far as to physically shove her out of his establishment. She touched her shoulders; she still wore the bruises from that encounter.

She had one last place in which to inquire, Gose Inn and Tavern, just ahead and to her right. Larka paused at the entrance and took a breath. She pushed a heavy and ancient looking door open then stepped inside. Warmth suffused her skin as her eyes adjusted to the lower level of light. The door shut of its own accord behind her.

Several strides in front of Larka stood two doors, both rough and splintery. The right one opened into what obviously served as the inn's kitchen; the other remained closed. To her left, a rather rugged and railed stairway led upward, sunlight dappling the steps from a window above the landing. A draft flitted the flimsy material of the window's curtain. Through the balustrade, Larka could see that the stairway terminated with a right turn onto the long, narrow landing that hung over the two rooms before her.

She leaned right to peer around the corner of the kitchen. The fore of the tavern and its tables stretched back nearly to the smooth wood of the bar. Several glass-paned windows speckled the walls and supplied the dimmest of daylight in that area.

"Well, what do you want?"

Larka started and looked up to find the voice's source on the landing: a stout woman, her lips pulled into a permanent frown and furrows dug deeply between her brows.

"I-I came to see if there's work to be had?"

A smirk lit the woman's face. "You?" She snorted and leaned against the railing before her. "You want a job here? You couldn't lift a mattress corner to change the sheets."

Larka flinched, and her stomach growled so loudly that the hollow sound of it permeated the room. The woman's eyes widened.

"I can . . . I mean . . . I'm sorry. I didn't mean to waste your time." Larka backed toward the ancient door. She found the knob and turned it to hastily squeeze her thinning body between door and frame.

Her boots clattered on the wooden plankway before she dropped onto the pebbly, dirt street below. Someone caught her shoulder as her feet impacted the street. Larka spun around, hands crossed over her face.

The woman from Gose Inn and Tavern stood above Larka on the slat boards of the sidewalk, hands on hips and buried within the pleats of her dress.

"Jumpy little thing, aren't you?"

Larka tried to overcome her disheveled breathing.

"I thought you might wash dishes, and I do need someone to launder the linens. I suppose it doesn't take that much to strip a bed." The woman paused and extended a hand toward Larka. "I'm Heta."

Larka withdrew a step before she realized the true import of the woman's words and gestures. A slow smile spread across her face.

"Oh, I'm . . . Larka." She grasped the plump hand and shook it.

"Well, come along. We'll feed you and board you. It's all we can afford at the moment." Heta turned on her heel and made strides with a confidence Larka admired on the way back to Gose Inn and Tavern.

Heta insisted Larka eat a bowl of porridge before she introduced the girl to the different bits of the establishment and the girl's duties in each part.

"This is your room." Heta pushed open a small door at the end of the upstairs hallway.

Larka peered into the tiny room. A narrow bed rested alongside the left wall. Next to the bed stood a night stand. A basin—pitcher nested within—sat upon the stand's surface. A closed chimney ran up the back wall, partitioning the small room. A small window to the right of the chimney lit the room. Larka smiled. It was more than Gilly had ever given her. The backroom of the cottage had served as a bedroom to both of them.

"My husband's building a fire in the backyard. You'll meet him soon enough." Heta started off downstairs, pointing to the closet under the stairway. "That's where we store dry goods, coats and the like."

Heta eyed Larka's shirt—too short of sleeve. Then she eyed Larka's rough wool pants—too short of leg—and said, "We'll have to see about those." She then guided Larka to the kitchen.

After the tour, Heta sent Larka to the upstairs lodgings that had been occupied the previous night. Larka removed linens from beds and toted them in a large woven basket to a small backyard enclosed with decrepit gray boards, many askew, like rows of crooked teeth. A fire burned, and over it stood a large metal washtub filled with water. Larka perused the two shelves attached to the inn's backside and found a jar of semi-liquid soap. She poured some into the water, stirred with a short paddle then stuffed sheets and pillowcases into the mixture.

As the water heated, she raced back up the stairs and retrieved the blankets from the three rooms. She returned to the small yard and hung the blankets on a clothesline to get them some sun as she had been instructed to do.

She finished washing the sheets and hung them as well. She then returned to the lodging rooms and proceeded to sweep, mop, and dust—giving the rooms a thorough cleaning, which it appeared they had not received in quite some time.

Heta appeared in the doorway of the last room. "Guess I was wrong. A skinny little thing like you could outwork the best of us. Guess Gilly taught you that."

Breath withdrew from Larka as the image of Gilly's shocked and enraged face swelled inside her mind.

"She can't hurt you here," Heta's warm voice assured and passed quickly over the subject. "We eat again at three-thirty o'clock. Gives us time to eat and prepare for the diners that'll be coming in around five."

Heta's expression took on a distant aspect. "Sometimes, people forget things" —Heta's eyes reattached to Larka— "until reminded. You'll help out in the kitchen, child. That should keep you somewhat out of sight. You can cook, can't you?"

Larka opened her mouth to ask a question but thought perhaps she should know the answer or should at least think on why she needed to be hidden. Recalling the eyes of the villagers, she shuddered and welcomed the haven of being out of sight. So few days filled with so many cold, rancid stares had put her stomach into a constant twinge of guilt and made her feel as if she should simply slink away.

"Can you cook, child?" Heta reiterated with a trace of anxiety. Larka nodded in response, fearing her blank stare had offended Heta.

"Good. You'll feel better soon. A few days more of food and shelter, and you'll be fine." Heta smiled, momentarily vanquishing the permanent scowl that had entrenched her skin. "See you in a bit," she said in a voice Larka had decided rich with melody.

Larka did see Heta a bit that evening as the plump woman ran in and out of the kitchen until good food had sated the inn's diners and they had made their way to either the lodgings upstairs or homes nearby.

Larka yawned as she washed the last plate, then dried and put it away. Finally, she straggled up to her room, cleaned herself up and plopped into her narrow bed, all the while examining the events of the last three days: her escape from Gilly, the air's help in that escape, the lack of food and adequate shelter during her homelessness, the odd and cold behavior the villagers had exhibited in her presence.

Her eyes raw and reddened by exhaustion, she closed them and turned away from the light beaming at her from beneath the door. She fell asleep, for once in the days since she had left Gilly, without a stomach churned by hunger.

The hours passed as she slept, the mischievous wind rapping at her window, wheedling its way inside until it curled like a snake around her head and struck with ominous intent.

Larka awoke to naught but a hissing in her ears and the feeling she was not alone. Gooseflesh prickled along her arms. She glanced around her room, found nothing and eventually felt nothing except the cold draft her window produced. Had she but looked at the crack under her door, she would have seen the solidity of booted feet blotting lamplight.

Larka shivered and thrust her blanket over her head, snuggling deeper into the mattress.

The feet shifted away.

CHAPTER 3

TRESPASS

Bustling out of the hot kitchen, Larka wiped her brow with the sleeve of her shirt. The creamy linen came away splotched with sweat. She leapt up the stairs, taking two steps per stride, and nearly collided with Heta, who half smiled down at her from the landing above.

"Larka, I'd like it if you'd go to Barter Post for me and pick up the things on this list."

Larka grasped the slip of paper Heta held out to her, peering up in question at the woman.

"You'll be all right, child. Wrap yourself in my shawl and make sure you keep the hood up." In spite of her words, Heta's brows inclined toward one another and doubt sang within her dark eyes.

Larka swallowed audibly, her throat suddenly dry. Her heart pumped madly within her chest. She tried to smile as she turned and slowly descended the stairs, reflecting on the rancor of the man who had bodily removed her from Barter Post upon her asking about employment within. She fetched Heta's old knit shawl and pulled the large hood down around her face.

She pulled open the front door and stepped outside on vacillating legs. Two steps away from Gose Inn and Tavern, the wind blew the shawl's hood down to Larka's shoulders. She cringed as a passerby stared at her for much more than a mere moment. The look in his dark eyes told her she erred within the bounds of Jaunty. Larka jerked the hood back over her head, clasping the extra length of it beneath her chin.

"Hi," a voice squeaked next to her.

Larka jumped and peered down her right side to find a little girl—perhaps six years of age—outfitted in a too-small, ragged dress.

"Oh . . . hello. Where did you come from?"

Strands of grimy, dark hair falling away from her face, the child peered up at Larka through pastel-green eyes then pointed at a line of trees separating the village from outlying farms. "Over there," she said.

Larka pondered the meaning of the girl's answer as she entered Barter Post, the child scampering in behind her. The man who had refused Larka employment ogled them. He and a tall, bony woman whispered, their eyes sliding toward Larka and the girl. The man then exited through a doorway behind the opposite end of the counter that ran the length of the store.

That shrew of a woman—long, skinny nose infused between beady eyes—peered at them from behind the store's counter, and her expression transitioned into a scowl as Larka approached with the list held forward, the child still tagging along.

"Get out of my shop!" The shrew pointed at the door. "Go on. Leave."

Larka ceased her steps, mouth ajar. "But Heta at Gose Inn wanted me to pick up some things for her."

"I heard all about you working at the inn. I don't suppose Heta's noticed a drop in business since you arrived, has she?"

Larka's mouth opened to reply, but her throat decided to choke her at that moment and she emitted an odd gurgle; heat rose to her face.

"Now, I believe I told you to *get out*, and after I am finished with her, take that filthy little urchin with you." The woman pushed up a segment of the counter and stepped through the cavity it made. She crossed the gap between them and grabbed the little girl's wrist so that the child dangled in the air, tiptoes just contacting the floor.

The shrew then proceeded to pat in loud, short claps over the remains of the child's frayed dress.

"If you want something to eat, you have to earn it," the woman said and turned the child's trunk to pat her backside without any relinquishment of grip on the thin wrist.

The child squealed and something inside Larka broke. Her hand darted out and grasped the woman's wrist, squeezing until the woman released the child.

The little girl landed nimbly on her feet and reached to cling to Larka's legs.

A cold, hard slap resounded through the store. Larka barely registered the back of the woman's free hand colliding with her face as she shoved a bony wrist and its owner away from her. The woman stumbled and regained footing.

The door to the store had glided open during the altercation, and several customers lingered around the doorway, watching the skirmish's outcome.

Noting the newcomers, the woman stood to her full height, smiling jubilantly at Larka.

Larka shoved Heta's list at the woman. "I'll just leave this with you. Perhaps you can explain to Heta why you tried to break this child's arm and attacked her messenger next time she needs supplies for the inn, or you can just deliver the goods, and she need not know about it.

"How much business, I wonder, does Heta have to lose before you start noticing a drop in your own profits? Or maybe the inn could look down the street a bit farther and do business with the tradesmen there."

The woman's triumph dissipated into slack jaws and sharp eyes rolling upward, as if calculating the damages to her trade, before she tore the list from Larka's fingers.

"I'll send whatever she wants, but you tell her to keep Gilly's bastard out of my store . . . if that you are."

The woman's last comment raised the hair on the back of Larka's neck. She pivoted on her heel and caught the urchin up in her arms to walk with a slow dignity by the spectators until she reached the boardwalk outside the door.

"How's your arm?" Larka put the child down and remained bent to feel the length of the girl's battered forearm. Nothing had broken, but the wrist would bruise, judging by the red marks encircling it.

"Okay." The child grinned, causing her pointed chin to sharpen. She brushed Larka's stinging cheek with her fingertip. "I never saw nobody do anything like that before 'cept my mom; she was brave like you.

"That woman don't like anybody. She 'specially hates the weather witch 'cause people would rather buy their medicines from her than the store."

Larka stood straight and sighed. "No one much likes the weather witch, do they?"

The girl shook her head. "Too scared."

The child grinned again. "Heta's good. She gave you work. She feeds us sometimes."

"Us . . . sometimes?" Larka repeated the words, her mind reaching into the distance between them and grasping the reality. A cold dizziness swayed her. Abused she may have been, but Gilly had fed and sheltered her, and the few days she had slept in the forest had not been pleasant.

A slow smile spread Larka's face. "What's your name?"

"Pentheya," the child replied, peering coyly at her feet before she burst into more dialogue. "I saw you in the woods. You were like us."

"Homeless and hungry?"

Pentheya hesitated then nodded.

Larka held her hand out to the girl. "Come with me."

CHAPTER 4

SPECTACLE

Larka had no more taken a step than she came face to face with a countenance so like her own she stopped and could only stare. Sun glinted off blue-black hair surrounding a pair of smoky-blue eyes so large they nearly overshadowed the pale, oval face in which they rested.

Larka released Pentheya's hand without realizing it.

Pentheya's mouth forming a small O, the child glanced from Larka to the older woman.

The woman seemed to break free of some invisible force then rushed down the street, not looking back at Larka, who turned and watched the gleaming dance of straight hair over the woman's back.

Larka compressed her lips, crushing the word they had formed: "mother."

Pentheya tugged at the shawl, which hung low on Larka, and pointed to the onlookers who had gathered in fascicles—like noxious weeds—on this and the opposite side of the dirt street. Larka gulped. Ominous stares surged at her, yet no one stood too near.

Murmurs rippled through the small crowds.

Movement to the left caught her attention; Larka turned her head and recoiled. Hollow, bleak eyes stared through glass where inside Barter Post people had lined up along the display window to peer out. Larka pushed Pentheya into the street in a race for Gose Inn. As she and her companion fled, Larka caught bits of conversation that only confirmed their vulnerability.

". . . weather witch's bastard . . . showing her face . . ."

One young, blond man pointed at Pentheya. "She's a thief, too. Watch your pockets."

Before Larka got by this man, his head lifted, his turbulent gray eyes pinning her with acrid accusation. Shock took her, and Larka tripped over her own fast-moving feet but quickly re-established balance.

"Go!" she yelled, as Pentheya had slowed for her.

Larka scooped the child up then pushed her own legs with frantic strength, passing the last of the onlookers. As she did so, air blasted the ground and lifted the street's matrix into a churning cloud. Then, with the dense volume of dirt and pebbles it carried, the wind shot into the crowd, scoring skin and lungs alike. Villagers coughed and gagged.

Larka heard the gale strike then the villagers coughing as the inn finally shunted into view. She dared look back to find the blond man staring at her through a blur of dust, malevolence in his mien. Larka dashed into the inn, slamming the door then leaning on it, the sound of her breathing defined by jagged chops. She put Pentheya down.

"Did you see the wind?" Pentheya whispered, pastel-green eyes huge in her gaunt face.

Larka shook her head.

Pentheya's lids blinked over wide eyes. "You could live with us. No one cares what we do so long as they don't see us."

"I live here." Larka stared at her feet, avoiding the child's haunted gaze.

Larka toweled off Pentheya's head. She was surprised to find chestnut-brown hair, with its reddish highlights, beneath the mask of dirt.

"You comb it while I get more water," Larka said and took the basin of dirty water to the squatting room where she dispensed of it down a hole sown into the wooden floor, a hole which led to the sewers beneath Jaunty. Larka then fetched another pitcher of water and scrubbed the rest of Pentheya's body clean.

"I thought a pretty little girl was underneath that crust." Larka grinned and tweaked Pentheya's small nose.

The child giggled.

"We'll have to wrap my sheet around you until your clothes dry." Larka enfolded Pentheya's frail body within the linen then grasped the child's hand.

Larka sniffed the air. The odor of onions and other vegetables melding with meats met her senses.

"I smell dinner cooking. You can eat while I make bread." She led the child downstairs to the kitchen.

Heta's husband, Jenin, smiled at Pentheya whose large eyes blinked up at him innocently.

"I think I know you." He laughed and pointed toward the counter where hot bread and other food awaited diners. "Help yourself."

Larka soon set a bowl of hot, thick liquid and a chunk of bread before Pentheya then used the other end of the sturdy block table to begin the division and final kneading of a large amount of bread dough.

Heta walked into the kitchen through its front entry as Pentheya poked bread sopped with chicken broth into her mouth. Flashing eyes locked on the urchin; Heta's lips dipped inhospitably toward her jaw line.

The muscles in Larka's neck tensed, and she felt the beginnings of a headache as she set dough inside a round basket to rise.

She looked up to see Jenin bend to stir the stew in one of the pots that hung in the fireplace.

"Don't do that," Heta screeched at Jenin and flew to snatch the spoon from his hand. "You'll make the vegetables fall apart."

Jenin met Larka's eyes and winked at her before scuttling away from Heta to fetch a piece of thick, green wood. He opened the brick oven's cast-iron bottom door then positioned the wood in the furnace—beneath the floor of the oven's upper compartment where bread baked—Heta squinting at him the entire time. As he worked, reflected firelight bounced off Jenin's bald pate and highlighted the silver horseshoe of his hair.

"You haven't fired it up until now?" Heta had at Jenin again, hands on her hips. "You'll burn the bread with all that heat," she huffed, though the wood was obviously not dry enough to burn fast and hot. "We've so many people wading into town now that the first frost's near. We can't feed them burnt bread!"

Jenin thumped the furnace door shut and turned to grin at Larka.

Larka refused to smile at the twinkle in that silly, old man's bright blue eyes, for Heta had turned to glower her way. Larka lowered her head and feigned attention to the bread dough beneath her hands, kneading it with a calm rhythm despite her frenzied heartbeat.

Pentheya's fist came to her mouth and the child coughed—very conscious to do so quietly. Still, Heta spun around to glare at the tiny girl. Pentheya scooted down in her seat and trembled, on the verge of tears. Larka gave a slow wink and smile to the child just as something white sailed through the air and hit the older girl's shoulder. Larka caught the garment before it landed on the dough.

"Put your apron on," Heta ordered and stomped out of the kitchen's tavernside entry.

Diners deluged the tavern as the sun sank into some other part of the world. Heta stayed behind the bar or took orders from the guests as they clustered around the small round tables scattered throughout the tavern. Relief flooded Larka as the woman's presence in the kitchen diminished to nothing other than requesting orders at the door and scurrying back to work, leaving Larka in the kitchen with the tinkering of dishes and Jenin's quiet patience.

Larka had sent Pentheya to their room to sleep while she worked.

The child's absence had done much to assuage Heta's anger. Feed Pentheya Heta might do, but housing the child seemed to be another matter altogether.

Larka had finished up chopping potatoes, onions and carrots for another pot of stew when Heta blustered into the kitchen, eyes wide and face wan.

"I need some help out there," Heta said, breathless, and commandeered Larka, pressing quaking hands against the younger woman's back.

Larka gasped as Heta propelled her into the low babble of the dimly lit dining area, feeling quite out of place until she realized most of the people here would not recognize her; they were not from Jaunty.

"Smooth your apron and go serve that side of the tavern." Heta shoved Larka toward a darkened corner where a particularly tall man sat. "Start with him. He's been here a while." With those words, the older woman whirled around and distanced herself greatly from Larka, standing behind the bar as if it were a shield.

Curiosity lifted Larka's brows as she stared after the innkeeper: Heta did have her moods.

Larka turned to note the tall man. His hands were folded under his chin as he surveyed her—*all too keenly*. Larka felt herself flush and ran her hands over her apron as Heta had ordered. Flour dust wisped around her as did the smell of raw onions; her flush intensified. There was little she could do about the mess she was in now other than draw more attention to it—and herself.

She smiled at the man and made her way into the shadows. Most of the tables near him stood empty, the other diners grouped in the fore of the tavern. Larka had to wonder with so many tables bereft of customers why Heta needed her help.

"Would you like a bowl of chicken stew or pot roast tonight?"

The man peered at her coolly through amber-colored eyes and smiled broadly within the handsome square of his face. "Is nothing honeyed on the menu?"

Larka tilted her head and assessed him before speaking, "Pie is baking and will be ready soon. Until then, there is bread of course."

"Of course." He paused and dropped his folded hands to the table. "The pot roast and bread, if you will."

"Of course," Larka heard herself reply before she ran back to the kitchen, certain by the humorous look in his eyes that she had missed something in the conversation. Something about the smooth baritone of his voice also nagged at her, but she quickly forgot the concept as she prepared the bowl of roast and vegetables, heaping it with extra portions then thieving bread still warm from the oven rather than cutting a cooled loaf.

"Enjoy," Larka said as she placed the dish before the man. As she turned to go, he grasped her wrist. All the villus hair on her arms stood up. She gave an involuntary jerk of her right arm, and he let go.

"A mug of beer, if you would, *pretty Larka*."

Larka's heartbeat quickened. She had never seen this man in her life. She stumbled backward and caught her balance.

She swallowed and nodded. "A mug."

Within minutes, Heta—hands ashake—gave Larka a beer mug overflowing with froth. It slopped down Larka's arm as she trudged toward the strange man. She kept her head down, trying not to look at him. She hastened to serve him, slapping the mug down on the table—not caring if it spilled, which it did—and dodging out of his reach lest he touch her again.

Back beside the bar, Larka wiped the spilled beer off her hands and arm with her apron. She scrubbed at her wrist where the man had touched her until the flesh there chastened red.

Larka served several thankful guests and began to feel like there were kind people in the world until a man with well-groomed, short blond hair seated himself near the tall stranger, who still watched her while sipping from his mug with a cool detachment that matched his words.

She approached the newcomer. Recognition set in, and her heart fluttered as if it would escape her ribs. The newcomer set his gray eyes on her and started at her appearance. She jumped back a scant step herself.

A sneer overtook what had been a gentle round face. "Bastard, last time I saw you, you left me with a mouthful of dirt," he breathed. He then raised his voice for all to hear, "I will not be served by Gilly's bastard!"

A hush fell over the tavern, smothering the clanking of utensil against plate, the burr of conversation. Larka felt herself shrivel into smallness, the eyes of many cast upon her. Though she wished to shrink further, to these people she had swollen into immensity.

Larka heard someone move behind her, out of the shadows and into the light. The blond man's gray eyes became turgid and his posture rigid with what Larka could only describe as fear. Hairs on the nape of her neck stood up; Larka turned to find the tall—no, hugely tall—man looming behind her, his long amber hair gleaming in the oil lamp's light. She scuttered away from him to watch the exchange that followed.

The huge man stepped forward, his long black coat swishing around him, and leaned to whisper into the blond's ear. The words, spoken so gently, did not immediately carry to Larka. It seemed to her they were eventually carried on a current of air that led directly into her ear canal though much out of synch with the movement of the man's full lips. "Order your dinner. Eat it and leave."

The tall man straightened to his full height and clapped the blond man on the back with feigned good nature. "There's a good man," he bellowed in a deep voice, a hearty smile spread deceitfully across his face as he looked around the room at the other diners.

Larka had no more troubles that night, but the next night, no one except the road weary entered Gose Inn and Tavern. Thus, she had retired early, just tucked her cold feet under the bedclothes, when a knock at her door caused her to cringe.

Larka grabbed a barrel key off the bedside table and unlocked the door. Her features pinched and anxious, Heta stood in the doorway. She peered around Larka. Larka followed Heta's gaze to where Pentheya lay in the bed, clean and asleep.

"You can't stay here after tonight." Heta stepped in and patted

Larka's shoulder as if that would ease the situation. "You're the best worker I've yet had, but I can't run a business with who you are and the company you keep."

Larka flushed and peered at Pentheya then back at Heta. "I didn't think you would mind. She's just a child—"

Heta held up a hand. "Not her, Larka. That man last night, the tall one. He's trouble. People go missing when he turns up. They're never seen again. He comes around from time to time." Heta looked down and inhaled deeply, puffing up her hefty chest, then exhaled in a long deflation before she met Larka's eyes again. "No one's ever been able to prove he's behind the disappearances, but I know. I saw him once when I was your age. He took a shine to my best friend, and she went missing the day after, and he's . . . he's not aged a day since that time, some thirty years ago.

"Larka, he's the Amber Man, and if he's set his eyes on you . . ." Heta shook her head in a somber motion. "Just be out before dawn."

Larka gaped, unable to speak for a long pause.

"Okay." Larka's voice finally strained forth, and Heta dropped her vision to the floor.

Larka swallowed then went to straighten the blanket on Pentheya, needlessly sliding her hands over the rough material several times after pulling it back up over the child's shoulders. She paused, shivered. The chill that had begun in her feet had crept into her scalp.

The sound of the door closing brought Larka's head up to view the solidity of its thick wood and the protection it offered. She moved to jam the key into its hole, her shaking hands taking some time before the lock clicked into place.

Regardless, Heta had, in effect, removed the door's hinges and left it open for anyone to walk through.

CHAPTER 5

WILD AND FREE

*L*arka lay awake many hours, unable to wrest sleep out of the fretful night, Pentheya occasionally shifting beside her on the narrow bed.

Soon enough, however, the room's tiny window leaked in information of a new day stirring. Larka arose to fetch a small oil lamp off the wall outside her door. She returned to the bedroom and placed the lamp beside the basin on the table then grabbed one of several fire-sticks from a crack in the chimney's mortar and lit the lamp. Shadows fluttered through the room.

Larka washed with speed and pulled loose britches up beneath a thinly woven shirt, effecting the same outfit she had worn when she had escaped from Gilly's cottage. Heta had found no time to replace Larka's clothing as the woman had bespoken.

"Pentheya." Larka ran her fingers over the girl's cheek. "Wake up. We can't stay here anymore. We have to go."

Pentheya yawned, her eyes opening a slit before closing again.

Larka dressed Pentheya while the girl dozed. The child's eyes opened and closed until they remained open, pupils dilated to the light level.

"Heta doesn't want me here?" Pentheya murmured as Larka wrapped the rough blanket around the girl.

"It's me she doesn't want here. She never has, not really." Larka picked the child up and grabbed the oil lamp. She shoved the door open then turned and peered into the room, shaking her head, a sad smile twisting her lips. She had left the bed unmade and dirty with the filth of Gilly's bastard.

Within the swing and flicker of the lamp's light, Larka carried Pentheya down the stairs to the kitchen, skipping the steps that would groan under their weight.

Larka settled the child on thin, swaying legs. The little girl yawned while Larka held up the lamp and studied the kitchen. Larka eventually placed the lamp on the table and took a bag of oats, wheat flour, dried beans, fire matches and other usefuls. She also took a batch of sourdough for bread making; it would last if she could nurture it properly. She placed the items in a large square of cloth and tied its four corners shut.

She reached into her pocket and placed a few coins next to the lamp on the block table. If nothing else, the Amber Man had left a substantial tip the night of his visit. Larka peered at the coins several seconds then repocketed the money. Heta had not exactly overpaid her during the past month. What's more, the inn's mistress had just fed Larka and Pentheya to the overstretched mouth of winter and any other iniquity that might await them.

Larka ushered Pentheya out of the kitchen, leaving the lamp behind. She placed the makeshift supply bag on the floor by the closet under the stairs, careful to be quiet; Heta and Jenin slept in the room between closet and kitchen.

Larka opened the closet door, cringing at its plaintive creak. She peered at the old shawl Heta had assigned her. Conscience fluttered in her stomach as she reached within the closet's dark maw. She grasped the hanger through the garment, hand trembling. Finally, she drew the shawl off the hanger and snatched it out of the closet. With stronger conviction, Larka wrapped the frayed knit around her shoulders, pulled the hood over her head, then gathered up the supply bag and Pentheya.

With twilight, Larka and Pentheya exited into the early morning air, the cold snipping into their flesh. Larka gazed up and down the street, muscles tense. No lamps burned to illuminate their way, and Jaunty's main thoroughfare held no onlookers. Larka blew out a breath and relaxed.

"Where do you stay?" Larka tightened the blanket around Pentheya's frail shoulders.

"The woods." Pentheya shivered.

"The woods," Larka echoed, eyeing the child.

"Well, what do you eat in the woods?" Larka asked as they made the brink of forest.

"Berries . . . apples from the orchards . . . cattail hearts, roots." Pentheya yawned and rested her head on Larka's shoulder.

Larka ducked into the forest then cast her vision behind them. The streets still lay abandoned to twilight.

"Which way? Pentheya . . ." Larka looked down. The girl had fallen asleep.

Larka peered through the umbrage of daybreak, lips pursed, then headed for and had almost reached a nearby spring when Pentheya stirred.

The child blinked, head still propped against Larka's shoulder. "Where are we?" The child sat up, eyes growing wide. "Not here, Larka. Not here!" Pentheya squealed and struggled in Larka's arms, causing Larka to nearly drop her.

"Pentheya, stop." Larka held the girl tight. "Stop, please, little one. Shh. Shh."

Pentheya grew still, face reddened, breathing stilted, as the silent forest bore witness, its musty breath shifting around them, its fingers playing through their hair.

Pentheya shuddered.

A queasy feeling struck Larka, the hair on her neck standing on end. She hugged Pentheya to her, glancing about, better able to see by the beginnings of day. She beheld no one and no thing. Still, a shudder spilled through her.

Larka looked back to Pentheya. "Where would you have us go, little one?"

Pentheya pointed over Larka's shoulder. "To the trees."

Larka gazed at the child, brow knit. "We're in the trees."

"Not these trees," Pentheya insisted, on the verge of hysterics once more. "In the trees with my brothers! That way." Pentheya pointed again.

"Alright." Larka nodded.

Something rustled behind them and she peered back over her shoulder as they started downhill. A dark shadow moved behind trees not far from them. Larka whipped back round, speeding her steps, barely noticing the sun's ascension or the golden glow it cast through the curtain of autumn-hued leaves below.

"How many of you are there?" Larka said, refusing to slow her stride.

"Don't know," Pentheya replied then held up the fingers of her right hand. "Maybe this many." Pentheya pushed her thumb onto her palm. "Or this many."

Here, Larka slowed, perusing those slender fingers. "I see," she murmured. "I'll teach you to tally soon. It's a useful skill."

Pentheya guided Larka on to a grove of well-spaced, thick-trunked trees. So silently as to be unheard, three more urchins emerged from somewhere within the woods: two babes led by an older boy.

Larka halted, breath rushing into her lungs. "Dear gods," she exhaled, blinking hard against abrupt emotion. The boys stood before her, clothes so bedraggled they were nearly naked, bony rib-cages and painfully thin limbs attesting to their starvation.

"Have you no food? No shelter?"

"We have the trees," Pentheya replied and struggled out of Larka's grasp, knocking the supply bag out of Larka's hand.

"This is Ian," Pentheya touched the older boy's chest; he was perhaps four. "And this is Arnt and Halty." Pentheya pointed at each small twin as she spoke his name.

The twins examined Larka for the briefest moment. Their eyes held a darker green than Pentheya's, and their hair grew paler, almost blond. One of them whimpered then the other.

"You can't stay here," Larka began. "There's the spring near here. We could build shelter there."

"Can't," Ian replied. "Land *belong*." He spread his scrawny arms, his green eyes as huge as his sister's. "All land *belong*. We hide." Ian's eyes broadened further as he looked around them. "Always hide."

"We have the trees," Pentheya repeated and pointed at a wide tree with a large notch carved into its trunk, a notch starting near the ground and narrowing several feet up. "This one's our house some-times. So big inside, good hiding."

"Hiding . . ." Larka cocked her head, studying Pentheya. At that point, the whimpering twins began to bawl, each embracing the other, neither looking at Larka. Understanding hit her like a fist in the gut.

Larka shook her head faintly as she reached for the bawling boys. "I'm not here to hurt you."

The twins began to wail, edging away from her. Larka withdrew, watching them. She turned back to Ian and Pentheya.

"How long have you been here?"

"A fall, a winter, a spring, a fall," Pentheya spouted.

"You've been through a winter with no shelter? How . . . what did you do to survive—to live?"

"We not. We die," Ian said, grief flitting through his brow, jutting his bottom lip. "Jonah die last winter."

"Oh." The word rang out of Larka.

"Pentheya, you never told me . . ." Larka began, but Pentheya crossed her arms and turned away, refusing to look at anyone.

Larka turned away as well. She rubbed at her stinging eyes, lungs nagging her to breathe. She sucked in several unsteady breaths then turned back to the children, her next words solid:

"Where are your parents?"

Bemused stares came as the response.

"Your mother and father?"

"Gone. Woke up one morning in woods and just gone. Ian and I take care of brothers," Pentheya said—sniffing, wiping at her nose— as she walked to Larka and leaned against the older girl's side.

Larka squatted and her arm curled around Pentheya of its own voli-tion while her eyes cast once more upon the now-whimpering twins, the small boys aged no more than three. Tears streaked through the dirt on their agitated faces.

"Was the Amber Man. Saw him. Thought it a dream when Ma take us into woods until woke up." Ian nodded, eyes round, fearful.

Pentheya whispered next to Larka's ear, "Ma hid us in the trees while Da fight him. She left. She don't come back, but we go back to the riverboat. Was gone."

Larka swallowed hard. She then grasped Pentheya by the shoulders, turning the child to look squarely at her. "Well, I'm here now, and tonight we're going to have better shelter . . . and food."

The twins quieted. Expectant eyes fell upon Larka as she dug through the supply bag to produce a small cast-iron pot. She then began to collect stones and rest them in a circle to contain a fire.

Without instruction, Pentheya gathered sticks and laid them beside Larka as Larka poured water from a skin into the pot to make oat porridge, which had to be eaten with grubby fingers because Larka had not taken any eating utensils; they were much more costly than a pot.

That night they slept within the hollowed tree. Larka had built a lean-to over its opening with sticks and leaves, which cut the chill breeze into a slight draft blowing over them. Larka still shivered most of the night, having thrown the only blanket and her shawl over the children. Her muscles eventually cried out at the cramped ball she had rolled herself into within these close quarters.

Odd, scuttling noises emitted often within the tree's wood as well. Yet clashing loudly over these noises were the unheard cries of homeless babes and their parents' fate. Thoughts of the Amber Man and where he might be lurking picked at Larka until her flesh screamed with a mixture of chill and fear bumps.

Eventually, she left the shelter of the tree and fed the near-dead fire, eyes darting to the forest, trying to pierce its darkness. She sat down next to the greedy flames, her hands and body collecting warmth.

A breeze carried the smell of lavender, blanketing her with it. So tired was she that she did not contemplate until the next morning how the scent had reached her this far from the Lavender Hills. She, instead, breathed deeply and lay next to the fire, finally relaxing into slumber.

CHAPTER 6

OLD JOETON IN THE TREES

Within the silence of sleeping children, Larka's stomach gurgled. She had become leaner in these woods, not eating so the children could. Her reward had been flesh on their bones and smiles on their faces, but food now ran short. The last bit of flour had been eaten yesterday morning, and the few coins she had possessed had been long spent by Ian in his trips to the village.

Larka sighed and shook her head as she recalled the ludicrously high prices the child had been charged for a bag of flour and beans. The merchants had known whom that food fed. No thanks to their avarice or ill will or both, Larka had found herself, with the moon's light as comfort, stealing apples out of a farmer's small orchard, digging up the few potatoes remaining in a vast field, collecting dandelion greens from the roadside, or digging cattail roots from land that "belonged" as Ian so often reminded her, but these influxes of food were not enough. In winter, when the ground froze deep and snow covered all . . .

Larka closed her eyes and breathed, hearing little other than the stammering fire before her.

They had a few handfuls of dried hawthorn berries left in one of the pine-straw baskets Larka had woven. Fortunately, barberries still hung in bright red globules on shrubs along the trail, but they filled her gut little. Larka added a handful of berries to the cook-pot's contents.

She rubbed her aching head, shoving apple slices and berries over heated cast iron with a piece of wood.

Near sunset, Larka built a lean-to against the thick bole of a red oak. Under Ian's advice, they moved the camp often; the children knew every hollow tree in the forest. When she had finished the lean-to, Larka peered overhead. The moon's near circle peeked at her through the red oak's bower.

Larka motioned for Ian to follow her.

"Can't I go?" Pentheya seemed to know instinctively where they were going and sat down in a resigned manner, as if she knew the answer before Larka shook her head.

"Someone has to watch the twins," Larka said. "Ian's better at climbing." Larka grinned, but Pentheya frowned and turned away.

Larka tucked the shawl around Ian. As she and the boy departed, a mist crept up around them, its dampness clinging to them, amplifying the cold until it pierced into their bones.

Ian shivered and hummed beside Larka under the starlight. Larka's breath fogged before her. How they would survive the full gale of winter she could not foresee. The lean-to she had built this day had been sturdier and thicker set with branches than usual. She had even plied mud and pine straw to the vertical cracks that aligned between the sticks, but the cold would be deadly.

She had listened to the stories the villagers had told Gilly of relatives and acquaintances freezing to death each winter . . . *and Jonah had died last year.* Larka pushed the thoughts from her mind as she and Ian reached the orchard's edge.

"Shh." Larka held a finger to her lips.

Ian stopped humming and nodded.

They scavenged a few apples off the ground. Several of the well-pruned trees also contained small quantities of fruit, most of which felt knotty. Larka wrinkled her nose as she groped the fruit: who knew what they would look like in the daylight. She tucked the apples into her front shirttails—no time to be choosy.

Ian tapped her shoulder and pointed upward. Through the night's vague haze, she saw the full, round shapes hanging above them. Even in the dim light, these fruits looked succulent. Someone had not been efficient in their apple picking. She helped Ian climb into the height of this tree—taller than any other in the orchard—and waited as twigs snapped and limbs shook above her.

Air shifted over Larka. She breathed in its coolness and grimaced. A musky odor had assaulted her sense of smell. Several heartbeats later, she heard a large animal padding through the orchard, snuffing as it went. Then she saw a dark shadow glide through the thin mist and stop beneath a tree to her left, its nose pointing toward her. As still as she stood, she knew the creature had found her.

"Ian, don't come down. It's not safe," Larka whispered. "There's a dog."

The boy's movements hushed.

A baritone growl met her, and the big dog stepped out of the night shadows into a mist lit by vivid moonlight. Air swished through her hair, followed by a thud; an arrow's shaft stuck out of the tree in front of her. Larka let go her shirttails. Apples thumped to the ground. She ran fast and far from Ian, the dog's snarling bark at her heels.

The dog bit into her ankle, and she fell forward into the composting humus on the orchard floor. She kicked at the beast with her other leg, yet the dog retreated only enough to open its mouth and sink its teeth into the meat of her calf. Larka screamed.

A burst of wind plucked the animal up and flung it, back first, across the orchard—a black streak against the twinkling night sky. Larka heard a thud along with the dog's pained yelp, and then all was disquiet. She looked in the direction the dog had been thrown and noted its dark form reclined at the base of a tree, a still and twisted shadow with a broken back.

She heard the farmer running toward her and crawled into the dark woods that encased part of the orchard. She stood and took a step. A spraying sound cast upon decaying leaves. Larka took another step, and the spraying resounded. Had she known a curse word she would have flung it at that moment, for with each step she took, blood arose within her punctured calf and spurted onto the forest floor before her.

The farmer shuffled around in the orchard behind her. Between Larka and farmer, the wind shifted, the mist thickened. Larka tried to speed her steps. She tumbled forward, but strong hands stopped her. Arms tucked underneath her knees and back, and Larka struggled to break somebody's hold as that somebody lifted her off the ground.

"Hush now, Larka. Es safe. Es safe." She barely discerned her captor, a man, point toward a lighted building in the distance, but she knew that voice, had heard it before.

Larka stilled and became intensely aware of the blood dripping off her leg as the man dashed toward the lighted structure and finally brought her inside. His face, illuminated by an oil lamp, turned into one she had seen before—the carpenter's son. Gilly's benches and cabinets had been built by this man and his father not so many years ago.

"Seems you meet Joeton." The young man set her on a high bench beside the door and met her eyes a moment before he examined her leg, his face contorting with concern. "Es not so good, so much bleeding." He tapped the area above the injury on her calf. "I fix— and your ankle." He let his hand rest around her ankle for a moment as he examined it.

A cot stood along the opposite wall. The man left her to pillage its cream-colored top sheet, tearing strips of cloth from it. A pitcher of water and cake of soap already sat next to her.

"With way it bleed, I think es not necessary this." He pointed to the soap upon returning. "But we make sure es okay." He lathered and rinsed her wounds at great speed, letting the rinse water drip onto the floor's wide wooden planks.

The room tilted. Larka swooned, a bleary dizziness—caused by hunger and bloodletting—overtaking her.

"Whoa." The man propped her up and pressured the wound with the heel of his palm. "Es not so bad. Old Joeton just bite you where it matter as far as blood."

"He's dead," Larka whispered, peering around the carpenter's son, taking in little of him other than his black pants and the splotch of blood on his pale shirt. She barely registered the many worktables and benches, which took up much of the shop's space.

"Yes, and a good thing. I hear him barking and come running. He bite into me once or twice as a lad. He bite more than his fair share of people." He cocked his head to peer into her eyes. "Wonder how such a slight thing as you manage to knock him so far. I see him fly before I grab you." The man grinned, mischief twinkling in his eyes.

Larka allowed contact with those eyes but a moment then stared over the man's shoulder at the woodworking tools lying about the shop, her silence stilling the conversation, her mind's eyes once more reliving that dog's death and hearing its cry as it slammed into the tree. She had seen only one other event such as this occur: the ascendance of Gilly's whip to the cottage roof. She had tried to forget it—to dismiss it—but no more could she do so. She had heard the air whoosh by her and grab the dog: the same sound she had heard before the rawhide whip had been snatched from Gilly . . . as if the air had grown hands. She recalled also hearing the wind scour the villagers with dirt and rocks as she and Pentheya had escaped them at Barter Post. She could no longer dismiss that occurrence as unassociated with her either.

"Larka." The name sounded as if called from a great distance. "Larka." A hand waved before her eyes. "Here, drink this." He took her hands and wrapped them around a warm mug.

Larka smiled uncertainly at the carpenter's son. The pain in her calf had numbed. So lost had she been in her thoughts, she could not recall when he had stopped applying his hand to her calf and bandaged her wounds.

Larka leaned forward and sipped the milk. Warmth trickled down her forehead and dripped into the milk, spreading red tentacles into its whiteness. She reached up and brushed at her hairline. A red stain smeared her fingertips.

"Es no good. No good!" the man exclaimed and seemed to hop up and down. He lifted her hair and found blood staining her neck then began to clean her as if she were an infant. "What happen here?"

"The—an arrow. I thought it missed." Larka shuddered at the recollection of that weapon hurtling by her head.

"Farmer Smithen try to shoot you? That sorry old shat! That part of the orchard es not even his. I tell Papa and—" He stopped short of his full statement as he caught Larka's expression, one of stunned awe. "Sorry. Es the dark moon, Larka. Smithen think you cursed under it."

"Dark moon," she repeated, and her thin frame shook. A chill draft touched her, and a burst of memory assailed her with an image of Gilly, crow eyes cold and angry—always angry after that point—as she had yanked Larka out of her bed and out of her dreams: the first time she had beaten Larka.

> *"You pissed the bed again, girl. Get up! Why the dark moon gifted a stupid brat like you . . ." she had yelled, and her arm had risen and . . .*

Larka clamped her teeth together, not just to control the trembling caused by that recollection but also her present fear: savage persecution raised itself against those even suspected of being children of the dark moon. And this resurfaced memory, along with Guta's words, accused her of being such.

She gasped. Farmer Smithen knew. The villagers—they all knew. More than being Gilly's bastard had put itself upon her.

"I didn't know," Larka cried.

The carpenter's son perused her face with a penetrating stare then nodded. "Es okay. You know why now they treat you so." He pushed her wrist upward. "Drink. You need milk."

Ignoring the taint of blood in her milk, she drank of it. Lowering the mug, she peered into golden-brown eyes, which matched the highlights in this man's short hair.

"Where are you from?"

He grinned and bowed with a flourish of his hand. "Lands far beyond, madame. Me name es Guta."

He busied himself, folding what was left of the bed linen and placed it on her lap. "Your mother no give introduction when Papa and me call."

Larka straightened her spine with deliberate slowness. "Gilly is *not* my mother."

Guta hesitated before replying, "Es good. My mother never treat me like weather woman do you. I see what she do. Es good you leave."

Larka nodded though not certain wild and free was as good as she had thought it would be.

"You and the children been living in me Papa's part of forest. He and me Mama no mind. You find the apples we leave, me thinks. Ma, she try to feed the children, but they run, afraid because farmers like Smithen." He paused, lips parted, eyes growing distant. Those lips finally enclosed words, "Like they vermin or worse when they only children." A hard expression crossed his face; then he exhaled somberly. "And the way they treat you when you only a child."

"I am not a child. I have never been a child," Larka said without anger and jumped off the bench. Pain shot through her abused calf. The circumference of the blood on her bandage increased. Her ankle buckled.

Guta caught her beneath the arms and steadied her until she ventured to put a little weight on her leg.

"I no mean to offend." He pointed to the cot in the corner of the workshop. "You sleep there if like. I sleep in floor."

"No, I must return. Ian could be hurt. I've been here too long already."

"You make good mother." Guta shook his head, half smiling. "Wait here."

"But—"

"Only be a minute. I meet Ian few times. Es slick. With no Joeton, it take more than Smithen to catch Ian." Guta left and returned with a sack made lumpy by its filling. He placed the rest of the torn linen in it, slung it over his shoulder, and tucked an arm around Larka's waist in order to balance her.

"I walk you home. Es not far."

CHAPTER 7

PETIT THEFT

*B*efore Larka, the central vein of Jaunty stood covered in a thick snaking mist, the dawn sun brushing the fog with tepid light. She breathed in deeply, trying to rebuild the courage that kept seeping out of her. She then slunk through fog and street alike to a narrow alleyway and hid behind a stack of wooden crates. She sat there several moments, noting her leg poking out of the shawl. Her pants, ripped by old Joeton's teeth, gaped to display reddish scars on the pale skin of her calf. She grimaced and wondered what she had been thinking to come amidst these people. Her stomach gurgled in answer to that question.

The sack of food Guta had given her had run out two days ago, and the children's teeth clattered all too often at night: hollow bellies gave no fuel for warmth. Although she had accepted their charity once, it felt wrong to take food from Guta Wittin and his family to feed hers. She could not bring herself to ask for more.

Her wind friends had pressed sound into her ears once before when the Amber Man had defended her at Gose Inn and Tavern; she would see if they were willing to do so again.

She listened intently and waited for many hours, hunkered behind the crates, her muscles eventually complaining with cold and cramps, but the sound she wished to hear did not come. She watched the shadow between the wooden buildings on either side of her until the sun began to push it down the south-facing wall of the alley, giving her a bit more warmth.

She grew sleepy and shut her eyes, still thinking of her goal. A chill breeze stirred about her. Then her consciousness snatched forth in a burst of swishing air and careened through the streets, nearly entering the forest until she forced a stop. She hovered—it was all she could do until the shock of being part of her body yet apart from it wore off. As she gazed about herself, she was able to sense people and buildings as nothing more than blurs of multicolored light.

She tried to move her spirit forward and began to career once more. She halted, hovered. This incorporeal form mired her ability to think clearly; thus, Larka had to focus with great intensity on moving slowly, in a straight line, up, down, left, then right until she had gained enough skill to navigate. Soon enough, however, she prodded the bodies of passersby and picked up the vibrating friction of coinage in a pouch.

With that confirmation, Larka's spirit slammed back into her body. Her eyelids flipped open, and she gasped—a desperate wheezing sound. Larka peered about herself, eyes round. Naught but the silent alley greeted her.

She stood and, with legs shaking beneath her, shuffled into the street. After one last long draw of breath, she peered down the main thoroughfare. A plump gentleman, matching the stride and shape of blurred lights she had witnessed, walked toward Gose Inn.

Larka secured the hood of her tattered shawl. With surreptitious steps, she paced into the man's pursuit until she stood an arm length behind him. She held her breath and reached out, a knife—given by Guta—poking from beneath the knitted shawl at ready to slash tethers joining money pouch to belt.

Before she could act, the pouch lifted as if held by unseen hands. The tethering untied of its own accord, and the pouch slipped into her palm. As her oblivious victim walked away, Larka stood, rooted to the spot, staring down at the weighty pouch until she heard footfalls clunking behind her. She tucked the pouch into her tattered britches and scampered to her alleyway. There she counted out enough coins for supplies.

With her hood still over her head, she crept into a barter store. Larka felt the merchant's eyes on her, heard footsteps coming toward her. She coughed in a dry, hacking manner. The footsteps ceased then receded. Yet she still felt spying eyes on her back as she perused the shelves.

Face downcast, she placed a bolt of thick woolen material on the payment counter and feigned coughing again, angling her head down and to the side. She requested the rest of her order: various food items, thread, needles, a thick blanket, cotton cloth, and a large bag for carriage. She just managed to heft the bag over her shoulders without knocking off her hood.

Unlike Ian, she paid only the value of the items.

Larka entered the camp. The three boys sprang out of the tree, nearly knocking the lean-to over. Pentheya, however, crept out from behind the lean-to, hugging herself. Ian solely remained wrapped in the blanket. For the twins, Larka had rigged clothing out of the sack Guta had given her. She now took the woolen material out of her bag and wrapped it around them.

Kneeling, she carefully removed other items from the bag then held bread toward the children. Ian grasped the loaf and tore off chunks for each child, the twins giggling and squealing. Larka grinned at the excited chatter of her clutch.

Pentheya, however, stared at her bread and sighed then let it drop by her hip with the fall of her arm. As Larka distributed the rest of the goods into pine-needle baskets, she watched the girl. Pentheya stared at Larka as if Larka were barely there, with no trace of enthusiasm.

"How are you feeling, Pentheya?"

"Okay," Pentheya said in a thin voice.

"We have a new blanket. Would you like to use it?"

The child stared through Larka.

Larka rose and took a step toward the girl. Wind tore through the forest at that moment. The lean-to rattled. Larka stopped, turning her attention on the lean-to. She bit her bottom lip, tapped her chin.

"We must have better shelter before the full breadth of winter hits. I've thought a long time about it. I was lucky to find a good purse." She patted the coins in her pocket. "Ian, Pentheya, I have a transaction to make. Would you please start the beans while I am gone?"

Larka smiled at Ian's shy nod.

Pentheya sighed.

As Larka bent to hug Ian goodbye, her eyes lingered once more on the girl.

Larka tucked the woolen cloth more firmly about the huddled twins. "You two should get back behind the lean-to, into the tree. It's cold out."

Larka took the shawl off and moved to wrap it around Pentheya. When finished, she brushed Pentheya's forehead with her lips then leaned back to peer down at the child. The youngster's pale features imbibed upon a sickly, yellowish hue.

"You are warm to the touch."

"I just need some water," Pentheya murmured.

Larka looked to Ian and pointed to the edge of the road nearest them. "Do you see that white-flowered plant yonder? The one with the flat-topped clusters?"

He nodded, eyes locked on the plant.

"That flower is called yarrow. Lucky for us, it likes the cold. Collect two handfuls of the flowers and make Pentheya a tea from them." She looked at Pentheya. "Drink the tea for me and keep warm while I am gone. And eat something." Larka hugged the girl tightly and departed, foreboding gnawing at her heart.

Larka's quavering fist knocked on the Wittin door. It opened. Wittis Wittin's head popped out, looking much like an older version of his son's.

"Come." The elder Wittin beckoned her inside.

As she entered the warmth of the large home, she noted Wittis wore the same silly smile Guta often did.

Wittis waved her to a well-cushioned chair. Larka cleared her throat as she accepted the proffered seat then forced herself not to fidget. She refused the bread and tea they offered. She had eaten enough during her earlier walk home and wanted to cut through the pleasantries, as Pentheya's condition nagged at her.

"I came to ask if I could buy an acre of your land," Larka said.

Guta's mouth fell open for a moment before he clamped it shut, his eyes narrowing then filling with humor. She ignored his reaction, unsure of how to interpret it, and plodded on.

"You are kind to allow us to live on your lands, but I think it unfair that we accept your kindness without giving some form of payment."

Wittis held up his calloused hands. "You not pay me for use of land. You need it."

"I wish to buy an acre to *own* it," she enunciated with slow and deliberate care. "We need to build shelter before full winter hits. We can't have that without our own land."

"Ah," Guta exhaled and spoke to his father as much with his hands as in a language replete with rolling *r*'s and rapid speech, a language Larka would have found it hard to wrap her mouth around.

Wittis nodded his head and also spoke in the foreign language.

"He say one silver coin will buy an acre," Guta said, his brows arched well above his eyes.

"That seems a very low price," Larka said, shifting on the comfortable chair.

"Es worth little more," Wittis said, nodding as if the rapid motion of his head would cause her to nod in agreement.

"Two silver," Larka countered and pulled the coins from her

pocket. The rest of the loot had been tucked into a pine-needle basket, beneath the flour bag.

Guta chuckled and spoke to his father in a low voice, "Skull thick with pride."

Wittis chuckled as well, and Guta moved to accept the coins for him, giving Larka a wink before he returned to his father's side.

"You need help with build home. You accept this for extra coin. Yes?" Wittis offered, nodding.

Larka stared, uncomprehending for a long moment. Kindness had been so rare in her life. Then breath escaped her. Tears pricked at her eyes. She gazed at her feet, opened her mouth to speak but found she could not. She gulped in air and tried again but to no avail. Heat built in her face, and her faded boots peered up at her through crooked eyelets, the only witnesses to her crimson cheeks.

"Larka, you not accept our help?" Guta quipped. "Es cold. Snow come soon. Es late now!"

Larka cleared her throat. "Of course." She managed a hoarse agreement, lifting a discomfited smile to the men.

Agitated air tore at her, raising her clothing, crawling against her skin. Thereupon, anxiety pounced on Larka's heart and batted it about. Some wrongness churned without. Pentheya's bleak visage swirled into Larka's mind. Larka jumped to her feet and smacked into a flesh-colored object. She started, for Wittis stood in her path.

"Oh," she exclaimed and shook his outstretched hand. How long had it dangled there? She had not noticed, just as she did not notice the affectionate approval in Guta's eyes.

CHAPTER 8

RED-EYED MONSTERS

Guta trailed Larka as she departed his parents' home, his footfalls an evanescent echo within her head, apprehension a loud gnawing within her core. As she reached the edge of a Wittin field, she urged herself to greater speed, but Guta's hand caught her shoulder—a firm encumbrance in the late-afternoon sun.

"Where you go in such hurry? I must to speak with you." He nodded just as his father had done previously, and Larka caught her head before it bobbed to that inane rhythm.

"The children. I must return," Larka offered as reply, staring to her right at the trail and itching to be on her way. When she glanced at Guta, however, she met such a grave countenance she quelled the inclination and turned to face him.

"Listen to what I must to tell you." He shook his head just as emphatically as he had nodded it. "Es no safe for you and children so far from us. The villagers . . . they talk . . . say bad things 'bout you and children."

"What do they say?" Larka asked, fear lowering her voice to a husky whisper.

"They say you and children steal from fields. They say es blight on harvest. They say you daughter of dark moon and something make them forget what you are. This make them angry . . . like . . ." He tugged at his chin with his fingers then stopped and spoke, "Es like brooding. Es no good, this brooding. Will get worse."

"But we took so little. Apples no one else would have, potatoes left to rot, cattails no one else harvests." Larka felt blood thrumming wildly through her head. She pressed her left temple with her forefinger. "How could we have blighted their crops when they had already harvested them?" A tense strain in her shoulders reached into her neck. "And how could something *make* them forget?"

Guta placed a hand on Larka's shoulder. "So sorry for this worry. Es someone to blame for bad fortune. You come close to us and no so much worry. Es safer."

"Guta, what about birth under a dark moon do you know?"

Guta's hand dropped away from her shoulder and animated his speech. "Es birth under the second dark—uh, no—second no moon in month's time. Es not often to happen. In my home country they no give punishment for it." He chuckled. "I think old Joeton know, huh? That mean dog. He deserve it. You just be careful no one end up like old Joeton, and no one confirm what you are." He used the emphatic nod again.

Old Joeton knew . . . in the last moments of his life. Conclusions snapped into place within her mind; the villagers were right to fear her. Larka inhaled deeply, wishing her whacking heartbeat would lay off the walls of her chest. And, yet again, a separate source of apprehension pricked at her consciousness on wisps of wind. She gazed toward the children as if she could see them through the distance.

"Larka," Guta called through the haze of her thoughts. She looked back up at him. "Will be okay," he said, concern in his eyes, in the set of his brow.

"Thank you," she whispered and tried to take a step on the path home. Guta caught her shoulders, one hand on each, forcing her to peer up at him.

"You come tomorrow. Here." He pointed to the ground. "We pick land close by. Mama take care of children. She like little ones. But no more trips to Jaunty, Larka. Es dangerous, what you do. Maybe no one bother you if you no steal." His lips curved upward.

Larka's chest tightened, breath scalding that tightening each time she inhaled. All of her senses rang with alarm. Pure panic tugged her, and the children served as its magnet, yet Guta would not let go.

"You could ask for work if too proud to take more food. We would have give it." Guta's lips lost their curve, and he tapped her head with his finger. "Skull thick with pride." His palm slid around her jaw.

Larka jerked away, took a step back, not liking what she finally saw in his eyes.

"I must be going." She tripped over her feet and caught her balance to race the length of the trail back to her urchins.

Larka reached the children as dusk settled into night, her stomach a roiling churn of worry, yet she found nothing amiss amongst them except that Pentheya was not inside the shelter. As well, the youngster clawed at her left ear where she sat before the fire.

Larka bent and inhaled over the child's ear opening—as Gilly had once done to Larka as a child. The salty odor of pus emanated there. Larka fetched the cylindrical vial of lavender essential oil she had purchased earlier.

"Tilt your head right, Pentheya, so I can put some essence in your ear." Larka knelt. Using the vial's pointed stopper, she slid a few drops into the child's ear canal.

Pentheya screeched and clutched the outer flesh of her ear. Larka rapidly replugged the vial and tucked it into her pocket. She caught and rocked Pentheya gently in her arms, wishing the essence had been infused with some sort of oil to reduce the sting.

As she held Pentheya, the telling air swirled about her, and Larka's skin pricked into tiny mounds of anxiety. The burn in her stomach increased. She peered into the dark forest.

And screamed!

A pair of glowing red eyes leered at them from amongst the tree trunks then swung out of sight.

A vertical tunnel of wind built about Larka and Pentheya then charged toward the monster. Larka heard a thud followed by a grunt. The breakage of vegetation assured her that the large animal pummeled the forest's undergrowth in flight, the sound becoming distant and leveling to nothing.

Larka's fretting stomach fell silent and her heartbeat calmed. She sighed with relief.

Pentheya gazed up with her ever-haunted eyes. "When you make wind, you sparkle." She pointed to Larka's chest.

Larka followed the direction of Pentheya's tiny finger yet did not see the smoky-blue sparks the child had witnessed; they had already faded.

"The wind comes when I need it. I don't make it." Larka smiled and kissed the child's forehead. "You are safe now, and we will have a home soon. But, for now, go to sleep with your brothers in the shelter."

Yet another night did pass without Larka succumbing to slumber. She stared into flames through most of the dark hours, lying on her side, occasionally feeding the fire, and thinking. Of all the things that red-eyed creature had been, big was definitely one of them and hungry for human flesh more than likely another.

CHAPTER 9

LAYING THE FOUNDATION

*L*arka walked across the floor of her log cabin and relished the sound of brick underfoot. She and the Wittins had finished laying the floor yesterday, one of the last steps in completing the one-room home. Larka dipped her fingers into a bucket that contained a mixture of clay, sand, and some whitish material she could not identify. She smeared the compound between two of the many logs constituting her home's walls and smoothed it with a flattened block of wood.

Pentheya and Ian worked in silence on the cracks that rose to their height.

Larka shivered. Despite the fire burning in the fieldstone fireplace, the drafts between the logs remained too numerous, and the wind flourished its arms outside, battering against the walls, whistling into their new home. Larka rested the wooden block atop the mud then extended and flexed her fingers; the joints cracked like unoiled hinges.

Larka hugged Heta's old shawl around herself as she glanced at the children. They wore the thick sweaters and hats Kila, Guta's mother, had knitted for them as well as new britches cut from the bolt of cloth Larka had bought in Jaunty in what seemed like much more than the month since. The twins remained in Kila Wittin's care, warm inside the spacious Wittin abode.

Larka spread the muddy mixture and smoothed it with more rapid motions until she and her urchins had finished two walls.

The clop of hooves outside announced the arrival of a delivery. Guta's boisterous voice met her ears, and Larka's heart beat aloof. She had thought it would take longer for him and Wittis to return. She resisted the urge to open the shutters of her home's single window and peek out, but Ian and Pentheya had no problem following that compulsion. They stood on tiptoes, trying to see outside the small, square opening adjacent the door.

"Bring here," she heard Guta order someone, and a scuffling outside the door made her cringe, yet no one entered, and eventually she heard the clop of hooves withdraw.

"You ready for your furniture?" Guta boomed in the doorway, merriment dancing in his golden eyes. He did not await an answer before he disappeared to fetch her wares.

Pentheya and Ian ran to the doorway, retreating each time Guta and Wittis reappeared. The two men carried in a roped bedframe, a mattress, various bags and barrels of food, which they lined against the wall opposite the door, and lastly a small table with four chairs.

Guta settled the last chair around the square table and beamed at Larka. She paused long enough to simper then turned back to her chinking.

"Come now, Larka. Es all very nice. Will suit the children well, yes?" He stood there, a short coat over his usual pale shirt and dark pants, hands by his sides.

Larka resurveyed the mattress. It rested upon taut ropes tied in a latticework over the bedframe. She grinned at Ian and Pentheya, who had both lined up next to the bed. "Yes, I think they like it very well."

"I like it," Pentheya spouted and nudged Ian.

"Me too," Ian chimed, rubbing his muddy hands down his pant legs.

Larka shivered again. The cold had numbed her fingers and crept into the meat of her palms. Her fingers slipped, and the wooden block clattered onto the floor. She reached to pick it up but Guta intercepted, taking the tool and redirecting her with a light shove toward the fireplace.

"Warm up, Larka," he said then spun around to Pentheya and Ian, who eyed the bed with intent written across their faces. "And you two, no playing on the bed with so much mud. Go. Let Mama wash you up. We finish here, soon." Guta nodded, an overdramatized squint lifting his left eye, his lips puckered. The expression broke, melding into a grin. He chuckled.

Giggling, the children scampered out of the cabin.

Wittis—always quiet—smiled at Larka and grasped a wooden block. He picked up the children's bucket of muck to begin chinking the last two walls.

Larka allowed her hands to thaw partially—she could at least wriggle her fingers again—before returning to fill in gaps. The sooner they finished, the sooner Guta would leave. She felt guilty at such a thought. The Wittins had done so much for her, even taking her money and purchasing the furniture and supplies she needed, so she could stay tucked out of sight. Yet each time she looked at Guta, she saw certain expectations spilling out of him. Even now, Larka noted Guta's head rise frequently to look her way. She refused to acknowledge him or the concern she knew imbued his eyes.

She and the two eldest urchins had slept in the workshop since the day after sighting that red-eyed creature in the forest. Guta had slept in his parents' home—on the floor before their fireplace—and Kila had insisted the twins sleep in the Wittin's spare room.

Every morning, Guta had awoken Larka, Pentheya and Ian in the workshop. Every day, they had labored to finish this cabin. Every day they had all crowded into this very, very small space, working with frenzy. Every single day!

Larka longed for privacy, needed to get away from Guta's constant, hopeful presence. She wanted her home finished *now*, but her hands quaked from the cold, which by this point had snuck up her arm. With stiffened fingers, she tried to poke a stubborn bit of caulk into a crack; the piece fell out and besmirched the floor.

"Es all for you, me thick-skulled lady," Guta said, startling Larka. He grabbed her muddy hands and rubbed them between his own. "Go to Mama and get clean up and some food. Papa and I finish here."

Larka, in the habit of staring into a fire before she fell asleep, sat cross-legged on the hearth, occasionally sipping tea or prodding the fireplace's flames with a charred stick. She twisted around, peering behind herself. There, four children slept in a row parallel to the head of the bed, warm and comfortable between a cotton-stuffed mattress and several thick blankets. Larka smiled.

She resumed facing the fire and noted the way the chimney's stones fit together to form the fireplace's sides and upper reaches. She noted the joints of the crudely made mantelpiece—merely split logs—jutting from betwixt stones. Within her peripheral vision, she noted her small table's shadow flicker with the candlelight above it. Mostly, she noted the quiet, broken only by the fire's bright crackle or a log intermittently slumping to ash within the fire.

Larka gripped the warm mug in her hands and sipped her tea.

Not an hour ago, she had escaped Guta with the excuse that it was bedtime. She finally had her new home to herself.

A knock on the door caused Larka's whole body to twitch. She rose with trepidation and placed her mug on the mantelpiece, her fingers lingering on the warm earthenware surface before she crossed the floor to slowly unbind the rope that served as a lock when looped and tied over two hooks, one hook on the door and another on the adjacent wall.

Guta sauntered inside along with a brisk wind.

"Es cold." He shivered. "So, how you and little ones do in new home?" He grinned and nodded his head energetically. He held an object that looked like a long, wide pillow in his hands.

"We are well." Larka stared at the floor. "Are the Wittins still well?" Hesitantly, she closed the door.

"Yes." He grinned and thrust the dull-gray mat before himself then leaned it against the wall next to the door. "Sorry, I forget. Mama send you this pallet. She say you sleep on it. Es better than floor."

He nodded with such vigor Larka actually found her head and body bobbing along. She chuckled. The Wittin nod had at last caught her in its throes.

At the sound of her amusement, Guta's handsome features broke into a silly grin, his head starting to bob again. Larka took this in and chortled. Guta guffawed, his head bouncing up and down on his neck, if possible more jubilantly. At this, Larka slapped a hand over her mouth but was unable to stifle her next gush of laughter.

Guta grew still and silent, brow knit.

Larka paused, taking in his lost expression, then laughed harder still.

Guta cocked his head and his lips rounded to say, "Wuz so funny?"

Larka smashed her lips together; her trunk shook as she tried to hold back the mirth gathered in her core. It burst free in a snort. She then laughed as much at herself as at Guta.

Guta shook his head. "You plenty strange, Larka." He smiled and laid the pallet next to the bed, ever watching her.

"I'm so sorry." She stopped to breathe. "I haven't laughed like that in years." She paused. "Hmm . . . I've never laughed like that."

"Es good, you think?" She mimicked his accent and nodded her head with Wittin vigor.

Guta's mouth puckered then twisted with good humor before he spoke, "I no believe you, making fun of me. Es so . . . *mean*."

"Oh no, I didn't mean it that way," Larka sputtered.

"Strange girl," Guta murmured, shaking his head. "Sleep good tonight." He clasped her hand and squeezed it before he left, a slight smile still on his lips.

Larka looked at her hand then at the slatted logs of the door and sighed. She tied the door shut, made certain the shutters were likewise shut, then blew out the candle on the table. She gathered the shawl off a hook on the wall, grasped the sleeping pallet and moved it as close as she dared to the fire, then burrowed in.

"Es better than floor," Larka murmured and pulled Heta's old shawl over her weary body.

CHAPTER 10

WATER AND AIR

*L*arka awoke within the dark of night to the sound of an expulsive cough. She rolled off her mat and stood, the shawl peeling off her and falling to the floor. She blinked, forced her swollen eyes to focus through the light the fireplace's embers lent her. On the bed, Pentheya writhed in another barking fit. Larka hastened across the room and placed a hand on the girl's forehead. The skin there felt sweaty, a bit too warm.

Larka lit the candle on the table and peered into the fireplace; the water kettle still hung over the embers. She sifted through the stack of muslin bags on the flour barrel, sniffing each until she located the herb she needed.

Pentheya exploded once more. Larka glanced right toward the girl then whirled to the fireplace. She grabbed a clean mug and potholder off the mantel then ripped the kettle out of the fireplace's mouth. Then it was to the table where she assembled all-heal tea, steeping the herb in hot water before sweetening the liquid with honey.

She left the tea and pattered across the floor to the bed. She slid her hands underneath Pentheya then stilled and caught her breath. The girl felt as if flames had been stoked beneath her skin.

"Oh, little one," Larka murmured, lifting Pentheya out of bed.

Larka seated herself at the table, holding the child on her lap. She brushed her lips over Pentheya's forehead—the skin there hotter still and growing more so by the moment.

"Pentheya . . . Oh sweet earth, I should have noticed, but I was too busy putting in a floor and roof and chinking. . . ."

Pentheya smiled weakly up at her. "I should have said. I wanted home too." The girl inhaled—her lungs' clamor for air.

"Drink this tea then bed rest for you," Larka whispered into the child's sweat-dampened hair.

Pentheya sipped the concoction until it was gone and the cough eased. Larka then settled Pentheya upon the pallet and pulled the shawl over the girl.

"I'll go out and look for some yarrow for the fever."

Beside the door, Larka shoved her feet into a thick pair of socks and a sturdy pair of boots—the only items she had requested of Guta's shopping expedition for herself. Her gaze lingered on Pentheya as she closed the door between them. She turned around. The cold night greeted her, lit faintly by the hang of stars and the moon's slender crescent.

Along one of the lanes between fields, she bent and gathered a large bundle of yarrow flowers—stalk and all—then straightened her back and turned to go.

A huge, dark shadow loped across her path into the field on her left. Larka froze, the hairs on her scalp standing on end. Her eyes followed the path from which the shadow had run. The cabin stood stolid, silent at its end. The memory of red eyes glaring at her from amongst tree trunks collided with the knowledge that the cabin's door was unfastened. Clutching the yarrow, Larka sprinted back to her new home.

The door stood firm, still resting against the doorframe as she arrived at the cabin. She shoved through and rushed inside, already reaching to tie the door shut and peering around as she did so. All remained as she had left it. Larka exhaled then crossed the room to slump into a chair beside the table.

Pentheya coughed throughout the night. The cough worsened over the next five days until the hacking, dry sound of it sent a tremor of desperation through Larka each time she heard it. And now, Ian had disappeared. Not long before nightfall, she had noticed a certain disquiet in the room. The twins and Ian had been so silent during their sister's illness it had taken Larka some time to miss the eldest male.

Larka poured a spoonful of Kila's whiskey into a mug half filled with wild-bergamot tea then thickened it with honey. Guta had gone searching for Ian upon her request, yet much time had passed since then, and that red-eyed thing lurked out there somewhere.

Larka crossed the room, opened the shutters and looked out. Drizzling shards of snow rained through the darkness. Anxiety whipped its way through Larka, and she wiped its sweat off her brow. She smacked the shutters closed.

Larka returned to the table and stirred the tea again, preparing to dose Pentheya with the same concoction she had made many times under Gilly's instruction. This particular brew soothed Pentheya's throat enough for the child to claim much needed sleep, but the girl's tiny body still burned with fever. No matter what Larka tried, cool compresses or herbal remedy, the fever refused to fall.

The door to the cabin bammed open, and Guta pushed Ian inside, following behind the boy.

"Es by the river!" Guta boomed incredulous. His voice then dropped into chiding. "Could have fallen in, Ian. Es no good."

Ian offered Larka and Guta each a petulant look then bent to his knees beside his sister.

Guta grabbed Ian by the shoulders, thrust him to his feet and forced him to face Larka. "Apologize. Larka es worry sick about you. You no run off and not tell where going."

"I'm sorry," Ian huffed and shuffled his shoulders until Guta released him.

"You no act sorry." Guta grabbed after the boy. He missed as Ian once more knelt beside Pentheya. "Ian, you being very bad."

"It's okay." Larka placed a hand on Guta's arm, staying him.

Pentheya awoke and fought another bout of coughing.

"Did you get it?" she wheezed.

"Some, before Guta came along and poured it out." Ian whipped a waterskin off his shoulder, uncorked the opening and held it to Pentheya's lips. A brief stream slid into her mouth.

"Es worry for her. Es making him a little crazy I think," Guta said as he and Larka witnessed the exchange between the two children.

Larka gazed at the youngsters, puzzlement creasing her brow. She then shook her head, tucking the puzzlement away for later consideration.

"Give her a few spoonfuls of this too, Ian." Larka picked up the honeyed tea and wooden spoon.

Larka ran her hand over Pentheya's cool forehead. The girl had slipped into a fitless sleep just minutes before midnight. Larka tucked the shawl over Pentheya's shoulders and yawned. Facing the door, she sat at the table, folded her arms on its surface, then rested her head on them. The scent of lavender seeped into the cabin and suffused the air. Larka dozed, disturbed occasionally by Pentheya's light cough or the wind rapping on the door.

A rustling noise finally roused Larka. She lifted her head, blinking groggily. Her eyes focused on the drab light filtering through the shuttered window until a movement on the floor caught her attention. She looked down to find Pentheya sitting up on the pallet.

"I'm hungry." Pentheya grinned at her.

"Hmm." Larka returned a weary smile.

Ian popped up and flung his legs over the side of the bed. His feet hit the floor, anxiety giving way to relief as he scrutinized his sister.

"That stew sure smells good." Pentheya smacked her lips and peered at the stew pot hanging in the fireplace.

Ian grinned and raced across the room to serve his sister before Larka could lift her own stiff body.

Arnt and Halty awoke and swarmed Pentheya as she dipped her spoon steadily from bowl to mouth.

Larka's chin quivered as she watched the children, her lips battling to curve upward, eyes shiny with drawled tears. She finally stood and moved to the door where she untied the rope and walked outside.

To her left, sunshine had begun to dance within the naked for-est, a backlighting for the Wittin field in which lay shriveled corn stalks alongside the emaciated vines of pumpkins and winter squash. She walked around the eastern corner of her home and gazed into the corridor of trees lining the fallow field that was now her land— land that appeared much more than the acre she had requested. She shook her head, smiling, still peering into the trees.

Somewhere beyond that narrow thicket of woods lay the Lavender Hills—and Gilly; Larka shuddered and redirected her thoughts. In all, she felt lucky the Wittins lived a good bit beyond the outskirts of Jaunty, felt lucky they were good folk . . . felt safer here than she had anywhere. And tired. She had been awake, tending Pentheya for nearly a week.

She yawned, stretching her arms overhead.

A rooster crowed. Goats bleated outside the barn, which stood on a diagonal behind the Wittin house, close to the workshop.

Larka peered through the hedge of seedling trees between the Wittin homestead and hers. Someone already moved around inside the kitchen of the Wittin home. She inhaled and caught the smell of baking bread. Kila must have risen to get the day's baking done.

Larka walked through a gap in the seedlings to the Wittin well to draw a bucket of water. She returned to the cabin and heated the water, so Pentheya could bathe. Larka then settled in the children's bed for a nap. The twins tumbled into the bed and snuggled one on either side of her. She wrapped an arm around each of

them, and they slept, the babble from Ian and Pentheya's whisper-
ings occasionally inserting into Larka's dreams.

Larka awoke to a sharp rap on the door and Guta's coming in
without waiting for an answer.

"Larka, we must to talk. Es important." Guta's usually glowing
skin appeared sallow and his features strained.

"What is it?" She picked her way out of bed, careful not to awaken
the babies.

"Come." He grabbed her arm and pulled her out of the cabin,
around to its more westerly side.

"Es this." He pointed to the soft earth at the base of the chimney.

Larka blinked at the dark soil—so recently disturbed by the cabin's construction—then peered up at him.

"What is it, Guta?"

"You no see?" His hyperactive tone had returned. He swayed forward on his tiptoes, ramming his finger at the soil.

Then, all too clearly, the objects of his worry became delineated
in that dirt.

"Oh, sweet gods." Larka stumbled backward before her left foot
moved to catch her. "What made those tracks?"

"Es not in my knowing." He gave a troubled shake of his head. "Es
not good whatever. Es huge . . . like a big, big man but with claws
and four legs."

Larka gasped, hand flying to her mouth. "I saw something, last
week, something really big. It was running from the cabin when I
came back from gathering yarrow. I think it was in the forest too,
watching us, before we came here."

"And you no tell me, Larka?" Guta's hands gripped her shoulders,
his gaze locked with hers.

Larka grimaced. "I wasn't sure it was the same animal. Pentheya
was so ill . . ." Her words drifted into her thoughts as she stared at
the spread of the prints. The tracks looked fresher than last-week's
incursion. So clear were their perimeters, they appeared to have just
been made in the moist soil. In the direction they pointed, this thing

could have been watching her as she sought water from the well this very morning. Larka shuddered.

Guta's grip on her alleviated. "I no mean to make you nervous, but the tracks, Larka, they all over the place, all round the cabin." He ran his palms slowly down her arms and grasped her hands.

Larka's skin tingled from each shoulder down to her fingertips. She tore her vision away from the prints in the soil and gazed up at Guta.

"Papa and I hunt this thing. Stay inside. No going out unless you must," Guta said and shook his head, slowly and resolutely. "We hunt today."

Larka nodded and let him guide her back to the cabin's door. Guta opened it and nudged her into her home. She caught the door before he could shut it and held his gaze.

"Be careful," she breathed.

Guta grasped her hands in his once more and kissed her quickly on the cheek.

Shrill giggles broke out behind Larka.

CHAPTER 11

MALICE

"We no find the animal," Guta reported on the third day of the hunt. His bloodshot eyes spoke as to the magnitude of his valor.

"Es like it just disappear—into air." He snapped his fingers.

Pentheya coughed—a dry, hacking sound. The hairs on Larka's neck stood on end, and she whipped around to look at the girl lingering in the bed. Pentheya had regained strength and vigor over the last few days, yet she had not lost the shadows beneath her eyes, and the child's body still seemed so frail.

"I go to eat. We hunt until we find the animal. Has been here again. I see more tracks yesterday . . . today. Stay inside." Guta eyed Pentheya with concern then squeezed Larka's shoulder and slipped out of the cabin.

Larka immediately set to steeping herbs and mixing the resulting liquid with honey and whiskey.

Pentheya shook her head as Larka approached with the elixir. "I need water," the child's tiny voice pleaded.

"There's water in the tea, Pentheya. Drink it, so you don't get sick again." Larka placed a palm on the child's forehead. "You feel a little warm."

On that third night of entrapment, Pentheya's fever reignited, and the girl's body became so choked with cough she began to vomit.

The sound of that spewing ejection awoke Larka as it spattered the floor. Larka sprang from her sleeping pallet and found Pentheya hanging over the side of the bed, gagging. Larka picked up the small body in time to receive hot spew down her chest but felt relief, as Pentheya's throat had at least cleared.

After settling Pentheya on the sleeping mat, Larka swabbed the girl's face and touched the fury of heat resurfacing within the child's skin.

Larka cried, "You're too hot."

Nothing she did alleviated that heat. Ian and the twins looked on much of the next day with anxious stares, so quiet Larka barely discerned their presence.

After noon, Pentheya stopped drinking her teas and fell into a sleep much too deep to be normal. Thence, Larka submitted to the inevitable. A blanket she had washed hung dry before the fire, still smelling faintly of vomit. Larka wrapped it around Pentheya then enveloped herself in Heta's shawl.

"Ian, I must speak with you." Larka went to the table and squatted before him. She grasped one of his small hands. "I must take Pentheya to someone who can heal her. I must leave now before it's too . . ." Larka grimaced. "Before the sun sets."

"She will die like Jonah," Ian said, his voice muffled by the droop of his head.

Larka bit back tears. "We don't know that, Ian."

Larka kept her ear bent to Pentheya's breathing. She barely noticed the desiccated wild herbs lining the long-harvested fields on either side of her as she drifted off Wittin property. She also did not notice that she became once more what others had made of her: a spectacle.

Inhalation and exhalation both shallow and irregular—these were all Larka heard until the sounds stopped not far from Gilly's Lavender Hills.

With that, the impish smile Pentheya displayed when pleased with her world flashed into Larka's mind. She gazed down at Pentheya's face—so still now, so pale.

Disturbed clouds began to muddy the sky overhead, yet Larka saw nothing except the breathless girl in her arms. She fell to her knees, her bent body a paroxysm of grief. Thunder clashed with her sobs. Still, she did not mark the disquieted electric field playing almost transparently over her skin.

Then she heard it—a wisp of air. Pentheya's shallow breathing had returned, and the child's fevered green eyes opened to view Larka.

"What have you done to that child?" An irate baritone voice broke into Larka's inner world and brought forth a foe its speaker had not fully contemplated.

"I did nothing to her." Larka stood, barely taking her eyes off Pentheya. Still, she ascertained that three men stood in her path, each with a hunting bow slung over his back.

Pentheya opened her mouth to say something yet produced only a sigh. Larka saw the fire in the child's eyes and guessed Pentheya attempting to defend her guardian.

"Save your breath, little one. We'll be at Gilly's cottage soon enough." Larka scrutinized her enemies.

The baritone stared at her with turbulent gray eyes, the wind swirling through his blond hair—the young man who had taken a zealot's dislike to Larka. On his left stood another who bore a great resemblance to him, except this other was taller with darker hair.

"I can handle this, Rostin." A short, bald man with stubble on his chin stepped forward, a rope dangling from his fingers. "You will come with us. You are trespassing on Rollen and Rostin's hunting grounds." A mark on his coat named him law warden. "You are also guilty of stealing from the fields and murdering Farmer Smithen's dog. You will pay for these crimes by order of Albilar Decree."

Pentheya gasped for air, and Larka looked from her to the men.

"She's dying! I must reach Weather Witch Gilly before it's too late." Wind eddied about Larka in a wrathful spiral, flailing long blue-black hair wildly about her, picking up dirt, building momentum.

As if they were one, each man retreated a step. Hate and fear mingled within the three pairs of eyes set upon Larka.

"Sweet earth, look at her," Rostin cried. "She's drawing on her powers to strike us down."

Larka gaped at the man. What in this living nightmare was he babbling about? Then, she noted what she thought they saw as she glanced back down toward Pentheya: a smoky-blue current sparked around Larka's hands, her arms, her chest. . . .

Larka looked back up at her enemies in time to see a glint of steel hurling toward her. A flash of light exploded where the knife should have struck her heart, just above Pentheya's weakened body—too close to a dying child!

Larka's head snapped up. Her vision locked on the men. The maddened wind coursed through her. A horrendous blast of air smote her foes to the ground. Larka's hands tingled and an electric crackle whipped through them; Pentheya's body gave a simultaneous jolt

The child writhed and gasped once more, the sound of her want to breathe tremulous, truncated.

Leaping over Rostin's moaning frame, Larka raced death through Lavender Hills. She arrived shortly at Gilly's cottage and kicked the door to her old prison with vehemence. The crone took her time answering this particular house call. The door finally creaked open on its hinges.

Gilly's vision latched on to Larka whose odd energy remained astir about her slender frame. "Found yourself, did you?" Gilly said then scoffed at Pentheya's limp form, "Girl's cold. You should have brought her to me long ago."

Larka swallowed against what felt like ice in her throat. "Can you help her?"

"Humph." Gilly smiled. "Told you—she's cold." Knobby fingers lifted Pentheya's arm and released the limb to let it flop and dangle where it would.

Heat imbued Larka's cheeks as she surveyed Pentheya, desperate that the jolt she had accidentally driven into that frail body had not finished it.

"Can you help her or not?" Larka wailed.

"As cold as she is, my help will cost you. And you *will* pay," Gilly rasped.

Larka spoke through taut jaws, "I will pay whatever it takes if Pentheya lives." She shivered as Gilly's lips curved upward, etching into inelastic skin.

Gilly widened the opening of the door. "Put her on the table."

Larka did as told. Gilly shoved her aside and pressed a palm against Pentheya's chest. The gentlest of breezes whispered across Larka and almost indiscernibly lifted Gilly's long white hair.

Gilly smiled and shook her head without looking at Larka. "Go to where the river runs loudest. Bring me a bucket of water from there."

"What?" Larka breathed.

"Tarry not, girl, or she'll never be revived. Put the water inside the door when you get back but don't *you* come back in here." Gilly pointed a shaking finger at Larka. "*You* wait under the maple and think on how you will get me *my money*," she spat, a dead gleam in her rust-colored eyes.

Larka soon dashed toward her destination, Gilly's well bucket swinging in hand. As she ran, she listened for the loudest place. Water's fall crashed into her ears, carried on the wind. As if a hand pressed into her back, Larka was pushed to the falls—falls she had never desired to visit.

Larka stared upward at the gorged rock walls conducting the water's violent descent. Chills briefly overtook her. She forced herself to plunge the bucket into the river near as she could to that pounding water and then, careful of spillage, sprinted back to Gilly's.

Larka placed the bucket inside the doorway. Leaving the door ajar, she took a seat on the far end of the bench under the maple. Within seconds, she heard a sharp intake of breath. Pentheya's strong cough then reverberated within Larka's ears.

Larka fell to her knees and thanked the powers-that-be for the little one's life, but in the next moments she heard the door creak open, heard the scuff of footfalls. Ice crept into her heart as she felt Gilly's eyes on her, heard the elder's labored breathing.

"I want my money!"

Larka stared at her hands. Splayed before her on the cold ground, they had begun to shake. A tremor ran through her as well, and her breath felt like fists beating open her chest with each inhalation: all the old fears she had relinquished upon running away from here had returned.

"I want it tonight or little Pentheya could take a turn for the worse," Gilly crowed. Her words stopped for a moment then resumed, her voice lowered. "Look at me."

Slowly, Larka stood and rotated.

"The villagers all know how you get your money, *thief.* You think they didn't see you wrapped in that rag the day the man from Albilar was robbed? You think they couldn't identify that when they'd seen it a hundred times? A rag won't make them forget what you are, *girl.* Only I can do that."

Larka sneered, overcome by seething, her fear dissipated momentarily. "You'll get your money, weather witch, but if any harm comes to Pentheya, you'll get more than a few coins can fix."

Larka's seething leveled to a simmer as Gilly's last words sank into her. *A rag won't make them forget . . . Only I can do that.* Then Larka could only stare.

"What have you done?" she whispered.

Gilly snickered, amusement lilting in her eyes before she hobbled away. Then the front door slammed. Larka drifted around to stare at the cottage's face.

A grating sound carried to her—an old window being opened. Then Gilly pushed open the window's eyelid—the shutter—in a great scraping din. She remained in that space, the innards of the cottage dark behind her. The hag smiled then supinated a hand, kissed the palm, and blew over the hand's inner flesh toward Larka.

A breeze played over her, and Larka swayed in vertigo. Her stomach roiled. Her legs trembled. Despite the wintry ambiance, sweat dotted her brow, slid from her armpits down her side. Her skull felt like talons had enfolded it, one inserted at the core of her ability to manage fear.

She fell forward to retch and vomit until she curled into fetal position and shook uncontrollably.

CHAPTER 12

THE AMBER MAN

*L*arka tucked her thin shirt, tattered britches and Heta's old shawl beneath a fallen log, then washed up quickly, the frosty air nipping at her bare skin. Just as quickly, she covered her chilled flesh with a long-sleeved dress the color of lavender flowers, a dress she had stolen from the single clothing shop in Jaunty. Much to her consternation, she had found no one else with a fat money pouch to rob while there, and Gilly wanted her money *now*.

"As if nearly fifteen years of slavery shouldn't pay for something," Larka muttered and worked makeup she had likewise stolen into her skin. Several minutes later, she peered at her reflection in the spring's pool. Blue-black hair stacked upon her head, rouge on her lips and cheeks, she looked much like the older version of herself she had seen walking down the main street of Jaunty not so many months ago. She stood, wrapping a newly acquired lacy shawl around her shoulders.

With luck, the dress shop's owner would not be dining in the tavern tonight. Guilt twisting her insides, Larka wrapped slender, lace-covered arms around her empty gut and quivered.

"No one should hate or fear or . . . hurt." Her thin voice carried through the silent forest. She started—unsure why—and gazed around, fingers tingling, skin prickling. A tremor ran through her lower jaw.

Nothing more than skeletal trees greeted her, but she was sure glaring, red eyes watched her.

78

The last light of day bid Larka farewell as she slipped into Jaunty and headed for Gose Inn and Tavern. Braced against her desire to flee, she raised the hood of the shawl and moved on. She slunk to her alleyway and waited behind a stack of crates, shivering in the cold until no more footfalls sounded.

Larka stepped out of the shadows onto the boardwalk, attempting to be quiet but feeling that each of her footsteps crashed through the night. She reached the inn, heart hammering in her throat.

She stood with her hand quaking on the door knob, trying to manage her unsteady breathing. She finally twisted the knob and entered, head down, her face hidden under more than tatted yarn, as a haze of darkness lurked within the tavern, steeped here and there by the glow of an occasional oil lamp.

Larka took a seat, and a new tavern maid descended upon her. Larka kept her head down as she ordered food—for which she could not pay—until the tavern girl drifted to another table.

Larka closed her eyes and sifted out all noises save one. The sound of coins rubbing together eventually carried to her on the shifting air. Larka opened her eyes and peered up at the man leaning against the bar. Her breath disengaged from her lungs. He saluted her with his mug, his square jaw and amber hair highlighted by the nearness of a hanging lamp.

Larka clutched her seat and noted Heta skirt around the bar then flee into the kitchen. The tall man tilted the mug to his lips, eyes Larka knew to be pale amber transfixed on her. Larka scooted down in her chair as if the table could hide her.

Another figure crossed the space between them, blocking her view of the Amber Man for which she felt relief until she recognized the gray eyes upon her, a pleasant smile lighting those eyes until recognition reset this man's features into a glower with such fury Larka could not quite fathom its depths. Then again, she supposed being flung around like a rag doll suited no man's pride, especially this Rostin's.

Larka leapt to her feet and darted toward the exit. Rostin caught her around the midsection. He jerked the hood off her head. Larka kicked him in the shin and yanked out of his grasp. She snatched the hood into place and scurried toward the exit as a hush fell over the tavern's customers.

A bald warden and his substantial girth barricaded the front door. "I thought I saw you slink in here. That stolen dress marks you real good."

He smirked, persecution in his piggy eyes. Larka envisioned the rope dangling from his hand on Rostin's property, and shock swayed her. Had they meant to hang her? She had assumed the rope meant for a restraint. Now, she was certain it would have restrained breath rather than wrists.

The air shifted about her. However, it did not possess the intensity required to remove this man from her path, no matter how she tried to summon it. Soon, its movements became altogether absent.

Larka's skin convulsed into hair-raising bumps. She turned right to find the Amber Man beside her but no sign of Rostin. She watched the Amber Man as he advanced on the warden. The warden's self-satisfied expression withered. Regardless, he stepped to meet the Amber Man.

Larka took that opportunity to slip outside. As she closed the door against its jambs, she felt a weight about her right wrist and heard the clinking of coins. She held her arm up to view the bulging bag of money hanging off it. Her brow puckered. She cocked her head at the bag. She had not taken this pouch, but she had no time to ponder its acquirement, for a loud crash within the inn spurred her to a swift retreat out of Jaunty.

As she ran, she thought of her urchins, Gilly, Pentheya's near deaths, and the unabashed maligning Jaunty's people had committed against her. She felt her throat clench, her mouth tremble, heard herself whimper, felt hot tears sliding down her cheeks. Larka ran harder, swiping at the blur in her eyes.

They wanted her dead—to kill her! The arrow Farmer Smithen had shot at her should have been enough proof, but thinking that he or anyone else truly wished her dead had been too much to accept. And, it was no coincidence that the villagers had begun to remember what she was when she had appeared in Jaunty—after she had left Gilly. The weather witch had admitted as much. Larka bit her lip and ran on, lungs burning with the effort.

She finally drew to a halt, wiped her nose on her dress sleeve. She turned and peered through the woods toward what she had left behind. She gnashed her teeth, nostrils flared with more than panting. The villagers had not cared that she had been overworked and beaten most of her life, had not cared about starving urchins, but they certainly cared now!

A kind wind undergirded her with caresses, murmured through her hair. Larka took a deep breath then tried to exhale her disgust.

Coins jangled slightly in the breeze. Larka looked at the pouch on her arm and determined her path at that moment. She headed for Ian and the twins. No one could afford a horse in Jaunty; doubtless, no one searching her out would have yet had time to reach her home.

Larka arrived at the cabin and opened the door and entered the home for which she had worked so hard. A fire burned low in the fireplace, and the smell of stew wafted to her. Her stomach gurgled.

Ian sat up on her sleeping pallet and yawned, stretching his arms in opposite directions.

Larka put a hushing finger to her lips and bent to dispense half the coins under the mat.

"Pentheya's better," she whispered.

She rose and tucked blankets around the twins in the bed before she returned to Ian and resumed speaking in hushed tones.

"I have to go get your sister. I'll send for you soon. We'll catch a ride to Albilar, but just in case I don't make it back here, that money should hold you a long time. Hide it someplace better." She kissed his forehead.

"We can't go to Albilar," Ian whispered back, eyes wide. "We can't leave Pentheya."

"But she's coming with us."

"No." Ian shook his head. "We can't leave here."

Impatience brewed within Larka, but she prevented its onslaught to Ian. She stated softly, "I've no time to argue. We'll talk about it later. Tie the door and shutters and don't let anyone in. I saw the Amber Man in the tavern tonight." With those words she left for Gilly's bitter lair.

Larka gazed over the abyss of the open hills for several minutes before deciding to skirt them and move alongside the forest. The gibbous moon detailed too much on land made barren by winter's approach, spawning that domain into a snare to seize around her ankles—or her neck. She shivered against the cold as well as the depth of foreboding that weighted her stomach.

The scent of lavender diffused into her, and she plucked a dry segment from one of the many plants. Larka tucked the snip behind her ear as she took a first step around the Lavender Hills. This would be the last visit she made to these hills if her plan went smoothly. She would be free of Jaunty and its people.

In a city the size of Albilar she could easily blend in and hide behind a new name with an inspiring story of how she and her brothers and sister had lost their parents and decided to find work in the city. She had not worked exactly how her story would play out, but that she could do on the way to Albilar.

Larka hummed softly, occasionally plucking a lavender stalk and drinking in its smell. She tucked a bit behind her other ear, the sound of it crisp as it slid behind the lobe. The herb tinkled dryly as she walked.

About halfway to her destination, brittle vegetation snapped behind her. Larka froze, listening intently for the noise's repetition. She heard nothing, yet the hair on the nape of her neck stood up. Her next inhale came in a painful rush: only two creatures had caused her hair to stand on end before—the Amber Man and a red-eyed monster.

Larka quickened her pace slightly until she descended to a spot just on the other side of one of the hills extending into the forest. Under that glimpse of cover, she sprinted straight across the Lavender Hills, into the shallow moonlight.

Gilly's cottage was not far now, yet Larka heard the slippage of silence and doom in the booted footfalls overtaking her. She dared not look back. The footfalls hushed into surcease. The air parted as the being dove at her and slammed her thin body to the ground.

She sucked in breath as the heavy mass stood up. Hands settled beneath her arms, shooting a jolt of a foreign and savage emotion through her. The Amber Man pulled her to her feet, her back still to him.

"Look at me," he whispered.

Larka shook her head with the fervor of dread as she noted how far she had come, how close to her old home and its promise of safety. Light flickered in the open eyes of Gilly's cottage, atop the next hill.

Gentle hands gripped Larka's shoulders and turned her.

"We have been promised, you and I."

Larka heard his words but could assign them no meaning. Her flesh huddled into screaming bumps as his finger slid beneath her chin and tilted her head back. Her head shook with the tense spasms of her neck. She gazed into those disturbing eyes and whimpered.

"I gave you what you needed, did I not, *pretty Larka?*"

The way he said her name sent a preternatural chill down her spine, and she leaned away from him, the clangs within a half-full bag of coins playing distant notes.

"Did I not?" He reiterated in a quiet, hurt tone.

Larka wished for the air to help her, yet it remained still and silent, as if she stood in a void of its protection.

"*Did I not?*" He bellowed.

Larka winced and would have retreated were it not for the staying hands on her shoulders.

"Yes," she whispered.

His voice calm, he spoke again, "You are then cared for?"

"Yes," Larka repeated, voice quavering. She turned her head to see Gilly's cottage, and her lungs suspended function for a long moment. The eyes of the cottage had been closed, the sockets blackened and empty.

"You've grown into a beautiful woman, *my Larka*." He articulated the last two words in a bestial hiss.

Larka rotated back round to stare at him, terror reflected in her moonlit eyes.

He stroked the curve of her jaw with the back of his hand. Larka jerked away from that touch. The gentle hand then turned to stone and smote the span of her jaw. She wobbled on her feet, and stars blazed behind her eyes . . . like the universe remade.

A HIGH PRICE TO PAY

*L*arka stirred, opening her eyes a slit. Starlight twinkled down at her while snowflakes meandered through the air. She groaned. She ached—her arms, her legs, her back, her bruised shoulders and jaw. The night swished about her, and an eerie sound carried on the swirling wind, like the anguished howls of thousands of tiny animals.

Larka dozed several times more before her shivering body forced her awake. She sat up, her consciousness cued to the odd cries filling the air, like nothing she had ever heard. Wind blew over the hilltop, and the cries riled into shrieks. Larka tensed, eyes widening, pain shooting through her abused body. She clenched the rough fabric covering her to bare breasts and stood, searching for the sound's origin, yet the wails desisted as the wind grew still. Only clumps of overwintering lavender met her vision.

Blood slid down Larka's inner thigh and dropped to the earth. She flinched, driving back the memory of the night before, and slid the rough fabric around her shoulders.

Wind scampered through the Lavender Hills once more, refreshing the peal of sad cries. Larka started. Then a movement below caught her attention. Where she had lain, something wormlike worked at the blood, sucking her spilled juices into itself.

Larka gasped and jumped back, hands over the orifice of her mouth. That which should have remained underground—lavender roots—writhed in the spilling of her virgin blood.

A great gush of wind flooded the hills, and lavender shrieked throughout. Larka screamed, peering this way and that then returned her gaze to the earth. She stumbled away from the squirming roots, fell on her buttocks and frantically beat her legs beneath her, shoving away on heels and palms, temporarily unable to turn and take her eyes off the slithering mass of roots.

The sun doted in the eastern sky, filling Larka's eyes with the stirrings of day. The bag of coins jangled on her wrist, reminding her of the reason she had gone to Jaunty last night. Larka flipped around to face Gilly's home. The shutters stood open once more. Light played behind the window glass, shone through the twilight.

Larka's teeth began to chatter. With each moment that passed, her body shivered with greater intensity. She raised herself slowly to glare at the ostensible quaintness of that cottage, hugging herself beneath the rough fabric.

The strange vomiting fit from the day before spat into her mind's eye. Larka bit her top lip and allowed her eyelids to veil her sight but a breath before she staggered down Last Hill then trudged up the next to the cottage. By the time she reached the stone structure, her crotch seared between her legs. She clamped her jaws against the pain and banged the cottage's front door open.

Gilly sat in her rocking chair, back to Larka. Still atop the table, Pentheya slept like only the innocence of childhood would allow.

"Where's my money?" Gruff words struck Larka's ears.

Larka snorted.

"I need a bath." She slammed the money pouch onto a counter top, easing the loop from her wrist. "And clean clothes." Larka noted her bruised legs poking from beneath Heta's old shawl and gnashed her teeth. She spoke next through this countenance. "These coins should more than pay the price you requested. Count out your part. The rest is mine."

Larka drifted outside and drew water from the well, inducing more shots of pain through her body. She poured water into the washtub near the defoliated maple, not bothering to warm the liquid, until the tub was almost full. She dropped Heta's old shawl beside the tub then cocked her head to stare at the garment.

She had not been wearing that last night.

Larka shuddered. Eyes she knew to be pale amber, not glaring red, had fixed on her long before she had reached the tavern the night before. She raised her chin and squared her shoulders, blinking back remembrance.

Finally, she stepped with care into the metal washtub, lowering herself into the water. She rubbed at her bloodied thighs until the pale skin there turned lurid red. Larka gazed at that marred flesh then inhaled suddenly, sucking in a lone cry. She closed her eyes and hugged her arms around the crook of her knees, chest heaving with dry sorrow; all her tears had been shed the night before.

The door to the cottage creaked. Larka revealed then resealed her eyes and ignored Gilly until she felt a current of warmth slip around the submerged parts of her body. Larka opened her eyes and glared at the woman's back. Hobbling away, Gilly held a kettle in her hand. The tang of lemon balm invaded Larka's dark thoughts, and she noted its fresh leaves floating atop the water, yet the slightly camphorous scent of lavender also prowled the waters. Larka gagged on the scent of it.

Gilly returned with another hot water kettle, and a small jar of hazelnut oil to which she had added fresh lemon balm leaves—taken from an interior window box—and dried rose petals. Larka held up her hand as Gilly began to tilt a vial of lavender oil over the jar.

"Don't. I don't much like the smell of it."

Gilly gave her a searching look then nodded. "Suit yourself. Put this oil on your cuts at least twice a day until they've healed."

"I have few cuts, just the ones on my back," Larka said, refusing to lower her gaze.

Gilly's mouth compressed and tugged downward, her eyes assessing

Larka. "I assume you want to stay here. Word's all over Jaunty you're of the dark moon. Some men came looking for you while you were out, said a law warden and some men were hurt on your account. I told them you ran off, wouldn't be back."

Larka raised a brow. "Who is to say they believed you?"

"Oh, I blew them a kiss." Gilly cackled. "They believed me whether they wanted to or not." Gilly's expression then grew stern. "You can stay here as long as you agree to one thing."

Larka closed her eyes and pressed her forehead against her knees, hands still clasped over her shins. "I don't want to stay here."

"But you will and care for me until the day I die."

Larka's head popped up. She gaped at the crone. "But I gave you your money."

Gilly continued to speak as if Larka had said nothing, "Or, maybe I'll send word you're here." The crone's hands crept to her hips, and she stood as straight as her stooped back allowed. "Or perhaps I'll take back what I did for *little Pentheya*."

Larka jumped to her feet, barely noticing the pain that resonated through her. "If you touch her, the day you die shall come to pass much sooner than you expect."

Gilly's eyes widened briefly. She took a step back. Then the crone leered, stagnant breath filling crevices between missing teeth.

"Don't you think to challenge me, *girl*. I've lived long and learned much in my days, more than a mere shard of wind can overcome.

"Little Pentheya could grow ill again even so far away as that pissant cabin you built." Gilly leaned over Larka. "How many brothers has she? Three? One near her age and two younger. Perhaps they need a kiss before I *tuck them in*." Gilly's death-rattled laughter shook her frame. "Perhaps I'll blow you another and you'll obey me."

Larka felt heat creeping into her face despite the cold. How much bluff and how much truth did the crone's words contain? Larka knew first hand the puissance of Gilly's malcontent; it had controlled her own fear for years though unbeknownst to her until that nauseating display the day before. If she sought to challenge Gilly, what would the outcome be? Larka dared not think of it. She bowed her head.

At this, Gilly tapped the bare skin above Larka's womb. "You shall need me in time."

Larka shrank from the touch.

Gilly stooped and picked up Heta's old shawl. "Don't much like the smell of this anymore either, do you?"

Larka's eyes widened.

"It'll burn well enough," Gilly said then walked away sniggering.

Larka folded her legs and slid beneath lukewarm water. The weight of the liquid should have been soothing and light, yet it felt heavier, like an anchor to Gilly's madness.

CHAPTER 14

ARRIVALS

omeone comes," Gilly called from the cottage's doorway.

Larka dropped the water bucket into the well and rushed past Gilly, through the front room and into the back one, closing the door behind her. She sat quietly on her bed, ensnared in a dimness wrought by ever chilling days. She fingered the dull material of the shapeless dress Gilly had loaned her.

Somehow, Gilly always knew when company approached. The crone's head would perk up and a distant focus would come to her pitted eyes; thereupon, Larka would be sitting in here—just as she was now—pining for her urchins and the cabin beside the Wittins.

She wondered how they fared. Gilly had sent a messenger to Guta upon Pentheya's waking; he had arrived shortly thereafter to retrieve the girl. Larka had listened—pressed against the door between them—to the deep cadence of Guta's voice. Several weeks had passed since.

Larka jammed the heels of her hands into her eyes and rubbed doggedly at the moisture there. She would see them again. She would!

The opening scrape then thunk of cupboard doors soon assured Larka of Gilly's movements outside the backroom: fetching herbs, essences, tinctures, or herb-infused oils. Jaunty's villagers arrived often now to stock up on medicinals before the weather became too bad for the trip to Gilly's outlying cottage.

Larka heard the rustling of Gilly's voice and a deeper one as well. Larka missed the opening and closing whisper of the front door—the announcement of a second visitor—as she worried about her urchins.

She inhaled deeply, her blossoming chest rising and falling with her breath.

The front door thumped shut. Light soon fell across Larka as Gilly opened the backroom.

"Come out now," Gilly commanded and left the door open.

Larka stepped toward the living area of the cottage and halted in the doorway, her fingers clutching the frame. Skepticism lifted her brow as she gazed at the woman who sat at the table, on the nearer end of one of its benches.

The woman turned on her seat.

"Hello, Larka." The woman tried to smile, but the expression came out pained, shattered within the pallor of an oval face contrasted by blue-black hair.

"Your father is dead," the woman said—voice dull, nearly lifeless.

Larka drew herself taller. She recalled the sun flashing off this woman's blue-black hair as the woman had fled down Jaunty's main street. She recalled the dream of this woman she had finally stopped having. She recalled the cold, hungry nights in the forest this woman could have deterred. Mostly, she recalled the years of not knowing why she existed if it were to be tortured under Gilly's hands.

"What father?" Larka sibilated, not meeting the woman's gaze.

The woman sighed then clasped and unclasped her hands where they hovered above her knees. The woman's vision settled on those restless hands before she closed her eyes and mouthed silent words, praying to some god Larka did not know.

Larka stepped back into the shadows of the bedroom. She began to close the door, but Gilly clawed it open.

"You listen to Mentheleda. She's your mother."

"I know that!" Larka's thoughts snapped outward with electric fire. Her scowl smote Gilly with the visage of a smoky-blue aura flaring around an angry ghost before the luminescence settled then receded into nothing.

Gilly glared, and Larka felt that talon trying to slip back into her brain, yet somehow it failed, and a wide-eyed crone sought her rocking chair then collapsed into it.

Larka railed at Gilly, "I remember her . . . *you*" —her eyes fixed on Mentheleda— "never coming back, not once in all these years. I remember you, *your back*. I remember your back as you walked away from me!" Her voice rose and fell with the turbulence of her emotions.

Mentheleda twisted her fingers together and put a stop to the wresting of her hands. She overscrutinized her fingernails as her words quavered into the room,

"I-I thought I did right by you, child. You'd not have made it in my keep." Mentheleda's mouth bunched and trembled. "The townsfolk," she paused and closed her eyes a moment, strain written in the crevices of her face, inhalation audible before she continued, "your father, they'd have seen you dead."

Then, very quietly, the woman began to weep.

Larka chewed her bottom lip and stepped into the living area, vision transfixed on her mother.

She barely registered that Mentheleda continued to talk so low was her speech, and Larka heard not what her mother expressed; instead the woman's carriage singed its way into her daughter's mind. Larka's stomach heaved. The woman acted afraid to look at her, almost afraid to speak. Larka understood all too well this browbeaten mien; she'd certainly been Gilly's whipping girl long enough to recognize it.

Larka bent forward to hear and decipher what Mentheleda's low murmur pronounced.

". . . He was not the best of men, but he kept us fed and clothed."

Feeling as if she had been punched in the gut, Larka let out a small cry.

Her next words came out a tormented whisper, "But he abused you."

Mentheleda lifted her head to peer at Larka. "I do not defend him. The best thing he's ever done by me was to die younger than most."

Larka paused and closed her eyes, leaning back against a door jamb, shaking her head; there was something so wrong about that statement.

Finally she asked, "Why didn't you leave him?"

A meek smile flitted through Mentheleda's expression and was just as soon gone. "I couldn't leave you behind."

Larka rubbed her forehead.

"As for your father, I didn't wish him dead, Larka . . . just away." Mentheleda turned her clasped hands over and stared at the worn palms. "Funny, when you're young how you never think the person you love the most could become the one you dread to see, hear, smell."

Mentheleda gazed over her hands at the stretch of wooden floor between her and Larka. She sighed. "He's away now. I thought I could see you. When Gilly told me you had not fled—," Mentheleda choked in the midst of her sentence, and her next words grew hoarse. "She told me . . ." Shaking her head, Mentheleda pressed her lips between thumb and forefinger.

"She told you what?" Larka asked and shot an accusatory look at Gilly.

Mentheleda cried out, "She told me about the day you came back with no clothes, all the bruises, *the cuts on your back*."

"Oh." Eyes burning hot, Larka turned on the crone.

Gilly shrugged. "You need her. You need all those who would protect you now. You and the unborn." Gilly's gaze shifted to Larka's lower abdomen.

Larka grasped her flat stomach. "I am *not* pregnant!"

Gilly grunted, and Mentheleda wept like a river undammed while Larka's incredulity swept over the scene.

"I thought I could be here for you," Mentheleda breathed then winced as Larka's fiery eyes fixed on her.

"Listen to me, Larka." Mentheleda's voice firmed, and she held her daughter's gaze. "They would have hunted us down had I run with you. I was expected to kill you and cast you in the river. I couldn't do that. All I saw was a baby who deserved better than a murderer for a mother, so I did the next best thing to killing you. I just didn't know it at the time." Mentheleda's smoky-blue eyes blazed at Gilly. "I gave you to *her*." She jabbed a thumb toward Gilly then stood. "I'd no idea she'd treat you ill until the last day I saw you . . . bruised, switch marks on your legs, arms, everywhere." Face reddened, she swigged at the air. "And there was nothing I could do to keep you safest except leave you here."

Mentheleda came to stand before Larka and interlocked their fingers.

Larka half gasped, half cried out at that touch.

"Oh now, don't cry, child. I've come to stay, not to leave you again." Mentheleda dabbed at Larka's face with the sleeve of her own dress. "Everyone knows Gilly needs someone to look after her now. All I need is your agreement, daughter. We've finally time for each other. She can't hurt you now. She will never hurt you again." Mentheleda lashed out each word in her last sentence with a whip for a tongue, glaring at Gilly then murmuring to Larka, "Please forgive me."

Larka swallowed hard then nodded, biting her lower lip and sniffling.

A tiny smile lit Mentheleda, and she folded her daughter's trembling body into arms that had waited eleven hollow years to be filled by her youngest.

Larka closed her eyes and inspired her lungs with newfound air. When she unveiled her vision, she found Gilly staring through the embrace of mother and daughter. A look of longing hung the folds of the crone's skin.

Larka's vision aimed at her, the crone's focus returned. Gilly slowly pivoted her head to gaze into the fire. Then the crone coughed with a fist to her mouth and continued the creaking sway of her rocking chair.

CHAPTER 15

CATCHING UP

*P*eering out the back window, Larka slipped into the gray dress Mentheleda had made for her. Her mother wore a dress of the same cut and color. From afar, anyone could mistake Larka for Mentheleda, though no one had come to Gilly's home in several weeks, for the heavy snows—very late in coming—had spewed their forces upon Jaunty and its outlying areas, precluding all travel.

Larka pressed the dress pleats over her still-flat stomach. The worst pregnancy symptoms she had thus far experienced had been lethargy and nausea.

She left the backroom and seated herself at the table. Mentheleda set a cup of ginger tea before her and took a seat opposite, a sympathetic smile on her face.

"You'll feel better after you reach your fourth month." Mentheleda patted Larka's hand where it paused on the stem of the cup.

Larka gazed across the table into eyes wide and invigorated despite the slight bag of their lids. She grinned then concentrated on a table surface worn smooth with age.

"Your father didn't like it when I drank this. He said it stank." Mentheleda sighed then sipped tea, peering over her cup at Larka. "You remind me much of your sister."

Larka's head rolled up. In the two weeks since her arrival, Mentheleda had spoken little of their family.

"She was about two years older than you. She's been gone a few years. Took it upon herself to run off with some fellow." Grimness set Mentheleda's mouth. "You had three older brothers, too. None of them understood where you went when I disappeared and came back without a baby." Mentheleda's eyes lost focus as she drifted into memory, her tone descending into a low murmur. "It mattered little what your father told them or tried to explain about the dark moon. They wanted to hear none of it.

"Seems children know best what's right from wrong, before everything gets all mucked up by us grownups." Mentheleda smiled, a hard glint to her eyes. "They harangued your father about it for a long time and resented me until I told them I had not the heart for murder and why I came here."

Larka sat up straighter. "You told them?"

"Only your brothers. They left home as soon as they knew your father couldn't hurt me anymore, as soon as he died. At least two of them did. Your sister, Betta . . ." Mentheleda winced. "I don't know where she went. She left and never looked back I suppose, but Astla . . ." She sighed. "We write often. He's my oldest and part of the Overseer's Guard." Mentheleda breathed deeply and sat upright, her eyes atwinkle.

All the years spent without a family slipped over Larka like a suffocating body bag. Nausea threatened to overtake her, and she felt tears brewing. Thus she clamped her teeth together and gazed into yellowish tea.

"Tell me about Astla," she finally said and, peering up, smiled through the stiffness of her lips.

Mentheleda looked her daughter over. "Perhaps another time?"

Larka pressed her lips together then shook her head. "Now's fine," she said, unable to voice more than a whisper.

"It's the baby, daughter. It makes your moods more intense now with your hormones all stirred up."

Larka nodded. Then Mentheleda filled the tense silence with words of pride . . . and shame.

"Astla was the finest warrior, Larka. It came naturally to him. By eleven, he had mastered the bow and arrow, which I still can't handle, as well as defeating your father and any other man in Jaunty in swordplay. The Overseer's scouts sought him, and Astla left us at twelve years of age." Mentheleda wrung her hands.

"Sometimes I think he learned his skills so well because of you. Because he thought he could not save you. His being the oldest when you disappeared, he understood better than the rest what we had lost, and he hated your father with such . . . fury. He, of all the children, begged me not to go to the river the night you were born, until his father struck him down." Mentheleda drifted into reminiscence, eyes glazed, hands locked around her tea cup. A tear seeped from beneath her lashes. She cleared it absently from her cheek then gazed at Larka. "I suppose Astla was another child I lost because of *him*."

Mentheleda sighed, brow creasing. "I've been trying to talk about this since I got here, child, to let you know you are not alone in this world, that you never have been," she murmured the last few words, then her voice rose. "Besides, I never lost Astla, not really.

"You'd like him." She brightened. "I don't know where he got it, but he has such a sense of humor." Mentheleda stopped and leaned forward, regarding her daughter as if seeing some truth hidden far beneath Larka's surface. "He knows *all* that happened the night I birthed you."

"All?" Larka leaned back, a chill running through her. "What did happen that night?"

"Oh, child, strange things," Mentheleda whispered. "So many strange things happened that night. I had to put them out of my mind until I could accept them, but it started with the storm while I as working in the garden. So windy. So odd—the clouds closing in that fast." She pursed her lips, her gaze boring into Larka once more. "And again with the storm while I was washing dishes, like the wind was tapping at my window. Then my water broke. I dropped a plate, and your father saw me there with that water running down my legs, around my feet. He was so angry." Mentheleda shook her head.

"Astla was reading to the children in front of the fire. He sent them to their room when your father started yelling." Mentheleda's voice rose. "But Astla wouldn't go. He refused to leave me. They argued." Her voice fell. "Your father knocked him with his fist so hard on the head . . . It was so sudden, neither of us expected it. I'll never forget the way my son looked all shriveled on the floor that night." Mentheleda paused a moment, her breathing uneven, eyes brimming. She closed those eyes briefly then opened them to continue,

"Then he grabbed me and shoved me out the door, but I was ready. I had felt the contractions coming on in the garden. I had hoped he would be in bed asleep when the full labor struck, but it was not to be."

Gilly's rocking chair began to creak in the background as Mentheleda spoke. They had become so used to hearing the plaintive sway of that particular piece of furniture, neither Larka nor Mentheleda noticed the old woman had awoken from another of her more frequent naps.

Larka listened, rapt by the tale of her birth. When her mother finished speaking, Larka relaxed and slumped forward, placing her elbows on the table. She clasped her hands together, noting her own fidgety thumbs then peered back up at Mentheleda.

"I am still not certain how birth under a dark moon makes one person different from another."

The rocking chair's creaking halted, and Gilly snorted. "Strange magic walks the land beneath a dark moon. It claims those it would, girl, those worthy of its gifts. It makes from the ordinary a person so feared most would rather kill dark moon spawn than give them a chance, especially us females. Some of us survive by luck, others because their parents would rather have a child than follow the customs of fools."

Larka caught Mentheleda's flinch and apprehended the vaguest feeling of guilt pulsing from her mother. She reached across the table to touch Mentheleda's arm.

"You did not abandon me, Mother. You followed your heart."

Larka turned to assay Gilly's silhouette as the crone pumped the rocking chair into a drawling creak.

Gilly met her gaze with the empty stare that comes with age. Larka shuddered then ventured to speak her mind. "Perhaps bitter old weather witches with their odd insights and cruel ways are children of the dark moon abandoned to their fate?"

A cynical quirk lifted Gilly's mouth. "Took you long enough to figure that out." She snickered convulsively, the action drawing on dwindling reserves, the rocking chair's silence attesting to the immobilization of feeble legs.

Larka allowed her eyes to hold Gilly's a moment longer.

"Why females? Why not the males as well?"

Gilly's hands clenched into fists and she snarled, "Doesn't affect them the same, *girl!*" The crone struck the arms of her chair.

Larka's eyes widened, brows lifted.

Gilly's voice then dropped into its usual gruffness, her features reset. "Now you close your eyes and think on what you are and what you've done when desperate, and you think on what your mother told you of your birthing day, and you'll know how and with what the dark moon gifted you."

"I already have an idea of it," Larka said, shaking her head.

"Close your eyes and think on it, girl," Gilly commanded.

"No," Larka protested as her brain twinged. Her last thought was that Gilly aimed to hurt not enlighten her. Then a breath of air pressed on Larka's eyelids and closed them. The gate of her memories opened on the image of coughing townsfolk after they had been pelted with dirt and rocks; it shifted to three men being slung to the ground along with the crackling sound of her hands beneath Pentheya's frail body; the gate switched to Gilly's rawhide whip flying to the cottage's rooftop and then to the slap of air against a hidden red-eyed monster. Finally, images of lavender roots licking at her blood met Larka's consciousness. With much effort she quashed the latter image and forced the intruder out of her mind.

Her eyelids jerked open, the question of where the wind had

gone on that cold night when she had so desperately needed it foremost in her mind, yet the hypnotic air stirred about her and drew out that inquiry.

"Humph." Gilly glared at Larka then rasped, "Still, you see the outcome, girl, not the cause, not the link." The crone fell cryptically silent and started to rock again, the creaking of her chair more drawled, her withered body further weakened.

CHAPTER 16

HARBINGER

Larka held a palm against the round, hard structure that had usurped her abdomen. Outside the front room's glass window, snow again spewed forth upon the world, where it partially melted under the spring sun, stratifying into ice and shallow drifts. Larka pushed up the window then closed the shutters she had so recently opened.

She had suffered through those first months of snow with morning sickness until she had become an invigorated and very hungry pregnant woman. Then she had gone through much of the winter growing and eating, eating and growing.

Larka caressed her extended belly—a habit she had developed since the babe's first movements. Within a month and a half, the child would be born.

Larka had begun to pile wood in the fireplace when she heard the wispy rush of Mentheleda's gray dress behind her.

"Let me do that, Larka. You'll hurt yourself," Mentheleda fussed and garnered the wood from Larka's grasp before arranging it in the fire.

Larka smiled and shook her head. "I'm fine. I really am."

Mentheleda chided Larka with an upward sweep of her eyebrows then moved to the kitchen table to prepare a late-day snack of bread and raspberry preserves.

Gilly snoozed quietly in her rocking chair. Larka perused the drooping furrows of the woman's aged face and pressed her hands protectively to her belly.

She shook her head, certain Gilly's life failed with each passing day but also certain that Gilly could no more reach the urchins with harm than the villagers had bothered to reach out to them with care.

Something akin to pity for the crone had bloomed within Larka over the winter, yet she felt little remorse at having planned with Mentheleda to depart for Albilar soon after the baby's birth: the gleeful ease with which the crone had threatened Pentheya and her siblings left little room for remorse.

Concealed no more, eyes that reflected death studied Larka.

"Someone comes," Gilly breathed then straightaway nodded back into slumber.

The door burst open. Larka jumped and held her rotund belly. A tiny figure paused in the doorway then dashed into the cottage and clung to Larka, pastel-green eyes smiling up at her from beneath the hood of a coat.

Larka vented a sigh of relief.

"Pentheya, what are you doing here? It's cold out." Larka pushed the hood back and smiled at the healthy fill of the youngster's cheeks. "You look well."

"The Wittins take good care of us. I didn't tell anyone you were here, not Arnt or Halty or even Ian or Guta." Pentheya hugged herself. "The villagers . . . say bad things about you, about us when Kila takes us to the store. Guta says to ignore them. They can't hurt us because he's notified the Overseer of their threats, and they know it," Pentheya gushed and embraced Larka again. "I miss you."

Larka's lips compressed into a grim line. "It was good then that I left you, if they say such things." Larka smiled as best she could. "But I miss you, too."

"Oh." Pentheya patted Larka's protrusive abdomen. "When did that happen?"

Larka winced and heard Mentheleda cough at the table as if she choked on her food.

Mentheleda cleared her throat. "It makes no matter, little one."

Pentheya's brows arched, and her arms dropped by her sides. "Oh," she said with hurt inflection. "Well, the Wittins wanted some lavender essence."

The front door flipped open and banged back against its wall. Mentheleda yelped. Gilly awoke. A rectangle of pale daylight illuminated Larka and Pentheya.

A familiar man stepped inside, shaking snowflakes off his coat and cap. He closed the door before pivoting into a standstill and gaping, eyes flicking from Larka to Pentheya.

Mentheleda's voice arose within the strained silence, "Why do you stare at my daughter in that manner, Rollen? She's been gone but not that long." Mentheleda came across the room. "Well, what do you want?"

"Oil. Lav-lavender oil," he sputtered.

"Betta, fetch that oil." Mentheleda turned to Larka, her eyes gesturing to the cabinets.

Larka paused for an instant as comprehension flooded her, but it was a moment too long. She extricated herself from Pentheya's clinging arms. Her cheeks burned as she shuffled to the cabinets. She felt the man's eyes searing into her back the entire time she collected the essence oil.

Her hands trembled as she dropped the vial onto her mother's palm. She tucked her hands momentarily out of sight and seated herself—back to the man—at the table. There, she nibbled at the bread Mentheleda had prepared for her.

Mentheleda gave the man the vial. "Well, stop gaping and pay for it, Rollen," she snapped.

The slits of the man's eyes rested upon Mentheleda before he picked a coin from his pocket and dropped it onto her waiting hand. Rollen then fumbled for the door knob behind him and backed out, his eyes lingering on Larka until Mentheleda slammed that rectangle of wood between them.

"He didn't believe it," Pentheya murmured and shuffled to Larka's side where she plucked at Larka's dress sleeve.

Gilly snorted. "Well that was obvious."

Larka set her elbows on the table and rested her face within her hands, eyes closed.

"He'll tell! He'll tell!" Pentheya shrilled.

Larka raised her head.

"Nonsense!" Mentheleda retorted, yet her shoulders slumped with submission.

"Hush now." Larka put an arm around Pentheya then looked at Mentheleda. "She's right, Mother. Rollen was one of the men who blocked my path when Pentheya nearly died. You know what I had to do to him. He wouldn't soon forget me no matter my resemblance to Betta. I must leave here at once." Larka rose and Pentheya pressed her face into her adopted mother's side, sniffling and trembling.

Mentheleda raised her spread hands. "Where to go and what to do with you in your condition?"

"I can help," Gilly croaked from her chair.

"How?" Mentheleda and Larka asked in unison.

"A blight on his memory. It won't last long because the spirits may not help me, but perhaps it will give time enough." Gilly did something then that took Larka aback: the crone smiled a great, beaming smile. "Had to do it a few times for Larka. It kept the villagers from being too nosy. They remember too much now, ask too many questions. And I had to do it when my son was born." Gilly stroked the arms of her rocking chair, her smile growing serene.

This admission of parenthood shocked Larka. It must have shown on her face, for Gilly laughed—a joyous laugh.

"Yes, Larka, I had a boy. It was the sweetest time of my life." Her eyes became unfocused, and her mind carried her to another time. "A beautiful, healthy boy." She stopped then to glare at them and next spoke like a snake coiled to strike, "But you can't blame *me* for what he became!"

Gilly turned and stared into the fire. A multicolored flare of lights—like flower blossoms in spring—played around her then faded. She returned her rusty gaze to them.

"It's done. The spirits helped. Seems they wish the unborn unharmed." Gilly renewed her feeble rocking. Within seconds, she had fallen yet again to slumber, to stillness.

Larka and Mentheleda peered at one another, bemused.

"I should go," Pentheya spoke softly. "I think I caused enough trouble."

"You caused no trouble, Pentheya." Larka squatted to gaze into Pentheya's glistening green eyes. She ran a thumb over the child's reddened cheeks.

"But your sparkles would have warned you if I hadn't been here."

"You didn't cause this."

"But your sparkles—"

Larka placed a finger over the child's lips then paused, staring as if far off.

"My sparkles . . ." The information she sought squirmed deeper into her mind, but she finally pried it out, growing dizzy with the effort. "They don't always work when I need them." Larka raised herself, swaying slightly.

The memory of her most desperate want of the wind's protection on a cold, dark night with the Amber Man—as dim as it had been moments ago—now glared at her. She glanced at Gilly. Had the elder blighted Larka's mind as well? Why?

Larka steadied herself and delved into the cabinet for the last time. She moved back to Pentheya. "Take this oil to the Wittins and short-cut through the woods, so no one will see you." Larka hugged the little girl tightly. "I love you. I'll send for you when I can."

"Love you, too," Pentheya whispered and wiped her nose on her coat sleeve, tears shining down her cheeks. She spun and ran out of the cottage.

For what seemed a much longer time than the few seconds it took, Larka and Mentheleda stared at the door after it thudded shut.

CHAPTER 17

BIRTH SONG

Birth Song

embrace of the womb
relinquish thine arms
that i might be born

embraced of a mother
kissed upon the brow
sustenance, love
mother names me . . .

Larka hoisted a worn haversack over her shoulder. Mentheleda followed with her own bag. They had wasted no time in packing; less than an hour had passed since Pentheya's departure. Mother and daughter grew tenser with each spent minute despite Gilly's assurances of having slowed the message Rollen could deliver to the villagers. The old woman had fallen asleep one too many times of late.

Larka allowed her gaze to rest on Gilly's slumbering form. Sympathy infused her heart. The crone would die here alone, and she had volunteered this isolation to save Larka's baby. Larka swallowed against the burgeoning lump in her throat.

Gilly mumbled in her sleep, "Moon's dark tonight. Light snow coming."

Mentheleda opened the front door. Pentheya nearly fell into the cottage, poised as she was to enter. Cold rushed in around the child.

"They're coming! They're coming! Rollen didn't get to his house. It was like he wasn't right. He kept stumbling and falling and talking about the weather witch and her bastard and me. Another man found him on the way. I think the other man was waiting for Rollen. He saw me and started yelling about a curse. They're coming up the road now, lots of them!"

Larka's heart failed, or so it seemed. She gasped for breath and staggered backward. Only her baby's kick brought her back to right thinking and an upright stance.

Mentheleda shoved Pentheya. "Get out of here. Run! Do you hear me? Go!"

"Stay off the road," Larka called after the fleeing child.

"I'll stall them," Mentheleda said. She darted into the backroom and returned with a pillow that she stuffed under the pleated belly of her dress. She then began to cinch a cord around the lower quarter of it. She peered up at her daughter as she tied the pillow in place.

"Go, Larka!"

A drift of air mingled with thoughts of murder settled over Larka— a warning come too late of her air allies. A chill ran through her.

"Mother, they'll kill you."

Mentheleda clutched Larka's shoulders, a wild defiance in her eyes. "I've lived long enough! Get out of here. Save yourself. Save that baby!"

Larka nodded, ignoring the sting of tears in her eyes. She launched out the front door into the graying day and dodged through the trees, hands supporting her tumid belly. She headed toward the river, slipping frequently on the ice where it clung with tenacious grip to its solidity. She wished spring had come earlier—when it was supposed to have—yet the snows kept falling, thawing and freezing just enough to retain slippery footing.

A low shriek soured the air and encompassed Larka's head like a full helmet until it withered and was no more.

"Gilly," Larka whispered and turned toward the cottage. She found only the pale, bent trunks of birches in her view.

Pain wracked Larka's womb, and her baby fidgeted beneath her skin.

"Not now. Not now," she moaned through gritted teeth. She grasped her stomach and sped the gait of her legs.

A sharp snapping of twigs and stems sounded not far away.

"Mother," she stopped and called then chastised herself. It could be anyone, yet the semidarkness did not answer Larka. Hair, instead, raised on her scalp and neck—it should have been warning enough.

Within seconds, the sounds of pursuit ran straight through her. She shook her head against all the emotions, unfamiliar and rumbling through the air. She smelled spilled blood on snips of wind, perhaps Gilly's blood, perhaps not.

"Mother," Larka sobbed. Along with her panting breath, hot tears steamed into the surrounding cold.

The sounds of pursuit began to close in. She fetched a knife from her bag and burst into a sprint. But, a pregnant woman, she could not outrun the unencumbered.

The last bit of the sun's light had sunk. Larka's dark dress blended with the overwhelming shadows that had cast themselves upon her world. She blotted her eyes with that dark material, still running despite the contractions revolting through her womb and the broken water freezing down her legs.

She reached the roaring river and could see little of it, though she knew it swollen and thaw fed. Here, she slowed her steps, and something spattered her dress. Larka raised her bare hands to feel the snow's descent. Everything about the weather seemed ill-timed on her behalf. And where had the moon fled this night?

Larka recalled the crone's last words and murmured to herself, "You told me, did you not Gilly?"

"Ahhhh," Larka groaned and pitched into a descent caught by

her knees; her sack fell from her shoulder, the knife from her hand. She folded into the pain and rose into a squat, legs far apart. The baby wanted to be born—now! The pursuit grew ever closer, and she shifted her position, snow and ice scrunching beneath her booted feet. Light from oil lamps and many torches flared between the vertical lines of tree trunks. Soon they would be here. And all would be lost.

Larka gazed into the dark sky. "Help me, please. Whatever powers be with me, don't leave me this time. I need you."

The wind began to rip at her dress as her last word broke forth. Lightning pulsed within the belly of the sky overhead. Thunder, harsh and throaty, bellowed its dissent. Smoky-blue sparks flared around Larka's body. She gasped: the mob would see her like a beacon. The air, however, began a slow ascending swirl, its circumference broadening and glowing as it built strength.

Larka nearly toppled backward into the river at the sight of that vortex spinning around her but for Mentheleda's plowing past, running full speed on long legs with a slender, pale-haired man on her heels. The heavy tread of many feet paralyzed Larka, and the entire posse shot past in pursuit of her mother. Larka blinked. Certainly, they had seen her, even as hunched over this birthing as she was.

She heard voices—snippets carried on currents of air.

"You are not the dark daughter!" one man blared. "That's Mentheleda," said another.

"Where is she?" someone bellowed. "What did she do to Rollen?"

Larka recognized the third voice—Rostin—and closed her eyes. She gritted her teeth as another contraction shook her. She pushed but the baby did not come. She caught her breath, blew it out, ready to push with the next quake of her womb.

A shriek of pure agony slammed through the curtain of spinning air. Another shriek came and trailed into a gurgled moan.

"Mother. Oh gods, what have they done to you?" Larka whispered, chest tight with emotion.

"*You killed her!*" Mentheleda shrieked somewhere in the distance.

"Mother?" Larka's head snapped up, her heartbeat crazed but hopeful.

Mentheleda emerged into a small clearing, her arms held behind her by Rostin. Dark stains splotched Rostin's coat above the dagger sheathed on his hip.

"Where is your daughter?" he bellowed again.

The angry mob came into view. Nobody glanced Larka's way; they could not see her, could not hear her. Her body relaxed. Her baby was safe, and Mentheleda appeared unharmed.

"She's away from here," Mentheleda screeched and struggled to break Rostin's hold on her wrists. "Away from you murdering bastards!"

"Over here," a man called.

Larka had heard the odd inflections in that voice often enough to know its owner: Wittis Wittin. He stood so close to her, she could nearly touch him.

"Her trail end here." He pointed to the edge of Larka's whirlwind then peered into the river. "She must have jump," he said in raised voice and lowered his lamp. He spoke softly next, "If anyone survive, Larka, es you."

As other men came to examine her footprints, another contraction struck. Larka squeezed hard this time. She felt between her legs. The baby's head had crowned.

"You! Had you killed her upon birth, we would not be here tonight!" Rostin yelled into Mentheleda's face, angrier now than he had been before thinking Larka had fallen prey to the river. He reached inside his coat.

"Mother!" Larka screamed, sensing Mentheleda's peril, yet the sound did not extend beyond the whirlwind. It bounced inside of the air tunnel until its echo dissipated.

Larka slammed her fist into the vortex's wall as Rostin raised a club and banged it into Mentheleda's head.

Wittis caught sight of the action but too late to stop it. He ran and leapt at Rostin, the scant oil in his lamp sloshing.

Mentheleda lay at Rostin's feet when he began a repeat action with the club.

"She hurt no one." Wittis caught the younger man's arm.

The rest of the mob glared at Rostin, disgust languishing in their expressions.

"That's enough. We've enough blood on our hands for one night." A big man with broad shoulders started toward Rostin

"Rollen was my brother, Durk. He's addled beyond repair now because of her. He's slobbering like a baby." Rostin wrested his fore-arm from Wittis's hold and raised the club to strike at the aging carpenter.

Spread flat on the vortex wall, Larka's palms crackled with energy. Blue-gray lightning thrust forth from that flesh to sear into Rostin. The man blew backward and landed several feet from where he had stood, eyes unblinkingly open, smoke rising from his chest.

Durk and the rest of the mob cast about, looking for the source of an oddly colored horizontal lightning.

The vortex's swirling began to slow, and Larka screamed as she pushed the baby out. The newborn fell into the cold ice below, and Larka's scream resonated through the weakening vortex, echoing through the crowd.

"It's the girl!" Durk shouted. "Her ghost has come back for us!"

Wittis watched as the men fled the forest, shaking his head with condemnation.

He bent to Mentheleda and took her hand in his. "Me wife and I care for you."

Mentheleda shook her head feebly. "He hit me too hard, carpenter. Go home. I want to die as near my daughter as I can."

Wittis tarried over Mentheleda for a long moment before he rose in a slow, sad manner. "Es your right to die as you wish."

As Wittis and his lamp's light disappeared into the dark night, so too did the vortex. Larka picked up her baby and, still squatting, pushed once more to let the afterbirth slip into the ice, where snow flurries would meet its heat. She took up her knife and severed her child's umbilical cord just as the winds took their light with them.

"Please, I want to see my baby," she said.

A breeze lifted and lit around her, showing her the little girl's perfect face. Larka rummaged in her sack for string then tied off the baby's cord.

"Oh," Larka breathed. "You're so cold." She dug in the sack again and pulled out a small blanket she had made especially for the child's birthing day then wrapped the baby in that warmth.

"Larka?" A voice called.

"Mother." Larka went to Mentheleda's still form.

Blood ran in rivulets down Mentheleda's forehead, over the right brow, into her eye, and down her cheek. Mentheleda pressed a palm to the injury.

Larka bent with much discomfort in her swollen genitalia and, using her own dress sleeve, wiped the blood out of Mentheleda's eye.

"I thought you dead, child," Mentheleda said then peered long and hard at the glow shimmering around Larka's form. "You are of storm, born with the wind licking at you and lightning dancing so near my feet I thought certainly it would be our death." She smiled a pained smile, wiped her bloody hand in the snow. "Let me see the baby."

Mentheleda turned enough to lie on her side and hold the infant girl Larka sacrificed into her arms.

"There's a woman just over the ridge there. She was birthing near the river when the men found her. *That Rostin . . .*" Mentheleda spat through gritted teeth, shaking her head, unable to finish the sentence.

Larka looked at Rostin, at the dark splotches on his coat and hands. A breeze carried the smell of his seared flesh, of blood. Larka fought her gag reflex. She then grasped what comprised the coagulated fluid on Rostin's clothing and hands—a stranger's blood—and gazed back at her mother, who blinked with hazy vision.

"Another woman—that was who screamed?"

Her mother nodded. "Go quickly. See if you can save her baby. It may not be too late."

Larka kissed her own baby girl on the head. The newborn cooed.

"It'll be good for us now," she told the infant and whispered the child's name into Mentheleda's ear.

As her daughter left, Mentheleda began to sing in a low, sweet tone. Larka joined her mother in singing the song of birth and hobbled up the ridge, yet as they reached the last verse, the baby's name became lost in a bluster of snow and wind.

CHAPTER 18

DEATH SONG

Death Song

sing of life given
life lived
life passed
of grief born mighty
within my family's chest
tears strung from their hearts
ripped from their eyes
sing unto them
upon the shattered wind

On the ridge above, two pallid forms protruded from the darkness. As Larka neared, the light circulating around her further illuminated the protrusions; she realized them to be legs, knees bent and fallen inward to rest upon each other.

Larka paused, the hair on her neck bristling in warning: much evil stalked the forest this night. She glanced through the darkness toward Mentheleda but could not see her mother or her newborn. Thus unaware of the misfortune happening behind her, of the madness she would soon shed like tears, Larka took a deep breath and ascended the last few steps.

Blood pooled beneath as snow drifted over the woman's body,

where it lay within a patch of sapling trees. The woman's dress billowed in the wind, hiding her abdomen and upper thighs. Clenched in this stranger's hand was a large kitchen knife—a weapon that had proved useless against a rancorous man and a cruel dagger.

Larka bit her tongue against the cry that reverberated in her throat. She stared for vast moments, eyes fixed on the stranger's face, until anguished words spilled forth,

"I am sorry that our paths crossed this way. It is too late to help you . . . you or your child but sleep knowing Rostin will hurt no one upon this Earth again." She bent to close the woman's eyes.

A baby shrieked. Larka jumped back. The smoky-blue lights about her heightened in a swish of wind. She bent and squinted toward the angry wail and saw the newborn sheltered by the bridge of the dead woman's legs and the cloth of the dress. The babe thrashed about in a muck of mixed soil and blood, little hands flailing over her head; then the newborn began to slide downward in the muck, nearing a slope that would hurl her small body toward the river.

Larka caught the newborn up in her arms, and the child immediately quieted.

As she tried to straighten her back, Larka met resistance on the upward pull and hesitated in that bent pose. The baby shrieked. Larka spotted the cord still leading into the mother's womb and realized her mistake. She bit her lip and peered at the baby's squinched features. Then out of the side of her eye, Larka saw the umbilical cord moving forward. Quickly deducting the cause, she grabbed the cord —its slippery surface nearly escaping her fingers—before the placenta oozed out of the stranger's corpse.

Larka tucked the squalling infant more deeply into the crook of her left arm then transferred the cord to that hand, freeing her right hand to pull the kitchen knife from the stranger's death grip. With a flick of wrist, the blade severed the line from mother to child. Birth blood spattered rocky soil and sapling alike. The stench of it smote her, and Larka fought down rising gorge. The placenta, meanwhile, dropped into the muck and slid downward on slick rock to perch precariously on the ridge's edge, threatening descent.

Larka surveyed the yowling infant for damage. The babe stopped crying and stared at Larka's sparkling lights, as if the newborn could already see with matured vision. Cold wind slashed at them, giving Larka impetus to cut away pieces of the dead woman's dress and wrap the baby in that bloodstained material. The newborn wailed.

"Shh," Larka breathed and held the baby girl near. The infant pummeled her with tiny fists.

Larka's eyes fell once more on the dead woman. A guilty pall clenched Larka's gut. She placed the kitchen knife into the snow beside the stranger then spun to pick her way toward her mother.

Back down the ridge, Larka noted dark footprints in the snow ahead and left of her, as if someone had walked through barefoot and veered into the forest. Perplexed, she moved closer to the prints until it became obvious they belonged to no human, whereupon fear tightened her chest. Her aura blazed.

She had seen these immense tracks but once in her life: beside the cabin she and her urchins had built. Larka bit deeply into her lip as the dark color demarcating these tracks made itself known to her.

Blood.

It was blood!

"Sweet earth, no," Larka whispered and dashed along the bloody trail, knowing where the tracks would lead before she arrived.

"Oh, sweet earth." Larka shook her head. "Oh gods, no." She backed away from the sight.

Mentheleda lay there, form frozen in a defensive posture, left arm raised across her face, rosettes of blood gushing from her chest.

"My baby," Larka cried.

"Mother . . . my baby. Where's my baby?" Dizziness swayed her, yet Larka's eyes followed back along the bloody trail arcing into a dark and silent forest.

Larka ran to the trail's forest entrance, yet here the tracks disappeared as did her wind lights. A tremor of hopelessness surged through her.

She begged of her wind friends, "Please, help me. Please, where is she?" The air stirred not. All remained disquiet and shadow.

Larka asked, voice low, tremulous, "Is she dead?" She peered into the heavens. The sky remained as silent as the wind.

A mournful shriek rose in her throat. *Death Song* spilled forth in ululation, carried forth on strands of wind.

Larka ran toward the river, its gushing noose drawing her near. For reasons she did not care to contemplate, an oil lamp glowed by the river's edge, and she launched there to join the water's rushing oblivion. A vise caught her waist midair, dragging her back and down. She kicked against its grip, foot hitting the lamp, her heart yearning for the calling river as she moved through free-fall and thumped against the body beneath her. Meanwhile, lamplight flew through the darkness, descended, then succumbed to the river's waters.

"Larka, es not so bad. Es okay now. You and your baby," an out-of-breath voice uttered into her ear.

"My baby?" She shrieked the infant's name, and, yet again, the wind absorbed it.

He pointed to the fat babe in her arms. "Es right here. Shush now. Others hear you." Guta stroked Larka's hair.

Sitting up, he dragged them both backward on their buttocks, over rock and ice as far as he could from the river's edge before picking Larka, and thus the baby she clung to, up and carrying them through the woods to his family's home.

"We come back for your mother," he said in a gentle voice.

Larka awoke the next day, sunlight dappling the linens drawn across her shivering body. Her skin gleamed pink and clean, no trace of blood left on her.

"Finally awake, I see," a woman's voice drifted to her.

Larka lifted her head, focused on the woman. She knew her from somewhere.

"My baby?" Larka asked hoarsely.

"She's doing well, and such a healthy, strong babe I've never seen, though you'll not be nursing her for a bit. You've a fever, and these herbs could do her harm. I've been expressing your milk to keep its flow." The woman nudged a mug of steaming tea at Larka. "Your vagina ripped as well, but I stitched you up best I could."

Larka sat up and pushed the tea aside. She slipped a hand to her stretched stomach where just yesterday her baby had wriggled within her. The image of a tiny amber-haired baby cooing gently in Mentheleda's arms tore at Larka, releasing a deluge of sobs.

"Oh, now, Larka, you are safe here." The woman patted Larka's shoulder then placed the tea on the table to Larka's left. "You drink this," she said and exited the room.

Larka's mind cleared to recall this dark-haired, short woman to be Kila Wittin.

Guta appeared in the doorway, his expression somber, and a fussy baby cradled in his arms. Larka saw and heard him as if separated by vast space and time.

"Larka, sorry about your ma. Pa go back for her and—" The voice seemed to strangle in his throat.

The sobs gradually left Larka, but her mind insisted on reviewing the events that had brought her here: the first steps she had taken away from her mother and newborn baby, the sounds of snow falling as she had trod toward the dead stranger, the cold all around, the last panicked steps back to her mother, the absence of her newborn.

Her mind, nevertheless, focused on those first steps, snow and ice having protested underfoot—steps she need never have taken. Her head whipped up, and she glared at the baby Guta held.

Guta cast an eye of perplexity on her while trying to cover the baby from her sight.

Larka lowered her head and mewled.

Outside her room, she heard Wittis Wittin ask, "How she es?"

"Not so good," Kila replied. "She sang *Death Song* all night, and I don't think she even knew it. It was almost like she was in a trance, sitting there staring and singing that way.

"I heard it everywhere this morning. It was like the sound was there no matter where I went. I know others heard it . . . in the market . . . in the square. I heard them whispering about hearing the ghost girl. Others pretended not to hear. . . ." Kila's voice trailed into the distance.

Guta bent and kissed Larka's forehead. "I should been there, but it take so long for Pentheya to tell me . . . make me understand. Am sorry." He shook his head.

Larka sank down on her pillow and began to weep.

"Oh, no, Larka. Am sorry, really. I come back when I not so stupid."

Guta pulled the blankets over her. She did not notice him leave.

CHAPTER 19

REBIRTH

_L_arka drifted into the cabin, spied her quarry.

All the girl's brothers slept in a row beside her, dim firelight kissing each child. Larka placed a finger on the girl's temple, leering as she did so, the finger sinking through the girl's head up to the second knuckle. The girl squirmed, caught as she was in her nightmares. Larka cackled. She pulled her finger out then cocked back an ephemeral hand and smacked the girl across the face.

Pentheya awoke, jerked upright, blinked. Her eyes focused then widened. The girl began to scream, tears shimmering in her eyes.

Laughing, Larka wafted through the walls of the cabin. Many more minds slept this night, prey to this huntress.

"Es the song. Every night when asleep, you sing it, Larka. The villagers scared to wits' end. Their nerves fray, no one sleeps. Say they see you at foot of beds in night, hanging like ghost . . . with much screeching." Guta smoothed the blanket wrapped around the infant in his arms and seated himself at the foot of Larka's bed.

Pentheya stood beside the bed, pastel-green eyes as large and haunted as they had been when she and Larka had first met, frame almost as thin.

Singing *Death Song* was not all that happened to Larka when she slept. Her air allies had taken her on journey upon journey into the past to witness betrayers and their betrayals: Guta taking his time to get to her; Pentheya not being calm enough to relay her fears to Guta; Pentheya requesting the air allies not to warn Larka of the girl's surprise visit, asking the allies not to spy on them and Rollen showing up; Wittis leaving Mentheleda alone to die; the villagers, their mob; and that woman walking down the riverside, in labor and in the way; and finally the baby who had stolen her daughter's life—the only betrayer the huntress had been unable to prey on.

Larka scowled at that baby.

Guta caught the gesture. "Why you look at her like that, Larka? She need a mother." He uncovered the baby's pink face and held her out to Larka. The baby squirmed.

Larka stared blankly at the infant, feeling no compulsion to take her, and Guta finally snuggled the newborn against his chest, eyeing Larka with concern.

"You have not named her," Guta said with perfect syntax, emphasizing the importance of his words. "Does she not exist for you?"

"Let *her mother* name her," Larka hissed and turned on her side to count the cracks in the plastered wall next to her. These were the first words she had spoken in many days.

Guta inhaled sharply. "Where es the girl I remember? Kind and sweet no matter what." His legs snapped beneath him, and he marched toward the door.

Larka slipped into catatonia once more. The few strands of goat hair jutting out of the wall's plaster held much more interest for her than a dead woman's baby. She heard Guta pause in the doorway.

"Fine. I name her. You are Brina. You hear me, daughter of Larka, you now Brina. Es a good name for such a pretty girl." The door bumped against the frame.

A small, cold hand slipped over her shoulder.

"Larka, please look at me," Pentheya said behind her.

Larka remained engrossed in the walls, unable to escape the trap of her mind. She poked at a tuft of goat hair.

"I'm sorry. I told Guta as soon as I could. He couldn't get there. Larka?" Pentheya's little voice broke. "*Please*. Ian and I need you. Arnt and Halty miss you." The hand on her shoulder trembled. "Brina needs you." Pentheya shook her. "You have to wake up . . . stop hurting my dreams. I'm sorry!" Pentheya sobbed, and her footfalls beat swiftly from the room.

Kila stormed in seconds later, Brina cradled in one arm. She snatched the bedding off Larka.

"Get up!"

Larka rolled over, could only stare.

"I said *get up!*" Kila pulled Larka's upper earlobe until she sat upright. "I don't know what happened to your baby, but I can only guess with the tracks Wittis described. I don't know whose baby this is. No one knew the other woman out there, but this baby deserves a mother, not a resentful child who thinks of no one but herself."

Larka tensed as Kila's words seared into her. Tears welled in her eyes, and she swallowed against the lump that had taken root in her throat over the last two weeks.

"Take this baby." Kila tucked the sleeping infant beside Larka. "We are leaving for a week to see my kinfolk in Tree Lane. Guta will be in the cabin with Pentheya and the others. He will check on you from time to time. You are on your own other than his bringing you water. The cupboards should be full enough to last you until we get back." Kila placed her hands on her hips. "Guta will help you in no other way, and you are to water my seedlings while I am gone." Kila crossed her arms. "Understood?"

Larka nodded a dazed assent.

"Humph," Kila grunted then swept out of the room, taking her tempest with her.

Awaiting the air essence and another journey outside herself, Larka gazed at the shuttered window before the foot of the bed until she fell asleep. The air, however, did not stir and her mind rested, beginning a restoration of its agility in the absence of that which she had deemed friend.

She awoke from a deep sleep to the cries of an infant. Her daughter? Larka turned to see the baby, off balance and on the edge of the bed, little fists whirring above her body. No, not her daughter. Her daughter remained dead. This was just the burden with which the stranger had replaced Larka's child.

The baby's fists whirred with a more frantic beat, and tears spilled down her reddened cheeks. The infant dropped over the mattress edge. Larka's hand shot out and caught the babe just before she slipped out of sight; with that movement, Larka's madness shattered.

She placed the infant between herself and the wall nestling the mattress. The baby held silent but a moment then bellowed with fury.

The baby's visage renewed Larka's memory, flicking it over the image of a dead woman's face, the mouth a rictus—stretched with horror, agony. Had it not been for Larka's flight along the river, that woman and this child would likely be united as mother and daughter.

Larka bit into her bottom lip.

"I can't go back and change any of it," she whispered. "And you, I even hated the milk you took from my body." Larka ran a finger over the baby's moist cheeks.

The babe quieted and gave a soft murmur. Her dark-blue eyes seemed to flash up at Larka with approval.

Larka bared a breast, and the baby greedily latched on. Larka half smiled. She listened to the baby's grunting breaths as if she had never heard them before, watched the child suckling as if she had never seen it before.

Birth Song slipped out of Larka—a wispy, wavering sound—placing "Brina" as the babe's official name. Larka smiled a broken smile when done and smeared the dampness on her cheeks.

"Brina," she whispered, "welcome to my heart."

Unbeknownst to her, that night as she slept, Larka sang the song of rebirth, one sung every spring as the world awakened from its dormancy.

CHAPTER 20

THE BEST OPTION

*L*arka lay still. Something had awakened her. She heard the clank of wood being stacked and a stirring of the fireplace. The door to the Wittin home opened then shut.

A dim light flowed into the shutters before the bed's foot. Larka turned to see Brina's lips suckle the air as the infant slept. Larka grinned. She had lost herself far too long in a vengeful dream world.

She frowned. Had she truly hurt Pentheya's dreams? She sighed. She could recall little of the travel she had taken outside her body, though the shadowed faces of terrified villagers flitted through her mind. But she had honed the skill of snapping free of her body; that, she remembered and remembered well.

Larka closed her eyes and let herself wander. The air swirled about her, gaining strength as she commanded it. Her consciousness entered tendrils of elongating air until it stretched a radius of many miles, searching but not finding the beast that had stolen her baby.

Larka's eyes flipped open. A gasp almost became a sob as she recalled once more the cooing babe tucked into Mentheleda's arms . . . the bloodstained tracks leading to a silent, hollow forest. Larka bit back against the passion threatening to overtake her. At least the beast was gone, far enough she could not find it.

"We are safe," she whispered to Brina, lips pressed into the infant's soft hair.

Larka slipped out of bed to dress by the waxing light of day. She stuck a pillow next to the mobile Brina, careful to keep its top at the babe's waist. Brina had woken, and burbled reproachfully as Larka pulled on the slate-gray dress she had worn throughout her pregnancy.

In the living room, the front door to the house opened again. Larka heard a thump and slosh before the door closed. With Brina in her arms, Larka tentatively entered the living area. Two buckets—one small, goat milk; the other large, water—sat before the door, but no one was present. As Kila had commanded, Guta was leaving her alone.

Larka stuck Brina in a basket she supposed the Wittins had used for the same purpose then set the basket, replete with squiggling baby, near the fireplace but distant enough that sparks would not catch in the infant's blankets.

Larka's stomach gurgled, and she set to perusing the cupboards for oats to cook. As she sat to eat, Brina raised a howl. Larka dashed to the baby, a certain realization surfacing. Kila was barren with age; people would know this child to be none of hers.

Larka stuck Brina on a breast and continued breakfast, ruminating over more than simple oatmeal.

She peered at Brina for the twenty-thousandth time since yesterday. She could barely take her eyes off the little fusspot with that thick head of light-brown hair and clingy temperament.

Brina leaned back and looked up at Larka, brow wrinkled and mouth set with what looked like suspicion. Larka grinned and switched breasts. Brina latched on and suckled noisily, her little hands kneading away at glandular flesh.

Larka chuckled. "You are a pig."

The next few days passed with Larka awaking hungrier and hungrier. On the sixth morning of isolation, Larka eased a snoozing Brina into her basket then tiptoed away. Miraculously, the infant remained asleep.

Larka inhaled the fresh morning air and reveled in the sunlight starting to mottle the room as she collected breakfast goods from the cupboards. She placed a few pieces of thick wood on the fire.

As she watered the seedlings in the glassed kitchen window, the front door opened, and Guta stepped inside to place a full bucket of water and another of goat milk inside the entryway. He shut the door behind him and paused to take Larka in, a huge grin on his face.

Larka returned the smile, flushing. She peered down and had to stop a self-conscious slide of her hand over the droop of her midsection.

"Am lulled to sleep each night with the song of spring—um, *Rebirth*—by a sweet, sweet voice. Hope villagers hear it. Will give them some confusion—more than already they have." His head bobbed up and down with good humor.

Larka's hand fluttered to her mouth as she stifled a laugh.

"Ha, see! Am so hurt. You laugh at me still. You feel better, yes? Es good. Very good." He produced the Wittin nod once more, lips puckered and eyebrows arched comically.

Larka grinned and went to the pot in the fireplace to add oats to the heated water.

"Are you hungry?" She faced Guta.

"Plenty much," Guta replied and patted his stomach.

He moved to the basket and bent over Brina, cooing in a silly rhythm to the sleeping babe.

"Es sleeping hard." He glanced up and locked eyes with Larka. His body tensed and reticence reset his expression before he looked away.

Larka frowned as she watched Guta sit—back to her—on the floor beside Brina, where he stayed and hummed until Larka served breakfast.

They sat at the table. The only sound Guta made as they ate was the clank of spoon against bowl and an occasional sip at his milk.

Larka tried to eat slowly, but her stomach got the best of her. "I am so hungry these days."

Guta looked up and smiled, his golden eyes revived to their usual humor. "You eat for two—almost three now. Brina es big girl. We give her goat milk, not much of yours when . . . when you not well."

The muscles of his jaws then tightened, and his eyes pierced her. "I must to speak with you, Larka. Es something I must to say. The villagers regret a little what happen to you but more what happen to Rostin and your mother. They still danger to you. We cannot stay here. They crazy mad." He passed his hand over his head. "Es my wish for you to marry me. I become father to Brina. We leave here and be safe."

"I can't ask you to do that," Larka replied, her voice so low it was almost inaudible.

"You no ask me. I ask you. Es best for you and Brina. Es best for me, Larka. My heart carry no joy when you are not in it. I know. I lose you once already." He reached across the table and grasped her hand. "Think on it. Pentheya say she and kids go with us."

Larka closed her eyes and inhaled, envisioning herself in a safe home with all those she loved around her, yet a bloody trail arcing into nearby woods met her hopes for a future with Guta. Her eyelids flitted open, and she squeezed Guta's hand harder than she meant to.

A weary smile curved her mouth. "I'll think about it," she murmured.

"Good." He tucked a tendril of hair behind her ear and began to say something just as Brina squalled.

Larka jerked her hand from his—too readily—and rushed from the table. Guta exhaled long and loud behind her. As she lifted Brina, a soft thud announced the door shutting. Larka looked up to find Guta had gone. The room had seemed so full, warm with him in it. It now resounded with emptiness. Tears leaked from her heart, and she swallowed against the fate caught in her throat.

Larka plunked into one of Kila's overstuffed chairs. She bent her knees then propped Brina's back against her thighs. She stared at the snickering fuss for a long time then pulled the baby close and dropped her nose onto the tussocky head, inhaling the salty-sweet smell of her daughter. Larka returned a quiescent Brina to her thighs and gazed into the inquiry mirrored in the babe's dark eyes.

Larka blotted her face with her dress sleeve and gazed at the ceiling.

"I'm fine," she told the newborn. Her vision then fell anew on the child. "May you never know what you are, Brina," Larka said and stared over the crook of her knees at the door. "May Guta forgive me."

Larka fed Brina and set to baking bread and packing a haversack with several pouches of dried beans and meats. She also added a hard square of cheese, feeling the thief once more.

She sought and found a sparse supply of paper and ink in a kitchen cabinet. She sat at the kitchen table with quill poised over paper for the longest time before she wrote her message to the Overseer, leaving the cottage and everything she owned to the urchins. She signed Gilly's name for the signature. No one could prove that Gilly had wished otherwise. The villagers would say nothing, being that they had murdered an aged invalid barely able to walk.

Larka wrote to Pentheya and her siblings but mostly to Pentheya, telling her to stop blaming herself for what had happened, though Larka knew the child probably never would. She also apologized for hurting the child in any way. She refused to cry as she wrote to the little ones. Her memories of them would always be of the love they had taught her to share with the world's urchins.

On the next sheet of paper, she wrote to Guta. As she did so, she rubbed futilely at her cheeks, no longer able to hold back, tears smudging ink here and there on the page.

That night when all was dark and Brina rested in a makeshift sling, head against her mother's chest, Larka departed the comfort of the Wittin home and crept across the yard. Light flickered through the windows of the workshop, and Guta's form moved with the pounding of a hammer. Larka's legs started for that building with a "yes" on her lips.

Halfway there she halted. The image of blood-red tracks on stark-white snow taunted her, along with the bloated rage she had seen in Rostin's eyes, even after his death.

Larka gazed through leafless seedling trees to the cabin she had worked so hard to build and reached out a hand as if to touch it and all those she loved within; it was the last time she would reach for these children.

Chapter 21

ALLIES

The door creaked open under Larka's touch. She entered but could discern little in the darkness until she thought to use her aura. With that, smoky-blue light flared around the fringes of her body. Larka gazed about. Gilly's cottage seemed as hollow as Larka felt. Even the cabinets had been gutted; the doors stood open to reveal emptiness stretching back into shadows, not a vial or jar left. Larka shook her head.

A deep chill settled over her. Larka shuddered and made strides into the backroom, where she promptly ducked beneath one of the beds, careful not to drop Brina. She quickly dug up a floorboard to gain the half-pouch of coins she had wished never to see again and another pouch brimming with more Albilar currency—Gilly's stash, little spent by the miser.

Larka stood and turned. Her eyes widened.

She screamed!

Then covered her mouth, feeling the fool. She thought she had met Gilly's aged eyes for a mere blink of time.

Larka snatched a few blankets from the beds and rushed from the cottage, not wanting to look back at the vestiges of her life or the ominous stain beneath the rocking chair.

Larka lashed her spirit forth into the air, checking for danger once more. She found none.

Through the blanket wrapped around her shoulders, Larka's aura radiated a faint light into the darkness. Intermittently awake, Brina would stare at her mother's glow, brow puckered, then burble and pat at its occasional flares.

Larka trekked until the sun rose. Yawning, she peered about. She needed sleep. Yet the forest offered spare cover without its supply of broad leaves.

Air meandered around her, ever whispering, guiding her face upward. Larka spotted a patch of evergreens a short distance ahead, seedlings and older trees alike lurching with tenacious roots up a rocky hill to fluff their needles out along the edge of a plateau. Larka quickened her steps.

Minutes later, she glanced up a fairly steep incline. She parted the blanket to gaze down at Brina. The babe remained asleep, dressed warmly in woolen wear made by Kila Wittin.

"If you could only hold on to me, Brina," Larka murmured.

The babe stayed asleep, but her little fists bunched the material of Larka's dress. Larka lifted a brow yet dared not stop to question. She took the blanket off her shoulders, laced it through the haversack's straps, then placed a wearied foot on the rocky ascent and journeyed upward, using tree limbs or sapling stems as leverage when need be, scree spilling behind her. Brina swung back and forth off Larka's front, fists not releasing the folds of her mother's dress; regardless, one of Larka's hands constantly hovered near the infant.

Upon reaching the plateau, Larka discerned that the young white pines grew too closely together to allow her entry in front, not without scratching her and Brina up. Thus compelled, she aimed for a side of the plateau and squeezed behind the trees to find they formed a tight alcove in front of a tall upshot of granite but left enough floor space for sleep.

Panting, Larka peered down through a blur of green needles at the road. A cold wind stirred the pines. Larka shivered, chills accosting her so soon after the warming climb. Perhaps she was not as well recovered from childbirth as she had thought. She shivered again then peered overhead. The rock and trees surrounding her blocked the warm rays of the rising sun.

She reached up and released the heavy haversack from her shoulder. It hit the hard ground then fell against the rock wall beside her. Careful of Brina in the sling, Larka soon had one blanket unrolled and spread on the ground. She sat down. A small opening formed on that level between the pines, giving her a clear view of the road.

Brina opened her eyes and yawned with breadth. Larka picked Brina out of the sling and placed the babe on the blanket beside her.

"We'll be on the road for a bit," Larka informed Brina while making a small meal of bread and cheese. She gulped from her waterskin then reclined to offer Brina a breast before pulling the other blanket over herself and the babe. Pine needles pricked Larka's feet through blanket and socks until she curled around Brina, gathering in the child's warmth.

Larka lashed her spirit out and yet again found no danger near. With that, she welcomed sleep.

Larka jerked upright, skin prickling. She blinked against the sun slanting into her treed alcove. Something had awakened her. She realized what when air once again slid beneath her blanket, skirring over her skin.

Larka peered toward the road, cast out her senses. They soon confirmed the presence about which her air allies had warned her.

"Cover my tracks," she whispered into the wind, and it whirled away from her, spiraling back along the path she had taken, raising dust and dead leaves.

She waited and fretted, peering through the aperture within the needled cover.

As the sun's rays became more horizontal, Larka felt the presence more strongly then heard soft footfalls on the dirt road. The traveler approached. She glanced at Brina. The babe slept, little mouth suckling though without a breast to fill it.

Larka held her breath. Guta passed by, his head moving left and right as he searched the trail, a piece of paper—a letter—clutched in his hand.

Larka's spirit reached out to him. Guta's anguish struck her full-bore. She stifled a cry, smacking her hand against crumbling minerals as it flew to her mouth. That action set those small rocks tumbling over the edge of the plateau. Air slashed by Larka. The rocks reversed their path, couriered back up to rest where they had, the sound of their fall blunted.

She stared at the rocks for a moment, the air slithering inside her head, siphoning her retention, leaving her without knowledge of why her finger bled. She sucked on her knuckle as she returned her vision to Guta. He did not look her way.

Brina stirred, and Larka found herself willing the child awake—awake and howling.

Larka had reversed the intended pattern of walking by night and sleeping by day to accommodate Guta's presence ahead of her on the road. She stared at the cleft of moon gaping in the sky, vaguely heard tree frogs singing to the night. Brina fidgeted on the blanket beside her. They had left the alcove about an hour after Guta's passing, far enough behind that he could not hear them.

Guta's feeling of helplessness had engulfed Larka the remainder of that day; it did so even now.

"Larka," the air carried Guta's faint call from somewhere in the distance.

"Guta." Larka sat up. She had reached out to him again.

She stood, started to ready for departure, to go to him. The wind blew through her hair at that moment, flinging an image of Mentheleda at Larka, of blood bubbling out of her mother's chest. Larka's legs folded and she reclined, feeling strangely calm, resolute. She thrust a nipple into Brina's waiting mouth and fell asleep. When she next woke, the strand connecting her to Guta had been severed; she felt no more than his presence ahead of her.

Two days later, Guta's presence began to grow stronger.

Larka sat down on the bare ground to gather in the view of his footprints on the trail ahead of her. She then stared into the dusk of an overcast day and sighed. Guta's presence grew stronger still. Larka's brows meshed. A warning eddy of air settled over her.

She ground her teeth together; she had known this day would come.

The wind erased her tracks anon. Larka dropped over the side of a hill and huddled there. The nearness of Guta scorched her as he passed, but that heat diminished each step he took away from her.

Closing her eyes, Larka drew breath into her tightened chest. The man had rarely stopped to sleep and had carried nothing in the way of food. He must have been exhausted after five days.

Larka yawned. Trudging behind him had wearied her mind just as Brina's constant draw of nutrients wearied her body.

After the sound of Guta's feet on the trail had long since faded, Larka hiked back over the hill and renewed her journey. The distance between Larka and Guta became greater and greater that day until the last strain of him faded.

Larka gritted her teeth, staring at his footprints, the fresher ones now and forever pointing away from her. Her mouth curved down, her chin shook. Breath flew into her then heaved out in a half-voiced cry. At that moment, Brina gazed up at her mother and revealed toothless gums in a bright smile.

Stunned, Larka blinked rapidly. The child's eyes had changed from dark blue to earth brown during that last nap.

Brina nuzzled back into her mother's chest. Larka's face relaxed and she hummed, peering down at the top of the babe's head.

She looked up. Before her spread the road to Albilar—bereft of promise but replete of dream.

CHAPTER 22

AN AX TO GRIND

Scant trees stood along the trail, allowing sunlight to fall across Larka and Brina, giving them some warmth in the chill air. Cows lowed in the grassy fields bordering the trail, their fodder green and thickening as spring overcame winter.

Larka had not yet stopped to rest this morning. Hunger pained her, but the thought of the few wild edibles spring had to offer—had offered her after the supplies ran out—turned her stomach. The frequency of outlying farms suggested another village would shortly greet them. Sleep could wait.

She caressed her daughter's head. "I should have stopped somewhere for food last week, but after Jaunty . . ." Larka shook her head. "I suppose we can't hide forever, can we, Brina?

"At least we aren't filthy now." Grinning at the wide-eyed babe, Larka referred to the bath they had recently taken in a very cold brook.

Brina peered upward, and Larka followed suit. "You never take your eyes off those trees, do you, little one?"

Brina gurgled.

Near midday, they reached the promised village. It expressed a greater diversity of labor than any thus far encountered, judging by the array of shops along its bricked streets. Unlike the other villages she had skirted, Larka stopped here—at this Basswood Village—and ascertained by eavesdropping that she had nearly reached Albilar.

She sought out a barter post and scanned the merchandise. She fingered a sky-blue dress made of a light cotton weave. The price seemed high, but a new dress fit a new life.

"I'd like to buy this dress." Larka gestured to the clerk.

The man, of middle years and paunch, took the dress and placed it over the counter, Larka following him.

"A lovely selection for a beautiful lady," he fawned.

Larka tried to smile but felt it come out lopsided. "I also need two pounds of oats, a round of cheese, two loaves of bread, and two pounds of beans."

"Stocking up?" He rubbed his hands together and walked behind the counter. Larka nodded, almost imperceptibly.

The man filled and weighed bags then wrapped the cheese and bread together in a thin cloth.

"Oh, do you have goat milk?" Larka asked before he totaled her order.

"Yes, indeed, fresh every day." The man turned and perused the shelves behind him then pulled off a skin. "Trying to wean the little one a bit?"

"I just have a craving," Larka replied. Brina was much too young to wean; though, the gods knew, the child did not look it.

Bright light flashed off the wall above the clerk. Larka started and looked up, eyes locking on to a shimmering object—a small, finely crafted ax mounted amidst other weapons. Even as she observed the ax, its smoky-blue glimmer faded.

"What is that?" She pointed.

The man twisted back and peered up. "Ah, miss, none of that is for you. They are weapons for men. As is, our farmers like to be armed. At times, people take it in mind to rob them."

"May I see the ax . . . the small one with the woman's shape for a handle? It's . . . *pretty*." She tried to use the empty-headed inflection this man clearly expected of her; it came out strained and squeaky, though the man remained oblivious.

He smiled. "Well, of course." With much effort, the man climbed a short ladder to finagle the weapon off its mount, finally placing the ax in Larka's hand.

As Larka gripped the wooden handle's figure, energy spiked into her hand and up her arm. She reflexed, nearly dropping the ax. She then forced a retightening of her grip, and a smoky-blue glow pounced around the ax's perimeter while wind danced around her calves. Once more, the clerk noticed nothing out of the ordinary.

"A gift to your husband?"

Larka raised her head to see him wink.

"Hmm?" Larka blinked. "Oh, of course, but this price is a bit high," she said, no longer bothering with placation. "Perhaps you would take four silver coins for it rather than eight."

The man's brows made a fitful meeting before he stiffly smiled, eyeing her worn dress and dusty boots. "I would if you could produce those coins *now*." On the last word, he jabbed the countertop with his forefinger.

Larka pulled a cloth from her dress pocket and unwrapped the coins it contained then counted out four silvers, placing each on the counter, feeling heat rise in her face.

"Ah." The clerk picked up a coin and held it to the light then bit it. "That's fine silver."

Larka felt her jaws stiffen, her heartbeat quicken.

The clerk eyed the leftover coins in her hand. "And one more silver coin and two coppers for the dress and food." He rubbed his hands together.

Larka took in a deep breath, eyes narrowing. She smacked the coins on the counter—the last from that pocket. "My husband might enjoy his gift better were you not acting as if his coin were not good enough for you!"

The man's mouth fell open.

He bowed slightly. "Oh, my apologies, fair lady. Please allow me to pack these belongings for you in this fine packsack, only a quarter of the cost to you for being such a good customer this day." He reached beneath the counter then placed the leather bag before Larka.

Larka started to scoff, but she needed a more balanced bag for carrying supplies; she switched her haversack from shoulder to shoulder many times a day.

"It *is* a fine bag." Larka lifted it and glanced at the price tag before she commented, "Fine, indeed. I'll take it." She reached beneath Brina's sling and pulled a cloth from her other pocket.

The man's eyes widened where they lingered on her hand then grew beady as Larka plucked one silver coin from the cloth and placed it on the counter.

"The amount you requested," she said, and allowed a smug smile to cross her face.

Anger flared through the man's features. He hurled the leather bag upright and reached for her purchases. His forehead wrinkles became lined with sweat as he crammed the supplies into the pack-sack, breathing heavily and eventually throwing the goat-milk skin atop her oats and beans, posed to leak.

Larka placed her hand on his as he began to snatch up the dress. "That, I would not wish wrinkled."

The clerk scoffed and walked away, nose high in the air. Brina made a noise. Larka froze then gaped down at the babe's smiling face. Brina blew out spit bubbles, little eyes following the clerk. Larka's lips tugged into a grin before she took the bag and righted the milk. She closed the pack, looped a dress arm around each of its straps and flipped the dress over the pack's top, then slipped the bag on her back. She left the store, chuckling as she returned to the trail, the new dress flapping behind her.

Brina smiled up at her mother.

Larka's own grin broadened. "Were you laughing in there, Brina?" Larka bounced the child, sling and all. "I think I was too, by the end. But I've had my fill of rude, greedy, patronizing . . ." Larka stopped her grumbling and shivered. "Well, maybe I should have asked for that cloak too, but it cost more than the ax."

Larka sought out the stash of her old haversack, blankets and the rest of her coin—all hidden inside a hollow log within a corridor of forest. She sat on the log and removed the ax from its place within the new bag. It warmed upon contact with the flesh of her palms, blue-gray fire dancing around it, tingling through her flesh once more.

The blade was little bigger than her palm. The handle appeared to be made of oak carved its length in the figure of a woman, her hair wild and uplifted as it ascended beneath either side of the blade.

On impulse, Larka drew her arm back and threw the ax forward. Air swished with the weapon's departure. The metal head thumped through the shedding bronze bark of a leafless yellow birch and into the pale meat of the tree.

"Oh," Larka said. "That must make me a warrior." She laughed as she spoke to Brina.

"Thank you," she said to the air.

Several more days passed in which Larka filled her travel breaks with ax throwing until the gates of Albilar finally waxed into view.

She dashed off the road at that point to change her dress.

Brina flailed on a blanket, angry at having been set aside and looking much like an inching, brown woolly bear caterpillar in her soft outerwear, which the babe had nearly outgrown.

"Oh, hush. We're almost there," Larka chided, pulling on the blue dress. "Ouch." She slapped at a small black insect on her bare arm. "And none too soon. The black flies are biting." She pulled the dress sleeves farther down her forearms.

Larka picked up the fidgeting baby and hugged her. "Soon, we'll have a new life. We'll learn new ways. We'll blend in with the people of Albilar, and no one will ever know who we are. We'll be safe, Brina. Safe." She kissed the silken hair on the baby's head.

Brina nudged about, her hands patting the material of the blue dress. Larka shook her head and bared a breast.

"And maybe we'll get a goat because you are eating me alive." The milk in Larka's breast let down with a slight surge somewhere between tingle and pain.

CHAPTER 23

ON GUARD IN ALBILAR

great length of wall buttressed the city of Albilar and enclosed it against the bluffs of Mount Bald. The wall mimicked the local colors of earth and stone, making it look like part of the mountain. Atop it, guards—made small by distance—paced behind parapet notches and between the turreted towers on either side of the entryway.

Larka took a deep breath and hiked through the river's grandly carved valley then uphill to the open gates. She stood in line for a short period of eternity behind a man who smelled of a sweat foul and crusty. As the line moved, she was steadily shoved closer to him.

From afar, she studied the portcullis overhanging the entry, its iron rods deadly spikes on either end. Larka leaned to the side, trying to see around the shuffling people ahead of her. Sunlight glinted dully off a segment of armored gate—it and the portcullis remnants of a long-dead war between Northwoods and Southwoods.

The clunking tread of guards pacing overhead drifted down, grating on Larka's fraught nerves. She closed her eyes to breathe deeply and got a good whiff of the man in front of her. She gagged and took a step back, eyes stinging from the oniony vapors. Even Brina began to squirm.

Several minutes later, Larka came a few steps closer to him. Fortunately, the wind shuffled the man's stench away.

From this point Larka could finally see the gateway in more than a glimpse. On its right, several guards stood around a long table, each dressed in lichen-green tunics and pale-gray trousers. Tied low around each Guardsman's waist was either a belt of gray, green, brown, silver, or gold—some with embroidered black symbols. No weapons were apparent on any of the men.

A silver-belted guard stood before the table, clipboard in hand. He spoke to a woman and checked the board; then a green-belted guard rifled through the woman's bag and allowed her to pass.

Larka swallowed. What were they looking for? She carried little other than food and money. She tried several times to hear what the silver-belt said to the people seeking entrance but caught only snippets of his sentences, for the closer she came to the gates, the more noise seemed to drift out of the city.

She stepped forward several more times until the stinkpot ahead of her took his turn. At this point, she could hear the silver-belt's questions.

"Do you have any weapons?" he asked.

Stinkpot shook his head.

Meanwhile, one thought whirled into Larka's brain—the ax! Then all thinking seemed to freeze.

"What business have you in Albilar?"

"Visitation. Came to see my mother," the smelly man answered.

The silver-belt's next words flowed in a humdrum monotone, "If you possess any moneys over the amount of thirty gold coins or items worth that much, you must pay a ten percent tax upon the goods or money. If you possess only goods of that value or over and no coin, your property will be seized, sold, the tax taken from that sale, and the balance handed back to you upon departure—" The guard opened his mouth to say more, but the smelly man cut him off.

"Blah, blah, blah, blah, blah. Do I look like I got thirty gold coins or even one to my name?" Stained teeth stuck out from beneath his raised upper lip. "And before you ask, Sesil Brown, and she lives on 234 Vermot Street."

The stout guard narrowed then rolled his eyes at the shabby man. He checked a list of what Larka noted with alarm were names and addresses then said,

"Go before I have every filthy inch of you searched!"

The younger, green-belted guard, who stood slightly behind the older man, wrinkled his nose and took a step back. Several other Guardsmen chuckled.

The dirty man muttered as he walked away, "Stupid rules. Used to be a day when a man had more freedom. Could just walk in here without . . ." The rest of his statement was lost in the shifting crowds of Albilar.

Larka took a few timid steps to the Guard's representatives and halted.

"What business have you in Albilar?" The stout guard asked, his bored thrum replaced by annoyance.

The young guard, however, perked up and perused Larka with an up-then-down slide of his eyes.

Larka blushed and stammered, "I-I, uh, came to find a man named Astla." She patted Brina's head out of nervous need.

The stout guard stiffened and his eyes narrowed, lighting first on Larka then locking on Brina, whereupon his eyes widened and his thick brows raised. He looked back to Larka. "And this Astla knows you . . . *well?*"

Larka peered at the Guardsman then at Brina, consternation setting her brow until the man's actions and words finally forged their meaning within her.

"Oh," she mouthed. "He knows me *very well*, but he has not seen me for quite some time." Larka gave a slight nod and another pat to Brina as she emphasized "very well."

"That dog!" the guard exclaimed. "Wait here." He pulled Larka aside. "You keep your hands off of her, Guardsman," he ordered the young green-belt, who seemed rather disappointed.

Larka leaned to her left and tried to peek around the right swing of the gate as the rotund guard departed, shaking his graying head and chuckling. She heard little over the noise of the city except for a door's opening then muffled voices.

Seconds later, a tall, gold-belted man of tanned skin and graceful physique emerged from behind the gate, sword on hip and chest puffed as he marched impatiently toward Larka. The rotund guard followed, a suppressed grin in his countenance. Upon seeing her, the gold-belt halted and gaped.

The curve of his jaw spoke of the oval facial shape Mentheleda had given Larka. Aside from that feature, Astla had greenish, cat-like eyes and blond-brown hair.

Heat crept into Larka's face under his prolonged scrutiny. Then his next words caused her to jump as he snapped them out.

"Monton, escort this woman and child to my house. I will be there shortly."

The rotund guard guided Larka through the streets of Albilar, its people generally standing aside to let them through, until they entered a house made half of earthen plaster and half of stone, the stone forming the base of the walls.

"You wait here, Miss . . . Miss?" Monton's eyes questioned but a moment before she answered.

"My name is . . . Lark and this is Brina." She peered at Brina, who yawned and gurgled before snuggling against her mother once more. Larka fidgeted; she did not know her last name, nor had she ever. Neither Gilly nor Mentheleda had informed her of it.

"A fine babe, fit and strong," Monton commented heartily then lowered his voice. "Astla is young but a good man. I told him years ago he should settle down and marry before it all caught up to him this way, but don't you worry. He will do what is right by you, Lark." He squeezed her shoulder and departed.

Larka sensed nothing except sincere concern from this jocular man. A feeling of warmth settled over her as she watched him go.

She closed the door then crossed the stone floor upon the silence of worn boot soles. She seated herself at a small round table near a fireplace, which had not been lit in what appeared months. She shivered, kissed Brina, and looked up to observe that this home's interior walls reflected the exterior.

The door banged open behind her.

Astla stormed into the house and clutched her shoulders, drawing her off the chair. "Where is our mother?"

Larka ducked out of his grasp and held his torrid gaze until the mental image of Mentheleda bleeding into snow caused her head to droop.

Astla closed his eyes and drew in a breath that hoisted his wide chest. When he opened his eyes again, the hazel-green irises reflected a calmer anxiety but an anxiety, nonetheless.

"Last I knew, she was trying to protect you. Where *is* she?"

Larka swallowed into the abrupt dryness of her throat.

"Answer me!" Astla shouted, grasped her shoulders, and then shook her, causing her neck to snap back.

Larka shoved with all her might but could not dislodge him.

"You will crush Brina if you do not back down. And do not think to abuse me. I've had enough of that to last this lifetime!"

Astla's mouth drew slack and opened. He threw his hands up and turned his back to her. "I am sorry. It was not my wish to hurt you." He pivoted back to face her.

Larka plopped into her chair, rubbing the back of her neck.

Astla joined opposite her at the table. "What happened, Larka, or should I say 'Lark'?"

Larka pressed her lips together then let them go with a light smack. She shook her head, already reliving the nightmare she was about to repeat. She barely looked at Astla as she began to explain the night their mother was no more.

Astla listened, his face becoming more pinched as the story crescendoed. Larka's voice thinned the nearer she came to the story's final point, thinned the more she wrapped lies around Brina's identity, until Astla had to lean forward to hear her.

". . . I do not know what sort of creature took her life. Only that she was in the wrong place at the wrong time." Larka peered up at her brother and ended the telling on the vaguest whisper. "We all were."

Astla stared at Larka for a long time then said, voice raw—thick—"Sounds like a big cat." He cleared his throat, but there was no hiding the excess shine in his eyes. "A cougar perhaps, probably attracted by the smell of blood. It is within them to walk at night and steal lives not theirs to take." He rubbed his hand over his mouth. "And what is it that you want from me, *Lark?*"

"Nothing."

"Nothing," he repeated, tilting his neck back to stare down his nose at her before settling his chin on his thumbs.

Brina screamed hungrily, and Larka moved to thrust a breast into the babe's mouth.

"You will stay here to be known as my wife. That guise would work best," Astla said as if she were another under his command.

"I did not come here to find you. I do not want to be known as your wife. I told Monton I sought you because I thought telling him I sought a new life would not be deemed good enough reason to enter Albilar," she spoke softly but swiftly.

Astla drummed his fingers on the table, raising dust from its surface. "And good that you did, or you would have been put out at the gate. We've enough whores and homeless children here."

"I am *not* a whore!" Larka stood, adjusting her backpack. Brina let go the conduit to her meal. Larka tucked the breast away as she stomped toward the exit, the baby scowling up at her.

Astla caught Larka before she opened the door, a hand on her shoulder.

"I did not mean it in that way, but you did not explain the baby, and Mother did not mention it in her letters. How did that come about?"

Larka spun round to face him. A torrent of emotion spewed forth through gritted teeth. "It was *not* by choice!"

Astla's face paled then burned hotly. "Who did this to you?"

"I do not know his name." Larka could not meet his eyes until she redirected the conversation. "I have money to start my own business here. All I need is a home with a bit of yard, and I can grow herbs—"

"No," Astla interrupted, and seeing Larka's ire, he expounded, "You could request permission from Overseer Flock for a Grant of Domain within Albilar, Larka, but Flock's taxes against outsiders are high. You'll have to pay them on any money you've brought in, by the way. Then you'll have to pay Grant of Domain taxes each year until you have been here ten years; that's on top of all the other income taxes. And a lone woman with a baby—you'd be a target for no good here. You would be seen as no better than a whore by most men." He ran a finger over Brina's head.

Brina peered around at Astla. Pale brows set inward, lips compressed in a frown, she batted at his hand. The babe then turned back around and squeezed Larka's breast through the dress.

A slight smile curved Astla's mouth. "Feisty, aren't we? Both of you." He gazed back up at Larka. "Not so long ago, we began closing the doors to women and bastards, if you'll pardon the terminology. It seemed the streets were becoming full of them, and they with no place to go. They were preyed upon by the worst of men, when they weren't selling their bodies for money. And their children . . . if you could see them. . . ."

"So you refuse them entry? They go unprotected in the wilderness?" Larka stared up at him with apprehension, her mind dwelling on the world's urchins and a large cat swiping frail lives.

He nodded, barely meeting her eyes, muscles awork over his mandibles. He finally met her gaze. "Stay with me, please. No one would hurt the Captain of the Guard's wife, as you would be in name only."

Larka hesitated and straightened Brina's clothing. "I did not intend to seek you out, Astla. It seemed—and rightly so—that I would be barred from the city for wanting the safety within it. Besides, my presence here endangers you."

Exasperation huffed out his next breath. "Safety! I am endangered every day, little snippet. I can protect myself, you see." He patted the sword at his side.

The air picked that moment to wind its way under the door, to whisper into Larka's subconscious mind.

"Will you teach me weaponry?"

Astla laughed. "You joke?"

Larka lifted a brow and drew herself to full height.

Astla's mien fell. "You do not. A woman knowing weaponry is not looked upon with favor."

"It seems nothing a woman does here, or elsewhere, is looked upon with favor. Had our mother and I some skill with weaponry, she might still be alive, and I would not be mother to a fatherless child," she spat, shocking even herself with such vehemence.

An amused glint arose within Astla's eyes and carried through to the uplifted corners of his mouth. "You've Mother's wit about you as well as the look of her. All the times I can think of her setting some logic before our father to stop him beating us. . . ." Here, his smile disappeared, and he gazed at the cobbled floor, a hard set to his mouth.

"I have a throwing ax," Larka offered.

Astla opened his mouth, then paused, brow knit. He spoke then as much to himself as to her, "It appears my Guardsmen are not doing their jobs. Weapons are not allowed past the gates. I'll have a word with them on that matter!

"But, regardless of how feckless my Guardsmen, dear sister, distance weapons are the weaponry of cowards." He raised his hand to quiet the protest twisting Larka's lips. "I did not say you are a coward. I dare say your journey here was very brave, especially with a baby in tow." He eyed the length of her. "You are too scrawny for our heavy swords, and the bows to our arrows would not bend under your effort. They are all made for large men.

"Wait." He held up a finger as Larka began to object then pinched the small mass of her biceps. "Yes, light weapons used at a distance would be best for you," he agreed with himself.

Larka dropped her head to hide the roll of her eyes. It was at that moment she noticed the layer of dirt covering the mortared rocks of the floor.

"This place is filthy," she quibbled.

He shook his head. "You sound just like . . . like our mother. I usually sleep and eat in the barracks."

He opened his arms to Brina. "May I see my daughter?"

Without thought, Larka lifted Brina from the sling and handed the child into his massive arms. Astla held the child against his clean-shaven cheek and bounced her.

Brina slid her eyes into right corners to peer at him sideways, nose wrinkled.

"I can see why Monton jumped to the conclusion that she was mine." He held the babe so that she hung before his face. "Her coloring is similar to mine." He clucked at Brina, and to Larka's surprise, the baby smiled at him—right before her small fist plunged into his nose.

Astla laughed, not taking his eyes off Brina. "I shall never hear the end of this from my men."

CHAPTER 24

TO PROVE A POINT

A copse of saplings stirred as Larka passed, Brina nuzzled against her chest. Brina squirmed to twist her head and watch, with a silly smile, the gentle flapping of fresh leaves borne upon long, flattened petioles.

Astla walked beside them. Over his muscled physique he wore brown pants of cotton-wool blend and a creamy cotton shirt, long of sleeves. Though out of Guard uniform, his sword remained sheathed at his right side. Whereas his right hand remained free, his left held a clay pot.

When Larka stopped and reached into her packsack, Astla walked on, carrying the pot to the rocky shore of a docile river's edge. Leaving the clayware settled amongst the rocks, he returned to Larka's side, nodded then crossed his arms. He held his chin within the cup of thumb and forefinger as Larka gripped her ax's handle and whipped it through the air. Even Brina stopped watching the recently unfolded aspen leaves and gazed after the whirling object as it whizzed into the distance and clashed into the clay pot.

Astla's body gave a slight jerk at the shattering impact. He stroked his chin then turned to Larka.

"You say you've thrown that ax but three days?"

"Yes."

His brow lifted. "That's quite a talent."

"It's not my only talent." Larka held her hand out. Where it lay on the shore, the ax picked itself up and charged at her before slowing and hanging in midair.

Astla's eyes widened as she plucked the weapon from the air's holding. He pivoted around, throwing his vision everywhere then pinned it on Larka.

"Don't do that! Someone might see!"

"Of course." Larka nodded, her face stinging with flush as she continued to speak, "You know I was born of the dark moon. I throw this ax with good aim and the aid of my air allies. Listen when I throw this time. Listen to the air about us." She gripped tight to the ax in her hand, feeling a nervous tremor run the length of that arm. "Give me a target."

Astla peered about then pointed. "You see that tree, the maple amongst the poplars? It is leafless still."

"Yes."

"Hit the knot on its west side; shave off a slice about the thickness of my thumb." He wriggled his thumb, a smug look settling over his face.

Larka's mind jangled with nerves. She sucked in a long, soothing breath before her right hand drew up over her shoulder then flung forward, releasing the ax toward the left side of the tree.

A swish of wind caught hold of the weapon. The ax spun until its blade split through the maple; a slice of wood fell. Without slowing, the ax turned around and whirled into Larka's waiting hand.

Astla gave her and the ax a reproachful look before he fetched the slice of knot wood. He held it against his thumb as he sauntered back to her and Brina.

"It's close anyway." He offered the piece of wood to Larka.

"It's the same thickness as your thumb," Larka said, a smile tugging at her lips.

"Hmm." He grinned then replaced that expression with one of somberness. "I felt the air move around us. It came about my thumb just before your ax flew." He flexed and extended his first digit. "As if it were measured." He held out his hand. "Give me that ax."

Larka released the weapon to her brother. He aimed carefully and threw the ax at the maple's knotty left. The blade whirred by the tree and bounced off one of the thin poplars in the maple's background.

Larka struggled not to laugh at Astla's shocked expression. Brina hiccupped, or giggled, as Astla stomped away and retrieved the ax. He then stalked back to Larka.

"Do it without help." He thrust the ax at her. "No air allies."

Larka grabbed the handle, asking for no help from the shifting air. She slung the ax—from waist height—up and over her shoulder and let it fly forward with an instinctive flick of arm instead of wrist. It landed soundly in the middle of the aged maple, its top tooth digging into the tree's hard flesh.

"You missed the knot." Astla beamed.

Larka smirked. "I wasn't aiming for the knot." She walked to retrieve her ax, letting that last statement sink into her brother.

Brina smiled up at Larka, her soft brown eyes atwinkle. Larka smoothed the child's hair then tugged the blade out of the tree, noting the boughs' swollen leaf buds—ready to unfurl into spring. Small, reddish flowers also dangled in clusters off the tree.

Of a sudden, wind hissed about Larka and Brina, whispering against the maple's trunk, through its flowers. Brina shrieked, arms flailing, legs thrusting against her mother, dislodging the sling. Larka caught Brina just as the babe fell through the sling's bottom then tucked her back in.

Larka wiped at the tears on the child's reddened cheeks.

"What's wrong, Brina?" she asked as she returned to Astla, but the babe had already calmed, the wind faded.

Astla sat on green grass, legs stretched before and sword beside him. He cocked his head and looked up at Larka, the sun on his back.

"I've a knife you may use to practice if you'd like, until we can have suitable throwing knives made. We can come here after my duties are fulfilled each day if you wish to practice." He paused, his gaze lingering on Brina. "I would also like for you to learn empty-handed defense with Master Ling in case you should need to defend yourself . . . again." His mandibles twitched with flexing muscle, and his vision lifted from Brina to Larka.

Larka stared toward the river, wishing it to roar and block the gush of blood that rose to her head, flushing her with memories anew.

CHAPTER 25

EMPTY-HANDED DEFENSE

*L*arka took a breath and tried to relax. Her first lesson of empty-handed defense would begin within minutes. She shifted her feet—shod in flexible, light-weight shoes—and gazed at the bricked floor of the practice yards. An incessant thunking echoed all around her. She looked up and peered about. Throughout the yards, sparring Guardsmen threshed the air, a wooden sword at the terminus of each sword arm.

"You are Lark?"

Larka started and spun around to find a man of medium height and thick, black hair standing near her.

The man smiled slowly and held up his squarish hands. "Captain Brandon said you were nervous natured. Do not be nervous. There is nothing to be afraid of here except lack of practice." He extended a hand. "I am Master Trainer Ling. Call me Ling or Master Ling if you wish."

Wearing a lopsided grin, Larka grasped his hand and shook it. "It's nice to meet you, Master Ling."

He smiled, adding a sparkle to the jade green of his tilted eyes. He appeared to be in his fortieth year, but his demeanor suggested a man much riper with age.

Master Ling surveyed the length of her then returned his vision to her face. "You have a look of intelligence about you and are pretty but do not seem to dote on your appearance. That is good." He glanced at her legs swathed in the loose fitting, light-gray fabric of her practice pants. "You are likely flexible—most women are—but you will have to build on your strength. You are too thin, but Captain Brandon can work on that at home." He chuckled.

"Well, let us begin, Lark. Stand with your feet shoulder width apart. Now, step your left foot directly in front of where it is, so that the length of your stance is about two shoulder widths." He demonstrated in front of her as he instructed. "And bend your front knee, so that it is over the area slightly behind the first joint of your big toe, not beyond. You're leaning too far forward if your back heel raises off the ground. Keep your back leg almost straight. Keep both your feet pointing in the same direction, forward or nearly so."

He rose out of the stance and walked around her. "A little more of your weight should be on your front leg, but your trunk should be centered. Yes, better." He nodded as she corrected. "Do not let your butt poke up so much right here. You get knocked off balance that way." He slapped the center of her buttocks, and Larka jerked upward but managed to tuck her tailbone further beneath her. "Good. This is forward stance. Draw your left leg in and do it on the other side, and as you do, repeat each instruction I just gave you."

Larka did as he asked, even patting herself on the behind and retucking its tendency to curve up. He requested that she repeat the instructions and demonstrate on each leg three more times.

"Alright, now, stand up and bring your feet together." Master Ling stood in front of her again, demonstrating. He turned his left foot perpendicular to the right. "You see how my heels are like the intersection of two streets?"

Larka nodded, taking the pose and comparing her feet to his.

"Bring your left foot forward in the direction it points, about two shoulder widths. Bend your back leg and put most of your weight on it and keep that back foot pointed straight to the right; do not let it swivel in or out." She maneuvered as he instructed.

He glanced at her front leg. "You see how my front leg is slightly bent. Do that. Do not overstraighten your knee like that. It puts too much weight on your back leg, slows you down; anyone who noticed that could sweep your back leg easily." He walked around her and examined her stance. "Tuck that butt in, Lark, and keep your trunk straight. It is leaning left. Remember, even if the weight is not equally distributed on your legs, you must center your trunk over them and keep that rear tucked down." He pointed.

She tucked, not having realized her tailbone had arced up yet again. He walked to stand in front of her. "I see the problem. My Misa had it after our firstborn. Your abdomen is stretched from carrying child. Hold your stomach in, and your tailbone should tuck beneath you more naturally." He grinned. "The strength to do this will come as you practice.

"Do not let your back knee sag inward. You should not let your knees sag inward on any stance unless that is the stance's true form, and it is in very few."

Larka pushed her right knee outward.

"You shouldn't be able to see your back toes . . . maybe your big toe but no others. Your knee should be blocking their view. This is back stance. Practice it on the other side for me and tell me what you are doing and what you should not do as you move into position."

She reiterated his words as well as the pose.

"Other side," he said several times, and the process repeated, Larka correcting herself as she went, her knees drooping more and more inward, until he nodded and smiled. "Good. You are a fast learner. You just need to build strength and endurance to hold the stances correctly. It will come."

Larka was finally allowed to draw her feet toward each other, succumbing to a more natural stance.

Master Ling stood squarely in front of her. "There are several more things I will tell you. Captain Brandon has a book of diagrams and instructions. He and I are the only Guard members to have these. Feel lucky in that because it is always good to study for complete instruction; it brings fuller understanding. Sometimes, a teacher's instructions may not be as precise as he, or perhaps she, would like." He smiled.

He then sobered. "There are also certain things you must keep in mind as you learn empty-hands defense. One is that you must never turn your back on an enemy. The other is that you must not pause in striking down an enemy. If your enemy has shown himself to you, strike until he, or perhaps she, is down. Do not stop. Do not pause. Do not think. Just do." These words Larka would hear many times throughout her training.

Master Ling grinned. "It is a serious business, defense. Now, do not come back for one week and practice those stances several hours every day until then. And remember, do not lock out your knees with overstraightening. Keep them flexible and ready to move. And read over the next lesson in the book."

Larka nodded and said, "In one week's time. Thank you."

Master Ling bowed. Larka emulated him.

Keeping an eye out for overzealous sparring matches, Larka strolled alongside the barracks, which were interred within a section of Albilar's protective walls. Monton noticed her and waved over his sweating trainees. She grinned and returned the gesture then peered up briefly at the towers keeping the gate.

As she reached the third door in the wall and touched it, a telling wind struck her. Larka's gut wrenched. Brina babbled away on the other side of the door as her mother turned the knob.

Larka entered and squinted about, closing the door. A single window shed light into this room, joined by an oil lamp hanging on the cobbled wall behind Astla's desk, his form still and shadowy beneath the dim glow. When her eyes adjusted, she saw a document in her brother's hand, his eyes moving over it, frown lines straining his mouth and brow.

Brina lay on a blanket Larka had earlier spread on the floor. When she saw her mother, the babe smiled then—much to Larka's surprise—pushed herself upright and held up her arms, calling "Muh-muh-muh-muh."

Larka scooped the babe up, kissing down several of the thick tufts of hair that stood on end on the child's scalp.

"What's wrong?" she queried Astla when he still had not looked up but remained bent over the paper, silently mouthing words as he read.

He shook his head, rife with what Larka determined disbelief. Then anger took him. He pounded his fists on the desk as he stood, letter still in hand. "I did not train these men to do battle against their own," he shouted. "Read this." He shoved the crumpled document at her.

"Decree 305" was stamped at the top of the paper. Larka quickly read the contents. As she did so, her heart pounced at her ribs. "This was decreed by the Overseer?" She read the signature at the bottom once more. "Cornt Flock?"

Astla nodded, expression dour.

Monton stuck his head in the door. "What's the matter in here? Lovers' quar—" Monton stopped mid-sentence at the hard look Astla gave him.

"Come in." Astla beckoned.

Monton complied and shut the door behind himself.

"Give him the decree, Lark."

Brina gurgled and nearly dove out of Larka's arms as she squirmed toward Monton. Larka held tight to the babe, just managing to hand the decree to Monton before he seated himself in the chair in front of Astla's desk.

Astla reseated himself and seemed to be considering what to say before he spoke, "Our mad Overseer has decreed that all street women and their children be escorted outside the gates. If they refuse to leave, we are ordered to 'use any means to be rid of them.' He also deems anyone who is homeless after the date of 30 June 3005 will be executed on sight, and I am to prepare hit squads to rid the forests surrounding Albilar of 'the useless' as well."

Monton shuddered then scanned the decree. He looked up. "This is insanity at its best. Does the man have syphilis that his brain is so affected?"

"He's been a bit off—a good bit—since his daughter disappeared, but this is much too far off, and I will not lift a sword to do his bidding in this matter." Astla leaned away from his desk.

"I understand, Astla, but we can't have you accused of treason before we've had a chance to sort this matter out," Monton said. "Perhaps we can say we never received such a decree."

"He will send another. Madmen tend to repeat their insanity." Astla folded his arms over his chest, looking thoughtful.

He peered at Larka. "You've dealt with a homeless situation before, Lark. Would you be so kind as to explain to Monton here how so."

Her eyes widened and mouth gaped briefly before she responded, "I . . . I gave the homeless shelter."

"Shelter! What a concept!" Astla whooped and slapped his hands on the desk, a certain gleam in his eyes. "And one Flock would never think of, the old fool." Astla rose then opened a drawer in his desk and brought out a fountain pen along with several sheets of hemp paper. He placed these items on the desktop and patted the wood of his chair's back. "Come sit here, Lark."

Larka tentatively stepped past Monton and seated herself then peered up at Astla in question.

Brina immediately grabbed at the fountain pen, Larka holding her back.

Astla plucked Brina off her mother and held the baby against his side. "Lark, outline for us how this shelter would work for the city and make it sound good. Give him a *pretty kiss* from all of us while you're at it. When you are finished, let me know."

Brina reached once more for Monton as she and Astla passed the chuckling man to enter the practice yards. Monton followed and shut the door behind them, leaving Larka in an abruptly still room.

Larka stared at the door several seconds then shook her head. When she gazed down, a blank piece of paper gazed back up at her.

She picked up the fountain pen, well aware that what she must scribe would be treasonous to the Overseer though certainly not his people. The cloth beneath her arms became limned with sweat as she wrote:

In response to Decree 305 dated 30 May 3005, I must commend our great city's Overseer on his foresight regarding the problem of homelessness in Albilar's population. Your Guardsmen are more than ready to comply with your orders.

I, however, believe—

Larka stopped and tapped the pen's butt against her chin. That would not do. No "I" should be seen anywhere within this document. That made it too personal. She set that piece of paper aside and started on a clean sheet.

In response to the decree dated 30 May 3005, commendations to Albilar's great Overseer on his foresight regarding the problem of homelessness in the city's population. Your Guardsmen are more than ready to comply with your orders.

It is believed—

She drummed her left-hand fingers on the desk's polished wood as she thought on how to further ingratiate the Overseer while asking him to change his mind. Larka sighed and once again pressed the flow of ink to paper.

—that the city would indeed benefit from a lack of street tramps. Therefore, the funds you offer so graciously to form squads to clean up your city could be better used in displaying the truly generous and noble nature of Albilar's Overseer.

Larka stopped to read what she had written.
"So far, so good," she mumbled and wiped the accumulation of sweat off her brow, thinking she would smell like sour milk after this dirty affair and need a good cleaning.
She wrote on:

An application of funds to the refurbishing of structures to house the homeless would, indeed, dispatch the homeless from the horrors of their deprived existence. While sheltered by the Overseer's generosity, the homeless could also be trained by artisan volunteers from the community with the skills that would enable them to lead a moral and rehabilitated life. All would be deeply indebted to the Overseer's forethought and leadership abilities in the matter, and the citizens of Albilar and beyond would praise even more so the daily kindness of their grand Overseer.

Larka rose and stretched. The better part of an hour had passed.

If the Overseer were as arrogant as she thought him to be, the flattery would overcome the overall insult in this letter. If not—she grimaced—Astla might lose his head.

Larka opened the door to note Astla and Monton in conversation not far away. She waved to her brother, and he entered Headquarters with Monton close behind.

"I believe that's what you ordered." She pointed to the paper on the desk and shook her head at Brina—who had finally gotten her way—cuddled within Monton's arms.

Astla stood behind his desk and took up the letter, expression stoic, until he placed the paper on the desk and threw back his head, laughing.

"Must be good." Monton, standing before Astla's desk, pulled a face at Brina who gurgled happily up at him.

"Very good." Astla beamed at Larka. "You've a flair for sycophancy, Lark, at least the written version of it." Astla seated himself.

Monton chuckled and took his turn in reading the paper, his face turning grave and remaining so even after he had returned the paper to Astla.

"There could be backlash."

Larka nodded her agreement behind the large man. "That is my fear as well." Astla placed the letter on the desk and looked from Monton to Larka. "What else can we do?" He leaned back and threw his feet up on the desk, careful not to mar the letter.

"I know just the thing." Monton's eyes narrowed and a smug smile took his mouth. "We've given him the sweetest kiss. Now it is time we give him a good, swift kick in the ass."

Astla sat up and let his curiosity meet Monton's devious countenance. Monton handed Brina to Larka, humming as he did so. He then picked up the decree along with Larka's letter and headed for the door. When he got there, he turned.

"After the men read this" —he flapped the decree— "and sign Lark's petition, he'll either amend the original decree or realize that full-scale revolt by the Guard could displace him as Overseer. Wouldn't Astla look pretty in Overseer garb, all surrounded by peacock feathers?" Monton opened the door. The sound of clanking wood met their ears for a fragment of time.

After the door had been shut, Larka turned back to Astla. "Peacock feathers?"

Astla nodded. "Peacock feathers, indeed."

"What if the men don't sign?"

Astla's eyes narrowed. "They *will* sign, though Flock may assuredly keep his precious cock feathers."

CHAPTER 26

FIRST STEPS

arka slept in her new home, feeling safer each night with her swordsman brother in the next room, yet the torturous wind did visit her slumber, whispering into her dreams, cloying her mind with seeds set to germinate during her waking hours.

Larka awoke, body rigid, vision darting around the bedroom. She jerked her head toward an abrupt noise. A chickadee's call soon followed. Larka let go a long breath. She smiled, feeling foolish, for outside her window nothing more than these small birds rustled amongst the flattened needles of young cedars.

She rubbed her eyes with the backs of her hands. Brina wriggled next to her and hummed a tune Astla was fond of whistling around the house.

"Happy, are we?" Larka grinned at the baby.

"We have a busy day ahead of us," Larka yawned as she sat up and dangled her feet off the bed.

Brina pushed up to all-fours and crawled toward the edge of the bed.

"Got you," Larka said, grabbing the child's diaper.

Larka leaned forward and placed Brina on the cobblestone floor. The baby instated her usual rapid crawl to sit under the window then peered up at the closed shutters. With the aid of her hands, Brina pushed herself to her feet and wobbled slightly then clapped her hands and burbled with glee.

Larka gaped. The child was only four months old. She should not have been crawling much less walking.

Brina teetered, and Larka leapt off the bed though in vain; Brina caught her balance before Larka reached her.

"It's something new and more ambitious for you each day, is it not? But you'll hurt yourself on this floor if you fall." Larka settled the baby on her bottom.

Brina sat for a minute, brow crumpled, then looked up at her mother and said, "Pooh."

Larka chuckled and walked to the wardrobe where she discarded her nightgown. She reached for her dress and pulled it over her head. As the blue fabric cleared her eyes, she found Brina standing once more on wobbly legs.

"Brina, stop that!" Larka exclaimed and snatched up the babe. "We have to open the shelter today, preferably without you cracking your skull first, you little imp."

Five days had passed in a silence preoccupied by plodding tension, by thoughts of Astla being arrested for treason—five days of wondering what would become of Brina if Larka were also arrested—but no arrests had come. An amended Decree 305 had, instead, arrived on that fifth day, giving Astla everything Larka's petition had requested.

Astla, in turn, had lent Larka the responsibility of finding a suitable building for her homeless shelter. She had found a ramshackle house on the outskirts of the city, nestled between another old home and an inner section of the wall surrounding Albilar.

The building had required a new slate roof and floors up to the Overseer's standards. Wood, he deemed a fire hazard. Furniture the exception, all material had to be of the earth: clay, stone, brick, or veneered with such materials. With Monton and several Guardsmen ever present, the shelter's refurbishment had been completed in ten weeks' time.

Larka had hired local craftspeople to make cot frames and mattresses for most of the shelter's floor space. Several homeless women had already taken to the midsized shelter and been employed in helping make the cots and frames. A mason had been hired to build the brick baking oven, and several youngsters had been apprenticed to him as well. The cots complete and the last brick laid, today the shelter would officially open.

Larka pulled a light dress over Brina's head then collected handmade powder and a bag of diapers.

"Let's go." She hefted the child to her hip and strode outside. A hazy day greeted her as she made her way to the shelter.

"Good morning." Monton met her on the front porch with a line of bedraggled women and children at the door, no men amongst them. The shelter provided separate quarters for each sex, though Larka had set aside most of the space for women and children.

Brina burbled at Monton.

Larka replied "Good morning" and slipped past the small crowd to push the door open. She nodded at a Guardsman posted in the hallway leading to the shelter's kitchen and rear entry, then took a few forward steps and seated herself at the small greeting area's table. With a pad of hemp paper and fountain pen, she began to take names, Monton sitting jovially by her side. Seated on Monton's lap, Brina babbled and slobbered on her fist.

Larka scribbled names and assigned apprenticeships based on each occupant's interests for almost half an hour. Near the end of the line, Larka assigned a woman and her daughter adjacent beds. They moved away toward the women's quarters. Still scribbling on the paper, Larka heard footsteps fall softly; a body stood before her.

"Welcome to the shelter. What is your name?" Larka said without looking up.

She received no answer and peered up to find a man's eyes

boring into her from beneath the wide brim of a straw hat. A jolt of unease struck her; Monton tensed next to Larka and would have stood to defend her, baby in hand, had she not caught his arm and tugged at him to sit back down.

Larka heard a shuffling noise, caught movement out of the corner of her eye. When she returned her vision to him, she saw naught but the stranger's stiff-backed shamble before his exit.

Brina had nuzzled closer to Monton, much quieter than her previous self, little eyes wide.

"You'll probably get a few loons like that. Can't say I got a good look at him under that hat, but I'll be on the lookout," Monton said. "Don't you worry, though. You'll have at least two men here to watch over the situation during the day and three of our most trusted at night."

Larka smiled. "I'm sure I'll be fine. Master Ling has taught me well over the past two months."

Monton's mouth twisted with worry. "He says you are a good student," he finally conceded.

"I'm not overly confident, Monton. I wouldn't put myself in a situation just to try out the skill of empty-handed defense, if that's what you think. I fear my training hasn't the depth to sustain me just yet, and as you said Guardsmen will always be here thanks to you. Don't worry about me."

"They say not to look a madman in the eyes, Lark. It would take little to offend one like that, and I daresay little time for him to assault you even with the Guard here." Monton relaxed despite the anxiety compelling his words, and the horizontal folds in his forehead released along with the added height to his brow. "But I am confident in your training, Lark, perhaps more so than you are. It is not often that Master Ling compliments anyone as he does you."

Monton bounced a terse Brina on his knee.

Larka grinned, and a thought unfurled in her mind. "Are there any midwives in Albilar?"

"Misa Swan-Ling is the best we have." Monton's brows shot up and creased his forehead once more. "And why have we need of a midwife?" He leaned toward her, great hands still around Brina's chest, his knee no longer moving.

Larka's cheeks burned as she realized her blunder. "Oh, it's not for me. I thought . . ." What had she been thinking? The idea's roots slithered more deeply into her brain and gnarled around her thoughts. "I thought midwifery would be a good skill to teach some of these women—those interested."

"I see." Monton wiped at his brow in mock relief. "I thought you'd another little one on the way. So soon after Brina would be unhealthy for you." His chubby cheeks glowed hotly.

Larka chuckled. "Just another volunteer for apprenticeships," she assured, yet a pang within her mind and the lurch within stomach told her differently.

Larka placed a sleeping Brina in the bassinet near her feet and turned back to the papers on the table. The bassinet had been a gift from one of the previously homeless women, who was now proving quite adept at basket weaving. Larka beamed. Thus far, her plans to "rehabilitate" those who desired it had been a success.

During the day, women left their children with Larka, freeing time to learn new skills. The children usually played on the porch or in the small yard under Guard eyes. Two times a week, Master Ling dropped by to give the children lessons in empty-handed defense, for which Larka was grateful; the children had non-contact sparring to keep them busy even when Master Ling was not present.

Larka read the shelter's list of occupants, summing forty now, and smiled. Footsteps sounded on the porch, and she lifted her eyes to see a man of medium height and build pushing open the screened door. Grey hair mingled with the short acorn-brown strands on his temples.

She straightened in her seat and watched him meander around the room, muttering to himself, staring up and supinating his hands as if placating the walls. He finally settled before Larka's table.

By this point, a Guardsman had come out of the kitchen and stood in its hallway, eyeing the stranger with suspicion.

"Do you need a place to sleep?" Larka asked.

"Hmmm." Hands clasped behind his back, the man stooped over her, got right in her face, and stared at her, madness glazed over his soft brown eyes.

Larka jerked back. This man had worn a straw hat upon his first visit to the shelter. Larka's air allies breathed warnings into her psyche.

"Are you all right, sir?" Larka maintained her demeanor, though a coldness ran through the length of her.

"Yes, yes, I am." The man laughed, a hard, mirthless sound. "It would be a shame had this place not been created." He straightened, jumped from one foot to the other, and grinned through wide, roving eyes.

Larka nodded and scooted her chair back.

The man stretched up and down on his toes, hands still clasped behind him.

"Indeed, a great shame. Gentleness can at times supplant aggression. Great shames. Great shames would have been!" He smacked the tabletop with his open palms.

Larka started then recovered as the man went back to stretching up and down. She sniffed. She smelled no alcohol about this man; she much preferred a drunk to a madman.

The Guardsman had stepped closer. He now stood in the hallway's entrance, to Larka's right. His stance had opened to a natural stance, feet hip width apart, knees slightly bent, ready to act if need be.

A young boy ran by the Guardsman and burst out the door onto the porch. The madman turned to watch the boy then back to Larka. His face had flushed a deep red.

"Great shames upon the people had the original decree been instigated."

Larka's breath snagged within her lungs. Few, outside the Guardsmen sworn to secrecy, would know of the great shames that would have been wrought upon Albilar's homeless had Decree 305 come to pass, and only one she knew of was a madman.

Larka thought quickly, searching for the proper thing to say.

"Overseer Flock, I must thank you from the depths of my heart for allowing this shelter its place within Albilar."

The madman jumped and glanced left then right with spastic motions of his neck before he stared back down at her.

"To whom do you speak?"

Larka bowed her head and peered at the top of her orderly desk. At that moment, Brina began to wail her frustration at being stuck in the bassinet. Larka reached down and picked up her daughter, who immediately quieted, staring wide-eyed at the crazy man amongst them.

The madman's eyes became focused and compassion creased his brow. He held out his arms for the babe. Brina turned away and pressed into her mother's breasts. Wind lashed about them, fluttering paperwork to the floor and slashing through the man's short hair in warning. Larka narrowed her eyes and held fast to her daughter.

The young Guardsman moved to stand beside Larka's table.

The madman's eyes darkened with savagery as he glanced at the Guardsman, but he dropped his arms.

"She looks so much like my daughter, Maja, when she was a babe." He closed his eyes. When he opened them, tears glistened there. "I miss her so." He bent toward Brina who flinched away from him. "She is about a year?" He asked, not looking at Larka, eyes still on the babe.

"Yes," Larka breathed the lie.

Footfalls on the tiled porch floor caused the man to flitter around in a most exaggerated manner. Monton pushed the door to the shelter open, and the Overseer scuttled out by him.

Still holding the door open, Monton stared after him. "Was that Overseer Flock? What did he want?"

Larka shook her head. "I don't know. He was a very . . . strange man."

The Guardsman by the table made a small bow to Monton and slipped away.

Brina thrashed impatiently in her mother's arms, wanting to be put down. Larka settled her where the Guardsman had stood. The baby wobbled then steadied herself by holding each of Larka's proffered second fingers.

"And dressed as a commoner," Monton added, finally closing the door.

"He was here the first day. The loon. Remember?" Larka took a deep breath after realizing just how shallowly she had been breathing.

"That was him?"

Larka nodded.

Brina released her mother's fingers and stepped forward. The infant squealed with delight. Larka and Monton gawped as Brina raised her other foot and pushed it into the second step away from her mother.

CHAPTER 27

DARK MOON RISING

*L*arrrrkaaa." The whisper penetrated her sleep. "Larrrrkaaa, you were told what happennned the night of your birth. You lissstennned without putting thingsss together but lissstennn well nowwww."

Larka tossed about in her bed. "You will know how the dark moon gets into you, girrrlll," the phantom hissed into her ear.

"Go away," Larka groaned.

The hiss concluded. Then the voice cackled, wisped about the room, and repeated, "Larrrrkaaa, Larrrrkaaa."

Larka jerked upright and saw nothing unusual in her surroundings. Brina rested peacefully beside her on the bed, wavy ash-brown hair spilling over round cheeks. Pale sunlight had begun its decay of the darkness, yet something felt amiss in Larka's room. She felt hollow, out of sorts.

She recalled tidbits of her dream—there had been blood and umbilical cords—but no more could she release from the foggy world of sleep, no matter the effort. Larka gazed at Brina, and foreboding bilged her insides. Her allies licked at her on tresses of air, soothing her anxiety, replacing it with a placid, if docile, mind.

"And what will you do with these babes once you've rescued them?" Astla bellowed later in the day.

Larka's brow puckered. "If you awakened each morn with the knowledge that your inaction would lead to the death of an innocent, then you would not take to such offense at what is right for these babes. And, as for the babes, I have connections within my shelter which will lead me to proper homes for them."

Astla turned on his heel and paced the length of floor from fireplace to front door, his boot heels echoing off the floor stone. Taut muscles worked his mandibles.

"I forbid it. I absolutely forbid it! You will go nowhere in two days time if I have to bind and gag you."

"You will do no such thing." Larka jumped to her feet, nearly toppling her chair, her hips knocking into the table.

"I'll have Monton help if need be."

"But then you'd have to tell him *why*," Larka lashed back.

Astla stopped in his tracks and whirled around to meet her eyes. His countenance, bloated with outrage, fell into frustration. He threw up his hands. "You can't do this, Larka. You'd not risk our family for one baby."

"No one would be the wiser."

"You could be caught while helping. Someone might find you on the trail and hurt you before you could even get to this stranger." He slammed his left fist into the flat of his right palm. "A lone woman out there, Larka . . . you well know what could happen."

Larka felt blood rush to her cheeks, and her vision dropped to the floor. Still, her next words remained level. "I am well trained in empty-handed defense, and I will have my throwing axes and knives as well as swift legs to allow my escape should I need one."

Astla shook his head, muttering, "Had I known for what you practiced with such fervor all these years . . . and all that Misa Swan-Ling taught you, I'd never . . ." He shook his head again and resumed pacing.

"I felt its tiny heart beating this morning when I scanned the area. The woman will bleed, and she will die. Without her, the babe will die." Larka closed her eyes. "And I'll live with the guilt of their deaths until the day *I* die."

The clacking of boot heels on stone died away. Fingers cupped her shoulders, and Larka unveiled her sight to find Astla's concern streaming down on her.

"I'd not have you bear that," he whispered and released her then walked quietly out of their home.

It was as much acceptance as he gave her, for over the next two days, he said nothing more on the subject as he said nothing more to her until she left, casting doubts on the urgency of her mission. Larka awoke on that day jittery and ready to leave long before her departure.

Larka smiled as she reached the gate where a seated Monton bounced a giggling Brina on his knee. Larka stooped and kissed Brina on the head, the child's wild ash-brown hair tickling her mother's nose.

This night, a dark moon would blight the skies of Albilar. This night, Larka would leave Brina in Astla's and Monton's full care.

Monton read Larka's expression. "Our girl will be well taken care of, Lark," he assured. "But I wish you would take someone with you. It's dangerous for a woman alone, even one with your skills."

Larka smiled. If only Monton knew the true breadth of her skills…

Brina leaned toward Monton, and her hand darted forth to clasp the dagger sheathed against his left side.

"Brina, no." Monton admonished, sliding the dagger back into place.

Brina pulled back to look at Monton. Tears brimmed in her eyes. She folded her arms over her chest and stuck out her bottom lip.

"She has quite an affinity for shiny things." Monton grinned up at Larka.

"Perhaps it's just a phase." Larka sighed, eyeing the weapon. "It is too bad Overseer Flock decreed the wearing of daggers at the gate, though."

"He grows more paranoid by the day," Monton agreed.

Waving her thick arms, Brina giggled as Monton bounced her.

"Bye-bye," she peeped at Larka.

Larka's mouth fell open. "You won't even miss me, will you?" She grinned and kissed Brina again before strolling out through the gateway.

Larka watched her boot-clad feet as she walked away. She took a deep breath, displacing some of the anxiety clenching her chest. She needed her wits about her today, but the last steps she had taken away from her mother and blood daughter over two years past, snow and ice crunching underfoot, echoed through her mind. Larka took in another deep breath. Brina would be fine. She had to be.

Larka stopped and turned to stare uphill. Monton and Brina had become small in the distance.

The sound of Larka's soft footfalls kept her company as she trekked and pondered many things, among them the dark moon.

It seemed too simple that the second new moon in a month could wax with supernatural gifts to those born under it, yet that slippage of black sky twice in a month was it and nothing more.

Blood and a placenta slipping down a rocky slope and descending into darkness spat into her mind's eye. Larka shook her head. She blinked hard and fast. Her brow gathered as she grasped the thought—a memory—and began to unleash its meaning. Anon, the wind streamed around her, like tentacles suctioning out her memories.

She blinked slowly, feeling stupefied. What had she been thinking?

Larka wrapped her lengthy coat more tightly around herself to fend off the autumn wind. Astla had given her the coat along with a terse "goodbye" before he had taken Brina to the training yards this morning. Larka admired the craftsmanship that had gone into the tan garment's design. It served its purpose well: to hold weapons as well as cover the hilts of the thin knives sheathed on either side of her waistline and the two light throwing axes that rested in an X on her back. Throwing knives also rested just inside each calf-high boot.

Her wind friends nudged her to the east, and Larka broke from the trail, sojourning toward Shady River, or Blood River as she liked to call it. A bit after noon, she reached the river's water and made camp in an area not far from Albilar.

Larka accounted for her surroundings as her beans cooked in their small pot. Tall hemlocks, lopsided white pines, and leafless white ash intermixed within the woods behind her while aspens fluttered golden leaves like forest fringe. Between her and the trees, large rock outcrops created natural shields. The river ran a few feet before her, a soft trickle in contrast to her last memory of a roaring Jaunty River, which seemed to burst into her head at the worst moments.

No matter how deep the avalanche of mental rock she used to bury her past, it was never deep enough to imprison the pain of losing her firstborn. Some of it always seeped out of crevices like ghost vapors and attacked her—triggered by a smell, a sound, a sight.

Larka sighed. She had avoided lavender for so long she had nearly forgotten what it smelled like, but she did not care. That plant had long ago exchanged its ability to soothe her with the sucking mire of its slithering roots.

Larka shuddered and stirred her beans. Tempted by her hollow stomach to eat them, she wrinkled her nose: they would have that odd raw taste to them. She added more water to the pot and waited, the wind telling her it would not be long now.

The sound of someone walking through the forest eventually sifted to her ears. Larka stood and gazed over the rocks behind her. A young woman—almost a girl—paused and turned to flee, a pale beacon beneath the shadow of the forest.

"Wait," Larka called and resisted the impulse to pursue.

The girl turned pallid eyes on Larka, her white-blond hair slipping from beneath a wool cap. She clutched at a midsection turgid with child, bundling the cloth of a thin dress beneath her hands.

Larka took a step, and the stranger stumbled in the opposite direction. Larka gritted her teeth, and her hand rested on her own flattened belly where, once inside her, a child had shifted and kicked. She swallowed remorse, and let her voice rise.

"I am here to help you."

The woman-child hesitated and turned, her nearly transparent eyes assaying Larka once more.

"I need no help," the stranger replied. "I will birth this child and do what is right by it. I need no help with that."

"And what is right by your child?" Larka tried to query without condescension, but she heard it, as did the pale one.

The woman's blond brow creased. Her breathing became audible, quickening as she leaned against a tree trunk. She answered, pain chopping her words, "You know what is right for the good of the people if this child should be a girl."

A swift wind rose around Larka like a fury. Despite the whirlwind spinning in and around her head, Larka heard herself say calmly,

"I offer you an option. I can take your baby and place it in a home if you would allow that. Many people cannot have children of their own."

"Leave me alone," the girl half yelled, half panted.

Larka turned her back to the woman. "As you will, but I have midwife skills should you need them."

Larka ate her dinner, quietly aware that the pale woman had seated herself beneath the patient arms of a hemlock. The only sound Larka heard from the girl was the ragged breathing the labor pain wrung out while the forest regaled Larka with other sounds—chipping birds, chittering squirrels, and chirring crickets.

Larka stood, careful not to look at her fair companion and began to walk north along the river's rocky bank. Out of earshot of the woman's panting, Larka sat on a boulder still warm from the sun and crossed her legs to begin her meditation.

Wind thrummed around her. Larka inhaled and exhaled. She lost herself in that process, her body relaxing until a flash of light dispersed her spirit into the wind. Airborne fingers of her essence searched for the pain of birth until she reached the limit of her stretched spirit, yet Larka found no one except the unfortunate woman near her campsite, just as her air allies had shown her in flashes of revelation over the last week.

As the moon masqueraded black and the sun slipped away, Larka returned to the campsite to find the pale woman had moved and lay wheezing and groaning beside the embering campfire.

Larka observed the recumbent figure but a moment before emptying the remains of dinner into the river, cleaning the pot, and filling it with water, all the while accompanied by the stranger's uneven breaths.

Larka gathered a bundle more sticks from the forest then dropped them into the embers. She placed the small spider pot over the rekindling fire. Water sizzled on the pot's exterior. Larka dropped several clothes into the pot.

"I don't want your help." The woman shot her a recalcitrant look.

Larka heard "humph" leave her own throat and bit her tongue, reminded of old Gilly. She seated herself before the fire and swirled cloth gently in water.

"My husband would kill you if he knew." Pale eyes flitted to Larka.

Larka raised her brows and met a terrified gaze over the fire. "This is your first, isn't it?"

The girl's face broke with vulnerability, and she turned away from Larka.

Larka sighed. It would be a long night.

DARK MOON ABASHED

*L*arka stared into the hungry tongues of flame shooting up to consume yet another thick stack of wood until her drooping eyelids concealed her desire to be alert.

"Help me . . . please." A frail voice cut through the dragging night.

Larka's head jerked up. She blinked back sleep.

The pallid creature groaned and grunted, face contorted with her efforts.

Larka shrugged out of her coat to wash her hands with a soapy cloth then poured some warm water over them. She brought the soap, remaining water, and her bag and placed these implements beside the stranger.

"I need to see if you are ready to push." Larka knelt before the crook of the girl's knees then reached in to measure readiness for delivery with her right hand's fingers.

Larka sat back. "You're not fully dilated. Stop pushing."

"What?" the girl wailed.

"If you push now, you may never get this baby out. Pushing when you aren't ready causes swelling where the baby must pass." Larka rewashed her right hand. "You'll be ready soon," she said, drying that hand.

She rifled through her bag and set aside things she would shortly need.

"I'm going to clean you up down here."

Larka pulled a wet cloth from the spider pot and lathered it with soap to clean the laboring woman's genital area, rinsing with fresh water afterward; infection killed far too many women and left far too many children motherless, homeless, or both.

"Push now," Larka commanded where she knelt before her patient's knees.

The girl howled. With much effort and several more contractions, the woman finally pushed her baby into the world.

"Keep pushing. The placenta will follow."

Larka deftly cut and tied the umbilical cord, bundled the baby in cloth, and set the crying newborn on a blanket away from the stranger before hurtling back to the woman, whose vaginal opening bled with speed, the placenta dispelled. Hands stacked, Larka pressed their heels with force into the girl's abdomen, over the womb. The girl batted at Larka with weak arms.

"You'll die if you don't allow me to stop the bleeding," Larka warned, leaning away from the young woman's defenses. "You've bled a good deal already."

The stranger stared at Larka. Then the girl's arms fell by her sides.

Larka leaned back into her job and kept pressure over the woman's womb even after the blood flow had staunched to normal. She finally stood and shook the cramps out of her thighs and buttocks.

"You need to clean yourself up." She nodded to another cooling pot of water and the linens on the blanket beside the woman. "Massage and push on your womb throughout tonight to keep yourself from bleeding much more."

The woman raised her head.

"Is it a girl?" she asked through staggered breaths.

Larka raised a brow then went to pick up the baby. She peered into the infant's face. Memories pounced at her like a big cat intent on its kill: rosettes of blood spilling from Mentheleda's chest, Mentheleda's empty arms, Larka's hollow womb. She tore her mind from that chink in the past.

"What if the babe were female?" She projected a gruff voice.

"I don't know," the woman cried. Sitting up, she wrapped frayed skirts around her ankles.

"Is that so?" Larka's wry tone struck the air, and the air vibrated in agreement. She ran a thumb over the babe's brow. "So pretty."

"Let me see my baby," the stranger demanded, thin arms outstretched.

Larka peered at the woman, expression stoic, then began to sing *Birth Song*.

"Don't sing that," the new mother shrieked through tears, making fists of her hands and banging the herb bags beside her.

"Why not?" Larka held her breath.

"That is a welcome into this world only that child's mother should sing."

"And you claim the right to sing it?" Larka's brows advanced toward her forehead, her eyes challenging the girl.

The fair mother bowed her head.

"Yes." The mother raised her oddly transparent eyes to meet Larka's assessing gaze. "I wish to sing it to my baby." She outstretched arms for the babe once more.

The wind caressed Larka with knowledge, and she smiled.

"It seems you shall." Larka stood and handed the child to the woman.

The new mother hungrily pressed the child's head to her nose.

"Don't forget to pressure and massage your womb to keep the blood's flow down. Take these herbs as teas. They'll help, as well as keep fever away." Larka pointed to the small bags on the blanket beside the girl. "Don't forget to clean yourself down here." Larka pointed to her own crotch then spoke through taut jaws, "And clean the baby of your blood. I'll dump the rags in the river. We don't want to attract predators."

The beaming mother nodded, barely noticing Larka madly flinging bloody clothes into the river. The mother unwrapped the baby to count fingers and toes by firelight. Then the pale woman stared with consternation at the infant's lumpy genitalia.

It was a boy!

The new mother looked up to find the midwife gone.

"Thank you," she whispered into the night.

Carried on the air, the words reached Larka.

"You are most welcome," Larka whispered back where she sat not far downriver upon a slab of dry rock, her state trancelike as she searched yet again for danger. She found none.

Later that night, Larka retrieved her coat and covered the sleeping girl and babe with a fresh blanket, careful not to cover the newborn's face. She removed her cooking gear to her new site, leaving bread, cheese, fire matches, and a tin cup for the young mother. When, at dawn, still no peril prowled after the woman and child, Larka departed for home.

CHAPTER 29

SWORD IN THE SKY

Larka clothed Brina in a long-sleeved dress the color of terra cotta, its fabric reaching just past the child's knees.

The people Brina viewed as her mother and father presented her with a cake with five small beeswax candles recessed in its icing. Brina giggled upon receipt of a doll and immediately ripped its legs off with the blunted toy knife Astla had carved from oak—another gift.

Larka shook her head and picked up the abused doll.

Brina squealed and wielded her knife at Astla as if it were a sword. Astla feigned injury and plunked to the floor.

"Da. Da." Brina patted his back. "Da!" she shrieked.

"Boo!" Astla jumped to his feet.

Brina giggled, and the playing recommenced.

Larka placed the doll on the table.

"It's a bit chilly," she said before she grasped several pieces of split wood from the rack next to the side door.

Larka had no sooner settled the wood into the fire than Brina clamped her hands over her ears and screamed. After that day, neither Larka nor Astla could feed the fire with Brina in the room, not until the girl grew much older.

"What's wrong with my little Brauna?" Astla inquired, scooping the girl up—who was anything but little—and swinging her around.

Larka cringed at the use of that name, one Monton had assigned her child. She eyed the muscle that sheathed the child's calves. Larka had often compared Brina to other children her age. None, not even the boys, compared as far as musculature went.

Larka peered out the front window up at the foreboding cast of clouds. Astla had promised her something different in their training session today. The twinkle in his eyes had said it to be something good.

A shaft of sunlight threw itself between the shifting clouds as if it knew it would have few chances to speckle this part of Earth today. Perhaps they would have their session without rain. One could never be certain whether the clouds would pass quickly or slumber over them. The day disagreed with Larka's hopes, however, and produced a fine drizzle that misted her family as they walked by Guardsmen and out the gate.

Brina skipped ahead of her parents until she reached a copse of young aspens, which even Albilar's herds had not chewed into extinction. The swagger of leaves, dotted in an asymmetrical manner about their slender trunks, stilled Brina's gait just as they always did. The child stared at them, reaching out and brushing the leaves with her fingers.

Larka gave her daughter a light push when she and Astla caught up to the child.

"Up there, Brina," Larka chided and pointed toward the scarred maple so often used as a throwing target. "You know we practice up there."

"She likes those trees, Mum. They're growing like she does," Astla said and chuckled.

"Come on, Brauna." Astla picked Brina up and draped her over his shoulders, maneuvering the burlap bag he carried so as not to tangle its drawstrings around the child. Brina wrapped her arms around Astla's head, her feet dropping below his chest. The girl looked awkward, too long to be carried in this manner.

Larka shook her head—how Astla spoiled the child. Larka had found herself unable to lift Brina these days.

Larka gave the aspens one last look before she followed behind her family and eyed the area around her feet. Even the grasses in this area grew healthy despite the constant grazing and trampling.

Astla dropped the burlap bag—producing wooden clanks—in a thick carpet of dewy grass and placed Brina beside it. He dropped his sheathed sword next to Brina and tussled the girl's hair.

"Don't play with that sword, Brina. You could cut yourself." He laughed as he did each time he told Brina this. One of Brina's favorite games was trying to get Da's sword unstuck.

Brina smiled and struck the sheath with her toy knife. "Take that."

As the misting rain let up, Astla drew a quiver of arrows from the bag and handed it to Larka.

"Are we throwing arrows today?" Larka studied the gray-feather fletching poking out of the quiver, her heart daring to hope.

"If you like," Astla replied and sauntered to the red maple. He disappeared behind the wide trunk and reappeared to place what Larka perceived a target before it. He disappeared behind the maple a second time and returned, a lightly recurved bow in hand.

A broad smile lit Larka. "But it's longer and more slender than the ones you use." She pounced and pulled the weapon from Astla's hold.

"I had this made especially for you by me, and it needs to be longer and more slender. The changes reduce the draw weight." He chuckled. "Aren't you going to say 'thank you'?" He tapped the bow and waved toward the target stuffed with hay.

"Thank you." She grinned and ran her fingers over the smooth wood of the bow then plucked at its string.

"Stop that. It's not a guitar," Astla teased then retook the bow. "Now, you nock the arrow on the serving—the spot here with the extra string wrapped around it—with the bow parallel to the ground. Place the arrow on the shelf like so." He demonstrated. "When you draw, bring the bow up perpendicular, with the arrow held between your index and middle finger. Keep those two fingers and the fourth hooked around the bowstring."

Astla pulled the string back to his face. "Draw the string back and hold it against your chin with your index finger slightly under your chin. The string should divide your mouth and nose pretty much evenly, or I like a higher anchor point—by my mouth—and I don't like the string on my face." He hiked the drawstring up to the right side of his mouth and cocked his head. "Sight down and over the arrow's tip. Or you can figure out the best anchor point for you.

"These arrows should work for you. They're a bit short for me. Look at my hand. Note that I don't pull the arrow and string back upon release; that's called 'plucking.' I just release my fingers." He extended his drawing fingers, and the arrow sailed through the air to strike the clothed target in the distance.

He grinned with mischief. "You got all that?"

"Give me a few years," Larka mumbled, listening for Brina, who shuffled around in the wet grass behind them.

Astla showed her the proper stance and procedure again then gave her the bow and arrows.

A sweet pleasure lit her center as Larka let fly her first arrow. It fishtailed momentarily then sped up and hit neatly in the target's center.

Astla smirked beside her. "Had I but the talent of a redirecting wind."

"Oh, so you doubt my true aim." Larka grinned.

"With that awkward draw and wavering flight—" Astla's mouth fell open as he stared wide-eyed over her shoulder.

Larka turned. The sun shot out at that point, producing a glint off steel. Brina stood not ten paces behind them, haloed in the moment's golden light, the hilt of Astla's large sword held between her palms, the violence in that blade tip pointing at a low angle toward the belly of the sky.

Larka screamed, "Brauna, you drop that sword!"

Brauna's fingers opened and the sword fell into the thick grass. She gazed questioningly at Larka.

Blood swished through Larka's head. She closed her eyes against the world to be smote by the wind's cruel pleasure—unbidden and unhidden. As the elemental flounced about her, Larka viewed snippets of the woman Brina would become . . . of a sinewy warrior sleeping amongst a scatter of pillows in dim light. Tears seeped through Larka's lashes.

A tremor ran from her center to her extremities. She saw more than felt her legs give way, the ground rushing toward her.

"Larka." Astla bent to one knee, waving a hand before her.

Daughter of Air and Storm had surmised that her air allies scried something about the future she could not, that in some way and for some reason things had been set in motion—all facts she should not have known. The wind lashed into her with a merciless rage. Larka slumped into the grass.

For three days, the air allies whirled about Larka's consciousness, trying to assuage her doubts, to dismiss their relish of Brina's swordplay. They did not succeed. Larka refused to let go the notion that, somehow, they knew something she did not. The air element, nevertheless, battled without relent and finally cornered the concepts within the recesses of Larka's mind . . . close to the path she might have taken had a love-torn Guta heard crumbling rock spilling over a plateau.

Larka awoke to view the red-eyed anxiety of her brother, who sat in a dining chair beside her bed, light hair disheveled, a breeze ruffling his clothes. The breeze receded as she sat up and her thoughts expanded into the present.

"Thank the sweet earth," Astla breathed and held her. "It's been like a tornado in here."

Larka noted the room bare of its usual accouterments—basin and pitcher, candle and holder. Even the curtains on the window were gone.

"You repeatedly asked 'Why?' while you were under," Astla said and held her at arm's length. "What was happening to you, Larka? What were your *so-called* allies doing to you?"

Larka gazed at the span of quilted blanket between them, consternation crumpling her brow.

"I don't know," she murmured, yet nagging fueled her mind.

CHAPTER 30

TRYING TIMES

Brauna countered her father's lunge punch with a left upper block— an upshot of the arm into a nearly horizontal position— and right reverse-punched into his face, stopping just before her fist made contact. Larka shivered. It was too cold for these two to be practicing empty-handed defense outside in the yard, yet here they were, sparring back and forth and going so rapidly at times Larka could barely discern their movements.

Brauna had begun practicing this form of defense not long after her fifth birthday. The child had learned enough via watching her mother over the years that she had already known much of what Master Ling had to teach her. Larka shook her head, smiling, as she recalled Brauna's first practice session and the immediate execution of a honed forward stance before Master Ling could even instruct it.

A breeze brushed tenderly over Larka's shoulder and settled about her head, imbuing her with its need. A chill ran through her, and she pulled her shawl tightly about her shoulders. The fourth dark moon since Brauna's birth would occur tomorrow night. Since the last one, Brauna had grown from seven to ten years of age. She had also grown nearly as tall as Astla. Breasts had begun to arise on the girl's chest.

Larka gazed at her daughter with longing. Where was the little girl she remembered?

The wind appealed once more in an agitated gust, and Larka rushed into her home. Her eyes flitted from one thing to another: her tan coat, foods, herbs. She had so much to do. Or did she? The wind had at Larka again, spiraling around her. She shook her head. She really needed to hurry.

She flung objects and necessaries into the pack she used for camping. Her hands shook. Her breathing shallowed. Larka made an irritated shove at a loaf of bread, and her cooking beans spilled all over the floor.

Larka paced the floor with her air allies slinking about, further incensing her.

Astla glowered up at her, a book in hand, his candlelight extinguished.

"Cease the wind, Larka. It's disturbing everything in the house, and I'm sure Brauna is starting to wonder where a draft like *that* is coming from."

"Oh," Larka said, tone scatty. She closed her eyes and managed with much concentration to wrangle in the flux of air.

Her eyes popped open. "I should really be leaving."

Astla scrutinized her, brow contorted. "It is the middle of the bloody night!"

Larka heard him but did not understand. She looked at him but did not see. All she sensed was the urgency without.

She donned her coat and spread her arms, air shifting in and out of her hair. Her packsack and other belongings rushed in obeisance to take their places on her person, so many invisible hands guiding them.

Astla raised his brows and blinked.

Larka darted out into the night.

Larka awoke facedown the next day, farther along the river than she had ever traveled on a dark moon venture. She did not recognize her surroundings other than the vegetation of Northwoods and its typical sullen skies. She could barely recall her trek through the darkness. She could, nevertheless, recall Astla staring at her as if she were mad.

She pushed herself upright and shook her head. Her coat fell off. She had apparently used it as a blanket.

She had heard of drunks waking to the bewilderment of not knowing where they were. Larka now knew how they felt though without the hangover. She stretched her stiff back. Her bed had been granite, which, a short distance from her, sloped into the water of the river itself.

Larka built a small fire then breakfasted on crushed bread, hard cheese, and hot tea. She pondered the rocky, high bank across the river as she finished her tea. No pregnant woman in her right mind would negotiate that decline to get to the river. Behind her, the steep was no better.

Shivering in the chill autumn morn, she clambered partway up the slope and made a reconnaissance of the areas above her.

"Perhaps I should move my things up there."

The wind smacked at her angrily.

"Perhaps not," she said, slightly vexed. She had been given no visions about this mission, only the crazed urgency that had brought her here.

A scream blasted into her eardrums, perpetuated and exacerbated by her allies. Larka nearly cursed but caught her tongue. She slid back down the embankment.

Not far upstream, a man, long knife in his hand, stood over a dark-skinned woman who lay on the granite shore, her arms and legs tucked around her distended belly. Not far from him, an older woman—abdomen also turgid with child—watched with placid demeanor as the man menaced the younger woman.

"Get away from her!" The response burst from Larka. She reached over her shoulder.

The wiry man whipped around, and the older woman's head lifted.

"And who's going to make me?" The man sneered, rat-like incisors working against his bottom lip.

A throwing ax struck the back of his knife hand with the butt of its blade. That hand opened in flinch, and the knife clanged to the rock beneath him, nearly striking the young woman he threatened. At this, the young woman rolled up and began to scoot on her buttocks away from the man.

The man turned from Larka and started for his victim, missing the second whisper of wood sliding out of leather.

"Do you wish another?" Larka shouted, eyes flicking to the ax in her hand when the man swiveled back toward her.

Seeing her opportunity, the young woman hoisted herself to her feet then dashed to hide herself behind Larka's thin frame while the older, brown-haired woman moved to join the man.

The man bared his teeth. He looked as if he might propel himself at Larka but for the hand laid on his forearm by the brown-haired woman—the woman who had watched Larka pull another ax without a word of warning to her partner. Then this woman's breath heaved out of her, and she tugged at the man's arm.

Early labor, Larka surmised. The brown-haired woman would birth soon.

The man picked up his knife, not taking his eyes off Larka.

Abrupt knowledge and grief exploded within Larka. She cried out, tears pecking at her eyes, talons ripping at her throat. Whether under the dark moon or under the light of today's sullen skies, this couple's babe would die if left in their hands; neither wanted a child, particularly not a female and especially not one born beneath the darkest of moons.

Larka looked upon them anew, jaws clenched, lips twisted, ax hand twitching until the older woman's high, rounded belly began to glow through the grayish material of her dress, drawing Larka's eye.

The babe within made a slow turn to look at Larka, tiny mouth stretched in terror. Larka stared for a brief span of time then whispered,

"When the time is right . . . tell me when the time is right, and I shall be there."

The glow within the swollen belly faded.

"Be gone with you!" Larka then bellowed. Lightning streaked across a brooding sky. Thunder rumbled.

The woman yanked the man's arm, and they departed, the man glowering back from time to time until they reached a bend in the river and disappeared around it.

"I sought you," the youthful woman behind her spoke, "but found them."

Larka turned to the woman. "You sought me?" She tucked the ax back into place.

"A woman I know said you helped her sister years ago with the birth of her son. She knew my due date was close to the forecast of the dark moon and that I wanted this child more than anything. My husband's dead. Our child is the last bit of him I have left. . . ." The girl peered with heavily lashed eyes at the granite floor and inhaled.

"When I found those two, I assumed they were also seeking the dark moon midwife. When I asked, that maniac pulled his knife. I ran down a shallow bank upriver and ended up here." She gazed at the steep banks around them. "I got caught, but I found you." Her lips quivered. "I fear we haven't seen the last of them." The stranger's swollen abdomen quavered slightly beneath her wool dress. The woman's face tensed, and the length of her curly, black hair shook with the tremors of her body.

Larka reached to place her palms on the mound of life stretching the woman's belly.

"You did right. You have labored lightly for several hours, but with a first child labor can last long. You'll deliver tonight, I suspect, after the rising of the dark moon." Larka smoothed the pending mother's worried brow. "Do not think upon that man or his wife. They'll not harm us."

The woman tried to smile, but the contraction was still upon her.

"I'll have to move camp. Rest while I gather my things."

Illuminated by the bluish light circulating around her, Larka smiled down at the baby girl and wrapped her with haste against the chilled air. Autumn harvested winter too early this year.

"She's your thick head of hair and deep blue eyes." Larka paused then breathed, "She's beautiful." She placed the baby on Kara's deflated belly. Kara pulled the baby up over her chest and peered into the infant's face. The infant made a low grunting sound.

Larka turned and used her dipper to flush her hands with warm water, lathered them with soap and rinsed. She placed the dipper's bent handle back over the rim of the pot then fished out a cloth and shuffled on her knees to Kara, where the new mother lay on the blanket Larka had provided. She dabbed the cloth over Kara's sweat-soaked face, also pushing off strands of plastered hair. Firelight caressed both of them, flames crackling faintly between the campers and cedars lining the river, night dancing beyond.

Kara smiled. She sighed with contentment and shifted on the blanket to rest on her side. Relief and happiness trickled down her cheeks as she looked upon the newborn in her arms.

"You were lucky. You are bleeding little, and though I hate to leave you now, I have to get to that crazed couple before they kill their baby." Larka had tried to monitor the horrified unborn since seeing the last of the couple. The air allies had become silent on the matter, but the child had retained a link to Larka.

"I've little time, Kara. You need to clean yourself up to prevent infection." Larka stood and stepped to add wood to the fire then to untie another blanket from her packs. She returned to spread the blanket over Kara's legs and trunk. "I'll come back if I can, if you wish." Larka donned her coat.

"Oh, I do. What's your name? I'd like to name my daughter after you." Kara traced the newborn's face with a forefinger.

Larka thought for a moment, swallowed before she answered with thickened voice, "Mentheleda."

Kara peered up at Larka. "Mentheleda," she repeated dreamily. "Be careful."

Larka nodded then ran through the darkness, tan coat flapping behind her. After rounding a bend in the river, she stopped and held up a hand. Her aura flared out, and the throwing ax she had hurled earlier whooshed to her through the darkness. Larka caught the whirling ax's handle, peered at its female shape a moment, and then reinserted it into the loops under her coat.

The couple had climbed above the river not far from Larka's previous campsite. After a short run, she could hear the wife's raspy breath and moaning. Larka doused her lights and climbed stealthily up a more negotiable segment of the riverbank. She hid behind the trunk of an old spruce, fingers clinging to scaly bark as she peeked around the tree's girth, her long hair getting caught in low-hanging twigs.

A small fire lit the pair. The man knelt before his wife's spread legs, peering beneath the shadowy plateau of skirt stretched over her knees.

Larka ducked behind the trunk once more, slipping her hair out of the tree's grip.

"Just push the damned thing out," the man spat.

Larka's eyes narrowed. She stepped from her hiding spot and walked with brisk silence toward the couple, asserting as she approached,

"It's not quite time for her to push."

The man leapt to his feet and drew his knife from his belt.

Larka's fingers itched to grasp a throwing weapon, but she let that impulse be.

"I can help your wife deliver." Larka still maneuvered toward them.

"We don't want your help," the man hissed.

"Do you wish your wife to die?" Larka queried in a calm voice and stopped well outside the man's striking distance, beside the fire.

The man turned, gazed at his wife, shook his head.

"I have midwife skills," Larka offered once more. "I don't wish to see her dead either." Larka took off her coat, let it fall, then shrugged out of the harness belts that held the throwing axes on her back. She let the harness dangle on her fingers a moment before she let it fall.

The man watched with narrow-eyed suspicion as Larka disarmed herself of other obvious weapons. He grunted, looking her over when she had finished.

"You help her, but you leave once she's pushed the thing out." He gestured Larka toward his wife.

Larka stepped lightly, rolling up her sleeves. She knelt and checked the woman's cervical dilation. The man stood behind Larka, on a diagonal to her left. Larka looked over her shoulder at him, assessing more than his position.

"She'll be ready soon but not yet. She pushes now and she could die. It's as simple as that." Larka sat back on her buttocks, crossing her legs.

The man sneered at her. Larka looked back to the woman. The babe's image once more glowed through the woman's belly, and the unborn touched Larka's mind with a warning against the man's intentions toward Larka, the unborn, Kara and her own babe. Larka acknowledged this, and the child's head pushed into the woman's cervix, stretching it further.

Within an hour, Larka rose back to her knees and leaned forward to again check the wife's dilation.

"You can push now."

The woman screamed as she tried to eject the child. Although the woman was late in age, Larka surmised this child to be her first. This delivery would not be an easy one.

"Take a breath and try not to scream next push," Larka said and tapped on the woman's womb. "You need to use your strength down here, not in your throat."

With the next contraction, the woman pushed again, her body shuddering with the effort. She continued this pattern for almost an hour, Larka catching glimpses of the babe's head.

"Push like you are squatting in the squatting room," Larka instructed.

With the next exertion, the baby crowned and then the head thrust out fully. The infant's shoulders followed. Larka grasped them and pulled gently as the woman pushed. The child squirted into the world.

The man stepped closer. His mistake!

Larka released the newborn and backfisted the man's groin then immediately thrust-kicked into his right knee. Bone snapped. Cartilage crunched. He staggered, clutching his crotch. As her left foot landed, Larka rose and pivoted on it, delivering a roundhouse kick to the man's ribs then landing in a right forward stance.

He grunted, stumbled, then thrust his knife upward at her in a weak defense. She struck his right wrist with her left one, fingers closing around his forearm. She wrenched it counterclockwise. His palm rolled up with the knife. She grasped the long hilt and yanked it down, slashing through the meat of his hand to tuck the knife by her right side.

She still had not released his arm.

He stiffened, eyeing Larka with comprehending shock as she jerked him into the strike of a left front knee, slamming his middle abdomen, releasing his arm, circling her own right arm and thudding the knife's rounded hilt into the stranger's frontal bone.

Blood flushed out of his thinning hairline. His eyes rolled up. His eyelids sagged. He swayed backward and fell into crisp fall leaves.

"What have you done?" the man's wife screeched behind Larka.

Larka turned and backed toward the fire, eyes flicking from man to woman. She singed the knife's blade in the flames then side-stepped right, stopping where the baby had rolled along with the placenta. She severed the line that had connected woman and child.

Actions became automatic in freeing her hands as she bent to scoop the newborn out of the leaves. She pulled a piece of yarn out of her pant pocket and tied it around the babe's remaining cord to stop the ooze of blood.

The woman shrieked, "Is he dead? *Is he?*"

Larka maneuvered backward, slanting left to her gear, all the while watching the newborn's father. His mouth had lolled open, exposing the lengthy top incisors. He looked more rat now than man.

Furthermore, his chest still rose and fell with the pulse of his lungs.

"He's alive," Larka at last responded as she gathered her coat. She plucked throwing knives out of its lining, tucked them in her belt, and wrapped the contemplative baby within the coat's warm material. Shifting the baby from arm to arm, she slipped the ax harness over her shoulders, gathered the rest of her weapons.

"Give me my baby," the woman reached for the child, ostensible hope and hopelessness enrapturing her.

Larka eyed the woman, waiting, but her wind friends emitted no warning. Thus, Larka went to the stranger and leaned forward to extend the child toward her. The babe struggled and kicked as Larka's air allies—no, the babe's knowing mind; the wind was coincidence—assaulted her with flashes of what would come to pass if she conveyed the newborn to this woman. Larka lurched upright and the newborn settled, whimpering.

Larka stared down at the woman and took a wary step back.

"If I give you this child, you will break her neck the moment I leave."

A breadth of guilt-flecked eyes answered Larka.

The man wheezed. Larka snapped her head left to view him. His body twitched once then again.

Larka backed out of the campsite with the baby pressed safely against her.

Running, Larka recognized young cedars sketched by dying firelight. She hurried into the campsite.

Kara lay on her back, her newborn snuggled against her right side. Larka shook Kara awake then thrust the couple's stolen child into the crook of the woman's left arm.

Kara answered Larka with a groggy smile, her arm slipping around the Knowing Child.

Her aura leaping like a blue-gray inferno, Larka rushed through the cedars and fell to her knees beside the river. She shoved her arms in up to the elbows. She rubbed her hands together in a frenzy then sluiced water over her upper arms. The left biceps pulsed and stung.

As she sat up, something gouged into her thigh. She looked down her right side and saw it there: a long knife, a bloodied hilt. She shook her head, teeth gritted, nostrils flared, then jerked the weapon out of her belt and hurled it at the river.

She heard a splash, and a gust of wind rushed by her seconds later.

Larka pounded the granite shore with her fists. "Damn it, damn it, damn it." She jumped to her feet. "*Damned them!*" Breathing like mad, she slapped at her sleeves to get them back down over her wrists.

She stared out over the river until her breathing had normalized and her aura had calmed then returned to Kara.

"You saved their baby," Kara murmured, eyes more fully open. She raised her head to stare at Larka. "Mentheleda, you're bleeding!"

Larka glanced at her left biceps. Blood wet through the pale sleeve. "His knife hit me when I twisted his arm. It's a rather shallow cut," she lied. "I'll wrap it later."

Larka bent and clanked pots into her packsack. "It's not safe here. Can you walk?"

"I think so."

"I think I killed that man," Larka confided and peered at the newborns pressed against either of Kara's ample breasts. "I can't imagine he'll make it." Larka recalled his twitching form outlined by dim firelight, then recalled the Knowing Child's warning against the ratman. Her expression hardened. "He'd have killed us all."

"No doubt." Kara sighed then wriggled her way upright. "No one would miss a man like that."

"His wife would!" Larka spat and rammed the last of the camping gear into her packsack. She slung the bag on—over her axes—and took the Knowing Child from Kara, who grasped Larka's arm before the warrior could straighten her back.

"You didn't take care of her too?" Kara breathed.

Larka gawped at Kara for several seconds then shook her head. "I couldn't just kill her."

Kara's hand fell away. She stared down at her baby, shoulders slumped.

Larka righted herself. "She didn't attack us like her husband did."

"She did nothing to stop him either," Kara's voice quavered. Then a weak smile touched her face. "But in your place . . ." Kara accepted Larka's hand and slowly stood. "In your place . . . I'd have done no differently." Kara shook her head. "But dare I say neither of them deserved to live?"

"They certainly deserved no life I can think of." Larka gazed down at the Knowing Child, unable to look Kara in the eyes. "We can always hope the woman bleeds to death. I could not bring myself to tend her."

"Yes, we can hope."

Beneath Larka's gaze, the Knowing Child pulsed with a sheer yellow light. "She says we're to go to your sister's home." Larka peered up at Kara.

Kara's brow puckered then settled back into place. "She also says she shall stay with me if I will permit it . . . that you cannot care for her without many eyes of suspicion." Kara chuckled. "And your brother is a pain."

Two days later, Larka left Kara, Kara's newborn, the Knowing Child, and the tan coat behind at the home of Kara's sister, but not before the Knowing Child lent Larka images that showed the depth of malice the child's mother had employed against the ratman.

Several weeks after the dark moon, Larka heard chatter in the marketplace about a delirious, half-dead woman found along the roadside. The woman had told a tale of a mad, ax-throwing female who had killed the woman's husband and stolen the woman's son, males not being persecuted for birth beneath a dark moon.

Larka had scoffed. She supposed all tales could be twisted to so sad a pitch.

CHAPTER 31

THE THREAT

Brauna rushed through breakfast then slung her porridge bowl into the dish pan resting on a side table.

"Hurry up, Mum." Brauna shoved her mailed shirt over a thick lichen-green tunic. Gray pants hung loosely about her sturdy frame.

Larka finished washing her own bowl and started on Brauna's dish.

"Mum, the dishes can wait." Brauna grabbed Larka's wrist and tugged her toward her clothing.

Larka peered up into her daughter's warm brown eyes. "Alright, but slow down, Brauna. This is a day like any other."

Brauna nodded, but Larka could still feel excitement stirring around her daughter. She cringed at the sound of Brauna's sword sliding into its sheath.

"You don't need that. Empty hands today, remember?" Larka flashed her palms at Brauna.

Brauna pursed her lips. "Yes, I remember, but plans change. I'm training with a new man today. He's supposed to be accomplished with sword. We opted for swordplay and *against* the dummy swords."

Taken by a preternatural shiver, she paused to reassess her daughter.

"A new man?"

"Yes, Mum! Come on. We'll be late."

Larka changed from a nightdress into a short-sleeved tunic and baggy gray pants. She tied her silver belt in place below her belly button and allowed Brauna to push and pull her until they stood on the bricked part of the practice yards.

Larka breathed in the mist that pervaded the cool morning air. The sun would soon peer over Albilar's walls to singe through the vapors. Brauna shifted next to her, and Larka followed her daughter's gaze.

A young man strutted toward them, his dark hair pulled into a tail at the nape of his neck. His tan, symmetrically square face glittered with a smile that might have stolen any young girl's heart, but repulsion writhed through Larka as if she had stepped barefoot into something slimy.

"There's Ontar." Brauna took off toward the strutting man, leaving Larka to contemplate her daughter.

The gentle curves of a round face enclosed Brauna's pouty lips and almond-shaped eyes. Most of the girl's hair fell to her jaw line, though a fringe of bangs hung over her eyebrows—a boyish hairstyle not the fashion of the day. The girl's features had been carved into a distinct loveliness, but most men did not take the time to truly see Brauna.

Larka surveyed Brauna's new partner. A healthy sheen reflected off the bare, golden skin of his well-muscled arms. He was tall, as tall as Astla. Despite this young man's height, Brauna was taller and just as muscled, though her shirt sleeves and long pants covered the sinew. Still, the muscle became apparent under cloth as Brauna moved, no matter how the girl tried to hide it.

Brauna and Ontar crossed swords and bowed to one another. Then it began, a game that would see many years pass before the victor was announced. Brauna's sword beat Ontar back within seconds. At the last moment, however, a falter showed itself in Brauna's usually perfect swordsmanship; Ontar whipped the sword out of the girl's hand.

"No," Larka breathed.

Some of the men watching along the walls of the yard laughed.

Larka marked them serenely—trainees and probably from Ontar's class, judging by the lack of hands or other weapons embroidered into their low-ranking gray belts. Ontar himself wore a gray belt, a sword already embroidered into it.

One of the young men noted Larka watching them and elbowed the men on either side of him. A faint gesture of heads up and down the line alerted each neophyte to her presence. Stifled laughter and a slightly twitchy demeanor overcame the group.

Larka ignored them and returned to observing Brauna dance and flit before Ontar with a flexible grace that belied her muscled body.

A hand slid onto Larka's shoulder. She turned to find Monton behind her.

"I'll keep an eye on that one for you, Lark," he said as he came to stand beside her, his own vision filled with yet another parry and losing riposte from Brauna.

"You are a good man, Monton." Larka smiled and patted the hand on her shoulder.

"There's Thadus. We're to spar today." Larka marked the youth— about her height and not much thicker of frame—searching through the gangs of sparring bodies. She waved at Thadus, then squeezed Monton's hand before she set off.

"We'll start with the front snap kick, Thadus. Don't forget to snap your heel back to your buttock without hesitation, or I'll catch your foot and throw you down," she said as she searched out an area free of sparring bodies and found one beside the wall. Thadus followed. "I assume you've warmed up?"

"Yes, Trainer Lark," he replied with enthusiasm. "I've been practicing."

Larka smiled and stopped a few feet away from the wall to turn and face him. "Good. No one improves without consistent practice." Larka laughed. "I sound like Master Trainer Ling."

Thadus eyed her belt and the empty hand splayed in embroidery on either of its ends.

Larka gazed at Thadus's barren gray belt.

"It took me five years to earn the hands and another ten to reach a silver belt." Larka grinned. "But belts and symbols aren't everything, Thadus—Master Ling never wears one. Honestly, I've seen men with high-ranking belts and poor form as well as egos so inflated I thought they had mistook themselves for gods."

Thadus grinned, the expression holding briefly then slipping into seriousness. "I like the grandeur of the belts as much as the next man . . . or woman, but I could truly be student to this art the rest of my life without the acknowledgment."

Larka breathed in slowly, a feeling of nirvana suffusing her lungs and spreading to her extremities. "I felt that way too, many years ago.

"Now, for that kick. Show it to me." She watched and corrected for several minutes. "That's much improved since last time; your hips are into it now," she said, nodding. "Let's spar. Fall into left forward stance, and I'll do the same."

Alternating legs, Thadus executed three front snap kicks, Larka in turn stepping back and twisting away from each strike. Larka then took her turn to kick as he dodged, the sparring going back and forth several times more until it was her time to dodge again. As Thadus began to kick, a supernatural cold pricked Larka's skin, and she looked to find the source of that power.

Hair glowing like amber fire beneath the sun met her vision, and the ball of Thadus's foot smote her gut. Larka lost her breath and fell forward onto her knees.

"Spar Trainer Lark! Trainer Lark!" Thadus called, yet his voice sounded secondary.

Larka remained bent over her stomach, her tendrils of air reaching out and lacing around this redheaded newcomer. A backlash of hate struck Larka as if another foot had pounded her gut. She moaned and rolled to her back.

"Mother of Mercy! Help!" Thadus yelled.

Larka's eyes focused on the outcry above her.

"I'm fine." She stood up.

Thadus's eyes flitted from surprise to relief. "I thought you were badly hurt. The Captain would have killed me."

Larka suppressed a smile. "I told you not to worry about Astla when you and I spar. My lack of focus caused that mishap." She rubbed her aching ribs. "Nothing's broken. Just learn from this. Lack of concentration will get you injured, or killed, in a real fight."

Thadus nodded.

"Off with you. Find someone else to kick. I've something that needs to be done," Larka said in a light-hearted manner.

Thadus bowed to her, lips in a timid smile, then found another trainee with whom to spar.

Larka shivered as once again the grips of intense cold caught her. She looked up. In the middle of the yards, the possessor of straight, amber locks glared at her. A pail rested before the stranger, a ladle's handle curved over its side.

Brauna rushed by the girl toward Larka, but the girl caught Brauna's arm. Brauna stiffened at the girl's touch and did not relax as the girl lifted the ladle to offer a drink of water.

Brauna waived the offer and came to stand next to her mother. "Mum, are you all right?"

Larka nodded, her appraisal still on Ontar, who had stopped and gladly accepted water from the redhead. Ontar also appeared to be having a quaint conversation with this willowy creature. A coy smile and downcast eyes had overcome the water bearer.

"Well, what happened?" Brauna asked.

"I wasn't paying attention and Thadus kicked me."

Brauna scowled in Thadus's direction, emitting a rush of heated anger.

Larka touched the girl's shoulder. "I am fine. It was a well-executed kick. Don't worry about it. It is what I am training him to do. I think he will make an excellent empty-hander. He's the flexible, swift body type."

Brauna rolled her eyes and shook her head. "Is that *all* you ever think about?"

Larka's lips curved upward. "No."

"What's all the noise about?" Astla had arrived.

After hearing what had happened, he poked at Larka's ribs.

"I'm fine," she insisted, shaking off Astla's touch.

"You may be, but I think you scared Thadus out of his wits. He screamed like a girl." Astla guffawed.

"Like a what?" Brauna snapped, her gaze on the conversation between Ontar and the water bearer. An annoyed pout marked her lips.

"I'm thirsty," she announced then stalked off.

"I don't like that at all," Larka murmured.

"She's a grown woman, Lark. She'll have a crush from time to time."

"She's sixteen, more girl inside than woman outside."

Astla squeezed Larka's shoulder and departed. He stopped where Thadus and another young man sparred; the two partners froze. Astla patted Thadus's back and said a few words that slackened the high set of the young man's shoulders before the Captain sauntered back to his quarters.

Larka barely noticed this scene, as she watched the water bearer dip the ladle into the bucket and give it to Brauna. Larka let go her airy fingers. Yet again, she was struck with spite, and the water bearer's head had jerked up. The stranger once more glared at Larka.

Larka shuddered. She had not been mistaken. Her first attempt to read the girl had been intercepted and turned back on her.

Larka marched to stand beside her daughter. Before she could get there, the water bearer said something that caused Brauna's head to snap back and Ontar to laugh. Eyes never leaving the newcomer's face, Brauna dangled the ladle over the water bucket then let the utensil fall. Clear liquid splashed on the water bearer's long dress. The water bearer gasped and jumped back, an aura of dark moon power starting to shimmer about her.

Larka arrived in time to step between the young women's stare-fest.

"Might I have a drink?" she requested.

The water bearer's rankled expression transitioned into a beautiful smile curving full, pink lips. "That was quite a kick you took," the water bearer said.

"She is your superior, Lichena! Address her as 'Spar Trainer Lark' and *apologize*," Brauna barked.

Ontar pretended to look in a different direction at that point.

Lichena locked wild amber eyes on Brauna. The newcomer's aura pulsed and swelled. A shard of cold so bitter struck Larka that she took a step back. Several ticks passed before she regained her composure.

"It's all right, Brauna. She's new here."

Brauna peered down her curiously tall height at her mother, earth-brown eyes flashing ire despite the calm set of her shoulders.

"I suppose you are right, Mum. She *is* new here." Brauna turned back to Lichena, smirking. "Of the gypsies, are you not?"

"We are People of the Wheel!" Lichena bit back.

The whitest aura Larka had yet seen of a dark moon child leapt around Lichena, and purity was the last thing that glowed within it. Larka shivered and rubbed her arms, but the coldness within her expounded, raising her flesh into livid bumps.

Lichena's next dazzling smile would have disarmed Larka had she not witnessed this child's animosity with such clarity.

"It is nice to meet you, Spar Trainer Larka," Lichena said and extended her hand.

Larka's hands fell to her sides briefly as her eyes locked with Lichena's. She tried to return the girl's smile, but apprehension mitigated the expression. Had Larka's ears deceived her?

"Nice to meet you as well, Lichena." Larka reached for the handshake and nearly snatched back as Lichena's icy palm slid against hers.

"Well, I think the dishes are waiting," Larka spoke to Brauna.

A puzzled look crossed Brauna's face. "Dishes," she repeated as Larka tried to pull her away from Lichena.

"Wait." Brauna easily stood her ground to once more lock eyes with Lichena. "My mother's name is Lark."

The girl flinched and shrank back. "I thought you said 'Larka.'" She offered in timid explanation. "Someone said it."

"Hearing voices, are we now?" Brauna scoffed.

Lichena stood there dumbfounded, her mouth agape and eyes going wild once more. Before the water bearer could retort, Brauna placed an arm around Larka's shoulders and whirled her mother around to move them toward home.

"Is there anything you need to tell me, Mum?" she asked when out of the training yards.

Larka peered up at her daughter as they ducked away from an area where several mourning doves perched on a particularly jutting rooftop. They turned onto Market Street.

"Stay away from that girl," she said as their shoes patted the cobblestones of the stall-lined street.

Brauna's brows arched into her forehead. Her mouth opened to let go an amused chuckle.

"I can't exactly avoid her, Mum, but I don't think she'll be poisoning my water anytime soon."

Larka paled and halted her steps amongst the milling crowd, Brauna stopping beside her.

"It was a joke," Brauna quipped.

"That girl is full of hate when she looks at you. This matter is not the least bit funny. Hate like that can warp a mind," Larka said then proceeded toward home.

Brauna rolled her eyes and followed. "Mum, I think I can take care of myself." She patted her sword.

Larka peered at the sheathed weapon then into Brauna's face.

"Danger is not always at the point of a sword, daughter."

Larka shivered in the hot summer sun while, somewhere overhead, a mourning dove released a slow, plaintive cry.

CHAPTER 32

MADMAN'S FOLLY

Larka strolled along the quiet streets of Albilar. A slim fog coiled as she passed through it. A swirl of mist then enveloped her. She froze within it, seeing glimpses of a russet-haired woman girthed with unborn child screaming so loud and with such terror—

There the image became the glimpse, the severed vision. This child would be born tomorrow night.

Larka tried to squeeze air into her panicked lungs. The weather witch had predicted falsely this year.

The allies faded into the regular currents of air traversing Albilar. Larka's body relaxed, her mind calmed. She sighed long with relief then set out again and soon turned a left corner, hearing nothing except the sound of her feet on the cobbled walkways. Before she made it up the porch steps of Albilar's Rehabilitative Domicile for the Homeless, Monton charged through the front doorway.

"Have you heard?"

Larka drew her spine straighter and stared at him.

"What is it, Monton?"

"The weather witch renounced her calendar prediction of no dark moon this year. The Overseer has sent members of the Guard to *oversee* those women who are pregnant and might birth under the dark moon. No women are allowed outside the city tomorrow or tonight."

They stood there a long moment regarding each other.

"That is bad news." Larka's brows drew inward. "I can't think of any woman Misa Swan-Ling and I have attended who is due at this time."

Monton grimaced then intoned breathlessly, "There's more. Women with babies near dark moon age will not be allowed to enter the city without proof of the child's birth date. All births are to be registered with the Overseer's Registrar from here out." As he spoke, his usually pinked cheeks became enhanced by a more florid hue.

Larka passed a resigned breath.

Monton remained in front of her, leaning his weight from foot to foot.

Larka eyed him, brow knit. "Is there something more?"

Monton gave her a pained smile and patted her upper arm. "The decree is retroactive. Children of or near ages relating to past dark moons are to be weeded and, uh, culled unless they have registrar proof otherwise. A month's been given for Albilarians to obtain such proof." Monton stared at his feet, shame and duty at conflict within his features. "Flock posted the decree without Guard concurrence this morning. He sent no copy of it to us."

"Culled," Larka whispered.

Monton reached to pat her arm again, and she backed down the steps.

Hurt fretted Monton's slightly convex brow. "Lark . . . it doesn't apply to you."

"But what of Brauna? She was born in the year of a dark moon. Does that justify culling her?" Larka's air allies swooped about her.

Monton opened his mouth to speak, but no words did he emit. He simply stood there, staring down at the slate-tiled steps between them.

"I don't know," he finally said. "With the proper papers—"

"What difference would it make to whom it should apply if any child were culled just for being born of or near the age of a dark moon? How many will die, Monton?" Larka's heart slammed at its captivity. "How many? And just *what* are Guardsmen ordered to do if they are present at a dark moon birth?"

Monton squeezed his eyelids almost shut, the rest of his face squinched as well. "The rules are so vague. So many interpretations could be made of them."

"Dear gods, Monton."

A swirl of secerning wind settled over her head, and Larka found suspicions she had long harbored regarding Cornt Flock confirmed. Heartbeat normalizing, body losing tension, Larka spoke,

"I want to see the Overseer."

"Lark, he'll have you executed if you stand against him alone."

Larka smiled, a wicked glint to her eyes. "Monton, I am not alone."

Astla and Monton stood grimly aside as the Overseer's assistant escorted Larka away.

She followed through a hallway outrageously adorned with stuffed peacocks, that fowl's feathers also painted in disarray over the plaster walls. At the hallway's terminus, the assistant parted two wooden doors and allowed her entry to the Overseer's quarters.

Several ornately framed painted-glass windows lit the room. Cushions littered the floors. The only real furniture that held stake with the floor was a plush, high-backed, lichen-green chair trimmed in gray cording. Upon its seat, Overseer Flock stared at her, his chest puffed as if it were a peacock's thrown train of feathers.

The assistant closed the doors and maneuvered to stand beside the Overseer, his pointed face a maven in petulance.

Larka stopped about five paces in front of Flock and made a slight bow. She raised her head to narrow her eyes at the assistant.

"I have information on why Maja ran and where she ran to."

"That, I've been told." Flock disdainfully lifted a brow and tapped an index finger on the arm of his chair.

"I will divulge her whereabouts to no one except you. Those were the conditions laid out to you." Larka pointed at the assistant. "He must go."

Flock stiffened. His chest ceased to move. Finally his ribs expanded with one great gulp of air.

"Leave me." Flock flicked his wrist, flipping his hand toward the door.

The assistant whined, "But, sir—"

"Get out, Cun!" Flock's eyes conceded no challenge, their madness fastened unwaveringly on Cun's taut features.

Cun shot a haughty look at Larka and marched out through the double doors. Larka dispatched a wall of silencing wind, which served to block the voices that would soon emanate from this room as well as hold shut the two unbarred doors. No one would be eavesdropping today.

Cornt Flock fingered the buttons of his finely cut gray vest, which covered a silky, lichen-green shirt. He peered up as if just remembering she were there, finally drawling, "Well, where is she?"

Larka held her aspect stoic. "Buried somewhere near Jaunty River I would assume, her murder well avenged."

"Dead!" The man cried and raised himself from his seat. "I shall have your head for this ruse!"

Larka walked toward him, looking directly into those all-too-familiar earth-brown eyes.

"You shall have no one's head. No one's. Not one person's, *not one child's*." She stopped before him. "Culled or otherwise. Do you understand me?"

Flock seemed sane at that moment, absolute cognizance roiling within his eyes.

"You impertinent wench!" He struck at her.

Larka swayed her trunk back, employing a kick to his testicles, a blow she thought he quite deserved.

Flock hunched over and grabbed his crotch.

Larka bent her lips next to his ear. "Sit down, and I shall tell you how your daughter died . . . though not before she birthed your lineage."

Flock's head lifted in a slow rise until his vision was on level with hers, sanity binging on the hope within his eyes.

"Yes, the child lived, *Cornt Flock*," she hissed his name and pushed his chest. He fell back into the chair.

"Your daughter was dead when first I met her along Jaunty River, but from her womb, I gathered a child. You see, she was murdered for birthing beneath a dark moon. And now you should also see your most recent decree requires that Brauna . . . be culled."

"Brauna? The child you held at the homeless shelter?" His eyes became sheeny with moisture.

Despair reached from him and hooked into her. Larka stepped back. She thrust down the pity that tried to well up in her chest. Maja, Mentheleda, and Larka's blood daughter had died because of this man. Had he not laid the course for tragedy so many years before, perhaps all of them would be alive today.

"Yes, you and Brauna share blood, *much blood.* Am I to believe you would kill her, the child you wished so much to conceive?" Larka stepped back once more, careful not to trip on a cushion.

"One person knows all I do and so shall many if I do not inform this person that I am safe within the hour. And make no mistake about it, the person who shares this information with me is some-one you would least expect." Larka's mind drifted momentarily to the Knowing Child and Kara.

Overseer Flock sat as if frozen on the throne, not even his eyes reflecting life. Then he shifted his buttocks, leaned back and crossed his legs, smugness overtaking his expression.

"I have seen her spar in the yards. She is magnificent—the best we have." He smiled. "But you shall make no more threats on me. Deliver Brauna to me at once, and I shall lift the decree."

Larka shook her head and spoke through gritted teeth, "I shall do no such thing. Did you not hear me speak of her conception? I shall not give Brauna to a man who tried to breed his own daughter to make more pure the Overseer's bloodline.

"You see, no one would understand why a nonhereditary title needed a pure bloodline. No one would appreciate their right to choose a leader being stolen from them."

Larka decided on a lie then, one which might offer Brauna some protection. "It was fortunate your daughter was already pregnant when you tried to breed her. It was most unfortunate your actions repelled Maja, caused her to flee . . . to walk the path to her death." Not even Flock's closest advisers knew why Maja had run.

"She was not pregnant when I—" The Overseer lowered his head and rubbed his orbits. Red-rimmed eyes then met Larka's. "And your man on the outside also knows the reason my Maja fled?"

"Let me repeat that everything I say, my informant knows."

"Consider the decree rescinded. As to Brauna, I shall hold my tongue regarding her mother's identity, for now, if you shall hold yours regarding . . . other matters." Flock leaned back in his chair, a reflective stance in the eyes he turned upward.

"I give you my word, but if my colleagues begin disappearing . . . Or let me put it this way, if you try to find out who else knows the reasons to Maja's flight, I shall hear of it. Do you understand, Overseer Flock?"

He nodded without looking at her, still staring at the ceiling and appearing once more quite mad.

CHAPTER 33

THE THROWER

*L*arka mulled over Brauna's distraction. The girl chewed her dinner with a lack of zeal, mooning over the food, eyes fixed on the front door.

It had become clear over the last few weeks that Ontar and Lichena had become intimate. Over the past few days in the practice yards, Lichena had purposefully taunted Brauna with the fact.

Brauna had never mentioned Lichena and Ontar's relationship to her mother, and Larka was not certain exactly what to say to her daughter. Other than familial, Larka had little to no experience in the field of love, though a fleeting thought of Guta panged the beat of her heart.

Brauna sighed and poked at the lumps in her bowl of stew.

Larka played with her food, mimicking Brauna, who took note and spooned a portion of stew into her mouth. After that, the young woman quickly finished the bowl's contents then bent her arms across her chest, a reflective look sequestering her expression. She sat in that pose for several minutes, gazing at her mother.

Brows lifted, Larka finally met Brauna's gaze then smiled at her daughter. Brauna's expression did not change. Larka's brow furrowed.

"Da says you are to go camping tonight. I wouldn't mind getting out of Albilar for a few days," Brauna said.

"Oh." Larka nearly spat forth a chunk of potato but forced herself to masticate and swallow. "No, that's not a good idea."

"Why not?" Brauna drummed her fingers impatiently on the table. "I'm certainly old enough. I guess it can't be anything to do with that nutball's decree. Some hot-headed upstart put that bullshit down before it got going. Marched right into the Overseer's quarters this morning and let him have it. I'd certainly like to know what was said there." An admiring smile twisted Brauna's mouth before she carried on,

"Hmm . . . it can't be my age." Brauna cocked her head and slanted her eyes toward the ceiling. "It can't be my lack of training or lack of practice. It can't be that I'm not *big* enough. It can't be that I'll *understand when I'm older.* Can it?" Brauna held Larka's squirming expression, a sardonic glint in her eyes. "No, I guess it's not my age, not anymore, so what is it this time, Mum?"

"This is just-just my time alone, Brina . . . and watch your language." Larka stared into her own partially consumed stew and blinked against the dry weariness that had settled over her eyes.

"Oh, so I'm 'Brina' now, am I? And I mustn't curse. I suppose it *is* my age." Brauna tilted her chair backward, propping on its rear legs. "You know, it seems to me that you spend a lot of time alone when Da and I aren't here."

Larka felt guilt pinch her face as she looked up at her daughter.

"Next time, sweetheart, I promise." After the calamity that had filled most of her day—arguing with Monton about talking to Overseer Flock then arguing with Astla about talking to Overseer Flock, finally talking to Overseer Flock—Larka sounded much lighter in tone than she felt.

"You always say that. I'll tell you, Mum, I don't know what goes on here, but Da says secrets are hard things to hold by yourself. Rumors are circulating."

Larka's heart fluttered. "What rumors?" She spooned stew into her mouth and chewed.

"Bad ones." Brauna dropped her chair to all-fours, slapping the table with open palms. "You and Da never sleep together. One of you is always on the floor when I wake up early, and I'd like to know if you are seeing another man?"

Laughter welled up from Larka's vocal chords, leaving her choking on her dinner. She coughed and sputtered.

Brauna patted her back. "Mum . . . Mum, are you breathing?"

Larka cleared her throat. "Yes, I'm fine," she said then giggled until her eyes watered.

"Stop laughing, Mum. It's not funny," Brauna said, brow fretted.

Larka glanced at Brauna, tried to set her face, to hold her breath, but her lips twitched and tugged themselves upward. She finally snorted, setting off the giggles once more.

Brauna threw her hands into the air. "I give up!" She stood, towering over the round table and her mother.

"No, Brauna! Please sit down. We need to talk about this." Larka patted the table.

Brauna sat, crossed her arms and tapped her foot, mouth twisted in a frown.

Larka took in a deep breath then, all traces of laughter gone, said, "I am not having an affair. If you want to go camping with me, perhaps we can go next week. Is that all right with you?"

Brauna eyed her mother with a depth of suspicion but nodded agreement.

Larka leaned toward Brauna. "Now, I think we should talk about Ontar."

Brauna leapt to her feet. "There's nothing to talk about."

"I think there is, Brauna."

"No, there *is not!*" Brauna reiterated before she stomped off to her room and slammed the door behind her.

Larka steepled her fingers beneath her chin and shook her head.

The swish of the front door opening and closing brought Astla within their home. Anxiety fumed off him like a firebrand. Larka's heart spasmed as he came to the table and sat beside her.

She waited in silence, finally spoke, "What's wrong?"

"You can't go tonight," he stated, meeting her eyes with fervor.

"Why not?" she asked quietly.

"That incident with the man and his wife a few years ago has come back on you. It's just too much risk. The Overseer has newly decreed that Guardsmen be posted along the river each dark moon to watch for anyone helping in those births, essentially to capture you, to capture the woman they are now calling 'the Thrower.'" Astla paused, his eyes boring into her.

"Flock dismissed the retroactive part of the original decree and the culling, but birth papers shall be required of all those newly born from this day forth. And women are still disallowed exit from Albilar during a dark moon, all women, Larka, not just pregnant ones. That includes this dark moon.

"His intentions toward dark moon offspring remain vague, but it seems he wishes to monitor their activities. What he truly does is marks them as what they are; any mishap or unfortunate event will be blamed on them."

The truth sank into Larka little by little. Flock had not deceived the terms of their meeting, but it felt as if he had.

At length, she murmured, "But no culling?"

"Not at the moment, but the man swings on whim." Astla eyed Larka. "I don't suppose you'd like to inform me what was said between you two today?"

Larka shook her head.

Astla's brow quirked. "Didn't think so.

"Larka, Flock's convinced that dark moon magic bespells him at times. He's insane, and that makes things more dangerous for you, not less. Stay home this once. *I am begging you.* Change the pattern of your aid before you are caught."

Larka rose to her feet and gazed down at the gray streaks, which daily became more numerous, in Astla's hair. She would be giving him more of that coloring soon, she feared. She smoothed his shortened, wavy locks and spoke in a low, calm tone,

"I must go, my brother. I feel someone out there who will soon have great need of me."

Larka caught another glimpse of the unknown woman's future. The woman would make a risky abscondence from Albilar through the lightly guarded rear gate—an exit reserved for the Overseer's escape—desolation scribed within the tense folds of her face.

"I won't let you." Astla stood and faced her.

"You will." Larka stared up at him.

Something akin to pain flitted across his face. "Larka, give your own life some value for once." Astla grasped then pressed her left hand between his palms. "Please."

"My life would be valueless if I simply let someone die. You know that, Astla."

Muscle twitched under the skin of his jaw. He nodded.

She swallowed. "I've more to ask of you."

"And what is that, dear sister?"

"Post no guards at the rear gate this night." She squeezed one of the hands surrounding hers. "And tell me which areas along the river I must avoid."

Larka pulled a light cape around her shoulders and dozed in the rocking chair on the hearth until early morning. She awoke and yawned, stretching her arms toward the ceiling then rubbing fingers over groggy eyes.

Astla slept beside her, splayed out on the floor. She shook her head. He should have gone to the bedroom.

With stealth, Larka gathered her bags then strapped her weapons around her trunk under her cape. She buttoned the thick cape shut.

She looked in on Brauna. The young woman lay sprawled on her bed, sleep giving a droop to her mouth. Larka smiled warmly. Few people slept as hard as Brauna, but few worked as hard.

She covered Brauna with a quilt, which had been kicked to the end of the too-short bed. She then pushed tresses of dark ash-brown hair off Brauna's sleeping face, the plumpness there suggesting the child who still played somewhere within the young woman.

Larka bit her lip as memories washed over her—memories of a fluffy-haired toddler, arms raised to be picked up; of a helpless baby cooing happily; of a young child transfixed on fluttering aspen leaves; of a tanned, sleek adolescent. These memories of Brina merged with the sarcastically defiant woman the girl had become, with Brauna.

Tears stung Larka's eyes.

"My little Brina," she whispered, her mouth a crumpled smile. She watched Brauna for long moments, eventually kissing the girl's forehead. "I'll see you again soon."

Once at the door, she took a last look at her daughter then slipped out.

Astla stood before the fireplace. He turned to Larka as she joined him on the hearth, her boots clacking softly across the floor.

He held her, pressing her to him with ferocity.

"Take care," he whispered then released her.

Larka stepped back, peering up at his solemn face. "Keep Lichena away from our child. She's an odd power about her, and I fear she has every desire to use it against Brina."

Astla nodded. "Go. This guard shift ends soon."

Larka picked up her backpack and a basket beside the door.

Astla's weary eyes watched Larka depart into a gaping maw of shadowy air.

Something about Albilar's dark streets spooked Larka. The few lit oil lamps glowing through house windows did little to assuage the darkness. At this time of morning the streets did not seem unusually quiet, but a preternatural chill crept up the back of her neck. She then realized the thrum of crepuscular life absent. No insect chirped. No tree frogs called. Not even a bird twittered in the near-twilight.

She reached the gates too soon, however, to define the familiarity of it all.

Once there, she drew up short. The Guard shift had already changed. Thadus was not at the gate. Instead, she found Ontar leaning against the long table. A lamp sat next to him and several hung off hooks on the gate, releasing light and the stink of burned oil. Ontar smiled at her, all the while ogling her backpack.

"I couldn't sleep," she explained. "I thought I'd gather a few herbs before breakfast." She shifted the herb basket she held from one hand to the other, Ontar's eyes following the movement.

Ontar stretched his arms and yawned before patting his belly. "I've an empty spot for that meal."

He sounded agreeable—too agreeable. She had counted on Thadus being on duty, on his quiet demeanor, on his being off duty soon and not knowing if or when she returned.

"It's all right if I pass? I know as a woman I'm really not allowed—"

"The Captain of the Guard's wife, you are an exception." Ontar smiled, his dark eyes raking over her.

Larka's brows shot upward, and she tried to draw shut her already buttoned cape.

"Thank you," she whispered and made a brisk escape.

She stiffened as the zing of his heated desires struck her, or was it something more? A desire to dominate? She had felt that kind of cruelty but once before, on a cold night that had laid the path for the rest of her life. Larka hastened her steps.

How had a young woman as intelligent as Brauna fallen for a man like that? Larka shuddered. Brauna usually judged character with a crafty caution.

Larka smiled, thinking of Ontar's angry shock when Brauna had finally tired of his game and beat him back with her sword—not gently, not kindly, but with cold brutality. Brauna had then left him standing there humiliated, the other Guardsmen laughing at him. Perhaps the water-bearer's presence had been useful after all; perhaps Larka should even be grateful to Lichena.

Under her air allies' guidance and closer to Albilar than usual, Larka set up camp in a small clearing on a low-grade bank of the river. She gazed at swift waters running over slick rocks, the fishy smell of the river catching in her nose.

Most of the Guard had been sent farther along, closer to her previous campsites. Larka grinned. Having Astla for her brother had its advantages.

Larka folded her cape lengthwise and laid it over the many upright stems of a speckled alder. She built a fire then seated herself. Back to the flames, she drank in the gentle light the rising sun's expert brush painted upon the trees across the river. As the sun peered more and more upon her, its rays licked the forest into surreal grandeur, giving serenity a dwelling within her mind.

"Thrower?" A female voice called behind her.

Larka started. She turned to find the sun's rays glinting like fire off amber hair. Her eyes narrowed.

"Why are you here?"

"Just curious." Lichena approached and seated herself cross-legged before the fire. "You have become somewhat of a legend far and wide." The girl supinated her hands, indicating the world about them.

Larka turned on her haunches to face Lichena. She sensed none of the hate Lichena cast off in Brauna's presence. Larka smiled wanly at the girl but gave no response to Lichena's initial question; the decussating axes strapped to her back had spoken their own words.

"I knew it was you. You're the only woman I know of who can throw so expertly, and you fit the description of the Thrower perfectly."

Larka's lungs refused to inflate. She had to force her next inhalation. How many others might make—or had made—that same deduction?

"Lichena, you should not be here. There are certain dangers for a woman alone, and I would not see you hurt. Actually, I'm surprised Ontar allowed you out."

Lichena's disarming smile spread her full lips. "I've my way with him, and you came here alone, did you not?" Her face became plastered with anger the next moment, and she peered around. "I'm surprised Brauna didn't follow you?"

"*She* respects my wishes." Larka scrutinized her companion. "Does your mother know you are here?"

Lichena's brow crumpled. Her shoulders slumped. "If I had one, she would perhaps know." The girl turned her head aside and peered into the forest.

"I'm so sorry." Larka could think of little else to say. Suddenly, Lichena seemed less the seductress and more the child of her actual years, about the equivalent of Brauna in age.

Lichena turned back to Larka, her entire aspect brightened. "May I stay with you? I could help you in what you do. I've heard about the Guard postings. I think you could use some help."

"The Guardsmen are posted well away from here," Larka said, then muttered, shaking her head, "but at the moment, I suppose I am stuck with you." She inhaled deeply then sighed. "Still, Lichena—"

"Please," Lichena begged. "Please, please, *please.*"

"Alright." Larka half smiled then became grave. "I suppose you heard of the woman who died a few years back, her baby stolen by an ax-wielding mad woman and husband murdered by the same?"

Larka received a prompt nod from Lichena.

"Had I blatantly used dark moon power on them, Guardsmen would have been sent to search the land high and low for me and anyone suspected of being of the dark moon. Astla stayed the Guard that time, saying they would never find me." Larka halted speech, momentarily reflecting on that long night in the woods—on Kara, the Knowing Child, the ratman, his wife—before continuing.

"I interrupted the murder of the woman's child by her husband's hands. I did steal their baby, but I tell you now" —she paused for breath— "when I left, that woman's husband lived. Although I had injured him, her own hands finished him."

Lichena's eyes had grown wide. "Really?" she breathed.

Larka nodded and peered into the fire between them. "I suppose that makes me the Thrower, doesn't it?" She smiled sadly then gazed up at Lichena.

"It's all in the past. The woman killed her husband and died of an infection shortly after being found, but it just shows you how a story can be twisted to make someone look the victim when she is not. That child—she was the victim. She still is.

"Had I blatantly used dark moon power . . ." Larka shuddered. "Imagine the retelling of it with that angle. It would have been like a war cry. Guardsmen, ordinary folk, they would have hunted me from that point on. Persecutions would have risen once more, based on little more than suspicion.

"Lichena, you must promise me you will not use your powers, that you will run if things get dangerous. I will not lose another child." Larka drew in a short breath, a familiar ache squeezing her lungs as she pushed back the abbreviated memory of her firstborn.

Lichena nodded. "I will not do anything unless absolutely necessary," she said adamantly but failed to meet Larka's eyes. "And I will run if I have to."

Larka cocked her head and gazed at Lichena through the squint of her right eye. The young woman had not really promised anything.

"If Master Ling taught me anything, he taught me it's much harder to *not* fight than it is to fight, especially with the weapons you and I possess. It is unfair to those who cannot retaliate with such force."

Larka said firmly, "No dark moon powers, Lichena. I mean it."

Lichena leaned back, muted a grin and nodded, but Larka could still see the grin playing beneath the surface of the girl's features.

"I've one more question to ask of you, Lichena." A mellow smile belied Larka's billowing insides.

Lichena's brows rose with the slightest inclination. She leaned forward again.

"Why did you call me 'Larka' when first we met?"

Lichena sat for a moment in thought, her eyes pocketed in upper corners. She finally sighed and shook her head.

"I don't know. That name just came out . . . like it was just . . . put there."

It was Larka's turn to raise her brows not with indignity or disbelief but with surprise for the truthfulness she recognized in Lichena's words.

CHAPTER 34

THUNDER AND LIGHTNING

arka sat illuminated by her aura, smoky-blue bouts of tiny lightning jolts circulating around her and occasionally striking outward. A gentle breeze lifted her hair, whispering into her ear. A few bites of fish left on it, she placed her tin plate on the ground and stood to peer into the forest.

Bathed in her own bright white aura, Lichena lifted her head to follow Larka's rise.

Larka peered down at the girl. "It is time."

Lichena set her fish aside.

Another breeze wisped around Larka as she scanned the area. Gooseflesh prickled down her scalp and on to her neck, tingling through her arms.

The scan had snared on something rotten. "Dear gods, what horror stalks this woman?"

"What?" Lichena turned toward the woods.

Larka grasped Lichena's arm and dragged the girl along at a run. Lichena scrambled behind Larka, their auras throwing against the trees, forcing out patches of elongate shadows as they ran.

Larka halted abruptly, and Lichena would have collided with her had Larka not stepped aside and grabbed the younger woman to arrest her movement.

"Lark, what is it?" Lichena clung to Larka's arm.

"Look." Larka pointed. Her heart quaked with repulsion, fear, rage. Fresh-made tracks glared up at her from the forest floor, delineated by a misty swirl of dark moon aura. The same disquiet she had felt before leaving Albilar settled over Larka, her mind at last defining its familiarity.

"It was there, near the gates," she breathed. "It was waiting. Almost like it knew—" Anguish dug into Larka's throat. "I lost my firstborn to that thing." She closed her eyes and whispered, "Gods, but it was quiet then too."

Larka looked at Lichena. "I saw tracks like that the night I gave birth to my first daughter. We had escaped the villagers. I thought we were safe. I thought *they* would be safe, my mother and child. I left my baby with my mother, *and when I returned . . .*" A frantic note rang in her voice.

Larka closed her eyes and breathed, chest heaving wide. When she opened her eyes several seconds later, it was to Lichena's concerned visage. She took in another breath then continued in a more level tone,

"When I returned, I found my baby gone and my mother's chest gushed with her heart's blood . . . her blood in those tracks." Larka clamped her jaws on her emotions then lifted her head. The animal's prints crept into the darkness before them.

Lichena rested a hand on Larka's shoulder. "I'm sorry."

A woman shrieked—a prolonged, gut-wrenching sound. Larka bolted toward the source, cursing herself for having become so lost in the past. In less than a minute, she reached the scene and drew up, Lichena right behind her.

Not fifteen paces before her, red eyes glared into the night. Outlined by a flaring brownish aura, an enormous bear stood over a woman, its mouth over hers. A path of luminous mist traveled between the two mouths. That path faded into tresses of luminosity then slender tendrils until it waned into the shadows. The bear then snapped its jaws shut. The woman slumped.

"That thing just sucked the soul out of her," Lichena said, eyes locked on the scene.

A small body next to the woman stirred and wailed.

Larka shot forward, hands raised. Wind whipped about her while blue-gray energy rushed in a wave from every deviant point of her body to spew from the palm of her right then left hand and strike the bear in succession. The monster swayed—losing its brownish glow, losing the red-lit eyes—and then crashed onto the forest floor beside its victim. The smell of singed hair and flesh drifted on vapors of smoke.

Larka reached the soulless woman's side and nabbed the crying newborn.

Lichena yelled, "It lives yet! It's aura is back!"

The bear rebounded to all-fours and swiped halfheartedly in Larka's direction. Larka felt the gliding air coalesce and catch the great paw before its claws could rake her. She raised her free arm and hit the bear with another bolt of lightning. A high impact wind then slammed audibly into it, lifting the beast and sending it crashing through the woods. A conclusion to its flight—the monster thudded into a tree and fell to the ground. Its aura dimmed but did not disappear.

The bear lifted its head and gazed at Larka, eyes once more aglow.

Larka stared, mouth agape, at the red-eyed monster.

Lichena shifted behind her, and a shot of whiteness flashed by Larka, followed by a severe cold. Vision swayed. Legs failed. Larka collapsed to her knees, aware of little other than her desperate hold on the mewling baby.

Her eyes cast forward to the bear. Through the blur of her vision, she interpreted a glow of gray swirl around its form but then the blur gave way to focus. Ice encircled the prone beast, and the white aura surrounding Lichena reflected off its glassy surface—nothing more. Larka's own aura had vanished—just as drained as the rest of her.

"Come on." Lichena's hands plunged beneath Larka's arms. "I can't kill that thing for some reason. It still lives beneath there."

Larka's teeth chattered. "You . . . are . . . of . . . ice."

Lichena nodded, grimacing.

As they fled, they heard the ice shattering behind them, but the bear gave no pursuit. It lumbered off through the woods in the opposite direction.

Larka staggered back toward the campsite with Lichena's gentle yet sturdy support. Larka's teeth continued to rattle against each other, the only sound she heard other than their slow retreat through the forest.

"Take . . . the baby," Larka said with difficulty. She could barely lift her numb arms to hand the newborn over.

Lichena plucked the infant from her. Larka wobbled within those few seconds without an arm beneath her until Lichena re-established that support. Nothing more than fear prevented Larka's legs from giving way until they reached the campsite. Once there, she wilted before the fire, teeth chattering with a maddening beat on this warm summer night.

Lichena added fuel to the fire and stoked it. "I am sorry I hit you with the cold, Larka—Lark. I just didn't know what else to do. It seemed that thing would have stood again had I not done something while it was still weak."

"I'm fi-fi-fine," Larka managed to say, hands stretched over the fire. "At least . . . you did not hit . . . the baby."

Lichena gasped. Her free hand shot to her mouth. "I did not think of the baby. I was stupid." Lichena's great, stricken eyes gazed at length upon the baby in her arms until she plopped before the fire.

"You . . . were brave, n-not stupid. Bad range of aim." Larka smiled and tried to steady her voice but could still hear a tremor in her next words. "You need practice, but you did well."

Lichena beamed and shyly appraised the rocky ground between herself and the fire.

"Will you help me practice?" She peered up at Larka.

A bit of warmth crept into Larka as the flames jumped higher.

"Of course. On a weekend day but not with Brauna. I haven't practiced with her since she was five. She doesn't know who or what I am."

"I should hope not. She's just self-righteous enough to turn you in."

Larka appraised the sudden difference in Lichena—the angry sneer, the bristled posture.

"You really don't like Brauna. Do you?"

Lichena's lips smashed into a thin line before she answered, "She doesn't like me. She's called me a gypsy whore since the moment I arrived. I saw her point at us and call us 'gypsy whores.' She said it even before I started my duties as water bearer." Lichena stopped speaking and stared into the fire.

"That doesn't sound like Brauna. She's generally very defensive of women and their plight. If you could see her work at the shelter, the things she says and does for the women and children—pretty miraculous," Larka responded, her cold-stunned brain stimulated into contemplation. "Perhaps you two should speak to each other about it. Antagonizing each other as you do seems a great waste of energy." Larka leaned sideward and scooped a blanket out of her pack then draped it around her shoulders.

Lichena nodded, her expression unconvinced.

Larka gestured toward a speckled alder and the garment suspended on it. "If you get cold, put my cape on."

"Thanks, but I'm fine." Lichena thought for a moment then asked, "Was your first daughter born under a dark moon? You said you thought you were safe from the villagers. I assume they were after you because you were birthing beneath a dark moon." The girl added another handful of sticks to the fire.

"Yes." Larka nodded with abrupt contention. "But Brauna knows nothing of that child! Tell her nothing!" Her aura returned almost full force, and storm clouds seemed to dance in her eyes. Lightning gashed the darkness above them.

Lichena gaped up at the starlit sky then back at Larka.

"I suppose we all have our touchy subjects."

CHAPTER 35

AFTERMATH

*L*arka doubted the bear would trouble them again that night, but she insisted on holding watches, for the quiet had deepened as the night had paced on. Apparently, that thing lurked out there too near, and her allies had once again given her no warning of it. Had she not scanned the area, she'd not have known of its presence earlier.

Larka shuddered and added a few more sticks to the fire. She had taken the first watch. She had known her mind would disallow sleep, regardless of the silence orating through the forest. Her brain was too eager to assess the night's events and what that demonic bear— not a big cat—had done to the unknown woman.

The implications that monster's actions held for her mother's death and her blood daughter's absence began to repeatedly slam through Larka.

It seemed the past had opened its pitch-black maw and now groaned around her, seeping through her weakened mind, awakening in this night a coldness just as soulless and lost as the bear's victims.

Larka's shoulders began to shake, a tremor that eventually consumed the whole of her, a weeping so deep its unearthing unleashed lightning to slash into the forest.

Like tentacles feeling for prey, it fell from the sky, searching one large block of space then moving on to another.

Horrified but awed, Larka watched, the lights reflecting in bluish tones off her pale skin. Then she began to shake her head.

"Stop," she whispered and reached toward the sky. "Before someone is hurt."

The lightning withdrew into the belly of a cloud, leaving in its wake a guttural thunder and the smell of oncoming rain, not the odor of singed trees as Larka had expected. It was then that she realized she had not heard the lightning strike anything. It had simply searched with silent precision.

Larka slouched into herself, feeling colder, weaker, much unwell. For the second time this night, her aura had faded altogether.

Larka shivered, eyeing Lichena's slumbering form. The cold that had surged into the bear should have killed it, judging by the effects a brush of it had given her. Lichena had unleashed a great and untamed power. Larka felt lucky to have survived it.

She pulled her blanket more tightly around her shoulders and huddled closer to the fire, her mind drifting closer to home. Lichena's story about Brauna calling the girl a "gypsy whore" sounded truthful, unflinchingly so. And the great gods knew Brauna's tongue to be a whip, but saying such a thing to a stranger, in snap judgment—it just didn't fit the Brauna she knew. However, being raised by men had, if anything, enhanced Brauna's blunt nature, and the Guardsmen were known to call gypsy women "whores." These women acted with a freedom to which the men were unaccustomed, yet the men still went to them. . . .

Sounds emanated within the shadow-ensconced forest. Larka tensed, straining to see beyond the tree trunks, aided none by the fire's vague ring of light; Lichena's aura helped little either, having faded greatly since the girl fell asleep. Something shuffled long-dead leaves and twigs underfoot. Larka reached over her shoulder for an ax.

A skunk sauntered into view, sniffing at the air. It skidded back into the darkness upon spotting Larka, leaving a puff of its musk behind.

Larka relaxed and pulled her blanket more tightly about her. She attempted a scan of the area and felt nothing, but her sensory perceptions had cast without much radius since Lichena's ill-aimed burst had hit her. After the search lightning, her perceptions appeared to have further contracted. She could no longer sense the bear, but the disquiet in the forest marked its presence—Larka was certain of that.

Lichena mumbled in her sleep.

Larka gazed over the fire at her companion. The girl lay on her side with the rescued baby snuggled against her, her dress gaping open, exposing the sparse mounds of her breasts.

Larka allowed her vision to linger on the girl's skinny frame. Her eyes registered something that took her weary brain a bit longer to recognize: an odd mark lay between the girl's breasts. Larka leaned forward to get a better look and nearly fell into the fire. She steadied herself then shook her head and rose to her feet to carefully skirt the fire's flames. She soon knelt on one knee beside Lichena.

Larka squinted at the mark. She held a hand over the area, wobbled and fell back, then rebalanced herself by tucking her heels beneath her buttocks, things clicking into place within her mind as she did.

It was a scar! A jagged scar emerged from between Lichena's breasts and ran downward beneath the material of the girl's dress.

The scar began to pulse with an amber glow beneath the sheer material, running nearly to the girl's navel. Larka reached with her forefinger and traced the length of it, her touch remaining on its terminus. Before she could lift her finger, an image formed in Larka's mind—that of a blood-spattered newborn squirming under a bear's prying claw, a river screaming in the background, a familiar lament echoing through the background. Larka jerked her hand away. The image snapped shut.

She stared at the sleeping girl for a time long and long.

"No," Larka whispered, head shaking. "It cannot be. Dear gods, it cannot be!"

She fell forward and her forehead pressed into the rocky earth. Her eyes squeezed shut, head still shaking.

An abrupt hush then fell over Larka. Her eyes flew open. Teeth gnashed, she surged upright and tossed her head back to wail at the dark moon.

Cold hands shook Larka awake.

"The sun's coming up." An oval face framed by straight, amber hair hovered over her.

"Oh," Larka groaned. She found herself on her knees, head pressed into the earth. She raised herself and torqued her creaking neck to see that her blanket and axes lay on the other side of the fire.

Lichena assessed Larka with a look of deep concern. "I awoke and you were screaming above me. Then, you just fell forward. I couldn't move you no matter how I tried. I took your axes off, so you couldn't fall on them."

"I was screaming?" Larka rubbed the rough impressions on her forehead.

Recollection trickled into her. It seemed her air allies did their best to allay her thoughts, but Larka reeled in her memories with a tenaciously hooked lure and pushed her allies away. Then recollection poured into her. Her head snapped upward, eyes fixed on Lichena.

Larka jumped to her feet. She grabbed Lichena's shoulders to stare down the girl's dress, yet no mark met her; Larka found nothing there except freckled, pale skin.

"You are acting very . . . strange, Lark. I think you caught more cold than we first thought." Lichena rested a palm against Larka's forehead.

Larka blushed and wrenched backward.

"I . . . I'm sorry. I didn't mean to be . . . inappropriate, and I'm fine," Larka asserted. "I must have been sleepwalking, dreaming last night."

Larka swayed on her feet, and Lichena assisted in seating her on the flat ground near the fire before picking up Larka's discarded blanket and wrapping it around the older woman's shoulders. Lichena then inserted a mug of hot tea between Larka's palms.

The smell of beans cooking caught Larka's attention. She glanced at the pot over the fire and sipped her tea, stomach gurgling. Lichena soon set a plate of food before Larka.

While Lichena fussed about the campsite, the newborn in tow, Larka ate beans and a crust of bread with a slice of cheese. Warmth crept through her body.

Larka set her empty plate aside and held her arms out. "Let me see that baby."

Lichena grinned and kissed the infant's forehead before passing her to Larka.

Larka smiled at the sleeping face peeking out of a blanket.

"Has she eaten this morning?"

"Uh-huh, the goat milk you brought," Lichena replied around a mouthful of something. The clatter of utensil against plate assured Larka of the girl's activity.

Larka looked up and nearly laughed at the girl's zealous consumption of breakfast, as if she had never eaten.

Larka then recalled her own hunger at Gilly's hands, and her expression drooped. The girl's reedy body and tattered dress attested to lack of nourishment. People of the Wheel were notoriously poor.

Larka dropped her eyes from Lichena to the baby then pushed the blanket off the infant's head. Breath caught in Larka's throat. She ran her fingers slowly over the babe's soft amber down. She closed her eyes and gritted her teeth, re-interring visions of her own cooing amber-haired babe into the overused graveyard of her mind.

Larka opened her eyes to find the babe in her arms still asleep.

"She's got your hair." The thought leapt out of her.

"She does?" Lichena perked up, glancing at the infant. "That poor baby," she said and turned, searching the woods. "I must make a quick trip. I have to go." She jumped up and ran off, disappearing behind a hill in the forest.

An amused smile spread the thin planes of Larka's face.

"She's a good person unless you mention Brauna," she whispered to the sleeping baby then situated the child on a blanket.

Larka had begun to wash dishes in the shallows of the river when she heard the crunch of footsteps behind her and an odd sound, as if something dragged the ground.

Hair pricking from neck to scalp, she stood and turned. The tin plate in her hand fell and clanged on the stone below her.

"No," she rasped.

The Amber Man stood there, towering over the baby, his hand tangled in the back of Lichena's dress. Faceup, the girl dangled unconscious below him. He released his grasp, and Lichena's upper body fell into a flaccid heap, her head thumping against the rocky ground.

CHAPTER 36

ATTEMPTS

"What did you do to her?" Larka's voice thundered.

The Amber Man glanced at Lichena's inert body then back at Larka.

"Just a whack in the head. She'll come around soon." A smile spread his face, and he stepped toward Larka.

She retreated one step, and water swirled smoothly about her boot. Behind her, the river thrummed over the rocks, beckoning. She snapped her leg out.

The Amber Man laughed, taking the long strides his height dictated.

Larka raised her palms and would have struck him with lightning but for his speed and a surprising alacrity for a man so thickened with muscle. He ducked before the energy discharged from her hands. It struck near Lichena and the baby, shattering earth and sending up a plume of rocks and dust, which landed on the two unconscious forms.

Larka glanced at her palms, lowered them. The Amber Man caught her wrists in one big hand. He drew her against him until her face nearly pressed into his chest.

Larka simultaneously wrenched her arms and hips in trying to free herself. The Amber Man clenched her harder. Wind bashed into him. He laughed and steadied himself, his other hand probing at her shirt buttons.

Larka screamed, head-butted his chest, stomped the instep of his left foot, but his hands never stopped their actions.

Her rescue was heard before it was seen: Astla's charge pounded over the rocks like a hoofed beast. The Amber Man lifted his head and turned. He thrust Larka toward the river and moved to meet his attacker. Before she tumbled backward, Larka noted Brauna kneeling beside Lichena. The injured girl's head lifted feebly, her lips moving.

On impact, water splashed up around Larka's buttocks. Seconds later, Astla bellowed. And, even over the river's call, Larka heard a sword lisp angrily out of its sheath.

Larka scrabbled to her feet, slipped on algae-coated rocks. As she caught herself, hands behind her, she saw Astla swing his sword at the Amber Man in a wide, over-arcing maneuver. Astla's opponent smirked and moved to catch the Guardsman's wrist. Bones' shattering reverberated through the air.

"Astla!" Larka screamed then recalculated her efforts in fighting the clinging river. She crept forward on all-fours, picking her way through the rocky water as the Amber Man's fist slammed into Astla's face once then again.

A shriek echoed through the woods. Larka looked up to see Brauna vault toward Astla as the Amber Man kicked the now prone captain's ribs.

Larka's hands and knees finally touched shore. She tucked her feet beneath her and rose to full height. Her arm drew up over her shoulder, hand seeking a throwing ax. Yet her weapons lay there— near Lichena and the baby.

The Amber Man moved to meet Brauna's approach. He hooked a punch at her. Brauna deflected it with a sweep of her arm so powerful it threw him off balance. Shock registered on the Amber Man's face just before Brauna's other hand banged into his jaw, slinging a spray of blood onto rocky soil.

Doing something she had so often been told not to, Brauna backed off the Amber Man to ascertain his injuries. Teeth gnashed, he plunged his fist toward the center of her face. Brauna upper-blocked and landed a hard punch to his solar plexus then slammed a knee into his gut, lifting him off the ground.

Wide-eyed, the Amber Man landed on his feet to crash forward to his knees. Brauna leapt back. Before he could straighten his spine, her right hand caught around the Amber Man's throat. The warrioress then lifted that immense man off the ground.

"Sweet earth," Larka gasped and stood there entranced by the cold calculation on Brauna's face. Then, it became obvious to her—the olive aura enveloping Brauna, almost an extension of her daughter's smooth, olivaceous skin. Brauna's dark moon powers blended so naturally with her own strength the girl did not realize she used them.

The Amber Man kicked desperately at Brauna as the bones and cartilage of his throat began to give. Brauna simply dropped the man. He landed on his feet, and it appeared he would have fled, but Brauna's fists pitched into his left then right jaw. He staggered and plummeted.

Between Larka and the fray, Astla remained where he had fallen. His groan called her attention, and Larka darted toward him. Once there, she traced over the blood trails on his face.

"You sacrifice too much, my brother," she murmured.

A movement of pale material caught in Larka's peripheral vision. She raised her head to discover Lichena walking slowly, face stoic, dress swaying about her. The girl passed Brauna, laying a hand on the tall warrior woman's back. Brauna froze in place, white lights sparking around her own yellow-green aura.

As the Amber Man regained his footing, Lichena laid her hand against his chest, and sparks of gray shot into him—the same gray swirl Larka had seen on the bear and mistakenly dismissed the night before. The Amber Man, too, became paralyzed under Lichena's assault.

Wind whispered into Larka's mind, and her lungs suspended function. More than mere cold had grazed her last night. Lichena's powers originated from more than one source, the other source being much more sinister, the other source being death.

Larka's gaze whipped to Brauna. No gray-death swirled around the frozen warrioress. Relief deflated Larka's lungs.

In a last struggle to live, the Amber Man broke the contact between Lichena's palm and his chest. With what seemed like hesitation, he backhanded the girl. She staggered backward, tripped over an upshot of stone. As the young woman's fall would have thwacked her against rock, Larka sent a swift cushion of air to catch and ease her down.

The Amber Man took one last look at Larka and fled, gray energy pulsating around his chest. However, even that pulsating energy disappeared as he ran . . . as if he simply absorbed it.

After a reassuring touch to Astla's head, Larka left him to advance on Brauna's and Lichena's positions. She slowed as she neared Brauna then stopped and cried out. Flecks of gray power circulated within the cold white that had captured her daughter.

Larka held her finger just above that energy. A power like ice shot through her hand. She jerked her arm back, the hand momentarily numbed. Recovering, she lifted her hands and began to make a request of her air allies. The bits of death ray, however, fizzled with each circuit they made, Brauna's aura quelling them to give rise to itself.

Brauna's body jerked. She blinked wide eyes, shook her head to clear her stupor, then pounced toward Lichena, who remained prone on the ground.

"What did you do to me?" Brauna bellowed. A sneer on her lips, she leaned down and grasped Lichena's dress front.

Larka moved to seize Brauna's hand. Their eyes met and Larka shook her head.

"Look after Astla. We've had enough bloodshed today." Larka knelt beside Lichena.

Brauna retracted her position, earth-brown eyes the narrowest of slits as they traveled down her mother's torso.

"At least cover yourself." Those words spoken, Brauna strode toward Astla.

Larka glanced in the direction Brauna's vision had traveled. Her shirt front had been opened with the exception of the two bottom buttons. Her fingers trembled, fumbling over buttons as she refastened them.

Larka then redirected her attention to Lichena. "How badly hurt are you? Did he . . ." Larka grimaced. "Did he force himself on you?"

"No," Lichena responded, staring up at the sky. "My head hurts."

"Your head's been struck several times." Larka hesitated, drawing in breath before letting it go in a long exhale. "Lichena, I must ask you. Did you try to kill Brauna when you bespelled her?"

"No" came the brusque reply, Lichena's eyes still not meeting Larka's.

Larka stiffened, perused the girl's face for several seconds then whispered,

"I hope that's true."

CHAPTER 37

FAMILY AFFAIR I

Brauna rested back against her heels, eyes dancing nervously over Astla's wounded body then moving up to her mother's face.

Larka examined the wrapped splint around Astla's wrist.

"You did well in attending him, Brauna," she assured and plied her fingers along Astla's rib cage, moving from left to right side.

"One of his ribs is broken."

Guilt flitted across Brauna's face. "I should have stopped it sooner. I thought he could handle one man." She glared over Astla's waist at Lichena where the girl sat cross-legged beside Larka. "If it weren't for you . . ."

Lichena glared back at Brauna. "He'll be fine and don't blame me for a lack of good judgment. Most people know better than to tangle with the Amber Man."

"Lack of good judgment! How ironic—," Brauna yelled then paused and straightened. "That was the Amber Man?"

Then she erupted again, "Well, I didn't know who he was!" She smirked. "You sure seemed to have tangled with him alone and got your butt kicked real good while you were at it."

"I was taking a squat in the woods," Lichena exclaimed. "I, at least, didn't know the biggest man on Earth was there until he whomped me in the head." She effected a smug smile. "Of course, he's not much bigger than you, but I'd bet he's not as dumb."

"You little bitch!" Brauna's hand shot across Astla.

"Girls!" Larka admonished, brushing aside Brauna's attack. "Stop this bickering at once! None of us could foretell what happened. It just did, and none of this blame you two are pitching about will change anything."

"I wouldn't be so sure of that!" Brauna glowered, if possible, more heatedly at Lichena.

Astla's eyes opened slowly. "Fine greetings to you all as well." He smiled and flinched. "Ouch, my face hurts."

The three women stared at him.

Larka's mouth compressed into a thin line. She shifted her gaze to note Brauna's fretted brow and Lichena's meek smile.

"It's good to see you back." She clasped her brother's hand. "I believe you'll live, with a few stitches and some bandaging."

"Much more of that beating and he wouldn't," Lichena mumbled, sliding palms over her knees to smooth the wrinkles of her dress, vision primly placed on the backs of her hands.

Brauna's nostrils flared. Her top and bottom incisors clamped together, upper lip curled back. When she finally spoke, anger chopped into her words.

"Astla . . . and I . . . would not . . . be here . . . had you not followed Mum and told everyone," Brauna paused to breathe, "in Albilar *why*. We had to make sure your big mouth did not get her killed." Brauna stood abruptly and stomped off toward the river, muttering under her breath.

Larka eyed Lichena. The Wheel child's lips parted. Her neck reddened and curved forward so that she peered at the strip of granite soil between her and Astla.

"I told but Ontar," Lichena said and peered up at Larka, a plea in the girl's pale, amber eyes.

"Told Ontar what?"

"He—," Astla gasped as Larka set his rib. "He told a tavern full of men how much the water bearer panted after him. As he got progressively drunker, he told them of Lichena's guess work on who the Thrower might be. I'll be ever grateful for Thadus's warning on Larka's behalf."

Larka tore a strip off her sleeping blanket—already ill-used for the wrist splint—with a bit more strength than necessary, preparing to wrap Astla's ribs. She should have warned any and all women Ontar was no good, but she had sat back and said nothing to either Brauna or Lichena.

"That jerk!" Lichena blared, causing Larka to glance up at her. Lichena refused to let go the meeting of their eyes. "I am truly sorry, Larka. Please forgive me."

"My name is Lark." Larka peered down, ripped another strip off the blanket.

"Please," Lichena said hoarsely.

Larka winced. Her mind flashed back to Pentheya's high voice begging for forgiveness while Larka had remained with her back to the child, doing nothing more than staring at goat hair in a crumbling plaster wall—her final encounter with Pentheya. Larka bit her bottom lip.

Astla grunted as Larka began to wrap his rib cage, though she did so with care.

"Lark, please," Lichena called to her.

Larka's mind whirred. At Lichena's sharp inhale, she looked up. The girl's lips had begun to tremble and tears brimmed in her eyes.

Larka shook her head. "Next time you wish to impress someone, Lichena, think about what you are telling them and the possible effects such shared knowledge might have on them and others."

An outcry banged into the air.

"The baby," Lichena said then mumbled, "I am sorry," before running to the squalling infant.

Larka finished wrapping Astla's torso then proceeded to poke and prod him until he said,

"You forgot my little toe."

Larka smiled ruefully.

Astla touched her shoulder. "We can't go back to Albilar, you know. Overseer Flock will surely have heard the rumors by now, if Ontar did not tell the man himself."

Larka ran a finger over Astla's swollen cheek. "He's already told

Flock, I assure you. Ontar was on guard duty when I left, a full hour before the new shift began. His being there was no coincidence.

"I suspect the man took his chance at advancement and let Flock know who I was at some time before I left, sometime yesterday." Larka shook her head. "It must have been after I'd confronted Flock on the decree. I'd have been arrested then had the madman even an inkling of my identity." She sighed.

"Flock—he can quiet me now with the law and will of the people behind him, even the Guard. My threats would be nothing, no more than gossip, a prisoner blowing smoke. And he would have Brauna."

"Brauna?"

Larka studied Astla's puzzled face. "I'll tell you all, soon enough." She drew away from her brother and stood up, turning her back to him.

"Astla, your men would vouch for you, you and Brauna. You could return, take care of each other."

She heard Astla stir and turned to see his body jerk as he tried to sit up.

"I think not," he grunted then sagged against the rocky ground. "It goes too deep. Besides, I can't leave you by yourself. Who knows what you would get into?"

Despite herself, the corners of Larka's lips tugged upward, producing a tremulous smile. Tears trickled down her face. She didn't bother to wipe them away.

"Astla, your career, all that you have built since you were but a child—"

"Had you not come along when you did, I would have returned to Jaunty to find you and Mother." He managed to push himself upright then rubbed the nape of his neck and gazed out over the river.

"But—"

"You will not change my mind!" He desisted rubbing his neck to give her a hard look. "We will be fine, Larka. Things will work out right for us."

He paused, cocked an eyebrow at her, began to speak, stopped himself then had another go. "Was that fellow truly the Amber Man?"

Larka responded with a grim nod.

"I might have lasted longer had I not lost my temper. When I saw what he was doing—"

"Let it go, Astla, please."

They moved camp. With a little effort to obscure that she did so, Larka sent her air allies to cover their trail, hoping to throw anyone who might pursue them off the mark. They moved steadily away from Albilar until sunset, avoiding the areas where soldiers might loiter, though Astla had sent orders before leaving Albilar. The Guardsmen were supposed to have returned to the city at sunup to report to Monton.

Brauna flung a line into the river a good distance ahead of where Larka and Astla propped beside each other on a fallen tree, its surface nearly debarked by time. Larka pushed a long stick through the fire before her, readying hot coals for the fish Brauna was catching for dinner.

"You need to talk to her," Astla said. "Tell her everything."

Larka could not look at her brother. There was more to tell than even he knew.

"I can't," she declared. "She'll hate me."

"She won't hate you, Larka." She peered up at her brother as he spoke, "She loves you. She's a smart girl. She already knew you'd been keeping something from her all these years, but she doesn't understand why you didn't tell her you were the Thrower. She thought your cause noble when I told her why I had to come find you. She insisted on coming with me, not that I would have left without her."

"She's still angry with me. She's not spoken to me all day," Larka said and gazed back down at her toes.

"It's not you. It's Lichena she's angry with. And she's a little upset because we can't go home. You know how Brauna is. She cannot speak to you now or she might take that anger out on you."

Larka leaned her head against his shoulder, peering at Brauna, who stood highlighted by the sunset.

"She at least spoke to you today."

"If you call a grunt here and there speaking." He chuckled.

Larka smiled.

Lichena emerged from the woods south of Brauna. Larka sat up, watching the young woman approach and stand next to the fishing warrior.

Lichena stood on tiptoes and leaned toward Brauna, lips moving in unheard syllables. Even from this distance, Larka could see Brauna's lax body snap rigid. Larka pushed off the log, ready to stop any harm from this interchange. Then she realized Brauna had not moved to strike but keenly observed the squirming newborn in Lichena's arms. If not for that baby, things might have gotten ugly.

Brauna threw a string of fish at Larka and Astla a few minutes later then stalked into the woods, not reappearing until well after dinner had been cooked.

Upon Brauna's return, Larka offered the terse warrior a fish wrapped in scorched maple leaves. Brauna accepted, sat on a raised chunk of granite and unrolled her cold dinner.

"Brauna, I need to talk to you."

Brauna's glower competed with her grunt for the highest level of contempt displayed.

Larka turned to Astla. He held up his hands and shrugged.

Larka scanned Lichena, who sat before the fire, back to the river, and found nothing of depth there except the usual discord that brewed within the girl when Brauna was present.

"Is there something either of you need to tell me?" Larka looked to Lichena then Brauna.

Lichena's upper lip lifted fine wrinkles into the skin of her nose, and her eyes rolled with adolescent rebellion. Brauna stuffed her mouth with flakes of fish flesh and refused to look at her mother.

Tension needled between Larka's shoulder blades. The makings of a headache shot up her neck. She let go a long sigh and readied a sleeping spot for herself then sat parallel to the river, the soles of her socked feet facing the fire.

Larka spoke in measured hues to Lichena, "Astla has first watch. I have second. You and Brauna can argue about who goes after that.

"I assume Brauna heard that." Larka glanced at her daughter.

"Humph," Brauna acknowledged.

A low noise in Astla's throat told Larka he was laughing or trying not to. She glared at him, lay down, and yanked a blanket over her head.

Larka's watch passed and ended when she had to fetch Brauna out of the woods to replace her on the fallen tree.

Larka lay down and found it hard to sleep next to Astla, both of them under one blanket. She rolled over several times and once found Brauna throwing an unrestrained glower in her direction. At that point, Brauna slapped at something—perhaps a mosquito—on her bare forearm then turned her head, an eerie play of firelight demonstrating the depth and breadth of the warrior's muscled arms.

Larka watched the girl for a short span of time then shut her eyes, her head finally swimming with sleep. A sound like a muffled cough awakened her not long afterward. Larka opened her eyes to see Brauna's face sunk into her hands. A quiet suffering rippled through the warrior's body.

Astla placed a staying hand on Larka as she moved to get up then whispered into her ear,

"Let her be. She'd never forgive herself if someone saw her like that."

CHAPTER 38

FAMILY AFFAIR II

*L*arka's weary mind drifted over so many occurrences in her life as she slept that the sounds at first did not disturb her. She assimilated the rummagings into her subconscious, into her dreams. A sharp intake of breath from so close to her head, however, brought her out of that realm.

A musky smell invaded her nostrils, and she groggily noted a dark blur hanging over Astla. A misty glow flowed from her brother into that looming shadow then ceased. Astla's body slumped to the ground. Eyes that burned red in the darkness flashed to her.

Larka's mind snapped with clarity. She shoved herself upright, screaming,

"Astla!"

Larka raised her hands, energy crackling about them. The red eyes swung out of sight as the beast began a retreat. She shrieked, blasting the electric surge into the beast.

The bear emitted a bray-like bawl upon impact then exploded into a race toward the river, its injury coruscating through the dark woods.

Larka sought along the ground beside her and whipped forth a throwing ax. She heard it thump into its target.

She barely noticed Brauna jump up from her bedroll as the bear crashed through the forest. Its bright streak evaporated into the dark night as a splash announced the animal in the river.

"Was there a lightning storm?" Blinking back sleep, Brauna pivoted clumsily about in a crouched, defensive posture.

Larka's aura leapt angrily about her while her air allies stole back along the river, slashing through tree and branch to reach her. She cradled Astla's body in her arms, her cheek against his warm forehead. *Death Song* hummed forth from vocal cords long unused for its purpose—a lament enhanced and once more spread by the wind.

Brauna stared wide-eyed at Larka's blazing aura then yelled over the singing,

"Mum, what is wrong with you?" Brauna's vision then dropped to Astla's limp form. The warrior froze.

The dead fire between her and the fallen log, Lichena lifted her head and straightened her hunched spine, Larka's cape slipping off her.

"Who sings *Death Song?*" Lichena asked and marked Brauna's fixed gaze then followed it to where Larka sat rocking Astla's body. The girl leapt to her feet. "Gods! What happened?"

Brauna shook her head and went to her parents. "I don't know."

She had to yell over Larka's singing, "Mum, please . . . is Da . . . Sweet earth, he can't be . . ."

Larka quieted and stared through Brauna. Seconds later, Larka retreated from self-pity to force her regurgitation into reality. She focused her gaze on the traumatized face of the young warrior who stood above her.

Hoarse words emitted from her vocal chords. "He's gone, Brauna. It was the bear."

Larka closed Astla's sightless eyes. "You sacrifice too much, my brother," she intonated quietly—but not quietly enough.

Brauna's mouth fell open. Bewilderment set her brow. She whipped her head toward Lichena. Something akin to a smirk adorned the Wheel girl's lips while an indignant cry escaped the warrioress.

"Brauna," Larka called, her aura settling. The rousing light of day then lent them clarity by which to see.

Brauna dropped her hands to her sides and locked fierce eyes on Lichena. The skinny girl slunk away as Brauna stepped toward her, yet the warrioress tripped over Astla's motionless legs then caught her balance and stopped to stare down at the man who had claimed to be her father with blind madness until it crumpled into grief.

"Da?" Brauna bent to touch Astla then backed away, shaking her head.

Brauna's body then snapped rigid and her head jerked up, her eyes locking once more on Lichena.

"You! You fell asleep on watch, didn't you?" Brauna launched at Lichena and shoved the girl's shoulder, causing her to rock backward and nearly fall.

"Didn't you?" Brauna shouted and shoved the girl again.

Lichena fell sideways and caught herself on her knees, rocks scattering beneath her. Lichena's right arm jerked up, the forefinger pointing at Brauna's chest.

Larka's eyes widened. Gray death shined within Lichena's aura and pumped down her outstretched limb, arming that one slender finger. Larka's own hand shot to an object by her side. She flung the hard matter and hit her mark.

"Ow." Lichena's hand drew to her mouth. She sucked a trickle of blood from the forefinger's middle knuckle and got to her feet.

Larka stood as well, wiping her cheeks on her shirt sleeve as she reprimanded the girl.

"I won't use a rock if ever I see you do that again, Lichena."

"It wasn't what you think. I didn't mean to—"

Brauna snorted, shaking her head. "You never mean to do anything, do you? You wheeled, nomad filth! You've been nothing but trouble since you first appeared, and now my Da is dead because of you . . . *you and your big mouth.*" Brauna stepped toward Lichena.

Lichena began to shift away. "I was so tired and my head hurt so. I'm sorry. I just thought if I closed my eyes for a few seconds . . ."

Larka noted the sun licking the sky with a warm color scheme as it peeked over the trees across the river, falling on Brauna's back, on Lichena's front, and outlining the disparity between the girths and heights of warrior and water bearer.

"Leave her alone, Brauna." Larka stepped between the two girls. "Her head is injured. We should never have used her for watch. If you are to blame anyone, *let it be me.*"

Lichena's chest puffed with pride while Brauna visibly deflated, head hanging but eyes flashing to the Wheel girl. Brauna then shifted targets and spearheaded Larka.

"You called Da 'my brother,' Mum," the girl breathed.

Larka swallowed audibly. "There are some things I must tell you, Brauna, but here and now . . . it is not the time or place." Larka flinched at the hurt look Brauna gave her.

"You have time to answer one simple question, Mum. Was he brother or husband to you?" Larka hesitated, and Brauna bellowed, "Tell me! You owe me that much."

"He was not my husband," Larka whispered, unable to meet her daughter's eyes.

"Why? Why lie to me all these years?"

"I can't explain it all now, Brauna. The bear that killed Astla could come back." Larka felt her heart swell with wrath at her own inaction when she had first heard the thing enter the camp—when she should have insisted Astla return to Albilar yesterday.

"What bear?" Brauna reassessed Astla. "What bear did this?" she quipped. "There's not a blood mark on him, not a new one." She sneered at Lichena. "Maybe you did this with that dark moon power of yours."

"I wouldn't hurt Astla." Lichena went to her bedding and scooped up the sleeping newborn. "The bear did it. We saw him suck this baby's mother's soul right out of her the night before last."

"Uh huh, a soul-sucking bear," Brauna drawled, nodding her head. "I think Overseer Flock would like to talk to you about your special brand of magic."

"Brauna, stop it," Larka admonished. "The bear is real. He doesn't kill in the usual ways. He is a monster made of the dark moon. His aura speaks it true. And we must leave here before that thing comes back because we can't kill it." She paused, trying to sense whether the beast was nearby or not. She gained no sense of its location, and a chill ran through her. It could not have gone that far.

"We must bury . . ." Larka's words stilled as her eyes fell on her brother. She went to Astla's side and tucked his blanket around him, leaving his face bare.

"I am so sorry, Astla," she whispered and brushed at her redampened cheeks.

"What about the babe's mother. Shouldn't we bury her?" Brauna approached, stopping short of Astla's feet and eyeing the now-crying baby, whom Lichena tried to calm by pacing around the campsite.

"Had we not needed to move so quickly yesterday, we'd have done so then." Larka shook her head. "She's too far behind us, Brauna."

Larka tried to shift Astla's weight. "Help me please."

"No! He deserves a burial fitting his rank." Brauna's expression said she would not be deterred. "He deserves a burial in Albilar."

"Did he tell you nothing of our plans yesterday?" Larka straightened to her full height.

"He told me, but he didn't know he would die before the next sunrise." Brauna threw an averse look at Lichena.

Lichena skulked closer to Larka and stood on the matron's left, feeding the baby with cloth and goat milk.

"We really need more milk for the baby," she said, not looking up from the newborn.

Brauna rolled her eyes.

"Brauna, I cannot return to Albilar. You know that—"

"That wasn't my plan, Mum. I could take Da, bury the babe's mother and meet back up with you—"

"No. That's too dangerous. We don't know what the Guard might do to you, and Astla said he would have returned to Jaunty had you and I not shown up when you were a baby. The Guard was not everything to him."

"When I was a baby . . ." Brauna repeated, brow knit, before she carried on. "He is going back to Albilar if I have to carry him all the way there by myself." Muscle bunched on her jaws. "He deserves that much."

"Ontar," Lichena breathed, staring past Brauna.

"He's a bit off subject," Brauna snapped then turned around to follow Lichena's gaze. Every muscle on the warrioress tensed. Her eyes narrowed.

Ontar swaggered toward them from the woods, his Guard uniform in place and his handsome face lit with excitement until he saw the rankling of all three of the women's expressions. He halted beside the rooty butt of the fallen tree.

"You ladies are making enough noise to attract half the Guard patrol out here," he said as he gazed at Larka, eyes sweeping the length of her. Larka caught herself before she took a step back, not liking what she once more sensed within him. Ontar then eyed Brauna, irritation flicking through his countenance so fast that had she blinked, Larka would have missed it. He finally looked back at her.

"I came to give fair warning."

"Fair warning?" Larka repeated, a touch of sarcasm lacing her voice. A gentle zephyr informed her that Ontar had lied—something she did not need her air allies to confirm.

"Monton sent out a small search party for Astla and the Thrower this morning under Overseer Flock's orders," Ontar stated.

Larka's guilt-ridden heart began to pound with a heavier beat as Ontar's vision fell upon Astla. The Guardsmen walked farther into the campsite, eyes locked on his captain. Brauna swung around to watch him. Lichena halted bouncing the baby as Ontar came to stand to the left of her, his shadow falling over Astla.

"What happened to Captain Brandon? His color . . . Did you . . ." Ontar's words strayed, and he leveled his vision on Larka, the unfinished question behind the lift of his brow.

Anger flared within her. Larka opened her mouth to retaliate, but Lichena cut her short, saying,

"A bear attacked us this morning before dawn."

"We were taking him back to Albilar," Brauna offered, her eyes challenging Larka to say otherwise.

"Oh, too bad. He was a good captain," Ontar said and poked at Astla's stiffening leg with a boot toe. Ontar then gritted his teeth and squinted.

Larka lifted a brow? Was *that* supposed to express grief? Disgusted, she bent and pulled the blanket over Astla's face.

Ontar's expression normalized and he continued, "But you can't go back. Overseer Flock demanded your head and Astla's if he was helping you. He added a substantial bounty for your head, the Thrower's head. I am sorry, Lark. This is so much my fault." Ontar stared with overdramatized forlornness at the ground. "I drank too much one night and told a few men—just a few—who Lichena thought the Thrower was." He turned to Lichena with an imploring cast to his eyes. "I hope you can forgive me."

"Idiot!" Three strides brought Brauna to Ontar. Her hands shot forward and grasped the tunic of his Guard uniform to lift and shake him. "Astla is dead because of you and this nomad filth." She jerked her head toward Lichena. "And all you have to say for yourself is you *had a few too many*. You're sorry, alright!" Brauna thrust Ontar away from her and dropped him.

The Guardsman landed on his feet, mouth agape until a look of pure hatred consumed him. Brauna stood her ground, eyes blazing, chest rising and falling like a bellows.

Larka moved to place a hand on her daughter's left shoulder. To her surprise, Brauna squeezed that hand.

Larka next spoke in a placating tone, "Forgive us, Ontar. We are a bit overwrought at the moment. I do wish to know, in your kind fair warning, if Flock seeks Brauna as well?"

"She's a bit odd for a woman." Ontar's face displayed the slightest vulnerability as he spoke, eyes flitting to Brauna. "It makes her a target."

"Is that a *yes*?" Brauna snarled.

Ontar took a step back before he nodded with smug affirmation. "Overseer Flock thinks you are a daughter of the dark moon. You've a bounty on you as well."

"Me!" Brauna roared then glowered at Lichena. "If anyone's of the dark—"

"Brauna." Larka squeezed Brauna's shoulder. At that moment, the wind caressed Larka with knowledge. Ontar had lied yet again: Cornt Flock had put no price on Brauna's head, though he did seek her.

Larka regarded Ontar for several moments then said, "The rest of the Guard believes Brauna of the dark moon?"

"Of course. It's all they talk about," Ontar replied, telling the truth for a change.

A wave of panic tumbled through Larka. No doubt Ontar had incited the Guard against Brauna; not one of them had liked being beaten by a woman. Many had even expressed concern about being trained by those of the female ilk.

Larka felt her hands crackle with energy, but as she would have aimed that power at Ontar, her wind companions blustered about her, showing her his violent ending. Larka smiled inwardly. She lowered the hands she had started to lift. No doubt Cornt Flock would kill anyone who set out to harm his granddaughter, whether directly or indirectly. Ontar had unwittingly chosen to walk a hazardous path in his clamber for rank, though Larka had to wonder what would happen to Brauna to result in the loss of Ontar's head. That thought cut short her smile.

"Who told the Overseer I was the Thrower? Which man?" Larka asked.

"I haven't the faintest idea," Ontar replied.

Brauna's use of the word "idiot" echoed through Larka's mind. She spoke next through the stiff smile of her lips.

"I see."

"What about Lichena?" Larka continued, feeling Brauna's shoulder tense at the mention of Lichena's name. "Is she seen as friend or foe to Flock?"

Ontar grinned fawningly at Lichena. "They wish to reward her."

Brauna lurched out of Larka's grasp, roaring indignation.

CHAPTER 39

HEART GAMES

Brauna just as soon clamped her mouth shut, coming to an abrupt standstill. The warrioress drew in breath, her body visibly relaxing, her blazing aura calming. She then looked at Lichena and Ontar with cold calculation—the same look she had given the Amber Man yesterday when her hand had suspended him by his neck.

Larka's eyes widened a fraction before she stepped between Brauna and the couple.

Lichena's mouth twitched, her eyes agleam, the girl much unaware of the peril implied by Brauna's relaxed posture and smoldering aura.

Ontar kept his expression still, though Larka noted a flare of satisfaction within his orbits. He held his hands behind his back as he spoke next, tossing his chestnut-brown hair over his shoulders.

"I bear shame for my part in this dilemma. I should not have bragged on my Lichena so that night, but with my feelings for her . . ." He held his hands open at his sides, doing a good job at mimicking sincerity for once. "I do understand the frustration this situation causes. Let me make this up to you, at least a small amount for the trouble I've caused you . . . Brauna, Lark." He nodded at each woman in turn. "Leave Astla with me. I'll ensure his body gets the proper care. It's the least I can do."

Larka erased alarm from her expression. She wanted this parasitic worm nowhere near her brother, but Lichena shoved the baby at her, and before Larka could speak, Brauna—mien softened—responded,

"That would do well, Ontar. May you accept my apologies along with my gratitude."

Ontar nodded. Brauna then walked downriver from them.

Larka rocked the whimpering baby within her arms as she watched Brauna walk away—reflective, silent, back stiff with pride—until the warrior became lost in the high timber surrounding the waterway.

"Don't be silly, Ontar," Lichena chimed sweetly.

Larka's head snapped toward Lichena. Had the girl swooned under this man's attentions as frugal and false as they were? A glance here, a smile there, a lie anywhere—was that all it took?

Lichena's cheeks glowed pink and her countenance mirrored coy as she gazed up at Ontar. Larka repressed a grimace and the bold desire to ax the conniving fleabag right then and there.

Ontar laced fingers with Lichena. "I would have a word with you alone?" He peered at Larka. "Would you mind?"

Larka scoffed, not bothering to hide her disgust. "There's plenty of space that way." She gestured toward the river.

A sneer curled Ontar's lip as Lichena pulled him away.

"Look out for that bear," Larka called after them.

With that thought, Larka reached out to Brauna with her sixth sense and found the girl to be fine. Still, Larka could get no status on the red-eyed monster. She gazed at the shadowy forest where she had last seen Brauna then toward the river. She frowned.

Lichena and Ontar had disappeared.

Larka looked up to see aspen leaves quaking on the forest perimeter as the wind whispered through. The drifting air pressed on, swirling around Larka for the briefest moment, speaking to her in words heard only by her subconscious.

An image spat into her mind's eye: blood and a placenta—Brauna's placenta—slipping down a rocky slope and descending into darkness. The night of Brauna's birth echoed through Larka, focused on

Brauna's birth blood and its spill into the dirt beneath Maja . . . where she had lain within a copse of whip-thin trees.

Larka gasped. Aspens—those trees had been aspens. She was certain of it. She had seen that pattern of clonal growth too often now to dismiss it. Brauna was within her element in the forest and attached to it as surely as her feet touched the earth.

"The birth blood . . . it's the birth blood binding us to the elements," Larka whispered.

"Yeeess, musssttt sssseverrr itttt," air made voice snaked into her ear.

Larka started. "Gilly?"

Did spirits reside within the air? Had Gilly not mentioned that on the night she had died?

A gale then smashed into Larka, bickering about her head before it dispersed. Larka raised her fingers to the stinging spot left on her cheek. Had her allies slapped her?

The baby began to wail. Larka glanced down at the blanketed newborn curved into the bend of her arm then at the blanketed body of her brother.

"That a blanket might hold new life and hide the dead . . ." Larka shook her head, feeling sorrow burn her eyes, tug at her mouth. "I made a blanket for my baby once, long ago," she whispered to the newborn.

Larka took the last milk flask from her bags and plunked down beside Astla's body. She dipped linen cloth into the flask, the smell of the milk telling on its soured state. Regardless, the baby suckled nourishment drip by drip until she fell asleep.

Larka touched the blanketed body next to her. "Astla, my brother, I owe you much, and yet I can give nothing, not even a proper death ritual, and now I must entrust you to a fellow Guardsman's care, a corrupt man if ever there was one."

Larka shook her head. "Had I not insisted on aiding these women . . ." She sighed, a prolonged release. "But my allies were more insistent than I." Her hand went to her cheek, her fingers tracing a raised, reddened area.

Clouds began to blot the sky above, and thunder grumbled in the distance. Larka felt the air shift around her, murmuring into her ear, trying to soothe her regrets, assuage her aching heart, to dismiss any blame.

"My family comes first from here out," Larka said to the wind, and it hurtled away from her.

Larka briefly gripped Astla's arm through the blanket. "Farewell, brother."

She placed the baby next to him then packed the camping equipment and gathered up other gear, finishing those tasks before she saw an incensed Brauna tromping out of the forest, the warrior's face crimson. Brauna seated herself on the weathered log and sank her face into her hands.

Larka moved to crouch before her.

Brauna peered down at her mother over the tips of her fingers, the whites of her eyes bloodshot.

"Oh, Brauna," Larka breathed. "I am sorry I allowed so many untruths for so long, but Astla will always be your father, and I will always be your mother, no matter what."

Brauna scrutinized her mother before answering with a shake of her head.

"I think not. Everything has changed. Nothing will ever feel quite the same no matter how much you sugarcoat it." Brauna removed her hands from her face, smearing the salty dampness there.

"Sweetheart, I am not sugarcoating anything. Don't you understand? I love you. Astla loved you. All those years he watched you grow into a woman, a warrior . . . who you are. Those years can't be erased by anything." Larka stroked her daughter's chin with her thumb. "Brauna, won't you at least look at me?"

"I find it hard to see you! That nomad filth has manipulated her way into our lives. Destroyed our lives! And she's made it quite clear she hates me!"

"Now, Brauna," Larka chided softly. "Perhaps she does not like you, but she has her reasons. She said you pointed at her and called her a 'gypsy whore.' Is that true?"

"What?" Brauna huffed. Her eyes took on a distant aspect then refocused. "That petulant little idiot!" Brauna rolled her eyes. "I said, 'Look at the gypsy horses,' when the wagons came into town. They looked so strange, and I was pointing. She was there. She must have thought I said 'whores.' So few people have horses."

Brauna's voice became hushed. "She set all this in motion over a misunderstanding. If she hadn't been with Ontar to hurt me . . ." For the first and last time, Larka saw her daughter tremble. "Da . . . he *died* because of a misunderstanding!"

Larka closed her eyes and inhaled, trying to let this newfound knowledge sink in. It would have been so easy to make Lichena the scapegoat for Astla's death.

"So you see she does hate me. Her need for revenge—to hurt me— and her big mouth have brought these times upon us, Mum."

Larka brushed bangs, grown longer than usual, out of Brauna's eyes. "Sweetheart, her lack of discretion was revenge, but she did not intentionally sabotage our lives. If you are to blame anyone for the path we walk, let it be Cornt Flock."

"Cornt Flock!" Brauna leapt to her feet, nearly knocking her mother over. "Cornt Flock is but a tool of her sabotage. How odd it did not occur to her that telling Ontar you were the Thrower might put a bounty on you if he leaked it. That's not lack of foresight, Mum. It's plain stupid!"

Larka rose out of the squat as Brauna ranted.

"She didn't hesitate to take Ontar for herself when it was obvious how I felt about him! She'd use anything to hurt me—you, Astla, Ontar, *Cornt Flock*! She enjoys it! And she's putting another knife in my back as we speak. What do you think she and Ontar are out there doing right now? You should have seen the way she smiled when I caught them." Brauna glanced toward the woods then back at Larka, lips twisted with outrage. "Not that I care anymore," she added ineffectually.

Larka's mouth fell open. Then, tentatively, she spoke, "Brauna—"

"Don't." Brauna held up a hand. "We're here now whether those were her intentions or not. Don't say anything more. Don't defend *her*." Brauna hesitated but a moment, eyes narrowing, anger surging behind the warm brown of her irises. "What I'd really like to know is how she knew before I did that Astla is not my father. She told me yesterday when I was fishing. How did she know, Mum?"

Larka's mouth gaped further. She blinked as if the actions of her eyes would keep this question inside her long enough to resolve it.

Finally she whispered, "I don't know."

Brauna snorted her disbelief and walked away. Larka pivoted to watch her daughter kneel beside Astla's body.

Death Song carried to Larka several ticks later, Brauna's voice melodic and strong. Larka's heart twinged. She swallowed over the lump in her throat, soon lifting her thin voice alongside Brauna's:

> . . . *life lived*
> *life passed*
> *of grief born mighty*
> *within my family's chest*
> *tears strung from their hearts*
> *ripped from their eyes*
> *sing unto them*
> *upon the shattered wind*

Larka wiped her eyes as Brauna stood and turned.

Brauna gazed through space and time at Larka, a sad smile on the girl's lips.

At that point something moved within the forest. Larka spun, reaching for a throwing ax. The woods then spat two people from its shadows. Larka's arm fell by her side, ax in hand, as she advanced to meet a flushed Lichena and a dreamy-faced Ontar.

Larka glared up and down the length of their disheveled clothing.

"We really *must* be leaving," she bit. "Everything is ready if the two of you are finished *saying goodbye*." Heat ensanguined Larka's skin. She next stroked the ax blade, looking with purpose at Ontar. "You'll take good care of my brother on his journey home."

Lichena's eyes widened while Ontar's narrowed.

Although Larka next spoke to Lichena, she refused to take her eyes off Ontar. "Lichena, if you wish to collect your reward, go with Ontar. If you wish to make up for the heartache you and Ontar have caused my family, you will care for the baby until we can find her a home." Larka slipped a lonely ax into place—the other irretrievable, lost to the bear—then peered at Lichena. "Am I justified in asking this?"

Lichena nodded and hung her head a moment before she stood on tiptoe and gave an overdramatized kiss to a soured Ontar. Her triumphant eyes then focused somewhere beyond Larka's left.

Larka refused to look in that direction. She knew where Brauna stood.

CHAPTER 40

GIVE AWAY

Larka spoke to Lichena while they collected their things, but she also remained aware of the exchange between Ontar and Brauna.

"No, Brauna." Ontar refused Brauna's offer to assist him in situating Astla for transport.

Having propped Astla's body horizontally over his shoulders, Ontar rose from his squat, obviously straining under the weight.

"You can't carry him all the way, Ontar. Mark a tree or something and come back here with Monton or—"

Ontar turned a look of fury on Brauna and snarled, "I need no help from you!"

Larka cinched her packsack closed and peered up. It seemed Brauna would have attacked the Guardsmen but for Astla on his back.

"Go then!" Brauna flicked her hands toward the road. Ontar left after a final sneer. Brauna then turned to her mother, brows raised.

Larka met Brauna's gaze then her own followed Ontar's withdrawal from the campsite. Even under Astla's weight, Ontar nearly ran through the forest. Frowning, Larka thrust her arms through her packsack.

Lichena flourished the cape Larka had given her and wrapped it around her shoulders before picking up the baby.

Brauna joined them and collected her own belongings.

264

Larka studied the camp. "Looks like we got it all. Let's go."

The women made their way to the road. They had almost reached it when the abrupt snort and neigh of a horse reverberated like discord through the air. Then hoofs beat the road in a burst of speed, quickly fading.

Skin crawling, Larka sped her gait, Brauna and Lichena right behind her.

Larka watched Ontar fade into the distance, Astla's body strapped behind him over the hindquarters of a large, black horse. Brauna came to stand beside Larka and echoed her thoughts, with a few modifications.

"I wonder why they gave him a whore—I mean a horse." Brauna let her vision stray to Lichena.

Lichena did not counter the jab but stood under a pall of introspection, her shoulders drooping as she watched Ontar ride away.

"I've an idea why," Larka replied at last, shaking her head. The Overseer lent out his horses for dire situations only. Ontar would have been a fool to think Brauna or Larka would miss that sinister a gesture. The animal had been tied by the roadside or their confrontation earlier might have been different.

Queasiness suffused by disgust overcame Larka as she wondered what the encounter with Ontar would have been like without Brauna or Lichena present. Given the cold lust he had aimed at Larka several times now, she delved into the certainty that Ontar would have attacked her—body, mind, and spirit. And she, no doubt, would have been forced to kill him. In a short time, she would regret that she had not.

Larka reached out to Lichena and placed a hand on the Wheel girl's back, trying to give some degree of reassurance. The girl had appeared crestfallen since Larka had explained the initial misunderstanding between water bearer and warrioress.

"I know an older woman about a day's walk from here who can

take the baby," Larka said and stepped into the journey down the compacted-dirt road stretching between Albilar and its outlying towns, moving in opposite direction from Ontar.

A familiar presence stirred within Larka's mind: the Knowing Child cast forth a warning. Larka looked with dismay on the babe pressed snug against Lichena.

"Perhaps we'd do best to keep the babe with us. Something tells me she'll be safer that way." The Knowing Child's touch vanished from Larka's mind.

Larka and her companions trekked on in silence for some time under a gray-white sky, the sound of stillness about them, giving Larka good reason to be edgy. Something had hushed the forest.

About midday, slack drops of rain pattered their clothing.

Lichena shifted the whimpering newborn to her left side.

"Give me that baby," Brauna said and stopped to fetch the little one from Lichena's arms. Nose wrinkled, the warrior held the female infant before her. "I'd cry too if a bag of bones held me against her rib cage."

The babe began to wriggle and whine more insistently. Larka mustered a half smile at the awkward way Brauna held the newborn, but that expression vanished as the Knowing Child re-entered Larka's mind. Images of Ontar further mutilating Astla's remains under the sheltering forest felt like a great spike driven into her heart. She gasped and placed a hand over her chest.

Brauna's eyebrows gathered, and she stopped alongside her mother. Larka waved her off.

"Keep moving. Speed up. We're in more danger than I thought."

What was certain to be the clopping of hooves along with the creaking of wheels then sounded off the trail behind them.

"Into the forest," commanded Larka.

Brauna asked no questions, but Lichena stayed where she was.

"Get over here," Brauna hissed at the girl from behind an aged red oak.

"Shhhh," Brauna responded to the grunting baby.

"These are my people. They would not betray us." Through the drizzling rain, a bedraggled Lichena looked affronted.

"They would not betray *you*," Brauna quipped. "We've a price on our heads."

"Leave her, Brauna, where she is safest," Larka offered then gestured into the forest.

Brauna nodded. They dodged behind thick tree trunk after thick tree trunk, weaving away from the road, Lichena watching sadly as they went, until horizontal branches and vertical boles along with rolling topography blotted the Wheel girl's existence.

The baby gurgled angrily, little face reddened, as Brauna shifted through the woods.

"Hush now." Brauna paused and bounced the baby with a stiffness born of inexperience.

Finally recognizing the babe's discomfort, Larka reached for the newborn but too late. A small explosion ricocheted through the thick woods. Brauna wrinkled her nose, and the smell hit Larka. The newborn began to wail.

"Shit!" declared Brauna.

Hearing footfalls in the forest, Brauna ducked behind a maple's trunk. She turned to peer in the direction they had come and freed a hand to retrieve her sword from the scabbard on her back.

Larka sidled next to Brauna and took the baby.

"Get behind me," said Brauna.

Larka obeyed and held the newborn close, rocking gently.

"Lark, Brauna," Lichena called through the sound of her approach.

"Maybe she's come to collect her reward," Brauna hissed.

A squat man with a shiny, bald pate—raindrops beading off—accompanied Lichena. His eyes fell on Brauna's sword, and a sage smile pushed wrinkles into his leathery skin.

"I am Warin, leader of this Wheel band. We are a simple people, Brauna. We have no weapons to counter yours."

Brauna slid a guilty glance down her sword but refused to lower it.

"I understand your anger at Lichena. She has shamed my family as well as yours with her actions." He spread his hands in an imploring manner.

Lichena met no one's eyes as the man spoke, her head bent and face flushed. Brauna's face seemed to melt into agreement, but the sword remained in place.

Larka listened with more than her ears. She sensed no danger from this man, but a certain power lurked about him.

"You must understand it was not with my permission that my daughter acted to revenge the insult she thought you put upon her. Unless justified, we are generally not a vengeful people." Warin's dark eyes fell upon the baby in Larka's arms. "I believe we have a woman who would be more than happy to take this dark moon daughter. Milla's own baby was born without a soul under the last dark moon, and her grief would be lessened by the presence of this child."

The allies breathed into Larka's ear, further assuring her of this man's sincerity. The Knowing Child whispered into her mind as well, but that message confused Larka. Realizing, several instants later, that Warin looked at her with a request in his eyes, Larka stepped to Brauna's side.

"Scabbard the sword, daughter."

With much hesitation and her eyes never leaving her perceived enemy, Brauna slid the weapon into its scabbard. Metal scraped casing while water drops plopped through the forest canopy. The rain itself had fallen to surcease.

"We've room for you all to travel with us if you seek refuge. We ourselves fled Albilar after the news of your identity broke, Lark. Our presence is usually tolerated only under great suspicion even in that great city. Many suspect us of giving refuge to dark moon children." He shook his head. "Alas, we fled before that suspicion turned to intolerance and before Overseer Flock decreed against us as well. Rumor has it, he's become convinced we're to blame for his daughter's disappearance. With Cun whispering in his ear" —Warin shrugged— "who knows."

"Come." He gestured toward the road. "Let us help you." He chuckled. "And perhaps we shall prove the many right." The squat man turned and sauntered away through the trees.

"We're safer in numbers, Brauna. Trust that." Larka met her daughter's skeptical gaze then followed Warin.

Brauna exhaled with an incredulous puff and reluctantly trailed her mother.

Lichena fell in beside Larka. "He heard the baby cry and just seemed to know who was out here," said Lichena.

"The baby's belly likely aches from hunger and sour milk, and Warin knew because he is of the dark moon, Lichena. Do not lie to me." Larka stepped around a patch of aspens growing in a tree-fall gap.

"Oh, I'm sorry. It's just—it's for our protection," Lichena replied.

Brauna mumbled something unintelligible behind them. Larka then heard her daughter pluck a leaf off one of the aspens and sigh.

"I understand." Larka touched Lichena's shoulder lightly then grasped with more strength as they walked. "There are some things you and I need to discuss about your need to hurt those you think have hurt you, about your lack of foresight. You must know with exactness why you act, Lichena. You must think about consequences, about whom you trust.

"Ontar is a terrible man. He had you and hurt Brauna, and he did not care. He put you in danger by leaving you with us. Ask yourself why he did not fight for you, for you to return to Albilar with him. Will a price be on your head next?"

Lichena opened her mouth, it appeared, to rebel, and Brauna muttered behind them once more.

Larka swivelled and eyed her daughter. "If you can't be any more helpful to our situation, Brauna, you can care for the baby." Larka lagged and handed the infant to Brauna, who accepted the child with a roll of her eyes. Larka turned to rejoin Lichena and frowned.

The girl had left her behind.

As soon as the two stragglers and newborn got to the wagons, Warin offered Brauna a wet cloth and a dry cloth then plodded away.

Brauna rolled her eyes, muttering to herself, and spread a blanket from her gear onto the ground. She placed the infant on that material and had to hunch low over her task. As she cleaned the babe, with much wry comment, Warin and a hobbling woman aged somewhat beyond Brauna's years approached. Brauna turned her head to view them, a question in her knit brow.

"This is Milla. I spoke of her earlier," Warin said, touching Milla's arm as he named her.

Larka watched. The Knowing Child had informed her to entrust the newborn to the Wheel folk if she wished the tiny girl to live but had warned against Larka and Brauna traveling with them. Larka reached for the Knowing Child and more knowledge to clarify but could not touch minds as the wind blew by the wagon train.

Milla held her arms out to the newborn. "My baby died two days ago," she said, her voice the faintest whisper.

Brauna stiffened, clutching the baby to her. The baby writhed.

Milla spoke again, "I've milk in my breasts and love in my heart."

Brauna's entire body went lax, pity sheathing her face, yet she still gripped the babe to her breast.

Warin patted Brauna's back, his fingertips glazing her sword's scabbard. "You will be a good mother someday but not today. Give Milla the baby. The child is our kind. I see the magic winding round her now."

With a crinkling of her nose, Brauna surveyed the newborn. "I see nothing but a stinky baby."

The warrioress stood and grudgingly handed the child over to Milla who smiled and began to totter toward the rear of the caravan, singing *Birth Song* as she did.

Lichena chuckled into the silence that followed.

"What are you laughing about?" Brauna barked.

Lichena reached behind herself and patted one of the animals hitched to her father's squat wagon. "These are not horses. They are donkeys."

Brauna's irises blazed brown fury. "I see nothing funny about that!"

Lichena sighed and entered her father's wagon. Warin indicated Larka and Brauna do the same.

Several hours later within the safety of the covered wagon, Larka was awakened by the thunder of what could only be the Guard galloping by on a herd of horses. She shuddered. For Flock to send out so many horses . . .

She lifted the curtain covering the wagon's small window and noted a familiar rider rounding a bend ahead of the caravan—Ontar. Larka swallowed the rancid lament in her throat. Though not usually one for vengeance, she gladly called up the images of Ontar losing his head. But, once more, what did that imply for Brauna? She gazed uneasily through the dim light at Brauna, who slept amongst the cushions lining the wagon's creaky floor.

An eerie wind swirled across Larka. With that, the past snatched her into itself. She viewed herself standing in the grass near a river, sensing the joy her air allies had released after a five-year-old Brauna had lifted Astla's heavy sword. There and then, Larka had also witnessed in a flash of unbidden imagery what lay before her now: a grown Brauna sprawled amongst a scatter of cushions, a slippage her air allies had tried hard to erase. She recalled the unconscious battle to retain her memory of that day, of that sword in the sky.

A concept crept out of the recesses of Larka's mind: her air allies knew something she did not. Somehow, they had dipped their fingers into the fires of fate and come away unburned. The idea that things had been set into motion flared back to life, not to be extinguished again.

Brauna stirred and opened her eyes to meet her mother's apprehensive gaze.

Larka dropped the curtain, leaving them in near darkness.

CHAPTER 41

SUSPIRATION

Mum, what's wrong?" Brauna sat up, delineated by vague light and fey shadow.

Larka held a finger to her own lips and whispered, "The Guard just passed, all on horseback."

Brauna cocked her head, listening. The echoes of hoofbeats dwindled until they could no longer be heard.

"Not good," Brauna said.

"No, not good," Larka said in a hushed tone. "We must talk, my daughter, about the night you were born. There are many things you must know. But first . . ." She lost her composure, voice quavering.

Brauna seated herself beside Larka on the slab of wood stretching across the wagon's rear and had to slide her haunches forward to keep her head off the ceiling. She reached to close strong hands around her mother's delicate ones.

Eyes closed, Larka leaned her head on Brauna's shoulder, staying there for several minutes.

Larka finally took a deep breath then sat up to lean on the wall behind her. "My daughter" —she kissed Brauna's hand— "Ontar has betrayed us in the worst sense."

Brauna drew in breath with sibilance.

"Shh." Larka pulled her hands free of Brauna's hold and caressed her daughter's cheek. "You must remain calm." She peered more deeply into Brauna's anxious eyes and swallowed the taste of bile.

"Ontar removed your father's bandaging, put an ax in his back, cut him with a sword, then took your father's body back to Albilar to prove we are a greater threat than they thought."

"Ontar is a dead man," Brauna hissed.

"Yes, he is, daughter. He just doesn't know it yet."

Brauna's steady respiration filled the darkness.

Lichena stirred amongst the cushions. The young woman's voice sifted through shadow.

"But, what if he didn't blame Astla's injuries on you two?"

Larka peered through the dim light to decipher Lichena propped up on an elbow.

"What if you are mistaken?" Lichena said.

"You know I am not," Larka said with asperity then softened her tone. "What other reason could there be? He said he was taking Astla directly back to Albilar for a proper burial ceremony. Did you not hear the horses ride by, Lichena? Did you not see the horse Ontar rode earlier?

"Overseer Flock is most greedy with his horses; they are expensive, at risk of the horse plague when they leave his grounds. He does not allow the Guard the use of them unless something is drastically wrong. No, Ontar has added fuel to fire, Lichena, and he's thrown us into its flames . . . all of us."

Lichena became ominously silent. Her form, spidery in the shadows, stretched and repositioned amongst the cushions.

"Mum," Brauna said.

"Hmm?" Drowsiness flushed Larka's thoughts.

"How did you know what Ontar did to Da?"

"I know much that is not obvious to most." Larka sighed and straightened her posture. "Why do you think I help dark moon children, Brauna?"

"Um, because it's the right thing to do," Brauna offered clumsily.

Light flapped on and off Larka's face as the curtain swayed under the wagon's movement. Brauna must have seen clearly how her explanation stung her mother.

"Because you are one," Brauna said, tightlipped.

Larka nodded. She leaned her head against the wall of the wagon and yawned.

"I was persecuted for being one. I lost my mother to the bear the night you were born because we were trying to escape the villagers rather than being safe at home." She bit her bottom lip. "So many things happened that night. . . ."

Brauna sat very still, very quiet, awaiting explanations, but under the sway and creak of the ride, Larka succumbed to a deep state of unconsciousness. She slept like this each night and most of each day for nearly two weeks, as her body had been pushed beyond exhaustion for far too long.

After risking some exercise on the thirteenth day, walking unconcealed beside the wagons for many hours, Larka felt weary once more. That night, however, her dreams gave her a restless sleep: Mentheleda held out her firstborn, and the bear ran by to snatch the babe out of her arms, the beast's red eyes flaring brighter each time. That same segment of dream repeated until Larka could abide no more.

She awoke to darkness without and a faint glow within the wagon. She located the source as Lichena, in particular her chest where once again the ragged dress had fallen open as the girl slept.

Larka gaped, shaking her head. A radiant trail ran between Lichena's tiny breasts and down toward her navel. Larka leaned toward the girl, hand trembling, and touched the scar's point of origin. As if someone grasped her hand and snatched her out of this world, her spirit tore from her body, flying back to a harrowing past:

A river roared in the background. Eyes closed, Mentheleda lay on her right side in the snow, her cheek resting atop a baby's head, both her arms wrapped around the babe.

Something snorted. A shadowy form lumbered out of the night. Mentheleda opened her eyes to find a bear hulking over her, its great paw lifted to strike. Mentheleda threw her left arm up. Claws rent the woman's chest and it gushed forth with lifeblood.

Regardless of her state, Mentheleda still clutched the babe to her when the bear bent to peer into the matron's face, his eyes now blazing red.

Mentheleda's lips parted in silent rictus as the bear opened his jaws over hers. A misty essence streamed from matron to monster. Under that stream the baby cooed and lifted her fist into her grandmother's spirit, stirring it with innocence. With that, transference of spirit to devourer ceased. The bear shut its mouth and cocked its head at the babe. The bear then snorted, a discontent sound, its glowing eyes fading.

The beast positioned itself over the baby and sank its teeth into the blanket wrapped around the newborn—the blanket Larka had so carefully knit. It then sauntered off into the woods, carrying the babe in the blanket's sling, leaving Mentheleda's body devoid of life, devoid of soul.

Above the matron's body, a misty form shifted from one amorphous shape to another. The form hovered, seemed to be watching as a young Larka returned, the girl stopping in her tracks, screaming at fate, a fat babe in her arms.

The essence then sped off, shifting through the limbs of skeletal trees until finding the stolen infant.

The newborn rested on the spread knit blanket in the new layer of snow the sky had dumped upon the land. Eyes glowing red, the bear stood over the naked infant and prodded her gently with a paw. The babe gave no response. Then, with more dexterity than a bear's paw should have, the beast raked one clawed digit down the middle of the babe's chest, nearly to her remaining umbilicus. The babe still gave no response.

The animal snorted then trotted off through the surrounding hemlocks and white pines, heedless of Death Song's echo on the wind.

The misty form swung down and seeped into the spreading blood on the babe's chest, sealing the wound. Little time passed before the spirit rose like roiling fog off the scar. It hovered over the babe for the passing of five sunrises. Finally the spirit left the dying infant then reappeared, accompanied by a younger Warin, who stood over the babe's body, a look of sorrow consuming his face. He picked up the infant, the body appearing stiff, unyielding, in his arms.

Still, the essence whirled over the babe's chest, finally vanishing into the ragged scar.

Larka broke contact with Lichena and thudded back against the wagon's locked door.

Lichena's eyes fluttered open. "I had the strangest dream," she murmured and looked down to note how bright her aura.

Larka, too stunned to reply, simply stared at the sleepy girl. The scar that whispered of their shared past had yet again disappeared.

Lichena smiled dreamily at Larka and fell back to sleep, her aura calming to nothing.

Larka reached out and brushed the soft red hair framing the girl's face, one structured in bone much like Larka's and Mentheleda's faces, one Larka should have recognized long before now.

In a whisper she completed *Birth Song* as she had started it for this child many years ago, and, this time, her words were not drowned by a bluster of wind and snow.

"Samara, I named you Samara," Larka whispered, jaws trembling.

Recollections of Brauna growing up over the years struck Larka anew. Then, new ones of a possible past brewed within her: an amber-haired baby breathing loudly as she breast-fed . . . a toddler with reddish hair just long enough to curl against the nape of her neck . . . a little girl with pale skin and freckles splayed across her nose, who finally grew into the lovely young woman who slept before Larka.

Larka blinked rapidly but could not still the sorrow pouring down her cheeks.

Her entire body shook as she cried, "I thought you were dead. By the gods, I left you there. Just a few feet into the woods . . . just a few steps . . ." She pressed her hand over her mouth, shaking her head. "My allies . . . they . . ."

The memory of a bear's tracks ending on the edge of a dark and speechless wood blended with the image of a swirling wind that had once erased her own tracks as Guta had trailed her on the road to Albilar many years ago. Her face hardened.

"My *allies!*" she spat.

A knock sounded on the door of the wagon's cabin. Larka pivoted on her buttocks. Her aura had become fiery, giving her no problem with visuals. She reached to lift the latch's bar and open the small, round wooden door to find Warin her visitor.

"We have much to speak of," he intoned kindly.

Larka nodded and tore herself away from the flesh-and-blood daughter lost to her so long ago.

A nearly full moon peeked through the starry sky as Warin and Larka tread a short distance of the dirt road. Larka had forced her aura to recede, having felt awkward at its telling brightness.

An oil lamp's glow bobbing beside him, Warin headed into the trees then sat beneath the shaggy boughs of an old hemlock. Larka followed.

Warin sat, situated the oil lamp on the side of his legs opposite her, then patted the ground nearer her. "Sit down, Lark."

She did so and felt herself relax in spite of this night's revelations.

Warin clasped his hands and placed them on his short legs.

He smiled warmly. "Many years ago, the spirit that resides in Lichena's scar showed me, as it did you, what happened to place Lichena in the snow and ice. I thought it too late when the spirit led me to Lichena, but I brought her into my wagon." He sighed. "I remember your sorrow in that telling clearly. I heard it for many nights afterwards in *Death Song* as it carried on the wind."

Warin stretched his clasped hands forward, palms facing away from him, and yawned. "Excuse me." He dropped his hands back to his lap and continued,

"When we rode through Jaunty, a woman named Heta informed us what had happened to you. Everyone in the village said you had taken your own life and that of your baby upon losing your mother, and the Wailing Ghost Mother, as they called you, was having her revenge upon those who had pushed her to do such a horrible thing.

"Some, I was told, spoke of seeing your ghost at the foot of their beds." He paused, and a warm hand slipped over Larka's shoulder to squeeze with a gentle kindness. "I found Lichena the day before we passed through Jaunty, so I knew differently than the townsfolk that your child was stolen from you, as was your mother.

"I also knew they left out their own part in your demise. Much deceptiveness lay within the story told me by this Heta. I asked why you were by the river in the darkness in the first place, and we of the Wheel were promptly run out of town.

"When my people were safe, I came back by myself to find you to offer you refuge and return your child, but the song you sang had become no more. I could not find you.

"Lichena knows nothing of you, Lark. I could not bear to give her false hope when she was younger. She believes her mother died birthing her." Warin sat for a long moment, staring away from Larka into the flame of the oil lamp. "I don't know what to tell her now." Warin's head rotated back round. Woe fixed the stillness in his eyes.

Larka could think of no response to his last statement. She let the silence part them.

Warin smiled in a pinched manner before he continued to speak, "I think the bear thought Lichena dead. That's why he left her to be blanketed by the cold. Had her birth blood not spilled into the snow and frozen, she might not have the gift of cold that gave her the look of death. I believe that to be what saved her from his spirit-sucking habit.

"Lichena is most remorseful for the way she has hurt you and especially Brauna. She regrets most telling Brauna that Astla was not her father, though even she does not realize her grandmother's spirit the source of that information." He paused and drew in a lengthy breath. "Perhaps, when our Lichena finds the courage, she will apologize to Brauna."

"Perhaps." Larka suspired and thought for a long moment. "I suppose it is with much good fortune that I have found Lichena, but," she paused then croaked, "but it does not stop the ache in my heart."

Warin placed an arm around her. Larka let it lie there, an ineffectual brace.

He spoke, "It was the best of luck. And perhaps, it was your mother's spirit who guided you and Lichena back to each other."

Larka wiped her nose then fixed Warin with her gaze. "The bear . . . it was stalking me before I conceived Lichena. It showed up in the woods then at my cabin. It killed my mother, stole my baby. I think—*I know*—the same bear killed my brother. Why would it do that?" Another thought spilled from her. "Why wouldn't my air allies help me find Lichena?"

"Perhaps they did not know, or perhaps the elements that claim us sometimes have their own ambitions." His arm slipped off her shoulders. "As for the bear, he's the power of the dark moon, Lark. Perhaps that same power within you attracted him." Warin shifted and stood before Larka could respond. "You should sleep now. Tomorrow will come too quickly."

A moment passed before she recognized the hand he offered to help her up. Larka accepted it, and soon they walked along the trail toward the wagons, lamplight bobbing.

Warin spoke no more.

CHAPTER 42

REACQUAINTANCES

Wheels thrusting through it, water splashed forward. Donkeys brayed. The wagon slowed. Inside, Larka's unconscious body lurched with its movements. Soon Jaunty River's intersection with the road had been forded, yet Larka slept on.

Larka flung off her blanket and popped up. She had slept too long. She looked around. Lichena and Brauna were gone. She had to tell them; she had to set things right. It was not an accomplishment she relished, however. Brauna would be heartbroken.

And what of Lichena? What would she think of the woman—the mother—who had left her to die?

Larka pictured Mentheleda sitting before her in Gilly's cottage, shriveled with guilt and wanting so much to reclaim her daughter. Had Larka but guessed she would be put in the same situation with Lichena . . . She sighed and rubbed her temple.

She rose to settle on the wagon bench then lifted the curtain and peeked out. Muted light penetrated her vision, assuring her of more rain to come. She exited through the side portal—not looking toward

Warin as she did so—hid behind a tree to relieve herself, then quickly caught up with the steady creak of the caravan's wheels.

She spotted Brauna talking to Milla while they walked. Surprisingly, Brauna had taken to Milla regardless of a ten year difference in their ages, and Brauna had astutely aided in caring for the newborn girl Milla had named Prin.

Larka pivoted her neck again. Her eyes pillaged the stream of Wheel folk strolling alongside the wagons. She could see Lichena nowhere.

"Warin said to give you this." A small boy offered Larka a chunk of bread.

She smiled and thanked him. The boy scampered away while Larka chewed breakfast absently, not perceiving her surroundings, not seeing or smelling the dampness on the donkeys. She had forgotten where she was . . . where she had come from.

Thunder rumbled overhead, and Larka's aura expanded about her, crackling in smoky-blue hue. Any breeze touching her swished with that color for several feet then dissolved into clear air. Each clap of thunder accentuated the crackle of energy in her hands, Larka's body answering to the skies.

Brauna drew up beside Larka and stared, eyes moving up and down her mother.

"Mum? What . . ." She tilted her head left then right. "You did that at the river, lit up the whole bloody place. And Prin, she glows sometimes. When I slant my head just right, I can see it."

Larka's throat went dry as she peered up at Brauna. She repealed her body's meandering energies, swallowed hard.

"Brauna, I must speak with you . . . about the night of your birth."

Brauna's head snapped up. She turned this way and that, eyeing their surroundings.

"Do you hear that? It sounds like someone crying."

Larka heard the faint sound, like the howlings of condemned souls, then came the slightly camphorous scent. Her stomach lurched. She stopped in her tracks, gazing west. In that direction and as far as the eye could see, Lavender Hills cried out. Wind danced through the silverish-green plants, ever renewing the chorus of their tortured song. Larka shuddered.

"We are very near Jaunty, maybe a half hour's ride," Larka said. "We should take cover." She headed for the wagon.

Warin peered over his shoulder from the driver's seat. Larka nodded at him, then timed her climb into the side portal of the rolling vehicle, Brauna close behind her. Inside, Larka seated herself on the back bench and listened. The sound of mourning lavender had been overcome by the clopping of hooves and clog of wheels on dirt.

Brauna seemed to have forgotten about the odd sound. She lay down in the cushions and shut her eyes, yawning. "Tell me about my birth now, Mum, before I fall asleep. I'm so tired. I stayed awake waiting for you to come back for so long last night. Where did you go?"

"I was talking to Warin." Larka waved her hand in dismissal. "We've so much to talk about, Brauna, you and I." She paused and met Brauna's half-lidded gaze.

"I don't know where to start," Larka said then suspired, pondering all the events that had led her to Brauna. Finally, she digressed to another beginning.

"My mother told me lightning danced about her feet, and the wind tried to steal me after my birth."

"Hmm," Brauna replied. Then a light snore emanated from her nose.

"Brauna," Larka called. She bent forward and touched Brauna's leg. How the girl fell to sleep so quickly was beyond Larka.

She closed her eyes, leaned against the wall behind her and meditated on how to tell Brauna the truth. Seconds later, the door clunked open and the latch dropped. Her eyes opened to view Lichena moving about in the shadows. Larka jammed her eyelids shut. And how to tell Lichena . . .

Time passed with Larka lost in thought, until she became aware that something felt awry. It took her a moment to realize what: the wagon's familiar creak and sway had stopped. She lifted her eyelids and sat up.

Brauna and Lichena lay sprawled next to each other, both asleep. Larka lifted the curtain to note the landscape without. What she saw made her heart stutter. Droves of people flooded toward them. Some carried knapsacks, but most carried nothing. Women wept and children bawled.

Brauna mumbled, recalling Larka's attention. The warrioress turned over and Lichena slung an arm over her, which might have been comical had it not been for the harried fright Larka had witnessed in Jaunty's fleeing villagers. She turned back to them. One familiar man—bloodied, distraught, staring into oblivion—caught her eye. She pushed the curtain aside and leaned her head out the circular window.

Hazel vision fixed slowly on her face. Guta halted the shift of his steps then waved a hesitant hand.

Larka motioned for him to join her inside the wagon. She picked her way over the sleeping bodies and reached outside the entrance portal to grab his hand and help him inside, noting Warin absent as she did so. She guided Guta to the empty spot on the short bench next to her.

His breath came unevenly, anguish jading his words. "I hear you wailing not so long ago, like you do the night we find Mentheleda." He blinked as his eyes adjusted, his sight falling on Brauna and Lichena.

"Es this my Brina?" he asked, not taking his eyes off the girl. "I thought after I hear you sing perhaps my Brina die too."

"She is well, gotten big and strong," Larka said softly then redirected the conversation. "Are all these people coming from Jaunty?"

"Es the Amber Man. Es gone mad in name of his mother. He rape and maim *and kill*," Guta croaked the last two words and rubbed at the crust of blood on his temple. "Also, the animal that slay your mother es back and in much the same rage."

Larka devoured the sight of Guta, drinking in the sound of his stilted language before she prodded in the patient murmur she had learned while working at the shelter,

"Who is his mother?"

"Es not in my knowing. Heta es to say when he rush the inn with

Overseer's Guard on his tail. We all scatter. But if not for Guard, I dare say Jaunty es nothing but ghosts. He make so many die." Guta shifted and peered directly into her eyes.

"I'm so sorry, Guta." She reached to hold him, and he leaned into her, gripping her waist and sobbing,

"He kill Ma and Papa. My wife, my little one. So many die at his hands. Cannot count."

"Who killed a child?" Brauna shot upright. "Ugh, get off me." She flung Lichena's skinny arm into the cushions. "And your wife, you said?"

Guta relinquished his grip on Larka and peered at Brauna. "Yes, my wife and child. My little girl, she was so small, just a—" Words caught in his throat.

Larka raised a finger to her lips and met Brauna's eyes.

Brauna fell silent.

"No one knew his mother live in Jaunty. Old ones say he es coming back once a decade since they just children, and he never find age. They say es Amber Man 'cause he last forever. His true name es Behrna."

"Behrna," Larka whispered. The memory of Gilly's argument the night before the commencement of the beatings of a then four-year-old Larka had clashed into focus:

> *A baritone voice had yelled outside Larka's room, "You promised her to me, Mother!"*
> *"Behrna . . ." Gilly had shouted—*

There the memory grew blotted by the fog of time.

"Gilly was his mother. That's why . . . that's why she tried to protect . . ." Who had Gilly been trying to protect? Larka glanced at Lichena, Gilly's motives becoming all too clear. The crone had given her life to ensure that of her grandchild's.

"Was Gilly?" Larka barely heard Guta ask.

Her mind held busy elsewhere. She recalled all too clearly the words Behrna had spoken to her on Last Hill, words of a promise, words she had not understood until now. And the cottage's eyes, the shutters—Gilly had slammed shut their invitation to safety and warmth—lidded in denial. A chill skittered down Larka's spine. She redrew her conclusions of Gilly, twice embittered.

She forced out her next words. "What of Pentheya, Ian, the twins?" If Larka flinched as she spoke the urchins' names, Guta's next words nearly stopped her heart.

"Gone, left long ago. We find the cabin burned and them . . . gone. No bodies inside the ashes. There some things you have no knowing about our Pentheya," Guta said then drew in breath to return to the present subject. "We try to stop Amber Man. I put arrow through him, Larka. Es still standing, laughing in most awful way. Even Guard no stop him for long. Es truly like amber."

"The Guard's here?" Brauna spoke up. "Monton's out there with that thing?"

"Monton" —Lichena yawned, sitting up and leaning against the wagon wall— "is no longer your friend."

"And Ontar is not *yours*. Besides, you don't know Monton. He would never hurt us."

Larka cleared her mind of the past, her focus reopening on Brauna's intent face. She shook her head as the path Brauna would surely take dawned on her.

"Brina . . ." Larka shook her head, unable to finish the sentence.

Brauna turned to her mother, quirked her brow, and then, having taken in her mother's stance, narrowed her eyes.

"Mum, I can beat him! I know it! If we worked together, an ax under his skin, my sword." She reached for the sheathed weapon where it rested alongside the wagon wall, disregarding the next shake of her mother's head.

"Brina, we can't—"

"Mum! He must be stopped!"

Larka felt the gravity of that statement, and her allies swished around her head at that point, encouraging her, yet she also felt the presence of the Knowing Child disapproving any action against the Amber Man. Larka closed her eyes and breathed. She could no more turn her back on the innocents dying here than she had on the babes born beneath the darkest of moons. At this decision, her air allies blustered around her, their excitement palpable. Larka shivered.

Fate beckoned.

"She's right," Lichena yawned again. "We almost got him at Shady River."

"We?" Brauna turned a wrinkle-nosed assessment on Lichena. "You mean *I* did. Had you not interrupted me, he would be dead now."

Lichena rolled her eyes. "You can't beat him alone, not just the two of you. My magic is powerful. I could weaken him first. I think you know that." Lichena smiled wryly at Brauna, who sneered.

Guta looked thoughtfully at Lichena then Brauna. "If what you say es true, you might be our good hope if dark moon make him, and it must be this way. No normal man lives through what villagers do to him. No man." He paused, still holding Brauna's gaze. "We fight like with like."

"Huh?" Brauna cocked her head at Guta, right eye squinted, brows flocked together. Larka's next words erased that expression.

"Might I remind you the Guard is no longer our friend, and the Amber Man's out of control. Who knows what he might do." Larka rubbed her forehead. "I'll go. Alone."

"Uh!" Brauna expelled the syllable and flung up her hands. "Really, Mum, you would prefer to take him on by yourself? I mean, we've all seen what he wants from you!"

Larka flinched, heat rising in her face.

"Larka, you not go alone. Look at Brina. Es strong. If she beat him before, she must do it again. I not be asking if there es another way. But me thinks three powers of the dark moon would kill Behrna dead."

"Three?" Brauna leaned back, peering through squinched eyes at Guta. "What *are* you going on about, man?"

Lichena scoffed, "Ah, but ignorance is bliss." The girl smiled at Brauna. "Isn't it?"

"Piss off!" Brauna blared, causing several villagers outside to stop and stare at the unmoving wagon.

A great sigh heaved out of Larka. She crawled out of the wagon.

All three powers might indeed be necessary if they were to defeat the Amber Man. And afterwards, Larka had every intention of hunting down what appeared to be his pet bear.

Larka's feet hit the earth and her head came up. She gazed around. Wheel folk milled about nervously. Warin was still nowhere to be seen. Milla, however, waved and concern crossed her face as she watched Larka return the gesture then move toward Jaunty.

"Are you two coming or not?" Larka flung the words over her shoulder.

"Get out of my way!" Brauna shouted behind her.

The sound of two people thrashing about in the small wagon portal assured Larka of her daughters' activity.

CHAPTER 43

OUT OF CONTROL

Clouds parted and sun shone brightly off the heads of warrioress, water bearer, and matron as well as those of the dandelions alongside the road. The many rays of some of these flowers waved at the travelers, whereas the mature seedheads of others spewed fluff into the breezes shifting around the matron.

Larka looked to her right at Brauna then to her left at Lichena. Guilt smote her gut. She opened her mouth, but no words came out. Silence ensued.

Eventually, Larka stopped on a gently curved hilltop, effectively stopping her daughters. She gazed around. The forest sighed today as the sun darted in and out of the clouds. White pines stretched their majestic limbs to the sky while hemlock reached for the ground. The patient crowns of maple, birch, and beech peered over aspen poplars while the scattered children of white ash plumed skyward throughout the forest.

Larka recalled that fire had struck this region in her youth, allowing aspens to pioneer the soil, but these shade-intolerant trees were now losing the battle for sunlight.

Vegetation rustled. Larka's arm whipped up, reaching instinctively for the throwing ax on her back. Her eyes lit on a groundhog ahead of them. The squat animal rose on its haunches beside a robust dandelion then darted into the shadowy woods, blending with the earthen tones of the forest floor. Larka lowered her arm.

"It certainly is pretty here," Lichena sighed.

Brauna wiped a mist of sweat off her brow, still watching after the groundhog.

"How much farther?"

Larka looked to the path ahead of them.

"Just ahead. You'll see Jaunty when we reach the next hilltop. It spreads out right below."

Larka forced breath into her lungs. "Brauna, if I don't make it through this, seek Guta and Warin. There are things they can tell you about the night of your birth, things you must—"

"I will not let you die, Mum! Never!"

"Much is set against us, daughter. . . ." As Larka spoke, Brauna's eyes drifted to the tall aspens on the roadside, their leaves set atremble by a gale. Larka watched the young warrior's face become unlined, peaceful. "We were burning aspen wood the day you turned five. Do you recall how you cried?"

"What?" Brauna murmured and turned a dreamy aspect to her mother.

"Aspens . . ." Larka smiled and shook her head. "Never mind, daughter. I'll tell you about your birth when I can."

Brauna's brow knit. She searched her mother's face.

Hoofbeats thundered through the air. A small group of mounted Guardsmen broke into view at the top of the next hill, unmounted guards and villagers pouring behind. They all drew to a halt.

"Do you see Monton?" Brauna leaned forward, eyes tapered as she sought the man's stout figure. Brauna then turned a sly smile upon Larka. "He'd never hurt you, Mum. He's been in love with you for years."

"Oh." Larka blanched.

Lichena peered at Larka and chuckled, but that sound was cut short.

"Sweet earth," she said, "there's the Amber Man."

He had broken out of the forest onto the road below. Villagers and Guardsmen chased after him. The Amber Man ran toward the forest on the opposite side of the road. Three Guardsmen on horseback burst forth from the tree line there, trapping him, then blocking his sprint toward the hill the three women controlled. The Guardsmen and villagers atop the opposite hill plunged toward the Amber Man just as clouds overcame the bright sun.

"It's time," Larka murmured.

Brauna peered down at Lichena and snarled, "Stay out of my way!"

Lichena rolled her eyes.

Brauna dashed downhill, followed by Lichena and Larka.

"Work together," Larka shouted as Lichena and Brauna outpaced her.

Brauna sprinted into the fray at the bottom of the hill, where the Amber Man had already pulled several Guardsmen off their horses; the men lay scattered upon the ground, injured and possibly dead. Before Brauna could reach the Amber Man, however, at least five Guardsmen pounced on her. The warrior woman took a tumbledown.

Larka coerced more speed from her legs. Just ahead of her, Lichena stopped near the foot of the hill, arm raised to send a cold death ray toward the Amber Man.

"No!" Larka screamed as she ran. The girl's ill range of aim precluded any aid. Even Larka could not use her lightning without possibly striking a bystander.

Lichena glanced back at Larka, dropped her arm, and darted elsewhere.

"Fall back! Let Brauna be!" Monton's voice boomed as Larka took Lichena's place near the foot of the hill. On horseback, Monton brought up the rear of the mob.

Larka peered down into the brawl of limbs and bodies. It seemed Monton's men had not heard him. A small group of them still abused a prone Brauna. With much regret, the Thrower whipped her favorite ax into a Guardsman's arm then reached to the belt on her waist. The crowd hushed as Larka's knives sliced through the air and found their marks in arms, legs, buttocks—areas not meant to kill.

Atop his horse, Monton worked his way through the crowd toward Brauna, shouting orders. "Fall away! Fall away from Brauna!"

Some of the men obeyed. Several still ignored their Captain, Ontar among them. Ontar's boot impacted Brauna's ribs even with the warrior woman's arms and legs tucked protectively against her. Larka's last knives slammed into each of his shoulders, though she had aimed for his heart.

Ontar grasped at the knives, teeth clenched, face twisted, eyes never leaving Brauna. Two of his comrades—already marked by the Thrower—dragged him away as the villagers began to more fully encircle the brawl.

Brauna regained her footing and began to shoulder her way toward the Amber Man, who had slipped farther away from the warrior woman and pummeled nearly through to the fore of the fray.

Larka had taken but four strides to help Brauna when she noted a bright aura emanating to the right. She stopped, pinpointing its origin: Lichena stood in a fore corner of the crowd, her powers brooding, collecting in her right arm.

Lichena lifted a hand to send her cold-death blast into the Amber Man—too near Brauna, too near the Guardsmen, too near the villagers. Larka countered Lichena with a powerful gust of wind, blowing the girl's slight form over. Villagers near Lichena also toppled. Then the Amber Man, chest heaving, turned to look straight at Larka and shouted her condemnation.

"Larka, help me!" He broke free of his attackers and ran to her.

Heads turned her way. Suspicion flew onto the faces of the few Guardsmen left. Villagers began to point and whisper.

She heard "Larka," "The Thrower," *Death Song*," and "Wailing Ghost Mother" imbibed by the wind and delivered to her ears—correlations made, conclusions drawn. Jeers rose off the mob.

"I can't help you," Larka said. And the first stone smote her head.

Larka staggered.

"Mum!" Brauna burst from the crowd, swinging fists and feet at friend and stranger alike—sword lost—a maniacal defiance in the clench of her gnashed teeth.

As she would have fallen, the Amber Man caught Larka, his hand pressing into the wound on her forehead. She felt it numb, and the pain disappeared as he placed her gently on the ground, rocks pelting the earth around them. The Amber Man stood as blood rolled into Larka's right eye. The wound remained despite the numbness, and a dreary blur of consciousness enveloped her.

Larka sat up weakly, wiping her eye, trying to see. More stones shot by her, one smacking its jaggedness into her shoulder. With no request from Larka, the air allies initiated her defense. A tunnel of air swirled around her, deflecting the rocks and hurling them back at the crowd. The persecutors soon stilled their pitching, their curses and raised voices stilling right along with it.

"Good," the Amber Man murmured, gazing down at her with a gentle smile.

Brauna placed herself between her mother and the crowd, turning so that one of her sides faced it while the other faced Larka and the Amber Man.

Peering around Brauna's defensive crouch, Larka's hazed vision cleared to show her Lichena had stood up. Again, the gray aura had amassed about the girl. Lichena lifted her right arm. The forefinger pointed at the Amber Man, but Brauna rose up in front of him.

"Lichena, no!" Larka shrieked, and a blast of air smote her birth daughter, tumbling the girl along with a quarter of the mob.

The villagers began to point and whisper once more, the sound growing louder, more insistent until the curses and shouts began anew.

"Desist! Desist!" Monton bellowed as his horse ambled to the fore of the crowd. "There's no need in all this! All three of you come with me, and no one else will get hurt."

Brauna deepened back into her crouch. "Piss off, Monton! We came to help!"

Monton appeared stung by her words. His sat unmoving, speechless.

"Work with us," the Amber Man said, his voice low, a deadly caress hissing into the tangled crowd.

Brauna swivelled her head toward the Amber Man.

"I will never work with a man who murders children and rapes women!" Brauna's voice boomed, silencing the villagers, just as an abrupt and chilling wind shunted through the hills.

Lumbering gray clouds seized the sky. A tingle ran through Larka as vegetation chuffed in a rush of air scented by oncoming rain while lavender shrieked in the distance. The storm stomped this way.

Lightning danced overhead, pulsing in Larka's veins as well, rejuvenating her. Thunder rumbled down upon them. Larka stood, trusting in the storm and the element of air.

"Let them be," Guta's stilted accent rang through the mob. "I ask help against Berhna from them. They come for helping us, not the Amber Man."

Monton nodded. "Give Brauna room to work!" He turned a bloated, red face upon all, marking the Guardsmen who had failed to obey his earlier command and daring any villager to defy him.

Brauna rushed the Amber Man as the crowd fell back. Shocked by the sudden change, Behrna was caught off guard. Brauna thrust kicked through his right knee, fired two punches into his chest.

The Amber Man careened and toppled.

Larka had stepped out of the way, between the crowd and the fight. It was now she who stood with one hip pointed toward either, her head turning back and forth.

The Amber Man had regained his feet, but Brauna's quick, efficient thrusts assured Larka the girl's outrage had settled into a calculated bloodlust, the warrior's expression impassive but her eyes hungry.

The crowd contracted and expanded as the dueling pair maneuvered. Rain splattered the throng of onlookers. Lightning rent the sky.

Lichena emerged once again from the arena of villagers with

a mass of horrific death pulsing through her. She threw Larka an agitated look.

"Brauna is winning. Leave it alone," Larka whispered on a current of air, directing it into Lichena's ears.

Lichena shook her head when she received the message and lifted her right arm, forefinger pointed toward the brawl.

Larka threw her lightning. It met the death ray in a midair explosion, dissipating that gray power in a fizzle of sparks. No one noted Lichena's part in the scene, only that the explosion occurred right after the lift of Larka's lightning-throwing hands.

"Larka, help me," the Amber Man gasped.

Larka turned to see him through a curtain of the sky's tears, he injured and losing under Brauna's rapacious pummeling. He remained upright, however, stumbling and blinded by his own blood.

She noted Brauna's hand turn into a vertical fist, the bottom of it aimed at his jugular—a killing blow.

"I can't," Larka whispered and turned her back to him. She heard the impact of that last blow and cringed. Then a prolonged thump gushed through the air. The Amber Man had fallen.

A movement of light-colored material and bright aura caught her eye. Lichena had moved farther to Larka's right and pointed yet again. Larka glanced where Lichena's targeting centered—right at Brauna.

With shaking hands, Larka aimed at Lichena to stun her with a weak jolt.

Her air allies hissed around her, hushed vespers forming into tangible words.

"Weeee doooo notttt ssssssslay innocccccenccccce."

Larka let go a flustered cry.

The gray death surged from its point of release toward Brauna. Larka leapt before it. It struck her fully on the chest, circling that area with precision. Larka's stiffened upper body hit the ground. She gagged as her frozen lungs failed to inflate.

The crowd hushed and rain stopped falling.

"Mum!" Brauna sailed toward Larka, leaving the unconscious Amber Man behind. She knelt beside her mother.

Larka choked once more on airless windpipes.

"Love you," she mouthed.

Her eyes then fixed on the grief-torn expression Lichena wore over Brauna's shoulder.

"Mum! Mum?" Brauna called then turned her head to follow Larka's still gaze.

The warrioress shot to her feet and rounded on Lichena.

"You!" Brauna roared, a primal, gut-wrenching sorrow that resonated through the core of every being present. "You did this! You and your dark magic."

The horde of onlookers fell briskly away from the two women.

Lichena turned and ran, but Brauna bore down on her with a swiftness made of grief. Her fist smacked into the back of Lichena's skull. The girl grasped at her head and spun dizzily to face Brauna, her mouth moving but no sound coming out.

"Ontar," Lichena finally managed to gasp.

Brauna's snarl deepened. Her hand shot out to close around Lichena's thin throat and squeeze as she lifted the smaller woman off the ground. Lichena kicked helplessly, uttering clipped cries. Bones failed and shattered.

When all was done, Brauna tossed Lichena away like a rag doll. The warrioress then stood very still and regarded what she had done.

At that, a swift wind rushed behind Brauna to be followed by a flash of smoky-blue light. She spun around, froze, and then frowned at a vacant spot on the earth but a moment.

"Where is my mother?" Brauna erupted, not noting the shocked expressions that had become the face of the crowd. "Where is she?"

Blood raged through Brauna. She barely heard the answer, as distancing thunder rumbled in the throat of a selfish storm.

"The wind take her."

"What?" Brauna took a crazed step toward the speaker.

"Es described no other way." Guta held up a placating hand. "The spirits wrap round her. Es glowing with such light. She . . ." Guta's voice began to shake. "She break into pieces of light . . . like color of her eyes."

"That's the biggest bunch of bunk I've ever heard!"

An older woman of large girth and melodic voice stepped beside Guta. "Those spirits . . . the lights winged into the sky. They came together again and faded. The wind that took her nearly knocked us down."

"Where is she?" Brauna took another step, her hand reaching for someone, anyone.

"Don't you hurt my daddy." A small girl no older than four dashed between the descending warrior and Guta. "He told you what happened. Now step off."

"Madow," Guta cried and he swept the child into his arms. "My little one." He held the child away from him, his eyes devouring her face. He then crushed her against him, his body trembling. "You no leave me again."

Madow patted his head and whispered into his ear, "The lady with green eyes saved me, Da."

A kind wind wisped around Brauna at that moment—an ethereal embrace—and compassion stole into her heart.

The crowd gasped as a smoky-blue electrical field danced over Lichena, yet Brauna did not witness this odd happening either, as she stood with her back to it. She turned after the electrical dance had grown faint and disappeared, guilt clouding her features as her gaze fell upon Lichena's form.

"Do something with her," Brauna barked. "And him." Brauna spun back around, paused then cast about. The Amber Man no longer remained to be seen, but a trail of blood led into nearby woods.

"He took her!" Once again, Lichena had stopped her killing the bastard, and he had her mother.

Brauna strode out of the crowd, looking for more signs of Behrna and her mother's departure.

Still on his horse, Monton nodded to Brauna as she passed him, his eyes bloodshot, shining with wet. She snarled at him in feral warning. His expression crumbled then, and he gazed into the sky, tears runneling unchecked down the crevices of his face.

"Larka," he whispered into the receding sigh of the wind.

GHOST WHISPERS

The Amber Man's trail led Brauna to Jaunty River. There it stopped. All Brauna found much later that day, after tracing back to the river, were the tracks of an enormous bear.

Brauna washed fully clothed in the shallows there, letting the blood on her flow into the rush of water, though its ichor had already stained her soul.

That night, she lay down upon a hill flushed with lavender to dream of her mother. The next morning, she stood up and glared at the empty eyes of the fieldstone cottage on the adjacent hill.

A breeze blew through the long, wavy hair falling around a tall warrior woman's face, its breath blowing upon her neck, a sweet murmur she could never quite understand. The warrior woman's head lifted from her task, earth-brown gaze ever searching yet never finding the eye of the voice in the wind.

Skin grown coppery-olive glowed beneath the evening sun as the warrior woman stooped back over a large granite boulder, engraving the rock's nearly flat top. She drew her tools away from the stone then blew off the last of the debris as a man of long raven hair and a stature that more than matched her own came to stand behind her. The man cleared his throat.

The warrioress clenched the mallet and chisel like weapons. She jerked round to face the stranger, revealing to the river the two axes harnessed in an X over her back.

A mellow smile met her. "What are you working on?"

The warrioress perused the stranger, finding little other than a guitar strapped to his back. She lowered the mallet and chisel, glanced at the engraving.

"A bit of poetry."

The warrioress grabbed an old packsack off the ground and stashed her tools.

"I am Anty Cole from Southwoods." The man approached, a light-hearted grace to his step, his hand extended. "What is your poem about?"

"My mother," she said and shook the stranger's hand. "I am Brina."

"It is nice to meet you, Brina." He indicated the boulder. "May I?"

The warrior's eyes narrowed momentarily, shifting over the length of him again. Finally, she stepped aside, gesturing to the stone. "If you must."

The stranger leaned in to read, mouthing the words:

Sweet Gale

Beloved whispering
Caress my skin
Tell me softly where you've been

Eluding mother
Rustle lightly through my hair
Avow my love you've borne another

Ethereal embrace
Blow your breath upon my neck
Murmur to me in vain

Sweet receding sigh
Brush tenderly against me
Until you've passed me by

The stranger smiled at the woman as he straightened his back. "I've music to set to your heart's song." He patted his guitar.

The woman gazed out over the river, longing in her eyes. She then looked back to the stranger, a sad smile on her lips.

"I would like that, Anty Cole."

The woman led the man away from the stone engraving, away from the past. Little did the woman know that each night thereafter a haze of smoky-blue lights would dance over the engraved words. Little did she know that, one day, the past would come looking for her.

About the Author

Sherryl King-Wilds holds a Bachelors of Science in Botany with a minor in Geography. She briefly attended graduate school.

Sherryl's next book *Daughter of Earth and Tree*, Book 2 of the Dark Moon Trilogy, is scheduled for publication in Spring 2009.

To keep up with Sherryl's literary endeavors, visit her online at www.sherrylkingwilds.com. You may e-mail Sherryl care of her publisher: darkmoontrilogy@badgirlspublishing.com. Or write to her care of Bad Girls Publishing, Post Office Box 275, Nashville, NC 27856.

If you wish to give a copy of this book to a friend or acquaintance, you may order it at your favorite bookstore, at your favorite online bookseller, at Sherryl's favorite online shop Mystic Spirit Gifts (www.mysticspiritgifts.com), or visit www.badgirlspublishing.com and place an order directly with the publisher.